I0760868

PRINCESS OF SHADOWS AND STARLIGHT

THE ZHENINGHAI CHRONICLES

PRINCESS OF SHADOWS AND STARLIGHT

THE ZHENINGHAI CHRONICLES

ANASTASIS BLYTHE

PRINCESS OF SHADOWS AND STARLIGHT

www.AnastasisBlythe.com

Hardcover ISBN: 978-1-960606-03-7

Jacket Cover design by Moorbooks Design.
Laminate Cover and Interior Design by Dragonpen Designs.

FOR THE WALLFLOWERS WITH DEEP SOULS.

READER'S NOTE

The events of this story begin a week before the events of Guardian of Talons and Snares.

CHAPTER 1

PRINCESS MEILING FOUND it unfortunate that the length of a person's shadows was not determined by stature, but by the turn of the light. Even someone as slight as herself could cast the longest shadows. It was a fact that made her heart pound with loathing, and her lungs clench until she almost couldn't breathe.

She took careful steps, watching where her feet fell more than the hundreds of celebratory faces. In her view, dainty jeweled slippers peeked out from gleaming silk robes, trailing sashes with beads that sparkled like diamonds in the soft lighting.

Breathe. In, out.

Those slippers skittered away from her shadow, a long dark thing cast by candlelight. If she moved too quickly, she sometimes caught a frantic whisper of a lord or lady who struggled to dodge her shadow fast enough.

Just a little bit longer.

It wasn't that difficult; people moved aside for her, be they graduates, Academy masters, or members of her father's court. No one blocked her path. Yet it took so *long*, and she couldn't increase her speed without looking like she fled from the sideward and the distinct *not* glances burning into every pore of her body, into the stitching on her sash and the starry embroidery of her hems.

One might have thought, with all the perfumed scents of floral arrangements and incense, combining with the mingling, heady aromas of a freshly prepared feast, the tinkling anklets on the dancer girls, the crowding new graduates in crimson robes, and the endless drone of conversation, there would be ample distraction from something as insignificant as her movements.

Apparently not.

Meiling forced her lips to twist upward in some semblance of a smile, forced her hands to remain unclenched by her side. If she could only make it through this crowd, she could find a less populated part of the celebration. A place where she could melt into the wall, vanish from view, where the shadows of towering support beams and darkened corners would swallow her up in one big gulp.

The courtyard opened in front of her, a refuge from the crowded reception room. She bit her lip to keep from gasping and charging through it, barely maintaining her dignity.

She cast one last glance over her shoulder, at the figure arrayed in fire-gold splendor on the dais, his chin tilted up and his mouth cut in a severe line.

His Imperial Majesty. *Pa*.

His roaming gaze caught her in the doorway, right before her slipper landed on the sun-warmed flagstones of the courtyard. His brow furrowed just slightly.

Meiling sent him the closest to a pleading look that she could muster in public.

He blinked slowly, and the subtle fall of his chest revealed how he sighed. His chin inclined in the briefest of nods.

Her shoulders sagged in relief, and the smile she sent him was the only genuine one she'd mustered all day. A desperate *thank you* for not making her stay any longer. His own lips turned up slightly in a sad sort of smile.

Whatever her obligation as princess, these people didn't want her here. Why ought she to torment both them and herself by remaining? She kept her footsteps stately, her spine straight, but inside she wanted to burst into a run, breathing in the clean, hot air of the night.

Not yet. She must endure this just a little longer.

A familiar voice sent her ears perking, and Meiling hurried down the stairs into the maze of gardens, past the lotus pond and a row of cherry trees. That bit of comfort the sound gave her drew her like a moth to a flame.

"I'm still *so mad* that Hu Fen graduated top ten," came her brother Yun's unmistakable voice from behind a row of tall, trimmed shrubs.

"She's about as fierce as they come," was the response. A voice Meiling didn't recognize. She pulled back, suddenly doubting her idea to join her brother. His friends would probably scatter at the sight of her.

"I *know* she's fierce," said Yun. "But she's so *nasty*. If there's someone you don't want to be on the bad side of, it's Fen. I guess I hoped she wouldn't do so well."

"What can you expect? She's a full shapeshifter. Of course she's got an explosive personality. It just means she's the perfect choice to lead that battalion north to secure our border against the barbarians. She deserves her appointment."

Meiling shook her head, slipping past the voices, remaining silent on her side of the shrubs. Yun rarely talked about anything but Academy things. Every road of conversation somehow returned to converge on fellow students, his magic classes, their most recent Hunt, or Night Game.

Things she knew nothing about. After all, the Academy was only for people with magic. She used to attend his arena battles as a spectator when she was younger. Before things changed. Now? She hadn't set foot on the Academy complex in years.

She intended to retreat further into the gardens, perhaps in hopes of finding her little sister Hou. But Hou was probably inside mingling with guests and enjoying the celebration, her robes doubtlessly stained or torn already and her headdress toppled.

If only Ma wasn't the queen and especially preoccupied with the coordinating of festivals such as this Graduation. Ma would let her sit by her side, silent and simply glad to not be so *alone* in a crowd.

Meiling kept wandering, seeking some darkened corner to settle into, but every time she found one, it was already occupied.

"Did you hear there's an evanescer in this year's graduating class?" asked an unfamiliar voice from his companion on the far side of the hedge. A nobleman, judging from the lilting cadence of his voice. "One son of the late Shi Mu, I do believe. A certain Shi Kai?"

"Evanescers make me nervous," the companion replied. "What's to stop them from going rogue in the palace, slaughtering and vanishing before anyone can catch them?"

Didn't they know that every member of the Palace Guard and Emperor's Guard was trained against such things? If an evanescer so much as stepped foot within the palace complex, every guard on the premises was notified. Besides, if any wielder went rogue, they'd be executed and their family stripped of title and wealth.

Meiling scurried past the conversation. Even outside, the air cloyed in her tightening lungs until the sight and sound of every person in the darkness nearly made her gasp. She came here to get away from people—but the gardens were filled too!

Her limbs ached with the need for the promised reprieve of sleep, the enticing freedom it beckoned. Did she *have* to stay? Maybe she had fulfilled her duty enough; maybe she could slip out and no one would notice. And if they did notice, they would be glad anyway.

Once she was free of this oppressing party, she could wrangle her emotions back under her control. Then she wouldn't be so hurt by the way everyone treated her. She would make herself remember that, to any outsider, she did certainly appear cursed. After all, to be the first princess without magic in a dynasty-long line of powerful fire-wielders was indeed suspect.

Could she blame them for not wanting her curse to afflict them?

At the moment, yes. Yes, she could blame them. Which was why she needed to get away.

She turned away from the groups of people milling around the gardens and made a beeline for the garden's exit. Each step was light and dainty, though the surging force in her muscles nearly made her break into a run.

But if she was caught running from the Graduation festival, how would that reflect on his Imperial Majesty, her father? She couldn't be a further cause of shame for him. She *wouldn't* be.

Guards lined the yellow-glowing entrance to the main celebration, flanking the path to the bridge spanning a lotus pond and leading away from the gardens. Beyond that bridge was a way through a lesser-used door back into the palace, and from there, to her rooms. Her refuge.

In her periphery, she caught sight of forms in red robes crossing the bridge. She instinctively dropped her head, focusing on her footsteps. For a terrifying moment, she was torn between waiting for them to cross, to give them space from her shadow, or whether she ought to act more like the princess she was and ignore them. She hated causing panic, but she *was* the eldest princess, not some servant. It would look strange if she waited for them, wouldn't it?

Her fists wound themselves into her sash, clenching around the soft fabric. She forced her feet forward. She was the princess. *Grace. Confidence. Elegance.* That was what she should be. Not some frightened little dove.

A mistake.

She wasn't looking up. Her focus was on her feet.

So she didn't see the red-robed graduate that was right in front of her until she collided straight into him.

Meiling let out a squeak, leaping back. Her rational mind told her she ought to bark a command to get out of her way, to straighten her spine and glare at the one who dared block her path. All that came out was a bumbling, "Oh! Forgive me! I—"

Her foot caught on the hem of her robes. Her balance tipped, and her flailing arms and faulty steps only sent her stumbling backward, falling, straight to the lotus pond.

An arm swept around her waist, catching her at the last second.

Meiling choked on another squeak, then found herself against crimson robes, staring up at a sharp-featured face and glittering black eyes. A handsome face—one that looked as if it had never smiled, with a pinched brow and parted lips. Her hands had unconsciously grabbed hold of the front of his robes, clinging to that bit of solid before she fell. He had one arm around her, the other propped for support against the railing of the bridge.

He wore a multicolored cord around his neck. A top graduate, then.

She was staring—gaping with open mouth at the young man who'd caught her. He stared back too, but the surprise on his face had quickly shifted into something else. *Recognition.* Following the recognition, he pursed his lips.

"Thank you!" she gasped, panic suddenly surging in her chest. How much did he care about curses? This had to be worse than walking into her shadow, right? "My apologies! Sorry—sorry!"

His brow furrowed further, his head canting to one side.

In a swift motion, he swung her back onto her feet, away from the lotus pond, removed his arm from around her, and with far more clip than she expected, said, "Your Highness."

He bowed crisply, respectfully.

Then he strode off in the opposite direction toward the group of graduates who had stopped to wait for him. Was it her imagination that his footsteps were . . .?

Was he *storming* away from her? Or was she just overthinking his briskness?

Mortification filled her belly. She pressed the back of her hand to her mouth, as if that could shield the heat of embarrassment flooding her cheeks. Careless—she'd been so careless! She'd upset the young man who had been so kind to keep her from falling, and on his Graduation, no less.

More reason than ever to get out of this celebration.

But when she looked up to ensure the bridge was now free, she found herself blinking into the sunny smile of a girl in white robes—the robes of a student.

"Whoops!" said the girl. "This is a bad sign. The evening is just begun and I'm already barreling into royalty. Don't you hate it when your tolerance for alcohol is so low that you get tipsy just by being in the near vicinity of it?"

Meiling blinked. Then almost checked behind her to ensure the girl was indeed talking to her, and not someone else.

The girl, either unphased by Meiling's stunned silence or used to setting people speechless, thrust out her hand. "I'm Feiyan, by the way."

Meiling stared at that offered hand. *Feiyan*. Could this be the healer everyone was so excited about? The first magic-wielder born in decades with the power to heal with a touch? With a timid smile, she reached out her hand and took Feiyan's. A gentle warmth threaded into her fingers, up her arm. "I'm Meiling."

With how many customs they were already breaking, it seemed silly for her to add "Princess" to her name. She wanted to pretend for this span of a heartbeat that she was just a normal girl. One without a curse.

"I know." Feiyan winked. She squeezed her hand, then withdrew and marched off toward the group of graduates the young man had joined a few minutes ago.

Meiling tried not to stare after her. What she would have given to hold on to that scrap of conversation and warmth for a few more moments. But she wouldn't act the fool and go prancing after the girl, as if she could join that group and be part of it now that someone had looked her in the eyes and smiled.

She quit dallying and crossed the bridge. The further she got from the celebration, the more the sounds of flutes and dancing and laughter died into the gurgle of foundations and soft chirps of summer bugs, and the more her shoulders loosened.

Slipping into the hallways of the palace, with moonlight trickling through papered windows and candlelight dancing on silk partitions and carved bamboo archways, she couldn't help but close her eyes and let out deep exhale after deep exhale.

The quiet of this distant part of the palace soothed the creases in her nerves, could almost make her forget the look on the young man's face, the clip in his stride away from her, and the smallest of smiles spread across her face.

"Almost there," she whispered to herself. "Almost free."

The guards remained silent as she passed them. She was always a smidge uneasy around them, knowing they possessed various magical abilities. She never knew which ones might possess the ability to hear her thoughts or smell her emotions. Ma said not to be worried because their magic enabled them to do their duty better, but that couldn't ease all Meiling's fears.

What if they found out about her secret?

What would happen to her—and her entire family—then?

She ducked her head, wary of losing her headdress and its rattling beads, and hurried beyond them.

Not much farther. When she reached an intersection of two hallways, she froze at the sound of swishing. Brows puckering, she glanced over her shoulder back the way she'd come. The stiff, armored guards stood at the far end of the hallway. They didn't look like they'd moved a muscle.

What was that sound, then?

Probably only her imagination. Her nerves were frayed to bits. It served her no good to be inventing sounds and creatures of shadow following her.

Setting her shoulders, she pressed onward.

She stopped.

That susurrus of silk hadn't been imagined. No, she'd heard it. But it stopped the moment she froze.

If only she'd been allowed to go to the Academy. Then maybe she wouldn't freeze in every situation that sent her hackles raising. She could be confident in her own abilities to defend herself.

"Useless thoughts," she muttered to herself. Being tired and emotional wasn't helping anything. She only needed a good night's rest, and she would be back to her rational self tomorrow.

She looked up.

And nearly leapt out of her skin.

She gasped, pressed a hand over her heart, and tried not to melt against the wall. "Ma, you frightened me."

Ma, who turned the corner just then of the hallway perpendicular to her, raised both eyebrows, her folded hands lost in long trailing sleeves. "Meiling! You look as though you've seen a *mó guǐ*! Why aren't you at the feast?"

Why had she thought someone was following her? It was only Ma. Meiling drew in another large breath into her lungs and straightened her shoulders. Her eyes, however, fled anywhere but that long, painted gaze of her mother. They rested on her towering, bejeweled headdress, the red circles on each cheek, the elegant and utterly unmatched violet and gold robes she wore.

"I wanted to leave," Meiling said.

Ma's heavy scrutiny swept her from head to toe, focusing on her face like she could read every thought that flitted through Meiling's head, all the anxiety that nearly drowned her at festivals.

"I know," said Ma softly, with a sigh not unlike the one that had escaped Pa earlier. "I know, little dove. At least you made an appearance. It is important."

"But why?" Meiling asked, more vehemently than she intended. "Why must I go out there? They don't want me to. I don't want to!"

"Because you are a daughter of His Imperial Majesty," said Ma firmly. "You must fulfill your duty. The people must see you. Your father and I will *not* hide you in a closet, as though we are ashamed of you when we are not. Regardless of what the people believe about your so-called curse, we know it's not true. Hiding you from the public would only confirm the lie."

The lie that kept her alive. The lie that even her siblings didn't know was false.

"What about just hiding me in the library instead?" Meiling offered with a timid smile and wincing eyes.

Ma rolled her eyes, the beads on her headdress clacking with the slight shaking of her head. But a smile played on the edges of her mouth. "Go on to bed, daughter of mine. I'm certain the library will be glad to see you again tomorrow after this long festival. I, too, could use some solitude. Perhaps I'll join you."

Ma leaned forward, careful of both their royal ensembles, and pressed a kiss on Meiling's forehead.

"I know things are hard," she whispered, "but they won't always be this way."

Meiling pulled away, something tight and rueful twisting her lips. "Won't they?"

She shouldn't have said that, should have clamped a firm hand down on her bitterness. But the words were out, and Meiling ducked her head and continued past her mother before she said anything worse that she regretted.

"I love you," called Ma.

Meiling stopped and fought the sudden prickle of tears. "I love you too," she replied.

Then she hurried away. She had to get to her room. Had to sleep. Had to be free. Just for these few hours of the night. Her soul tugged desperately at its confines, forever longing to pull free of her body, to soar among the stars.

"Almost there," she whispered.

When the shadows shifted as she approached her rooms, she told herself it was only a trick of the light on her tired mind.

CHAPTER 2

BY THE TIME the half dozen maids in pink helped Meiling climb out of her festival robes and scrub the paint off her face, her heart was pounding.

Sleep. Freedom.

Once she was alone, dressed in her silk nightclothes, she exhaled the deepest breath of her life and leaned on her windowsill, pushing open the shutters to gaze out on the sprawling expanse of the capital city, Suguan, before her. Lights twinkled everywhere from the dying festival, reflecting on the sea and dulling the stars overhead.

She closed her eyes and inhaled the fragrant, salty air.

Then she couldn't wait a minute longer. She latched the shutters, crawled into her bed, pulling up the embroidered quilt to her chin, and laid her head on the cushion.

Finally.

Falling asleep was rather like melting. As Meiling's body sank into slumber, her soul burned brighter, brighter. Her anxiety washed away into nothing. Gingerly, with the care of a creeping cat, her spirit slid free of her earthbound body and floated into the air above her sleeping form. She looked down at herself, her face pale against the darkness of the gloom. Black hair splayed across the pillow; hands curled under her chin with her knees drawn in toward her chest; long eyelids closed heavily as shallow breaths escaped her nostrils.

Her own sleeping body was the least interesting thing to see.

A soundless gurgle of excitement trilled along the tether anchoring her soul to her body. *Free.* Free to fly, to roam, to explore. Free from obligations, from pressure, from curses.

Funny how she never felt more herself than when she was nothing but a slip of shadow and starlight.

Meiling rose and flitted back to her window. The sky overhead was deep black, filled with a sea of whispering stars. They were too quiet to understand, so she usually ignored them, but tonight she floated through her window and flew higher into the air. She gazed in wonder at the dark expanse above her, stretching like an endless parchment sopping with staining ink. The stars whispered, but not to her—to each other? Incoherent, unintelligible murmurs and mumbles. Perhaps they only sounded so soft because they were so far away.

They glowed and sparkled, prompting and prodding.

Meiling promised herself that, the next moment she had a physical body, she would steal into the library and memorize every constellation.

Below her, the city of Suguan sprawled on the plain between the mountains and the sea, stretching its fingers into the shallows of the water. She wished she could fly higher, but even the view from her current height was breathtaking.

She glanced back toward the palace. How much more pleasant it would be to enjoy the celebration now, when she could take in the beauty of it while being invisible to human eyes. This would help her remember to not be so bitter about her lot in life. This would help her remember the beauty of her land, the people she belonged to, to see the world beyond books and libraries and holed up corners.

She drifted back toward her room, slipping straight through the stone, wood, and plaster of her walls into the corridor beyond. She was met with the familiar glows of the posted guards, both of their souls different shades of orange—an indicator of their feral magic. One had augmented strength, while the other had augmented hearing and smell. They'd guarded her for years.

A third glow entered the corridor.

Meiling froze.

This glow was violet. A glow she'd never seen in this part of the palace before. She drew back slightly, hugging close to the wall as she peered past her guards at the glow growing larger and brighter as it came closer.

The way the figure clung to the edges of the darkness made her heart pulse faster through her tether.

In a flash, the glow vanished.

An evanescer.

Something was wrong. Very, very wrong. Evanescers weren't allowed out of sight while they were in the palace, and there certainly shouldn't be one anywhere near her rooms.

The glow reappeared. Right next to her.

Meiling shrieked soundlessly, almost propelling herself straight through the wall in her fright. The evanescer was bony, white-bearded, and wearing filthy, ragged clothes. He stared at her door.

She needed to wake up and alert her guards.

Heart pounding, she zipped back through the wall and into her rooms. She snapped back into her body with a whirling rush as her terror yanked her through her tether. She burst up in her bed, sweat pouring from her face. Physical sensations slammed into her like a waterfall. She was hot, so hot, so dripping hot. Her hair stuck to her face, air filled her lungs quickly with each gasping breath. Clear air drifted in from outside, mingling with the mustiness of her room and the lingering scent of melted wax. Her lungs heaved so much that she pressed a hand to her chest.

Then she glanced to her side.

There, staring back at her with hollowed eyes and gaunt cheeks, was the evanescer.

Meiling screamed.

The door had already slammed open, and she threw herself from the bed as he dove for her. Bedsheets and night silks tangled in her legs, her hair getting in her eyes and mouth as she landed on all fours and scrambled backward.

Through her mess of hair, she couldn't tell if he'd vanished again as her guards charged into her rooms, and if he had, there was no way to know where he would appear again. It would only take one split second for him to reappear, stab her in the heart, and vanish again. Or grab her arm and take her with him.

Shouts echoed off the walls.

Meiling scrambled to her feet, pressing herself back into a corner and staring with wide eyes as her guards searched the empty room for the evanescer, their *jiauns* loaded and upraised to shoot.

The air shifted next to her.

Meiling screamed, dodging to the side as a hand came reaching for her, about to clamp down on her wrist. *No, no, no, no.*

A pair of arrows *zinged* through the air, and a sharp cry split the mayhem. The evanescer stumbled to his knees, right in front of Meiling, two bloody arrows protruding from his shoulder.

She was so stunned she couldn't move.

The intruder let out a pained cry and vanished.

She gasped, wrapping both arms around her shoulders and pressing closer into the wall. Her guards reloaded their weapons, prowling the space. One sniffed the air and shook his head. "I think he's gone."

"Stay with her. I'll get reinforcements," said the other as he ran out of the room.

Her whole body trembled, and not even the summer heat could stop the ice trailing down her spine. Her chest heaved with every gasping breath, and her mind could hardly fathom why anyone would bother to hurt her.

"T-thank y-you," she managed. It was so paltry compared to the service he'd just rendered, saving her life.

The guard looked up, then bowed and said, "It is my honor to serve, Your Highness."

Meiling stared at him, watching as he sniffed for sign of the intruder's return.

Someone had come for *her*. To hurt her or take her. Had they thought she was her younger sister Hou? Was someone trying to kidnap Hou?

The smell of smoke and the sound of pounding footsteps reached her before the door burst open again, and Pa stormed inside, fire sizzling on the tips of his fingers. His eyes found her immediately, scrunched up in the corner, her guard within reach.

He grabbed the foot of her bed and vaulted over it to her, planting his huge self in front of her and facing the room, blocking off any reach at her. She squished harder against the wall, sweating as his heat surrounded her, and let out a tiny whimper of relief.

Pa would keep her safe. Always.

"Are you hurt?" he asked over his shoulder.

"No," she managed.

"Report," he demanded of her guard, then shouted into the hallway, "Send the Emperor's Guard up here immediately!"

The guard explained catching the evanescer's scent, and how the episode unfolded. Perhaps Meiling ought to be more reverent to her father in the presence of the guards, but she couldn't help wrapping her arms around his waist and resting her head against his back.

"Keep your hands behind me, little one," Pa said firmly, albeit gently, as he pried them off his stomach. "I don't want anything happening."

She nodded, even though he couldn't see, and obeyed, tucking her hands against her chest. But she kept leaning on him.

Ma wasn't far behind Pa, her normally stalwart composure cracked to reveal her own panic. "Meiling? Are you hurt?"

"She's fine," said Pa, voice strained. "My Guard is coming. They'll investigate immediately."

Ma's eyes slid from Pa to Meiling's. Meiling chewed her lip, saying nothing.

"Liena." Pa stretched out his hand toward Ma, beckoning her to his side. He went to take her hand, but she flinched and gave him a small grimace. *Too hot*. "Sorry," he said, and the temperature dropped around Meiling. Ma took his hand, and he drew her close so the three of them were crowded into the one corner as guards searched the vicinity.

"Your vision," Pa said softly to Ma, his eyes never leaving her face.

Ma's face went pale, eyelashes fluttering in several quick blinks. "He must be looking for her."

"Who?" Meiling asked, standing up on her tippy toes to peek over Pa's shoulder.

"What can we even do?" was Ma's hushed response, as if she wished they could have this conversation where Meiling couldn't hear. "An evanescer, Nianzu."

Even from her limited angle, there was no missing the tension lining Pa's jaw.

"I'll stay with her tonight," he said. "We'll think of something and discuss first thing."

Ma nodded, and Pa reached out, pulling her face closer as he leaned down and pressed a kiss to her hairline. "Take extra guards of mine tonight. Send for Yun. Have him sleep on the floor or something."

"He's only a boy. I don't want to worry him."

"He's the Crown Prince, only a year away from his own graduation. He is a capable young man who knows his duty. I won't have something happen to you while I'm with Meiling."

"I'm not *entirely* helpless," replied Ma dryly. "I'll have you remember that, at the Academy—"

Pa rolled his eyes, the slightest of smiles breaking his intense façade. "Then send for Yun only for my peace of mind that you will get some sleep."

One more forehead kiss later, Ma was gone.

"Everything is clear, Your Majesty," said one of the guards after bowing to Pa.

"Very well. Double the patrol tonight, with extra security around my wife and children, and I want this corridor constantly monitored. You are dismissed."

"As you command, Your Majesty."

With that, the guards filed out of her rooms, shutting the doors behind them, leaving Meiling alone with her Pa. He stepped away from the corner, letting her slide out of the confined space.

"I'm sorry, Mei," he said, and for a minute he didn't seem at all like the Glorious Emperor, but a tired man with the weight of the world on his shoulders.

"Pa? What . . . just happened?"

He gave a great big sigh. "I'm not sure, little dove, but I will find out. You don't need to be worried; I will take care of this. Of you."

Despite the unease prickling down her spine, and the questions swirling in her mind, Meiling gave a little nod. "Thank you for keeping me safe, Pa."

His answering smile was sad and rueful. "Always." He planted a kiss on the top of her head, then pushed her gently toward her bed. "Go to sleep."

"But certainly you should take the bed. I will be comfortable on the floor—"

"Your emperor commands you sleep in the bed," replied Pa with a ghost of a smirk.

She obeyed, climbing under the covers. It was usually Ma who stopped by in the evening and pressed a kiss to her forehead, but tonight it was Pa. Then he sat against the wall, facing her. It was only now that she realized he had a *jiaun* holstered at his side, which he now set beside him, loaded and ready to shoot. Knives poked out between the folds of his ornate, golden robes.

Throat dry, heart hammering, she burrowed deeper into her quilt, rolling away from him and facing the door. She squeezed her eyes shut, attempting to block out the memory of that purple glow, of that haunted face, the sight of those gory arrows, the knowledge that Pa probably stared at her huddled shoulders. One breath in, one breath out.

It was a mercy she fell asleep.

When her soul slipped free of her body, she found that Pa fixed a hawk-like gaze on her sleeping form, his hand settled over the shaft of the *jiaun*. Once or twice, he blinked extra rapidly, yawned, and sat up straighter. His brow furrowed, his jaw tight, as if he were deep in thought.

Never once in the night did he sleep.

And never once did Meiling catch sight again of that violet glow.

CHAPTER 3

BEFORE DAYBREAK, THERE was a quiet tapping on Meiling's door. She sat on her windowsill in spirit form, gazing into the empty air above her sleeping body. Every few minutes she'd glance at Pa, find him awake and unmoved.

This night had been the longest night of her life.

At the sound of that tap, Pa stood, stretching and wincing quietly. He moved silently, belying his own size, and never once let go of his weapons. Opening the door slightly, he leaned his head out, then slipped into the hallway. Through the cracked door, Ma was visible, already dressed for the day.

Pa sent the guards away, but kept the door open, his eye hardly straying away from his sleeping daughter. He and Ma began talking in whispers too quiet for her to hear.

Meiling hesitated, fiddling with her tether, before floating closer.

"I can't think of any other option," Pa was saying.

"It sounds too dangerous! How could we send her off? Into the *mó guǐ* infested countryside?"

"If your vision is true, he hasn't forgotten you, and last night . . ." Pa shook his head. "He's trying to use her. To get back at me."

"Or me," said Ma, dropping her face into her hands. "It's been so many years, I never thought . . . But why Meiling, of the three?"

"Everyone knows she doesn't have magic. Perhaps he viewed her as an easier target."

"We should have sent her to the Academy."

"*No*," came Pa's vehement reply. "Her magic—you've seen what they're doing to that little healer right now at the Academy. If Meiling's magic was known, she would be like that healer, except far worse. She would be put to sleep for life. I *won't* have that for her."

"She's so unhappy, though."

"I know," growled Pa, shoulders drooping. "I know, Liena. After last night, I just don't see how she can stay at the palace for these next few months. With the barbarians growing restless on our borders, and all our intelligence points to *him* being their leader. If I must go there myself to fight—"

"Nianzu."

"If he knows where she is, and if he has an evanescer, one that can steal her away with him, he can send that evanescer back when we're least expecting it. Unless I keep her heavily guarded perpetually—fathers, I'd guard her myself!—there's no way we can be assured of her safety. She needs to leave, and no one can know about it."

"But where can she go? How long? How can we be sure she will be safe on the journey?"

"I've been thinking about it all night. Liafugan is our most secure fortress, and it isn't near one of the passes to Butagin."

"The journey would be a fortnight!"

"With proper escorts, she will be completely safe. One of this year's graduates has caught my notice in particular."

"Graduate! Surely we'd want someone older?"

"We need secrecy, Liena. Pulling established wielders out of their jobs will be suspicious and could lead to questions. For the Academy's faults, we both know the caliber of wielders it puts out. I've been thinking about this all night, and none of it is ideal."

"What if this is all a mistake? What if—"

Pa raked a hand through his hair, his jaw clenched. "It might be a mistake. But every minute she's here, she's in danger of being kidnapped, or worse. If *he* is trying to take her, she's in danger no matter where she is. Sending her away buys our military time to neutralize this threat. It should only be a few months. She could be back in time for the Festival of New Lights."

Meiling couldn't take any more. Heart pounding, she slipped back into her body, then sat up in bed. At the sound of rustling bedsheets, her parents turned, found her watching. They stared at her through the open doorway, their faces such a mixture of heartbreak and strain. For a long moment, no one said anything. They didn't need to ask if she'd heard, not when her eyes filled with tears, and she clutched the quilt beneath her chin.

"I don't want to leave," Meiling finally said, choking on the words.

Ma rushed forward. She looked more herself without her ceremonial paint, but it also meant that Meiling could read every line of fear in her face, each tear glistening on her lashes. Ma wrapped her up in her arms, as if she were still a small child.

"I don't want to leave," Meiling said again. "Pa? Please don't send me away."

Pa met her gaze, dark circles beneath his bloodshot eyes, and he was almost unrecognizable as the Glorious Emperor who had stood so tall and mighty at the Graduation festival the day before.

He turned away, but not before a tear escaped down his cheek. "I'll make the arrangements. You leave at dawn."

This wasn't real. It wasn't happening.

No maids helped her prepare for the journey. Just Ma, who seemed to magically produce proper commoner garb for her to wear: a long, wrapped tunic that secured over brown trousers with a threadbare sash. Sturdy, stiff, and practical for travel. Inconspicuous.

They didn't talk as they worked. She wasn't to say goodbye to her brother and sister either, and from the look on Ma's face when she asked, she wasn't sure they were even going to be told about her departure.

She should feel afraid, perhaps even betrayed, hurt. Instead, she was numb. Her brain refused to believe this was happening, that this wasn't some strange dream.

Except that she never dreamed, so she knew this was real.

In a fog, she bid her mother and father farewell while it was still dark, kissed their cheeks, and embraced them. When she was tempted to cling to Pa, he leaned down and whispered, "Don't tell anyone about your magic." Then he told her he loved her, that he would do everything in his power to bring her back safely as soon as possible.

"I love you, little dove," Ma said, tears leaking out of her eyes.

This isn't happening.

A tall form waited outside her door—a feminine form, cloaked with a hood drawn low over her face. Her clothes were likewise unsuspicious and common. Not at all the distinguished garb of a wielder. Yet there was no doubting that this was a trained warrior.

Pa placed one hot hand on her back and pushed her forward. She resisted, her feet sunken into the floor and rooted there, until he leaned down and whispered, "Go, little one."

She went.

Over her bowed head, Pa growled to the wielder, "Your life is forfeit if anything happens to her."

The woman bowed. When she spoke, however, Meiling was surprised by how young she sounded. "It is my honor to serve His Imperial Majesty and Her Highness."

The door to her rooms shut behind her, and the young woman set off down the hallway at a clip. Meiling trotted to keep up, glancing around nervously from beneath her own hood as she was led through the familiar corridors of her home.

Her escort clearly knew these hallways, and apparently even the servants' patterns, because she deftly avoided every eye. By the time they reached a side exit, Meiling doubted a single person had seen her escape.

It only made her heart beat faster at the sight of dawn's first blush painting the sky, and the three saddled horses tucked into the early morning shadows and another tall, cloaked wielder standing with them. He wore boots, dark breeches, and a long, plain tunic belted at the waist. The folds of his cloak couldn't entirely conceal the weapons tucked into that belt. The woman, too, was armed.

Leaving. For *months*, possibly longer. To not see her family, to not sit on her favorite cliff overlooking the ocean each night, to not spend her days in the library reading and studying on her own, to not—

The second wielder looked up, giving Meiling a glimpse of his face. Glittering black eyes met hers, set in a face like flint. Eyes that could slice her into pieces as they swept over her, calculation in their icy depths. They met hers with the force of a tidal wave, strong enough to decimate her in one blow. He was the same graduate who had saved her from a tumble into the lotus pond.

Hatred was etched into every harsh cut of his face. Apparently, he did care she was cursed. Apparently, he cared *very much*.

She stopped and nearly turned on her heel to run back inside.

No, no, no.

The woman whipped her head back toward Meiling. "Keep up!" When the young man's glare swiveled to her, she added, "*Your Highness.*"

Meiling's lips parted. She cast a furtive glance over her shoulder at the shut door.

Then she drew a deep breath, set her shoulders back, and strode forward. If her parents believed this was the best thing to do, she would trust them. She wouldn't cower. She would face this as the opportunity it was to see more of the world, to be free of the curse everyone believed she bore.

Well, perhaps not entirely free of that.

Hadn't she always wished she could accompany Yun on his travels once he graduated? This wouldn't be nearly the same, but that didn't mean she couldn't be brave and make the best of it.

The woman stuffed Meiling's pack into the saddlebag of a dappled gray mare and nodded to the man. "Help her mount," she growled.

He shot an icy look her way and jerked the saddle strap of his own horse tighter. She puffed and leapt into the saddle of her brown horse. Not waiting another second, she kicked her horse into a prance and headed out the gate.

Oh fathers, this wasn't boding well.

With another glare at the woman, the young man trudged to where Meiling stood by the gray mare. Her heart climbed higher and higher into her chest with each step until it rammed at her throat when he reached her side. Not sparing her the briefest of acknowledging glances, he bent over with his hands clasped in a step. "Put your foot here and I'll boost you into the saddle, Highness." His voice was low and cold.

Meiling swallowed and glanced toward the woman, who had mercifully stopped to glare back at them. Should she place a hand on his shoulder for balance? She reached out, then pulled her hand back halfway, hesitating. Her fingers curled into a fist as she mentally chided herself. Then, overcoming the sputtering in her brain, she grabbed hold of the saddle in one hand, and his broad shoulder in the other. She lifted her left foot and placed it into his waiting hands, and he boosted her up high enough for her to swing her other leg over the saddle.

Settling herself into the saddle and gripping the reins, she tried to process how high she was above the ground. She startled when the young man grasped her ankle and arranged her foot in the stirrup before swiftly turning to abandon her.

Meiling swallowed the knot in her throat, grasping at the bare bits of her courage. "Um . . . What is your name?" They couldn't travel as strangers, right? It didn't appear as though either warrior had any interest in introducing themselves.

He was already gripping his horse's reins, one foot in the stirrup. He paused, his shoulders rising and falling as though from a deep breath.

"Tan Shangdi," he said.

He mounted his horse with practiced agility and spurred it toward the woman's. With a kick into her horse's gut, Meiling awkwardly prompted it into motion. *Clop, clop, clop,* she followed her two escorts.

She needed to ask the name of the young woman, but she wasn't sure she had any courage left to spare. All her energy was focused on not turning her horse around and galloping back to the palace.

But Pa wouldn't be happy if she did. Her head sagged. She brought him enough embarrassment as it was.

Frustration burned in her breast. Why *hadn't* they announced her magic, like Hou's and Yun's? Why *hadn't* they enrolled her in the Academy? They were protecting her, that much she knew. But *why*? What could they be protecting her from that would justify the scorn she had borne since youth? Pa had said something about not wanting her "put to sleep," but what did that even mean? All she could do was float around and overhear conversations. How did that merit secrecy?

Who would be trying to find her? And *why*?

Taking a left after the gate, the woman guided their group along the road to go around the mountain. It remained dark and chilly enough that Meiling used one hand to hold her cloak tighter around her. She jolted with every movement of the horse beneath her, casting more than one forlorn glance behind her at the palace and city she abandoned.

Her companions were silent.

She chewed on her lip, studying the imposing backs ahead of her. Tan Shangdi was a graduate, and she'd seen yesterday that he wore honor cords on his robes. If she had to place a guess, it would be that her other escort was also a graduate.

Her eyes widened with sudden realization, her mouth dropping open.

Their appointments.

If they were graduates, they would have received appointments for their occupation. Positions in the military, bureaucracy, in the cities and towns of the empire. Academy students slaved away their lives to get the best appointment they could, because that determined their rank and position in society.

If these wielders were here with her, then they weren't at their new appointments.

"Oh no," Meiling whispered.

Had they forfeited their lifelong work and the prestige they earned to escort her to Liafugan? On a journey that was so secretive that even the Secret Services didn't know about it?

She was suddenly dizzy. It made sense now; the ice in Shangdi's gaze and the clip in the woman's tone. They'd given everything up for her. They'd been *forced* to give everything up for her.

Her hands clenched the reins so hard her fingernails dug into her palms. Was there any way she could repair this?

She could be sweet and smile, feigning ignorance, and hope they could simply brush this issue under the rug. Or she could address it directly, apologize for how this must be upending their lives, and thank them for their loyal and dutiful service.

One was easier. But easy didn't mean better.

Meiling closed her eyes, her hands breaking out in a cold sweat. She kicked her horse harder, urging the beast to quicken her pace and catch up to the others. Best to do this now before she second-guessed herself. The last thing she needed was to agonize over this for the entire day.

She struggled to muster enough courage to utter the words. Up they came. She opened her mouth—and shut it. Why was this so hard for her? Afraid of having to repeat herself, she finally leaned forward in the saddle and said loudly, "I know this journey must have cost—"

The woman pulled her horse to a stop. Shangdi's nearly bumped into it. She whirled in her saddle, her hood falling back to reveal a face that would have been pretty if it were not so incredibly fierce. She reminded Meiling of Hou, only grown and without Hou's characteristic mischievous glint. These eyes were wild, almost feral. Harsh.

Perhaps Meiling had been wrong about her initial judgement that Shangdi was the angrier of the two. The hood had hidden much.

The woman opened her mouth—

"Fen," growled Shangdi in warning.

"Don't *Fen* me," she snapped at him.

Meiling drew her cloak tighter around herself, something sinking like a stone into her gut. *Oh no.* This was even worse than she had expected.

"Control your tongue," said Shangdi. "She is the daughter of our sovereign."

The face Fen made in response was a mixture of scorn and disgust.

"It's alright," Meiling said, her knuckles white on her reins. "She can tell me. I want to hear."

Perhaps the last statement wasn't entirely true. But if they couldn't speak freely around her, there would be no resolution for this problem, which would make this journey far worse.

Shangdi's head half twisted back toward her, and she caught a wrinkled eyebrow and frown on his profile. He faced forward, however, without saying anything more.

"Thank you, gracious Highness," said Fen. Her words sliced through the beams of rising sun, almost sharp enough to sever the surrounding trees from their stumps. She looked like a volcano about ready to explode and spew lava across the countryside.

"Fen," said Shangdi again in warning.

"She said she would hear me, Shang, so shut your dragon-cursed mouth."

His shoulders tensed, but there was no other visible reaction to her words. Meiling waited with bated breath, trying not to huddle down into the saddle, trying to keep her spine straight and her face as cold and impassive as Shang's.

There was no doubt that she had failed. Her composure fractured by the minute. Her soul began craving that escape, that freedom from her body to fly free. It would be a long day before that.

"I suppose you can tell," said Fen, her eyes cutting like daggers into Meiling, "that we are not happy about this."

Meiling nodded mutely.

"Speak for yourself," said Shang.

"You are even angrier than I am! Don't try to play polite on me now."

No response.

"We aren't happy," continued Fen, "and I don't care if you're the emperor's daughter."

"Are you *trying* to get yourself executed?"

"Shut *up*, Shang."

"I'm not going to have either of you executed," said Meiling.

"See? She's *nice*."

Why did that sound more like an insult than a compliment?

Fen didn't stop, and apparently Shang had given up on telling her to control her tongue, because he didn't interrupt her anymore.

"Princess Meiling, you've never been to the Academy, so you wouldn't know how hard we've worked all our lives for an appointment, and you might not have realized everything we've given up for this. For you."

I do realize, thought Meiling. She said nothing, however.

"Shang and I did *not* work so hard to babysit a princess, understand?"

Did Shang flinch? If he hadn't, Meiling flinched enough for the both of them. Her fingers clenched into fists around the pommel of her saddle. She wanted to snap that this wasn't her decision, that she hadn't had any say in this, but trying to defend herself always made her feel pitiful.

"We lost our appointments because of you. Appointments we worked *very* hard for—for years! So please forgive me if I don't have interest in cozying up by the campfire tonight and exchanging pleasantries. I suggest you fold your hands nicely and let us do our job in peace."

Meiling was too taken aback to respond immediately. She stared, bewildered beyond belief, like someone had driven a knife into her chest. "I'm . . . I'm sorry," she said, but it was probably too quiet for them to hear. Fen forced her horse forward again.

Never in her life had she felt as small as she did now.

Her first instinct was to cry, but she swallowed her tears and dabbed her sleeve against the few that escaped the corners of her eyes. What would convince them more that she was the soft, useless princess they clearly thought she was? She was sheltered, possibly the most sheltered daughter in the entire empire, but she refused to break down into pieces at the first taste of the real world. If she took offense that someone should speak so harshly with her, didn't that just go to prove how sheltered and soft she was?

Fen might be harsh, and unthinkably rude to a royal, but her words were true. It might not be Meiling's fault that they were on this journey, but it was true that she was the cause of them losing their livelihoods. She ought to own that.

Dread seeping into her stomach, she kicked her horse faster, until she was closer to Shang's horse.

"I'm sorry, to both of you," she said, hating how her voice quavered traitorously, how her lip trembled. "I'm sure His Imperial Majesty will reward your service generously."

"My battalion will have left by the time I return," Fen huffed.

"He will repay you. I'm certain of it."

Neither responded. The silence stretched out into hours, and Meiling couldn't help but be relieved by the lack of attention.

How long this journey unfolded before her—an entire *fortnight* of travel with bitter escorts. For the thousandth time, she hated this plan, longed to understand. Nothing answered her, however, except the heavy, hollow sound of the horses' hooves finding purchase on the rocky ground and the clamor of the city coming to life as they fled it.

CHAPTER 4

MEILING HAD NEVER minded long, silent nights. Nothing, however, could compare to the dreadful length of this day. It dragged on and on as they rode and wound their way through the dense forest toward this fortress that was to be her salvation.

They hadn't stopped to eat. Shang and Fen only fished about in their saddlebags for food when the sun beat down hot on their necks without speaking a word to Meiling. Hoping she was similarly stocked, she gripped her saddle for dear life as she precariously leaned to rifle through her own bags.

Rice cakes. Hard strips of jerky. Apples. A sack of oats, and another of dried rice. Much plainer fare than what she was used to. Meiling swallowed her initial revulsion, telling her pampered stomach to be grateful. After all, she'd eat almost anything if it broke the endless monotony of the day.

When, at long last, the sun began to sink, and the heat subsided, Shang urged his horse up beside Fen's and leaned closer to her to converse. The distinct lack of nearby civilization was increasingly concerning. Surely they would find an inn to spend the night, right?

Fen and Shang both dismounted, and Shang handed his horse's lead to Fen. Meiling's heart climbed into her throat, throbbing wildly when he approached her. It was the first time either of them acknowledged her since this morning.

He reached her side, and the intensity of his black gaze nearly cut off Meiling's oxygen. "Toss your leg over the neck of the horse."

Was it not supposed to be the other way? Toss it over the back of the horse? Meiling obeyed anyway, struggling to get her stiff leg out of the stirrup and over the neck of the horse discretely, until she sat sideways on the horse.

Shang reached up, wrapped large hands around her waist—she looked anywhere but his face as she gripped his forearms—and pulled her down, setting her firmly on the ground. She stumbled, making his hold on her waist tighten as she clutched his sleeves.

"Forgive me," she managed with an awkward chuckle. "I'm not normally this clumsy."

As if there was anything normal about this situation.

Once her feet steadied beneath her, Shang withdrew his hands without bothering to respond. Then he strode off with her horse to where Fen was busy hobbling the others.

Meiling took a few stiff, aching steps to the nearest tree and leaned against it before her wobbly knees could betray her and collapse. Was this the feeling she'd heard described when people walked on land again after weeks out at sea?

The last rays of the sun cut through the forest and turned everything a fiery shade of orange. So, they would be sleeping out in the forest. She drew a deep breath. This would be a new experience.

Fen and Shang were busy setting up camp. Saddles were removed from the tired horses, a fire arranged and lit, and a small tent assembled.

Meiling stood awkwardly where Shang had planted her, watching the others work. Surely there was something she could do to help—something to lighten their load. Perhaps if she made herself useful, they would not hate her so much.

But summoning the courage to speak when her previous attempt had resulted so terribly, well . . . that was another thing entirely. Eventually, after a battle had raged in her head, she spoke up, "Is there anything I can do to help?"

"Actually, yes." Fen's head shot up from where she was striking two unfamiliar objects to create a spark for the fire. "Sit on that log and don't talk."

Shriveling into a tiny ball was tempting. Instead, she settled down on the log, ignoring the discomfort of the hard bark, and watched Fen closely. She noted how the other girl arranged the wood for the fire, watched how she struck the flint, observed how she coaxed the spark into a crackling blaze.

It was a while before Fen and Shang settled down by the fire with strips of hard jerky. Fen obliged to throw a few pieces Meiling's way. She tried to catch them, but only succeeded in catching one while the other landed on the ground.

She was keenly aware of the two pairs of eyes that watched her pick the food off the ground, brush it off, and begin eating it. But she wouldn't look in their direction, fixing her attention firmly on the fire. The sporadic movements of the dancing flames slowly calmed her, reminding her of her father and her siblings.

Her thoughts wandered. What would her life have been like if she had been born a fire wielder instead of . . . whatever the seven valleys she was. No matter how much she studied every subset of the five great categories of magic, the ability to separate her soul from her body didn't seem to fit anywhere.

Across the fire, Fen and Shang conversed in a whisper. Eventually, their tone grew, and they seemed to forget Meiling's presence. She listened with interest, scooting forward but trying to keep her eyes downcast.

"Honghui said the history part of the exam was so difficult. I don't know what he was talking about—it was so easy!" Fen was saying, gesturing with jerky.

Shang's hard mouth slipped into a small smile. "Honghui was always academically challenged. I never thought he'd be appointed to the Emperor's Guard."

"Which was why I assumed it *wasn't* just his brains. I thought I'd heard Nuo say something similar. Perhaps it was easy because I studied so hard—scared half to death by Honghui! I wasn't about to let the history section ruin all my hard work." She leaned against a tree, stretching her long legs out toward the fire. She absently tugged at the braid falling over her shoulder. "You were wicked during the fighting section," she said, turning a mischievous grin up to Shang. "I thought you might kill Master Gen for a moment there."

"Luck," he muttered. "And Master Gen was never at risk of dying. Not at my hand."

"I think he thought otherwise." Fen laughed. "There was one moment—you should have seen his face! I think he saw his life flash before his eyes."

Shang only chuckled and changed the subject. "I was sorry I missed your fight. I heard you did well."

She shrugged casually, but the movement couldn't disguise the way her face lit up at his praise. "This one wasn't very hard. I didn't have to change often."

Finding her voice, Meiling blurted, "Change?"

The sound seemed to startle Fen, but Shang might not have heard her for all the indifference on his face.

"Change. Shift," Fen barked quickly and turned back to Shang. "Wasn't it strange to walk down the city procession? Like we've seen everyone else do for years and years? To wear the red robes!"

Fen was a shapeshifter, then.

"It felt right, not strange," Shang said. "We worked for it. *Hard.*"

Meiling drew her cloak tighter around herself. Weariness dragged heavily on her lids, and her spirit tugged in angst, ready to flee her body and experience a few hours of freedom. She glanced at the one tent. It was painfully small. How would they all fit in there?

She didn't want to ask, that was certain. She hoped she never had to speak again on this journey. Hoped they would forget she existed and let her quietly follow their lead. Perhaps sleeping outside would be simpler. She had no need to fight over the tent, to make herself more despised. It would be different, but many people in the world slept thus every night. It would be good for her for a change. Resolved, Meiling slowly slid off the log to the ground and wrapped her cloak around her.

She was starting to lie down, her eyes already closing despite herself, when a voice jerked her straight.

"You sleep in the tent, Highness. Bedroll is over there."

It was Shang, who had evidently spied her attempts to escape notice. He jerked his head toward the pile of saddles and saddlebags.

Meiling blinked back her sleepiness to snag a quick glance at him, but he had already retreated into his conversation with Fen about the language and geography sections of their final exam from the Academy. Yet somehow, even though he wasn't looking at her, her senses prickled. She stood, brushing leaves off her cloak, and scurried to the mound of leather, canvas, and buckles.

She could have sworn his attention followed her movements.

After several minutes of rifling through saddlebags, she had only successfully found bandages, clothes, knives, more food—including what appeared to be a leftover lemon sweetheart cake wrapped in parchment from yesterday's festival—and a few other things. She took the coarse woolen blanket and was about to head to the tent. But she stopped, looking down at the blanket.

He said there was a bedroll. Unless she was mistaken—and she very well could be—a blanket was not a bedroll. Shang and Fen already thought she was stupid. No need to prove them right. With a deep breath, she surveyed the pile again.

Oh.

It was fastened separately to the back of one of the saddles, not stuffed into a saddlebag. She undid the ties and tucked it under her arm. With a deep breath, she braved the campfire again, but thankfully, no one said anything to her as she slipped into the tent.

It was indeed small, but a sense of calm and peace washed over her. It was small, but it was her own. Behind the thin canvas walls, she was free from Fen's bitter taunts and Shang's superior silence. She breathed a deep, relieved sigh.

The bedroll, combined with the blanket, was nothing like her bed at home. It smelled slightly musty, like it had spent the better part of its life in a closet. She tried not to care about how the bedroll hardly cushioned her from the ground. Most people slept like this—she should just be grateful she had the bedroll and blanket.

That was when she realized neither of her parents would kiss her goodnight tonight. Not tonight, not for months. It was stupid that she missed it; after all, wasn't she an adult now? A princess of marriageable age? She shouldn't be almost in tears over the lack of a goodnight kiss. But it wasn't the kiss she missed—it was the assurance of affection. It was a comfort that, no matter what their people thought of her, she was always beloved by someone.

Meiling fortified her courage, steeling herself up from tears. She would be home soon. This would be over quickly.

She drifted off to sleep, her spirit slipping free of the confines of her mortal body. Her spirit stretched like a lazy cat just waking up, and the anxiety of the last day and night rolled off her shoulders.

There were several things she intended to do tonight.

But first, she needed to breathe. Needed to simply exist. To feel free.

Then she slipped through folds of canvas to find the bright, angry red glow of Fen sprawling on the ground outside her tent. Shang sat awake and alert by the sparking flames of fire, a light blue emanating from his own soul.

Meiling drifted to the opposite side of the fire. She pooled into a little blob of spirit on the ground and stared at Shang, studying him.

He stared unflinchingly into the fire, the hard cut of his brow casting shadow over his eyes. His legs were spread wide, his elbows resting on his knees and hands tented beneath his chin like he was deep in thought. His brow furrowed as she watched. He was as silent as the mountain towering over them, oblivious to the excited chatter of the stars, of how brightly his own soul glowed. Blue—he must have magic pertaining to some sort of elemental manipulation. Water?

What was he thinking?

One of his hands curled into a fist as he closed his eyes and lowered his head, almost in defeat. But it was only the briefest moment, and then he had pulled every feature back into the stern and stoic mask he always wore.

He was thinking about his lost appointment, wasn't he?

If he was a top ten graduate, then his appointment must have been prestigious indeed. Fen clearly held Shang in a high regard that did not seem entirely reciprocated. Unless Meiling's guess was wrong, Shang was very likely *the* top graduate of the Academy.

She wished she hadn't ruined his life.

Meiling glanced back at Fen, whose face had softened significantly in sleep. It curved much gentler than Shang's, and while asleep, she looked deceptively sweet. Gone were the furrows and lines carved into her brow, the stern cut of her mouth.

Without a doubt, he was the smarter of the pair.

Suddenly, Shang's head snapped to Meiling. She let out something like a gasp as his black eyes piercing right through her. He had seen her. How had he seen her?

No, wait—

A snorting sounded behind her. She flitted out of his line of sight, but his gaze remained fixed on the noise. She relaxed so much she nearly fell straight into the ground. After the initial wave of relief, she stiffened.

What was that sound?

Was it a *mó guǐ?*

Her heart beat faster through her tether. Shang flicked his wrist slightly and, his formerly empty palms were now full of tiny, glittering ice shards. He didn't stand. Hardly moved beside the wrist flick, only staring into the darkness beyond the warmth of the fire.

The snorting grew louder.

Something emerged from the trees. Something huge, wide, hairy, and low to the ground. Moonlight caught on the sharp edges of long, protruding tusks. It snorted closer, its nose rustling into the ground.

A jolt shot through her tether. Fen still slept, blissfully ignorant.

The creature entered the firelight.

It was the ugliest thing she'd ever seen. Shaped like a barrel, with a tail rather like a rat's, it had saggy skin and a patchy-haired face.

It was only a hog.

Dangerous, indeed, but nothing near as dangerous as a *mó guǐ.* Meiling whooshed downward in the air with relief. Shang didn't move, keeping his eye on the beast as it nosed closer and closer to the camp, to the place where Fen and Meiling slept.

She darted about in the air above, flitting anxiously. *Kill it, Shang!* Why hadn't he moved? It could gore any of them in a second.

The hog didn't seem to notice Shang at all. It snorted its way near to the log where Meiling had been sitting earlier.

Shang stood.

"Go," he hissed, approaching it. "Get out of here."

At the sound of his voice, the hog's tusked snout shot up. Meiling caught her breath at the look in its eyes. It was going to charge him, wasn't it? Oh fathers—

Shang was so fast she hardly realized he had drawn back his hand and flung a myriad of small ice shards into the beast's body before it let out a squeal, waking Fen with a start. She leapt to her feet, almost losing her balance, her knife already drawn.

The hog toppled almost into the fire.

Fen, legs braced wide, blinked from the body up to Shang standing still behind it. For a split second, they both stared at it. Then Shang looked up at Fen. "Go back to sleep. Everything's fine."

Fen did not protest. She sheathed her knife, laid down, and promptly fell back asleep.

Not wanting to watch Shang gut the animal, Meiling decided it was time to go about the second thing she wanted to do tonight.

She fled away from the campsite and flew as high as she could go. Suspended far above the treetops, as close to the stars as she could get, she stopped and let her eyes soak in the glorious expanse of trees spreading for li upon li, so dark along the side of the mountain. The mountain itself loomed still higher above her, and she tugged at her soul tether, wishing she could float to the very highest cliff and overlook the landscape.

She could perch herself in midair like this, but it always felt strange to her mind—like if she wavered in her belief that she was only a spirit and not a physical body, she would fall crashing to the ground.

She floated around, looking for the perfect spot to sit. Unsatisfied, she flew lower. Once she was low enough to the ground to be beneath the canopy of the forest, she slid her shadow onto a tree branch.

Here, surrounded by the peace and quiet of the forest—so alone—Meiling could finally breathe. She was light, free. Her tangled web of emotions and thoughts from today unraveled, and she could make sense of things that had been so confusing and overwhelming earlier.

She had not realized . . . so many things. She was used to being ignored and shunned. This open antagonism, however, was completely new. To think she'd been sheltered from this her entire life because of her birth. There must be many people who were often treated this way, and far worse.

If she was honest, Fen and Shang had not done anything cruel to her. Fen's words were impatient and irritable, not cruel. And they were only words. Fen and Shang had given up so much to ensure Meiling traveled safely.

Despite their unkind actions, despite the unfairness of the situation, she ought to be stronger. She should not let their words bother her. They were good people. She might not have guessed it of Fen if she did not have such a similar little sister. But Hou, for all her sharp words, loved with a wild abandon like no one else.

After leaning her head against the tree trunk and running tendrils of smokey fingers along silver leaves for hours, thinking and thinking and thinking, Meiling decided she was brave enough to return to the camp.

With her soul tether, she could never be lost. Despite having no idea where the camp was, she only had to reach for that tether, and pull herself back—or, more aptly, let herself be drawn back—to camp.

When she flitted into the campsite, the fire had died some. It must have been many hours indeed, for Shang no longer stood watch. He lay sprawled on his back, one arm hooked under his head like a pillow, in front of Meiling's tent. Soft breaths puffed between slightly parted lips. He looked exhausted; even his glow was subdued.

Fen sat near the fire, blinking blearily. As the minutes passed, she began fiddling with her fingers and picking at her nails. She picked, peeled, and bit until they were stumps in her nailbeds. This accomplished, she pulled out a knife from her sleeve and a stone from somewhere else and set to sharpening the blade loud enough to wake Shang. He didn't stir.

"Dragon-blasted princess," she muttered. "Dragon-blasted emperor. Dragon-blasted *everything*." Then she set to vigorously digging out a wad of earwax from her ear.

Meiling pursed shadow lips, sinking closer to the ground.

After twiddling and fiddling and fidgeting, Fen startled her by suddenly melting into a blinding flash of red light. Where Fen had just sat, a wolf now snarled. It sniffed the air, red eyes blazing with intelligence. The wolf stuck its snout into the fallen leaves and sniffed the perimeter of the camp. Once or twice, its head shot up, held stone still, and sniffed the air. But after a few minutes, it plunked its nose back down to the ground.

Then there was another blinding flash.

The wolf was gone. So was Fen.

Bewildered, Meiling looked everywhere for that telltale red glow—and found it hovering high above in the form of a black hawk with a speckled breast. It glided over the treetops, screeching occasionally. It predominately flew high, but sometimes it careened into the forest, claws extended, and then shot back out for more circling.

Meiling's mouth dropped open. What incredible magic.

She sat by the fire and watched Fen guarding the campsite, imagining her life if she had been born with such powers. What her life would have been like at the Academy, the friends she would have, the pride she would bring to her parents.

She had so many questions for Fen; so many questions she could never hope to ask. Not unless she wanted a snappy reply.

Dawn crept so slowly that Meiling hardly realized the darkness had softened to gray and purple. She did not stir from staring at the fire, letting her mind stray to and fro wherever it wanted, until Shang roused a few feet away.

Meiling jolted slightly when he stretched out his arms and long legs. He sat up and rubbed the arm he'd been sleeping on, as though it needed to wake up too. Blinking a few times before awareness seemed to sink in, he stood up, quickly retied his hair into its long queue, and straightened his cloak.

Fen shifted back in her human form and smiled wryly. "Morning."

"Wake up the girl," was all Shang said in response, his voice deep with sleep.

The next thing Meiling knew, she was blinking foggily up into Fen's furrowed brow. Her body rattled strangely. Fen had her by the shoulders, shaking her none too gently.

"Up. We're leaving."

CHAPTER 5

BUT THE MOUNTAIN pass is so much faster!" Fen protested. "Your way adds a whole day!"

An entire day? Meiling groaned internally. Her backside suddenly throbbed worse than it had only a minute prior.

"It doesn't. The mountain pass is treacherous. It is a shorter distance, but it will be slower progress. The difference is irrelevant," Shang responded. "We go through the valley."

"We're supposed to make decisions *together*," Fen snapped.

Shang gave her an icy look. "The mountain pass will compromise our ability to protect the girl since my powers will be near useless. Should we come upon any dangers—"

"I could fend them off! You insult my—"

"Don't make this personal. We are discussing which route to take. The route through the plains will be easier, it won't be significantly longer, and one of us won't be severely disadvantaged. So unless you have a *real* reason to take the mountain pass, we'll travel the plains."

"Everything's personal, Tan Shangdi."

If the muscle flexing in Shang's jaw was any indication, he had no desire to continue this conversation. Nevertheless, after a few moments of silence, he spoke in that same cool, collected tone. "This assignment is strictly professional. We do our duty and serve our emperor as quickly and thoroughly as possible, then we return to salvage our careers. What we cannot salvage, however, is a botched mission."

Fen glared at him. Shang met that glare evenly, unflinchingly.

Meiling glanced between them, waiting. Shang showed no sign of breaking, but Fen seemed to be equally stubborn. Their strength was matched, though different. Complementary. Fen was brute strength and power. She was fierce will and stubborn grit. Shang, on the other hand, was calculated and strategic.

Their silent battle waged in the glint of their eyes and the set of their jaws. Meiling learned more about them in that moment than in all the previous days.

Fen broke first.

It was unacknowledged, but the tension in the air fizzled when Fen looked ahead first. Apparently, they were traveling through the plains.

One glance at Shang's ice-cold face when they stopped to camp sealed Meiling's lips shut. It didn't matter that she was too sore to move; she was just going to have to manage it.

Trying not to wince, she struggled to wrestle her leg over the neck of the horse. Shang's expression revealed nothing as he watched her. With flushed cheeks, she finally sat so Shang could reach up, grasp her waist, and pull her out of the saddle. This time, she peeked up at his face when he set her on the ground.

He looked off over her shoulder to where Fen had started setting up camp for the night, but then his eyes swiveled down to hers. Held her gaze.

He turned away, releasing his grip on her waist, and strode off to attend to the horses.

Now, it was time for Meiling to change things, even if they were small things.

She mentally fortified herself, every muscle bracing. She refused to be useless and helpless on their journey, but she knew that to prove herself useful, she would bear the brunt of Fen's, and possibly Shang's, sharp words. With a determined set of her jaw, she set to collecting sticks. The ground was littered with them, and her arms were full within minutes.

"What are you doing?" Fen snapped as she walked up with a little box.

"Helping," Meiling said, forcing herself to meet Fen's scowl.

The shifter's features eased into amusement. "You're going to light the fire? By all means, do it!" She threw the little box at Meiling, who just watched, arms full of sticks, as it landed in the dirt beside her.

It took every ounce of strength not to glare at Fen. She dumped her load into the midst of the clearing and arranged the wood like a tent, as she had seen Fen do yesterday. They tumbled into a pile on the grass. Meiling reset them.

"You skipped about five steps," Fen snorted.

Meiling's hands slowed. She looked up at Fen with narrowed eyes. "Would you care to show me?"

"You have to set up a few sticks at the bottom so the fire can breathe." She came to stand over Meiling with a cocked leg and folded arms. Her face pinched with impatience.

Meiling selected four sticks and laid them on the ground, parallel to each other.

"Not so close, spread them out. How can the fire breathe when they're so close?"

Deep breath. Meiling slid the sticks out farther from each other.

"That'll do. Now you add some on top—no! You lay them in the opposite direction, so they cross each other. Yes, like that. Wait, you didn't get any brush? You think those sticks are just going to catch fire from the tinderbox? You're hopeless." Fen threw up her hands and stormed away to rummage through her horse's saddlebags, which Shang had deposited nearby.

Meiling happened to glance up.

Shang had stopped setting up her tent to stare at them, watching their exchange with furrowed brows. Meiling's flush of embarrassment deepened. She grabbed the wayward fragments of her attention. *Be strong, be strong.* She would not let Fen's words get to her—wouldn't let them make her cry. She repeated in her mind the last few things Fen had said and deduced what she needed. Standing up, she searched until she had a little pile of dry leaves and dead pine needles.

Fen was not looking, so Meiling quickly added the brush to her pile. Then she added a few smaller sticks from her first batch of wood. Now, the difficult part.

She picked up the box Fen had thrown at her and slid it open. Inside were two unfamiliar objects. A rock and a flat, metal oval. Fen had used them to light the fire last night. Hesitantly, Meiling picked up the two objects and set the box on the ground next to her. She held one in each hand, feeling their different weights and shapes. She just needed to try. Fen would correct her.

She struck them together. Once, twice, thrice—

"What's this?" Fen growled, suddenly standing over her again. "You don't bash them together like that. You strike the steel on the flint. Do you even know which one is the flint and which is the steel?"

A shadow fell across the pile of sticks and kindling. Meiling looked up just as Shang came between her and Fen, folding his long legs to crouch silently beside her. Her eyes widened, her mouth falling open as Shang reached for her left hand.

"What are you doing?" Fen demanded from behind Shang.

He ignored Fen, touching the metal oval Meiling held. "This is the steel." He pointed to the rock in her other hand. "That is the flint. You strike the steel on the flint. You'll find it easier to switch hands."

Shang was . . . helping her?

Fen let out a huff and marched off. Meiling obediently switched the flint and the steel in her hands, and hoped the fading sunlight would disguise the heat rising into her cheeks. But she hesitated to strike the flint again. As humiliating as Fen's instruction had been, Meiling found herself caring much more what Shang thought.

She struck the flint with the steel twice before Shang's cool hand fell on her wrist, stopping her. She looked up at him, registered how close he was, and promptly returned her gaze to the pile of sticks before her.

"Let me show you," he said, and slid the tools from her hands. "It needs to be held close enough to the tinder so the sparks can catch."

As he demonstrated, a secret part of Meiling hoped he would just light it and be done with it. Instead, he returned the steel and flint to her, sitting back on his heels to watch her try again.

Six strikes and no spark. Shang leaned forward, and the sudden wave of heat turned the back of her neck warm. He wrapped one large, roughened hand around hers, tilting it to the side.

"Try like this."

She nodded stiffly and gave it a few more strikes. Finally, a spark caught on the leaves, and Shang showed her how to blow on it and coax it into a fire. It crackled to life before her eyes, sending her shoulders relaxing with relief.

When she turned to thank him, he was already getting to his feet and stalking off. Without a word. Meiling closed her eyes with a sigh, swallowed her thanks, and scooted back from the fire. Wrapping her arms around her knees, she lost herself to the hypnotizing flickers of dancing flame.

One tiny victory. A victory that had cost her nearly every scrap of pride and nearly shredded her patience to bits. Her body quivered from soreness, and the insubstantial travel food did nothing to strengthen her. She needed time to think, to rest her mind from the strain, to resolve herself for another grueling day tomorrow. To be free.

But she'd accomplished something. She'd learned something—made progress. And Shang had . . . been kind to her?

When she was finally wrapped up in blankets in her tent, when her spirit slipped free of the confines of her body, when the night fell dark and deep around them, three glows shone in their campsite. A blood-red glow curled up to sleep by her tent, an icicle blue glow staying up to guard, and the warmth of the fire.

But . . . where was that *mewling* sound coming from?

CHAPTER 6

MEILING DRIFTED CLOSER to that strange sound. She moved slowly, despite how the lack of a glowing soul indicated no magic. It made it more challenging to discover the source of the sound amidst a thicket of bamboo, and when she finally pinpointed the source, she learned why.

A small white-and-black body, half buried beneath a pile of dead leaves, mewled as it wiggled and bobbed its head.

A baby panda.

Meiling's mouth fell open as she flew to its side. But when she reached out to it, her shadowy hand went straight through the sad little cub.

You poor thing, she said, trying to stroke it. *Did your mother abandon you? Are you hurt? Just wait a few minutes, and I'll see if I can come find you. It's not safe to be out in the wilderness like this. You sweet little thing. Hold on until I get back!*

She hated leaving it by itself, but if she had any chance of saving the cub, she needed physical hands and feet. She carefully noted the spot of the panda as she flew higher, determined not to lose it when she returned. Thankfully, it wasn't far at all from their camp.

Her unfortunate dilemma only hit her when a certain ice-blue light glowed next to the flickering fire. Meiling halted short.

She couldn't march out of her tent, step over Fen's sleeping body, and prance off into the forest with a little wave at Shang. Neither could she tell him or ask for his help, because then he'd demand to know *how* she knew there was a baby panda.

Shang and Fen couldn't learn about her magic. That could get her killed—her entire family killed.

Maybe she could slip out under the back canvas of the tent and hope she was quiet enough to avoid detection. She'd always had a talent for being quiet.

When she woke herself up, she waited several long minutes, breathing to calm her racing pulse. Then she barely parted the canvas and peered out. Fen still sprawled in front of the flaps hardly a foot away from her, while Shang sat by the fire. The play of light and shadow from the flickering flames cast the sharp lines of his profile even harsher.

Good. She hadn't made any noise.

Now for the tricky part.

Meiling eased herself to the opposite side of the tent and slipped her fingers under the canvas, testing how much room she had to slip under. *Not much.* She might be small, but she wasn't *that* small.

Gritting her teeth, she crawled to the corner tent peg and set to work wiggling it loose. Shang had driven them deep into the ground, so it took her the better part of fifteen minutes to wrestle an opening wide enough for her to slide through on her belly. Frustration burned through her skin.

By now, her heart hammered so loudly she could barely think. She double checked Fen was still asleep, and Shang was still none the wiser at his post. Then she drew in a deep breath, eyeing the opening on the back side of the tent.

Nothing to it.

What was she supposed to do when she found the panda and brought it back? Cram it through this hole too? Hope it didn't make noise until Fen came to wake her up the next morning . . . and found her snuggling a panda cub?

This seemed more ridiculous by the second, but it wasn't like she could just leave a mewling baby by itself. It was clearly hurt. It would die like that.

She eased herself to her belly, lifted the canvas, and elbow-crawled her way beneath it. Very quickly, she discovered she'd underestimated her own size.

Dragons blast it. Getting her shoulders through proved to be one challenge, especially while not making a sound. Her hips, on the other hand? Why couldn't her figure have been more . . . stick-ish? The canvas pulled taut until it dug into her backside. It refused to budge. As did her hips.

A sudden flare of panic hit.

She was stuck.

Her hands balled into fists, and she sagged against the ground, cursing inwardly as she sucked in a breath between gritted teeth and squeezed her eyes shut. What now? She couldn't move backward—it was stuck too tight. But every time she tried to scoot forward, it only pulled the canvas tighter. She couldn't even angle herself to the side to keep working the stake up out of the ground.

She could always call for help.

The heat of mortification bathed her face at that thought.

It wasn't like she could stay here all night, though. The canvas hurt more with each passing second. There was also the baby panda to consider. She couldn't save it if she was stuck here.

Her only options were to call for help or keep wiggling to free herself. Her rational mind told her to choose the first option, but after much internal arguing, she opted to continue trying to free herself. Just for a little bit longer.

Her feet were starting to go numb. *Dragons blast everything.*

She pushed up on her elbows, hair falling in her face. Angrily, she swiped the rebellious strands to the side—and then froze.

That was a pair of boots. Not far from her face.

Her gaze traveled upward. Those boots were attached to a pair of legs. Which were attached to a torso, over which a pair of muscular arms were crossed. That was as far as Meiling could bring herself to look before she sagged back to the ground and squeezed her eyes shut.

Mortification seeped out of every pore on her body.

Maybe she could pretend she was dead.

When Shang said nothing, and the silence stretched out into what felt like a dozen miserable years, Meiling asked quietly, "How long have you been standing there?"

"Since the shoulders."

She winced. Instead of pretending she was dead, maybe she could actually die. Death would be a welcome reprieve to the scorching heat of embarrassment that flamed every inch of her. At least Shang hadn't woken Fen, so she too could participate in Meiling's humiliation.

She pushed herself back up to her elbows, this time not caring that her hair covered her face completely. "I suppose you didn't think to offer aid?"

Two steps, and those boots were right in front of her. Then a pair of knees, as Shang crouched before her. Finally, a hand entered her line of sight. Her heart gave a painful *thu-thud* as Shang's knuckle caught under her chin, tilting her face up to his. He seemed to ignore the strands of dark hair falling over her brow and cheeks, catching in her eyelashes.

His face was like flint, the handsome edges chiseled as though from the very night around them, and when he spoke, his voice was so low, so deep.

"What are you doing?"

Did he think she was attempting an escape? As if she would run off in the dead of night with no supplies or protection to brave the Zheninghai wilderness alone. When she opened her mouth, though, no answer would come. What was she to do? Blather to him about a wounded panda cub she'd found while using her secret magic?

He didn't release her chin. Fathers, he had the most intensely terrifying pair of black eyes she'd ever seen. They wouldn't leave her face until she answered him. As much as she tried to look away, she couldn't. As though she were a rabbit caught in a snare, staring up at the hunter about to bash her brains in.

"I heard something," she said finally.

He didn't move or relent—only waited for the rest of her explanation.

She licked her lips. "I think it's a wounded animal."

He tilted his head a fraction of an inch, and his unspoken question was almost audible. *"And you intended to investigate on your own? In the dark? With predators around every corner?"*

She tried to puff the hair out of her face. It didn't work. Neither was this conversation with Shang working. Perhaps it was time for something more honest? "I just wanted to go save it if it was hurt, and I knew you wouldn't let me, and Fen would probably call me stupid again. So I thought if I snuck out on my own, I'd have a higher chance of being able to save it. It's close—I think—and I had no intention of going far without one of you. But . . ." She trailed off, and when Shang removed his grip from her chin, she relaxed back against the ground. "Would you help me get out of this? It hurts."

He exhaled, and it might have been a sigh. Then he flipped a knife out of his sleeve, shifting from his crouch to one knee as he pried the tent stake out of the ground. The canvas relaxed, and Meiling let out a small groan when the pain finally eased.

But before she could push up on her hands and knees to finish crawling out from under the canvas, Shang stood and stepped one foot over her back, setting his boots on either side of her hips as he bent down, grabbed her under her armpits, and pulled her up to her feet. She wobbled for only a second before she spun around to face him, her arms wrapping around her middle.

She'd made quite the fool of herself thus far. Would it hurt to push her luck a little further? It wasn't as though Shang's opinion of her could be much lower than it already was.

She drew in a deep, fortifying breath. "Since you don't want me going off by myself . . . would you come with me to—"

"Go back to sleep, Highness," he said crisply, his broad shoulders set in a firm, unflinching line. "You need rest for our travels."

Her options grew slimmer by the moment. She could stomp her foot and throw a princess tantrum, *demanding* that he go with her. She could pull rank and see if that worked. It probably wouldn't. Or she could give up on the baby panda and let it die.

She rubbed her arm and peered up at Shang. "Please?"

His chest rose and fell. Once, twice, a third time. Then he gestured for her to walk before him to the front of the tent. It wasn't cold, but Meiling shivered as she obeyed, unsure if this was a yes or a no from him. She knew so little of him, but there was one thing she was certain of by now: He wasn't heartless.

"Wake up, Fen," Shang barked when they rounded the tent.

Fen scowled even before she opened her eyes. To her credit, she was on her feet in an instant. "What? What's wrong?" Her gaze slid from Shang down to Meiling standing next to him, still with her arms wrapped around her middle.

"Her Highness heard a sound and would like it investigated," said Shang.

Meiling couldn't stop her wince. Why did Shang have to discover her leaving? This was exactly what she had been trying to prevent.

Fen's brow lowered irritably. "A sound?"

When Shang said nothing more, Meiling realized she was supposed to speak. "Um, yes. It sounded like it came from there." She pointed to the stalks of bamboo at the far side of the campsite. "It sounded hurt."

"Did *you* hear it?" Fen asked Shang.

"I did not."

"What—why did you wake me up for this? Fathers, I'm exhausted, and we've got a long day tomorrow!"

"Then make it quick. I'm not leaving Her Highness unguarded."

Fen huffed, grabbed her broadsword, and stalked off in the direction Meiling had pointed, leaving Meiling behind to long for death for the dozenth time in the last half hour. Her nails dug into her sleeves so hard they probably left marks on her skin.

"Don't hurt it!" she called after Fen.

"You may return to your tent now," said Shang. "We will take care of this threat."

"It's not a threat!" Meiling protested too quickly, before catching herself. "That is, I don't *think* it's a threat. It sounded like it needed help."

Shang gave her a sidelong glance, a line appearing between his brows. Did he believe her lies? Perhaps he still thought she was attempting to escape, and this was only the excuse she'd come up with when he caught her. Whatever the case, Meiling lowered her head and shuffled back into her tent. Not a minute later, Shang's shadow moved around the canvas and pounded the peg back in place with the hilt of his knife.

Then he returned to the fire.

Meiling peeked out between the flaps, trying to catch a glimpse of where Fen had disappeared off to. Would she find the panda? Would she hurt it? "I'm doing what I can, little friend," she whispered.

She didn't stop studying the tree line until—*finally*—a figure reemerged. Carrying something fluffy in her arms. Meiling gasped, barely restraining herself from clapping her hands in excitement. Then she'd thrown aside the flap and bolted out of the tent toward Fen.

Shang shot to his feet, but didn't stop her from running straight to Fen.

"Is it hurt?" she asked quickly, reaching out toward it.

"Think so," replied Fen crisply, holding the black-and-white bundle to her chest. "I smelled blood on it. Move aside so I can get it to the fire. Shang! Look, it's a panda cub!"

Shang didn't look at the panda cub. He looked at Meiling, a muscle twitching in his neck. He suspected something, didn't he? She blinked and averted her gaze, focusing instead on the panda cub as Fen laid it on its back with surprising gentleness.

It let out a long mewl, trembling. Its fur matted along its belly, blood from a gash in its side staining its white fur. Meiling hovered nearby, peering over Fen's shoulder, hardly daring to breathe.

"Where's the medical kit?" demanded Fen.

"Still in my saddlebags," said Shang.

"I'll get it!" Meiling hopped up, desperate to do *something,* and ventured to the pile of saddlebags by the far side of the campfire. Once she was there, it occurred to her that she didn't know what the medical kit even looked like. Drawing her lip between her teeth, she dug into the canvas, searching for anything that could carry supplies. She found a compact leather pouch that, when she opened it, carried needles, strips of gauze, tinctures, various containers of what seemed to be salve, and several other things. *V*

ictory!

She hurried back to the fire and offered it to Fen. "Here."

Shang cast her a single, long glance from where he sat on the fallen log. Fen tore off a piece of her tunic and carefully wet it with water from her canteen. She accepted the kit from Meiling, barking orders for Shang to sterilize the needle. He didn't seem to have any interest in fulfilling them.

"Needle?" Meiling asked, back to hovering while Fen cleaned away the wound. "Is it that bad?"

"It's a little hard to tell with all the fur . . ."

The panda squeaked when she touched the wound, trying to roll away.

"Hold it down, Highness. I need it to be still."

Meiling squatted down beside the cub and reached out, laying a gentle hand on its chest. It was bigger than she had realized when she first spotted it. Bigger than a cat, with crusted fur and a mouth of yellow teeth. Perhaps it wasn't as young as she first thought. "It's alright, little one," she cooed softly. "Don't worry. We're going to have you patched up in no time."

"Don't make too many promises," said Fen dryly, using a knife to cut a length of bandage and then sticking the knife in her mouth for temporary holding. She spoke around the blade, the words slurring and jumbling together. "I don't think it'll need stitches, but if it gets worse, or the bleeding doesn't stop, we might have to. Can't say I've ever stitched something with so much fur. Did you bring a razor, Shang?"

Shang glared at her as if the answer should be obvious. He was clean shaven so . . . an obvious *yes*?

The panda gave a piteous mewl as Fen wound the bandage around its middle, peeling back the fur so the bandage could sit against the bleeding flesh. Meiling stroked it gently, trying to soothe it as she stared into its marble-like eyes.

"Oh, stop your whining," snapped Fen to the panda. "I'm saving your life. Be grateful. Shang, you need to take care of it for the rest of your watch. Then I'll take over."

"I'm not watching an animal. I'm guarding the campsite."

"You can do two things at once, you big oaf," growled Fen.

"I can watch it," said Meiling, hooking her finger around its paw.

Shang's irate gaze moved from Fen to the panda, then settled on her. "I will watch it. But there's no guarantee this animal is surviving the night, and you cannot be mad at me if it happens to die on my watch."

"Of course I can be mad at you. It's my specialty," retorted Fen as she pulled off her cloak and wrapped up the panda, ignoring its continued mewls. She took the bundle and held it out to Shang.

"I am *not* cuddling that thing."

Fen glared, but resorted to leaving the panda on a blanket by Shang's feet. "There. Sleep tight, you ugly fuzzball."

And with that, they both turned expectant expressions on Meiling—waiting for her to go back into her tent. She patted the cub on its head and rose to her feet. *Please survive the night, please survive the night,* she begged silently.

She returned to her tent and closed the flaps, letting Fen reassume her place on the ground and fall back asleep. It was much longer before Meiling finally fell asleep, and when she did, she slipped out of the tent to the fireside.

To her surprise, the panda wasn't in the blankets on the ground.

Shang was still sitting on his log, his face as hard as ever, his brow furrowed as he kept watch. He held the panda in one arm like a baby, checking it every few minutes. He gave it water, checked on its bandage at least twice, and then even got up to get it a shoot of bamboo to munch on.

Meiling smiled to herself.

CHAPTER 7

THE PANDA SURVIVED the night, much to Meiling's relief. Once they'd eaten another breakfast of jerky—which Meiling's stomach seemed to think was a breakfast of rocks—Fen and Shang packed up the campsite while Meiling gladly held the sleeping panda.

When something sharp burned into the top of her head, she looked up to find Shang staring at the panda in her arms, a hard expression on his face.

Meiling immediately tightened her grip on it. "We can't release it yet!"

"We cannot bring it with us," said Shang in that coldly reasonable tone of his.

Fen's head popped up over the saddle of her horse. "We *are* bringing it. It's not healed yet."

"It puts us at risk."

"Why? Because it might kill us while we sleep?" mocked Fen.

Were Fen and Meiling on the same team for once? This was a change!

"Don't worry," Meiling whispered to the cub, holding it close. Its ear twitched, and it wriggled a paw free to cover its closed eyes. "We'll take care of you until you're better."

"Because one of us has to hold it," replied Shang coolly. "That limits our range of mobility, should we be attacked. We cannot be protecting anything but the princess."

"I'll hold it," chirped Meiling. It wasn't like she needed to have limbs free for swords and spears. "You can worry about me, and I'll worry about the panda." She and the panda could be a little package.

Shang ran a hand down his face, rubbing his fingers into his temples. "This is why we need to get rid of it. It'll distract all of us."

"If we leave it, it dies," snapped Fen. "Do you want a baby panda on your conscience?"

Shang's shoulders rose and fell with a deep breath as he regarded her with another glare. Then he stalked off to saddle Meiling's horse, leaving Fen to stick out her tongue at his back.

Did that mean the panda was coming with them?

After saddling Meiling's horse, Shang pulled a leather-wrapped hatchet from his saddlebags and set to hacking down a few stocks of bamboo and chopping them into smaller pieces. He slid them into Meiling's bags.

Confirmed. The panda was staying with them.

"It might not be able to defecate on its own yet," said Shang as he helped Meiling mount.

She blinked, settling into the saddle. "I beg your pardon?"

He handed her the rather large bundle. "Baby pandas require their mother's aid to defecate. If it shows no sign of . . ." He seemed to search for a word besides *defecating*. "If it doesn't soil itself within a few hours, you'll have to rub it."

Meiling blinked again. "Rub it?" She was scared to ask, but managed a nervous, "Where?"

"Its low abdomen. The mothers lick them. Try to mimic a tongue with your hand."

She barely kept her nose from wrinkling. Perhaps she didn't succeed as much as she thought, because Shang's mouth twitched slightly.

"Stop knowing everything, Shang," drawled Fen from ahead. "It's disgusting."

Then they were off, and Meiling found herself unsure whether or not she was hoping for the panda to answer the call of nature in her lap onto one of the few sets of robes she had.

"Feels like rain," Shang muttered several hours later.

The panda slowly gnawed on a shoot of bamboo in Meiling's still-clean lap. It made little whimpering protests of pain whenever she shifted her grip and tried to wake up her numb limbs.

Fen squinted her eyes ahead into the morning sun. "I don't see clouds."

"I didn't say it *looks* like rain," he growled in return. "I feel it. It's coming. It will be here by the evening. We ought to find a town to seek shelter."

"I wonder if inns keep rooms available for pandas," grumbled Fen, shooting a glance back at Meiling. "Is it still alive?"

Meiling nodded just as Shang said irritably, "We cannot bring a panda into an inn, Fen."

"Watch me," growled Fen back.

They guided their horses through thick, lush underbrush. Around them, huge pillars of stone jutted into the air and towered above them. Meiling gaped as they rode between their palace-sized bases, certain they would topple and crush her. It was the most beautiful scenery she had ever seen. She stared unabashed, eyes wide and mouth open, almost forgetting the panda in her arms except for the occasional chomp of bamboo. She did not realize she had fallen behind, or that she was leaning precariously back in her saddle to stare up at the pillars, utterly enraptured in the most exquisite sense of smallness, of wonder, until Shang's voice roused her.

"Catch up."

She blinked, closed her gaping mouth, and swiveled her eyes to his. He stared back at her, one eyebrow raised in an expression that was . . . Was it softened just a tiny bit? It was so difficult to tell, since he always looked severe. It was a measure of *how* severe his face was. For a second there, it seemed slightly less severe.

She kicked her horse faster, but couldn't resist the way her eyes were drawn again to the vivid green against the cut of silver stone. What other beautiful places were out there in the world?

Would she ever have a chance to see them?

Sighing deeply, Meiling kicked her horse again, who seemed just as reluctant as her to move faster. The panda mewled in protest. Soon, she was directly behind Shang. Without meaning to, she spoke. "Your powers let you feel rain?"

His head turned slightly. Enough for her to see his sharp nose. "In a way."

She considered this. Encouraged by the fact that he had answered her first question, she braved another. She feigned ignorance, hoping to hear more from his own mouth. "You can manipulate water?"

"Ice."

"That is one of the subcategories of water manipulation, right? Which is a subcategory of elemental manipulation?" she pressed.

He kept his back hard against her. After a long pause, he suffered to respond, "Yes."

Meiling pinched her lips and rolled her eyes. Fine. If he was so inconvenienced, she would not prod further. At least he had answered three questions without snapping in irritation like Fen. His voice might have dripped with impatience, but this must count for something. She returned to gazing up at the stone pillars.

How did such a thing happen naturally?

"There are many different types of powers, but most of them fall under a few broad categories. Everyone's powers are unique, though. Like snowflakes."

Shang's deep voice startled Meiling. She stared at his back in surprise, arching her neck and raising an eyebrow. She suppressed a grin and urged her horse a little closer. "What are all the categories?" she asked. Of course, she knew them, had carefully studied them during her long days alone in the library, but it seemed the best question to continue the conversation. She did not want to let this barest shred slip through her fingers.

Fen barked a laugh from the front. Her horse whinnied nervously at the sound. "Don't get him started. There are too many subcategories, and he knows all of them. And I mean *every single one*."

Meiling smiled at the obvious tensing of Shang's shoulders. She shifted directions. "Can you tell me more about how two people can have the same power but have different abilities?"

There was a long silence.

She shook her head, fighting the urge to roll her eyes again. She must have reached her maximum allocation of questions for the day. Very well, he could be rude if he so chose.

She was surprised yet again—

"All magic has boundaries. Each person's powers are defined most by their constraints," he muttered, barely loud enough for her to hear him.

"Like what?" she prodded, not caring if she was bold or stupid to continue. "What are yours?"

Ahead, Fen scoffed. This time she turned in her saddle to look past Shang, back at Meiling and the panda in her lap. Her face was twisted in mockery. "You think a warrior will tell you his weaknesses?"

That was the end of the conversation, and the end of the short-lived camaraderie between her and Fen. She drew her cloak tighter around her, releasing a soft sigh.

But even this could not prevent her from growing distracted by the grandeur around her once again. Before long, she had resumed her gawking at the pillars reaching into the clouds. She ignored the painful jab in her neck when she arched it too far. It was simply too much beauty to take in.

"We must stop," Shang insisted. "Enough of your nonsensical protests. We cannot ride through this rain, and we cannot camp in it."

"It doesn't look like it'll rain that hard!" Fen fought back. "It'll be just a light sprinkling. See how far away the clouds are? We'll likely only catch the edge of the system. Besides, you said yourself that no one will let us bring a panda inside an inn!"

"We are *not* making decisions about where we stay based on a dying panda."

"It is *not* dying! It is *healing*!"

Shang had grown more restless over the last hour. He kept shifting in his saddle, smacking at imaginary bugs on his neck, and twiddling with his knives and the hilt of his sword. At one point, Meiling was sure there was ice in one hand, despite the absence of danger.

He rode alongside Fen now, his profile sharp and severe as he glared at her, and when he spoke, it was more of a snarl.

"We're stopping. It's a severe thunderstorm."

"But there are so few clouds—"

"Why do you challenge me?" he hissed.

"Because we were specifically instructed to avoid inns! Have you forgotten the orders of the emperor?"

"We have avoided. And now we have no other choice. Is there a town nearby?"

"You should know as well as I," Fen growled back. But before Shang could respond, she shifted, folding into herself, and was suddenly a large, speckle-breasted hawk. Shang snatched the reins of her horse as she soared into the sky, screeching as she went.

Despite knowing it was foolish, Meiling hugged the panda closer and asked softly, "The storm . . . It's making you anxious?"

Shang turned impatient eyes on her in silent answer.

"If the storm was great enough, could it make you lose control of your power?"

He let out a sigh of frustrated long-suffering and smacked at his neck. He checked his hand for bug guts. Apparently there were none, because he smacked again, harder than before. "No. Magic is a weapon. You should know that. My sword cannot kill unless I wield it. My magic does not act independent of me. It cannot *break free*. I can, however, lose my temper and wield it to an extent that I later regret." As though to demonstrate, he swept his hand through the air. Knife-sharp icicles stuck out from his hand. With one smooth, lightning-fast gesture, he flung them into the ground. They sank so deep into the ground that only the holes were visible. He turned his black eyes on her. "That is why most people think twice before testing the patience of a magic-wielder."

She held his gaze, refusing to flinch. The moment he looked away, however, she sagged in relief. The cub in her tired and sore arms squeaked. She gave it a fresh shoot of bamboo. It grabbed hold of it with padded paws, only to drop it a moment later. Meiling barely caught it before it fell to the ground.

Fen was back, shifting into her human form and dropping into her saddle. Her eyes held a wild, ferocious light. Was she still licking her wounds from Shang's words to her a moment ago?

"There's a town over the crest of that hill." She tore the reins from Shang's hands, glaring daggers at him, and led the way.

"Faster," Shang barked at Meiling.

As she followed, she found herself also glaring at Shang. She should be gracious; it was not his fault that the weather agitated him. But seven valleys—he could be a little nicer, could he not?

She was ready for sleep, and it had been a long time since she had floated through a thunderstorm.

Besides, as much as she enjoyed clean garments, this panda still hadn't soiled itself all day, and that seemed cause for concern.

When they reached the town, thunderous dark clouds hovered near the ground. A deep, distant rumble made her duck her head and pull the hood of her cloak lower. She had never seen a village before, but it reminded her of the outskirts of Suguan. The little houses and trade buildings were crafted of stone, with roofs of thatch and wood. Even in the village, the corners of the roof lifted in smiling eaves, like many of the buildings in Suguan. It was like riding into a small piece of home. The tiniest bit of tension eased from her shoulders.

The few people still milling about outside busily prepared for the rain. One, dressed in loose trousers and a long, colorless robe, strapped canvas over his woodpile. Another fought with a stubborn horse while it stomped its hind hooves. A woman bustled her children in front of her, away from the town square, a full basket fastened to her back.

No one paid them enough heed to notice the bundle of panda in Meiling's arms.

She was too busy looking around that she didn't notice they'd stopped in front of the inn until Shang was below her, glaring ice as he pulled the whimpering panda from her lap and shoved it in Fen's arms. Time to dismount, then. Meiling's numb limbs protested as she struggled to pull her leg around to the other side.

She couldn't finish. Shang wouldn't let her.

Impatiently, he snatched her waist with two hands and dragged her off the horse. She almost snagged her knee on the saddle and her breath swept out of her lungs in surprise. He dumped her on the ground and turned to snatch the reins. She stared after his retreating form, lips parting in shock and curling in revulsion.

She liked him less and less with each passing minute.

He said something to Fen, to which she snarled fiercely, "No, I'm not getting rid of the panda!"

"We can't release it!" Meiling insisted, running to Fen's side. "It's about to rain and it hasn't defecated today!" As soon as the words were out, her cheeks flushed hot.

Shang swiveled his glare from the panda to Meiling. "Then you get to be my extremely pregnant wife."

Meiling blinked thrice in rapid succession. Her tongue was too tied for her to even think of a cohesive question.

Fen came to her rescue, though probably not intentionally. "What kind of ridiculous nonsense is that? Did the rain wash out your brains with everything else?"

Shang snatched the mewling panda from Fen. "Get me a blanket, Fen."

He wasn't . . . was he?

"Hold this." He thrust the panda against her and grabbed the blanket from Fen. "Open your robes so I can tie this."

Apparently, he was indeed intending to tie the panda to Meiling's midsection.

"Open my *what*?" Meiling's face flushed hot.

"Your outer robes, for the father's sakes." The look he gave her seemed to say, *No, I'm obviously not asking you to strip in public, Highness.*

Meiling scowled back. But if she protested, he'd threaten to get rid of the panda. So she fought her blush as she shifted the panda to her hip, careful of its bandages. She unwrapped her sash with her free hand, pretending she didn't care when Shang arranged the panda against her tunic, suddenly leaning *very* close as he reached around her waist to tie the blanket into a knot at the small of her back.

"This is not going to work," growled Fen when the panda started wiggling.

"*You* wanted to keep it."

"Don't suffocate it!" cried Meiling, looking down at the wiggling bundle instead of straight at Shang's collarbone. He didn't deign to answer her, as if insulted she would insinuate that he wouldn't think to leave the animal a gap to breathe through.

"This is not going to work," Fen repeated when Shang finished binding the panda to Meiling's front. He backed up a step as Meiling hurried to pull her outer robes around herself—only to discover they didn't fully cover her new bump. Neither could it conceal the little squeaks and wiggles. It wasn't even the proper shape as a pregnant belly.

Shang's jaw clenched. Then he swept his cloak off his shoulders and wrapped it around her, fastening it in the front. The hems puddled on the floor around her, the garment almost swallowing her whole.

This was not going to work.

A few droplets of rain hit Meiling's head, spattered against her nose, and she tried not to care that her girth had tripled in a matter of minutes. Fen and Shang studied her, Fen with a dubious expression, and Shang with that critical, assessing eye.

Shang must have reached the conclusion that it would have to do, because he muttered something in Fen's ear and handed off the reins. Fen scowled in response but didn't protest. Overhead, the clouds grew thicker, darker, and threatened with thunder and bursts of lightning. The downpour was inevitable. Shang reached around Meiling again and yanked the hood over her head.

Then he placed one frigid hand on her low back and guided her up the creaky wooden steps.

The panda sneezed just as Shang opened the door.

Meiling clasped a hand over it, glancing frantically at Shang. Was the sling sliding lower toward her hips? A little paw wiggled its way free of the blanket. She pulled the cloak tighter around her and hoped she wouldn't trip.

His jaw clenched, but he said nothing as he pulled her into the inn.

It was like walking into another world. A world full of loud, rambunctious men and sly, winking women. Baijiu sloshed from small bowls across the room. The air was hazy, almost smokey, reeking of sweat and alcohol, clogging in her nostrils. Was that also the stench of vomit lacing everything else? Drunken laughter and shouts over gambling bets reverberated through her head until it ached. A knife slammed into a tabletop nearby. Meiling jolted.

She found herself holding back against the door, digging her shoulder into the hard wooden doorframe. She resisted Shang's tugging until he shot her a dark look and she reluctantly surrendered, following him. At least her hood was still low.

While the jutting pillars of stone had made Meiling feel small in a delicious sort of way, being dragged against her will into the tavern made her feel like a squeaking mouse in a cage. A disconcerting, horrible sort of smallness. A helpless sort. Shang pulled her relentlessly after him through the throng's center. Her breath snagged in her lungs with so many scary-looking men so close.

She'd grown up in close proximity to many dangerous men—including her father. Her guards and the members of the court were all magic-wielders and Academy graduates. As fierce as they were, however, each one of them was controlled.

These men were the type she expected to explode at slight provocations, dangerous and terrifying from their unpredictability and utter lack of self-control.

The ties of her cloak jerked hard against her throat. Meiling let out a little choked cry as the cloak parted slightly in front. Her heart skipped a beat—or five. She yanked it closed, only to discover the too-long hems were caught under an oblivious drunkard's foot. She would have spun to face him if Shang had not already bent and yanked the cloak free, then pulled her into his side.

"Is that your wife?" called another drunkard at the table, pointing at Meiling, whose face was no longer hidden beneath the hood of the cloak.

Shang merely tucked Meiling in closer to him, a possessive hand wrapped around her, and shot a scathing glare at the man over her head.

"Aw there, little brother, we was just curious," a different voice sounded from behind Meiling. "Is that your child she's carrying?"

Shang gave them no answer. He loosened his hold on her just enough to tuck her close to his side and keep walking, only barely increasing his pace. The heat of his anger coursed under his skin, emanating to her through his shivering touch.

"A room," he barked to the man behind the counter.

One? Would they not want one for her and Fen, and another for Shang? Or better yet—a separate room for each of them?

Then again, it *would* be strange for Shang to get separate rooms for him and his *pregnant wife*. As if on cue, the panda let out a squeak and batted Meiling's arm with its free paw. She tensed, hoping irrationally that the sound was lost to the din of the inn, and the movement to the bulkiness of Shang's cloak.

"One room? Drinks too? A hearty, warm meal for your lovely wife?" a much lighter voice responded.

Meiling looked up to find a round, happy face smiling at her. Warmth spread through her, easing an inch of her anxiety, even if her face flushed with the man's words. She offered her own tentative smile back. A meal sounded lovely.

"Just the room," Shang said.

This man could freeze with his words just as effectively as he could with his hands.

The innkeeper's smile faltered. She tried to catch his eye again, to offer a reassuring smile, but he did not look. He focused on counting the coins Shang slammed onto the counter.

A chill suddenly crept up through her body.

It had nothing to do with the stormy look on Shang's face.

She arched her neck to glance over her shoulder. Most of the men had gone back to their gambling and drinking and loud laughter. A few glanced at her every now and then. One—a bald man in yellow robes—grinned at her with one tooth missing.

Meiling laid a protective hand on the panda. It worked its snout free of its pouch and sniffed her side, but mercifully didn't squeal again.

There.

Toward the front corner of the room, three cloaked figures seemed to be watching them. *Her.* Two men and one woman? They sat situated against the far wall, easily overlooked. Were those red eyes peering from beneath the hood of one?

Shang's arm around her waist tightened as he dragged her toward the nearby flight of stairs. Meiling cast one last glance at the deflated innkeeper. This time, he did meet her eyes. She smiled, and his countenance lifted.

Right before they reached the stairs, a hand reached out and snatched one of hers. She started so hard she elbowed Shang's stomach in her attempt to pull back. Behind her, his sharp intake of breath mingled with a grunt. She found herself staring at a bearded man, seated between two women wearing more face paint than even her mother during the festivals. His thin eyes crinkled. He held her hand, turning it upward and tracing a finger down the length of her palm. She shuddered, trying to yank away.

"Get your filthy hands off my wife," Shang snarled.

The bearded man released her. He grinned, and cunning sparked in his eyes. "Soft hands," he said quietly, meeting Meiling's terrified gaze with a cool confidence that sent chills racing down her spine.

Shang immediately drew her away, all but dragging her with him up the stairs. As if she wanted to linger any more than he did! She was just as ready to be free of these frightening men as he was—and the way her low back ached with the strain of the panda.

They reached the top, both breathless for different reasons.

"You draw too much attention," he half-whispered, half-growled as he marched down the dimly lit hallway. The ceilings were so low, he instinctively bent while walking.

"I wasn't doing anything!"

They reached the room. Shang inserted the key, jangled it, let out another growl, and shoved the door open. He drew Meiling inside and shut the door behind them.

She thought he would let her go then, and perhaps storm to the opposite side of the cramped quarters. Instead, he whirled on her, gripping her arms, and leaned down so he could whisper to her. She was so surprised that she stumbled backward into the wall, staring up at his face, suddenly so close, tilted downward toward hers. The panda let out a squeak and popped its entire head free, poking its nose between the folds of Shang's cloak.

"Anyone with an ounce of sense in that tavern could see that you're high born. Anyone could—"

"What? *How?* I'm wearing commoner's clothes and I'm pregnant with a panda!"

"Because you *glide* everywhere. Disguise is more than clothes, Highness. You can't carry yourself like an elegant princess if we're to have any hope of getting you to Liafugan alive."

Her lips parted; eyes locked on his. Glide? Elegant princess? Was the way she walked that obvious?

She'd never thought . . .

Then his hands began running up and down her arms, her hands, her waist, and her panda as though checking for injuries. His voice was low when he spoke again. "Did any of them hurt you?"

For a second, she was too stunned to respond. She shook her head wordlessly.

His eyes returned to hers, held her gaze for several long seconds, then he dropped his hands and turned away, clenching them into fists. She dragged her attention from him to note the sparse, cramped quarters, which included only one bed.

The panda sniffed. Did it care about mustiness?

"Why would we not be able to make it to Liafugan? If they knew who I was, they would just avoid us more," Meiling said, her voice a tad high-pitched and squeaky as she struggled to untie the knot to release the panda.

Shang had crossed the room toward the window and was fiddling with the latch. At her words, however, he paused. Tilted his head half back toward her. Then he returned his attention to the window. It sprung open.

Why was he opening the window? It was starting to rain.

"Because," he said, keeping his tone quiet, "royal blood is still royal, even without magic, and people find many uses for it."

Her cold fingers struggled with the knot, and the panda squirmed. "Just be patient. I'm trying," she mumbled to it, going to pat its head to make it stop moving so much.

It bit her.

Meiling yelped, more from surprise than pain. Shang spun toward her.

"It bit me, naughty thing," she said, glancing at the side of her hand to make sure it wasn't bleeding. "It won't be patient while I untie this, and it'll hurt itself if it keeps struggling!"

As if on cue, the panda let out a shriek and flailed its one free paw, gnawing on its sling and drooling on Meiling's clothes. Shang's glower only darkened, as if to say, *See? This is why we can't bring the stupid panda along.*

He crossed the distance between them. With a flick of his fingers, he unclasped the cloak and pulled the trailing garment from her shoulders. Her heart skipped a beat when his arms went around her, his deft fingers working the knot at her low back. She tried not to register that the only thing separating them was this squealing panda, that Shang's mouth hovered only a few inches above her shoulder as he worked. Tried not to think as the smell of a clear winter day washed over her, wrapping around her like a quilt.

Apparently, the knot gave him trouble too, because when she stole a glance at him, his brow furrowed, and his fingers kept working at her back. Sensing her gaze, his eyes slid to hers. His hands stopped moving.

"What?" he growled.

Was she staring? Were her eyes too wide? Was she even breathing?

"Nothing?" she squeaked.

The knot gave, and Shang caught the panda before it fell, easing away from Meiling. She sucked in a greedy lungful of air, suddenly desperate. Then she remembered her robes gaped open and hurried to retie her sash before her face colored too deeply.

Flapping sounded outside of the window. A hawk flew through the opening and immediately transformed into a livid Fen.

"One room? You only got one room? You think I am going to put up with having your stinky self so close? What were you thinking? You are *not* making me sleep on hard wood."

Meiling stepped away from the bed, wanting to melt into the chipped, peeling plaster on the walls. Would they truly be here all night, packed into this tiny hovel with two of their party enraged?

"Keep your voice down; these walls are paper thin," Shang said, staring fixedly at Fen. "One room, because we can't risk being separated, of course."

Fen growled low in the back of her throat, and there might have been fangs gleaming between her lips. "Give me the bear. I need to check its wounds."

Meiling rubbed her arm and said in a small voice: "It still hasn't defecated."

Fen frowned, reaching for the panda in Shang's arms. "Let me look at it."

"You don't know how to make it defecate," growled Shang, refusing to give up the panda.

"You don't either!"

"Watch me."

"*Watch me,*" Fen mimicked back, then growled, "And *where* are you proposing this panda defecates?"

He didn't deign to answer, marching straight to the window and plopping the panda on the sill. It wiggled in his arms, squeaking and banging its head into his chest. With a grunt, Shang wrapped an arm under the panda's armpits, holding it so its legs dangled over the edge of the drop.

Meiling dug her nails into her palms, terrified that the panda would slip and fall. With monumental effort, she didn't say anything as Shang set to rubbing the cub's lower abdomen. To her shock, it only took a few minutes of rubbing before the panda did its business, leaving Meiling to hope no one happened to stand beneath this particular window at this particular moment.

"There," growled Shang, setting the panda on the floor when it was done.

It immediately rolled onto its back, spreading its limbs wide and letting out a long grunting sort of moan. As though it was greatly relieved.

Meiling might have smiled, except Fen was grumbling again as she set to checking the panda's bandage. It had slid down during the commotion.

"Couldn't you at least have gotten a room with two beds?" Fen complained, working just a touch too roughly on the panda for Meiling's comfort. "I've been sleeping on the ground for days now!"

"You can have the bed," Meiling mumbled.

Shang banged the shutters shut. "Her Highness gets the bed."

"Fen can have it," she repeated.

Those black eyes levelled at her, making her wish she'd swallowed her words. She shrunk against the wall. Then Shang's attention shifted toward Fen's efforts to rebandage the panda, giving Meiling a reprieve to let out the breath she'd been holding.

But now that the panda had been tended, there were other pressing concerns she'd prefer to avoid bringing up. For a long, blessedly silent moment, she gave into the desire to say nothing.

Then she could be silent no longer. She began softly: "There were people downstairs, who were staring at us—"

"You mean everyone?" Shang spun toward her.

He stood so tall in the cramped space, his shoulders framed by the window. It seemed utterly impossible that anyone downstairs could have seen his strong lean build or his calculating gaze and thought that he was anything but the trained, deadly warrior he was.

Her throat went dry, but she plunged onward. “No. Three hooded figures in the corner. One had . . . I thought I saw red eyes.”

“Bah!” Fen laughed a humorless laugh, tightening the last knot on the limp and sprawling panda.

“Go check,” Shang ordered her.

Meiling blinked. He believed her? At least enough to make Fen check?

Fen’s face contorted. “Why don’t you do it?”

“Because you can *literally* be a fly on the wall. And who knows what would be pounding on this door if those thugs thought the girl was alone?”

“You think I’d turn myself into a fly and get splattered? I’d sooner shift into a *mó guǐ* if I had that ability.” She huffed, shifted into a songbird with ruffled feathers, and flitted out the window as Shang opened it.

Quietness filled the space until he began pacing back and forth, crossing the length of the room in only four strides, stepping over the sprawled panda cub each time. Meiling slid until she was sitting on the floor, knees drawn up to her chest. Once or twice, she considered speaking, but thought better of it.

His nervous energy coursed from him in waves, and she was grateful when that energy didn’t focus on her but for the span of one sole glance. Then he went back to glaring in turns at the door, the panda, and the pattering rain splashing through the open window.

She would be even more grateful when the storm was past.

For now, she only had one escape from this hovel. *Sleep.*

Well, she knew she was sleeping on the floor tonight. She wanted to ask for her bedroll—anything to ease the stiffness of the boards beneath her—but couldn’t. She shuddered at the memory of the bearded man's calculating eyes, the strokes of his finger down her palm, and the glinting red eyes in the corner.

If only the bed were not so low, she could slide underneath and at least feel some semblance of privacy.

Shifting quietly down on her side, she curled in a ball in the corner, her cloak the only thing between her and the dirty floor. She pulled her hood down over her face to block out Shang's restless movements. It didn't stop her from feeling the prickle of his gaze, or the awareness that insisted he watched her carefully.

Falling asleep proved a challenge. The floorboards creaked and rattled with Shang's heavy footfalls, and every movement jolted through her jaw. Despite her hood, the world remained dim and awake.

Something thumped on the bed. Fen must have returned. Her familiar growl met Meiling's ears. "All's clear. Stupid fool's errand."

The bed creaked next to Meiling as Fen settled in.

"For all that is good and evil in this world, will you hold still for one minute?" Fen lashed at Shang. "I can't sleep with you stomping like that."

"You are welcome to sleep in the rain," Shang replied.

Sleep. She would be free if she could only fall asleep. It was nigh impossible.

But eventually, Fen quit wiggling in the creaky bed, and Shang's pacing grew quieter and more distant. Perhaps he stopped. In the half-light of near sleep, Meiling could not tell. Finally, finally—oh, blessed finally—she fell fast asleep.

Only to be haunted by red eyes.

CHAPTER 8

MEILING'S SPIRIT WANTED to tear free of the inn, twist loose of her soul-tether, and fly straight up into a sea of storm clouds. But her practical side urged her to flit downstairs and ensure Fen was right. That those cloaked figures were not a threat.

Shang's ice-blue soul glowed from where he stood by the window, staring outside and watching the rain fall. Fen curled up on the bed, a ball of brilliant red—and sleeping soundly in the crook of her knees was the panda.

Meiling sunk through the rafters to the floor beneath. The scene was even wilder than before, setting her on edge despite her safety in her spirit form.

The glows of magic-wielders immediately snagged her attention. Two in travel garb spoke to the innkeeper, a young man and woman.

His glow was a vivid purple, and his companion's a deep crimson. Just regular wielders—not a threat.

Three other glows, however, sent her heart beating faster.

They had abandoned their spot at the far side of the tavern and made their way through the crowd. She hadn't imagined it, then. They were magic-wielders. And there was something deeply *wrong* about them.

The first glowed a fiery red-orange. The color of a fire-wielder. When Meiling ducked closer, his unsettling red eyes became visible. Even though it was impossible for him to see her, she couldn't help the sense of *exposure* that washed over her. That sense that he was well aware of her, despite her invisibility.

Something was very, very wrong.

The second was indeed a woman. Her glow was a bluish gray, an odd and dull color, especially compared to the last glow of the group. Was it rose? No, it flickered—now was it purple? Blue? White? It was like staring into a shifting rainbow. It was . . . beautiful.

They made their way slowly, yet purposefully, to the staircase.

They were coming for her.

She had been followed.

There wasn't a shred of doubt in Meiling's mind. These wielders had been lying in wait for them and the moment that cursed drunk had stepped on her cloak and pulled back her hood . . .

She had to warn the others.

Zipping back through the rafters, she burst into her body with a force that sent her head reeling back into the wall. She shot up, gasping, "Shang! Fen! We must flee! They're coming for us!"

Fen moaned on the bed.

Shang fixed black eyes on Meiling. "You were dreaming," he said.

"No!" she cried, shooting to her feet. "Up the stairs—they're coming! I promise, I'm telling the truth!"

Either she was convincing, or Shang heard them in the hallway. His eyes widened and then narrowed. "Up, Fen." He grabbed her shoulder and dragged her to her feet.

Her eyes flew open, and she lurched out of his grasp. The panda rolled onto its back, blinking sleepily. "What kind of trick—"

"Take the girl out the window. I'll hold off the attackers." His eyes shone brighter than stars at midnight, brighter than lightning in a storm. It was as though his nervous energy suddenly had an outlet, and he channeled every bit of it into being alert and prepared.

Fen's battle instincts must have kicked in because she didn't badger him with questions. She bounced to the window from the bed and lightly leapt outside onto the roof, rain dampening her cloak immediately.

"How many, Meiling?" Shang whispered as he crouched by the door.

He called her by name.

"Three. A fire-wielder and two others," she said as she climbed onto the window. "Are you sure you can—"

He bristled at her words. "Go."

She'd just unintentionally insulted his competence. But there was no time for such thoughts, or for apologies. She scooped up the panda into her arms as it let out a surprised squeak.

"Leave it," ordered Shang darkly.

"No," growled Fen. She grabbed the panda from Meiling, and within a matter of seconds, unwound and rewound her sash to bind the panda to her front, ignoring its flailing paws.

Then Fen dragged Meiling through the window and helped her gain her balance on the steep, wet slope. She clung to the warrior as they inched their way to one curled corner. More than once, she slipped and caught herself, hating that she was only slightly more competent than a wounded panda. Within minutes, she was soaked.

Behind them, there was a loud *boom!*

"Hurry!" Fen growled, landing in a crouch on the edge of the roof. The panda's head poked over her sash, licking its nose before setting to obliviously gnawing on its own paw. Meiling almost lost her footing and plunged to the ground, but she caught a handful of thatching in one hand and Fen's tunic in the other and barely saved herself. Rain fell into her sputtering mouth and cringing face.

"It's not a far drop. Climb over the edge. I'll lower you," Fen said.

Meiling slid to the edge, her stomach lurching. A burst of flame out the window of their room made her clench her teeth and swing her legs over the side of the roof. Her arms quivered with the weight, and she leaned forward, the edge of the roof jutting into her stomach. Her feet scraped for a foothold and found the wall.

"Give me your hand!" Fen snarled. How was she supposed to help while carrying that panda?

"I've got it," Meiling grunted.

"Roll when you land!"

She had already dropped herself from the edge of the roof. When she landed in a painful crouch on the wet grass, pain shot up like knives in her legs and into her knees. She winced, but called, "I'm down. Hurry!"

A hawk flew to her side, a flailing panda hanging from its talons. When Meiling looked up, the hawk dropped the panda into her arms, and then Fen was running with her. "We've got to get the horses!" she shouted. "In the stables, there!"

A scream sounded from the open window.

Meiling's heart pounded. She glanced back as Shang shimmied out the window, a long burn on his bare shoulder. He blasted ice from both hands into the opening and then slid down the roof. Quickly, he dropped himself, rolled, and was up on his feet as a powerful gale of wind burst through the window, ripping the opening wider. Flames licked around its edges. The red-eyed figure emerged, his gaze settling on Shang.

He dropped off the roof to attack.

"Run!" Fen cried. "Faster!"

Meiling tore her eyes away just as the flame wielder threw a fireball right at Shang. She whirled on Fen, hugging the squirming panda tighter. "You've got to help him! He's one against three! I'll get the horses!"

Fen's brow raised in surprise, but she needed no more encouragement. In a blink, instead of Fen, there growled a huge, muscular, striped tiger. She bared her fangs and launched herself straight into the fray.

Find the horses. Find the horses.

It was so dark and wet. The rain came down harder. Lightning flashed overhead, and thunder boomed. Meiling ducked under the awning, arms wrapped around the black-and-white fluff ball, the world loud and threatening behind her. Smells of straw and manure clogged her nose, but she couldn't think about that in her panic.

She raced through the stalls of horses, dripping water onto the straw floor, until her eyes could make out her gray mottled horse. "Oh you beautiful thing!" she cried, rushing to its side and untying the lead, shifting the panda to her hip just before it bit her hand again. The other horses would be near, they must! Yes, Shang's horse was next to it. But where was Fen's?

That wasn't her worst predicament, either. How in the seven valleys was she supposed to get them saddled?

"Um . . . miss?"

Her head whipped up, wet hair slapping her skin as a wide-eyed youth, not quite grown into his long, gangly limbs, crowded himself into a corner of the stables. He clutched a pitchfork in both hands.

"What is happening?" he asked.

"Help me!" she gasped. "I need to saddle these horses!"

"Um . . ."

"Now!"

He rushed forward, still nearly petrified as thunder rent the air, but his fingers worked deftly in the dim light. She took a few minutes to tie the panda to her front, not caring when it set to chewing on her collar. Then she helped the stableboy heave the saddles onto the backs of the horses that Meiling was *pretty sure* were theirs.

It was the work of minutes, but every second cut like agony.

A roar sounded from outside, like a fierce cat.

The boy nearly leapt out of his skin, a tiny whimper escaping his lips. Why did Meiling's wet fingers tremble so dragon-spitting much? "Hurry, hurry, hurry!" she whispered as her nails fumbled on the strap of the saddle.

"There!" the boy cried as they untethered the three horses' leads and finally led them to the door of the stables.

"Fathers bless you," Meiling said, taking only the barest moment to reach out and squeeze his hand. She wished she had coin—anything to thank him. But the only thanks she could offer was doing her part to end this battle.

She led the three horses out of the stables, nearly tripping between them as the panda shrieked into her face.

Then she froze.

Before her, the strangest battle she'd ever witnessed played out in the middle of the village. She stopped for only that moment as her mind tried desperately to comprehend the flashes of ice and fire, smoke and rain, the roars of thunder and wildcat, the cries and screams as weapons and magic hit their mark. She tried to find Shang, but he was a blur of movement and flying ice. He moved too fast to be running. Was that *ice* beneath his feet? She spotted Fen's brilliantly striped coat quickly, snarling in the face of another enemy.

One, two, three, four wielders. Where was the fifth?

Meiling ran to mount her horse. As she planted her foot in the stirrup, a gale of wind blew her to her knees. Far too strong to belong to the raging storm. She knelt, trying to catch hold of something, one arm wrapped around the shrieking cub, but she was sucked too quickly toward the fight. Dread and panic flared in her gut—*the gray-blue wielder.* She clawed at the ground, her fingers digging into muddy grass. The fighting burst upon her ears, so loud and close that she let out a scream.

She was about to be *killed*. She could barely breathe. Whirling toward the overpowering wind, her heart almost stopped. But not for the reason she'd thought.

Right in front of her was Shang.

And at that very instant, a massive fireball plunged straight into his chest, exploding on impact.

CHAPTER 9

"SHANG!" MEILING SCREAMED.

Before her was the wind wielder as she clutched air to herself, pulling and pulling Meiling closer. A knife glinted in her other hand, catching raindrops as they fell fat and heavy, awaiting her arrival. Suddenly, a loud roar ripped through the air—and a tiger sank its fangs into the wind wielder's thigh. She screamed, and her hold on Meiling broke.

Meiling gasped, scrambling to her feet, a hand on the panda as it buried its face into her chest with a whimper. Where was Shang? *There,* lying on the ground. She choked, running toward him, away from a pulsing wave of heat behind her. She had to get to him, to see if he still lived, if she could help him. *Almost there.* His eyes were wide in shocked pain, his body and clothes blackened. Either she was crying, or the rain was getting in her eyes.

"*No Meiling!*" Shang's voice cut through the din behind her. "Get back!"

If Shang's body was lying in front of her, why was his voice calling from behind her?

She stopped, whirling in confusion. There, still fighting and launching volley after volley of knife-sharp ice, was Shang. His frantic face was set toward her. "Run!" he shouted.

She turned back to the dead Shang as his body rippled. Through the rain, a rainbow flickered—just for a second. Realization sunk like lead into the pit of her stomach.

A trap for her.

The third cloaked figure—nowhere to be seen—was an illusionist.

She turned to run just as the illusion flickered out entirely, replaced by a grim man with flashing eyes. A man that was terrifyingly close to her. There was no way she could outrun him. Her feet stuck like roots into the ground, paralyzed.

Something whizzed past her ear, breaking her shock. A wretched cry ripped from the illusionist as an ice bolt pierced his thigh and sank deep, blood spattering. Then something ice-cold grabbed hold of her arm and flung her to the side.

"*Run!*" Shang shouted, shoving her hard toward the horses.

Get to the horse. Get to the horse. Meiling ran as fast as she could, focused on her goal. The panda whimpered again, and she clutched it tight against her. *Almost there.* But then, just as she was close enough to reach out and grab the reins—

Her horse disappeared. Vanished, straight into nothing.

Meiling choked.

She reached for the reins of the Fen's horse. It, too, vanished before she could grab hold. Frantically, she turned and found the illusionist still fallen on the ground, but alert and concentrating hard. She gritted her teeth, facing thin air again. It was only an illusion.

Only vaguely aware of the struggle behind her, only noticing in her periphery the alternating blasts of hot and cold, she ran forward.

Her arms stretched out into nothing until her hands met a solid, coarse, muscular neck. Biting back a cry of relief, Meiling ran her hand through the air, along the invisible beast. The air shuddered and bent slightly, revealing the outline of all three vanished horses. It recovered, but not fast enough. She glanced back at the illusionist to see him standing, clutching his gushing wound. The ice bolt lay on the ground, covered in blood, by his feet. His face was puckered in focus and pain.

Meiling ran her hands quickly over the beast until she found the stirrup. Her whole body trembled with terror and adrenaline as she stuck her foot in it. She launched herself with all her might, flinging her other leg over the side of the air. Her judgement had been wrong, and she kicked the saddle. This was so much harder with a panda tied to her front. Biting her lip, she heaved again and then she was sitting in the saddle. The illusion of her horse flickered enough so she could quickly find the reins.

A loud bark sounded. Meiling turned her horse toward the fray to see a wolf attempting to maul the wind-wielder. The wolf caught sight of Meiling mounted on air, lifted its ears, and let out a surprised whine. Beneath Meiling, the illusion strengthened.

The wind-wielder seized her chance.

She thrust her clenched hand upward in the air and Fen gasped, a very un-wolflike sound, and her wolf shape broke. Fen collapsed to her knees before the wind wielder, clutching her throat, her eyes wide in panic. The wind-wielder drew back her knife in a flash. Fen squeezed her eyes shut and her face turned purple as she tried to break the woman's hold on her breath.

"Shang!" Meiling screamed.

He had already noticed. He raised his left arm and, with a fierce, swift motion, threw a sheet of ice across the entire town square. Launching a series of ice shards at the wind-wielder, he continued blasting the fire-wielder with another volley of bolts from his other hand.

The woman reacted, gusting away the ice, though not quite fast enough. She must have been hit somewhere because she cried out and slipped on the ice beneath her.

Fen gasped and fell.

They had to get out of here. They couldn't keep fighting—everyone was burned or bleeding or exhausted. But if Fen and Shang couldn't see the horses, they couldn't mount in a hurry. The illusionist worked feverishly to slow their escape.

Meiling turned her horse back to where the others had been and urged it until it nipped something in front of them. The illusion flickered until the outline of both horses was visible for a split second. She leaned forward and caught the lead of that horse. She squeezed her eyes shut.

"The horses are *right here,*" she said, flinging open her eyes in desperation. Fuzzy masses coalesced before her—just enough for her to snatch up the lead for the last horse.

The illusion shattered.

She rode a solid beast, led two more. Leaning precariously far in the saddle, she smacked the rump of one horse to run toward Fen, who caught hold of the saddle. Fen barely had the strength to hoist herself into it as the wind-wielder began pulling her back. The woman screamed again as blood burst on her shoulder—Shang's doing. The wind died in an instant. Fen mounted and turned her horse around.

"Run!" Shang shouted through the din. "Take my horse!"

"No!" Fen yelled back.

Shang winced as a dart of fire hit his forearm. *"Go!"*

Fen and Meiling kicked their horses into a gallop, Meiling still holding the lead of the third horse. Wind tried to snake around them, but it was cut off abruptly. She leaned as close as she could to the horse's neck, holding on for her life and the panda's life. Lightning flashed overhead and an ear-splitting peal of thunder tore across the world. Everything was wet, wet, wet.

The horses galloped through the muddy streets of the village, out into open fields of crops, trampling everything without discrimination.

"What about Shang?" Meiling yelled at Fen. She clung to her racing horse, still leading the other galloping one.

"He'll be fine," Fen shouted back. But was that uncertainty and fear ringing her pupils?

They gave no thought to the fields they ruined. They only pushed their horses as hard as they could. Chill seeped into Meiling's body, despite the heat of the horse beneath her. Her teeth chattered, and her hair plastered to her face. The torrent of rain stung her eyes. Darkness set deeper, so only the lightning flashing overhead illuminated their path. The panda huddled close to her chest, a warm and scared little bundle.

"Give me my horse!" a shout sounded to Meiling's right.

She whipped her head to see Shang zipping alongside them, his feet not seeming to touch the ground. Normally, she would have a thousand questions—was he *skating?* How in the seven valleys had he caught up to them?—but now she could only hold out the lead as she struggled to not fall off her horse. He snatched it away and, though it seemed utterly impossible, managed to mount his horse.

Meiling looked behind to see nothing except rain and storm. No pursuers dogged their steps. The relief was so great she almost loosened her death grip on her horse and plunged to her demise.

They were forced to slow when they entered the forest, but eventually the rain lightened to a steady downpour and the raindrops no longer stung. It might have been hours they rode in the cold, wet darkness.

Eventually, Shang called a halt.

They reined in their horses, but for a long moment, no one dismounted. Meiling glanced from Fen to Shang to the panda and back again. Fen sagged in her saddle, like she might fall to the ground any minute. Shang breathed heavily, his shoulders slightly bowed, but his eyes glittered in the flashes of stray lightning overhead.

"Are we camping here?" Meiling stuttered through frozen lips.

When Shang didn't answer, she assumed it was a yes. She dismounted, struggling a fair amount with the panda, and almost fell flat on her back, but still managed. She took her horse's lead and approached Shang's horse, holding out her hand for his lead. He stared at her blankly for one long moment, and then slowly dismounted. His clothes were torn where he'd been hit, gaping especially wide around his wounded shoulder. When he handed her the rope, his hand was so cold she almost drew back.

"I think Fen might need help dismounting," she said softly. She took both horses to a nearby tree and tied the wet ropes. They could be hobbled later, after she dealt with their more pressing matters, like how they were to sleep in this rain.

Shang placed another lead in her hand wordlessly. Fen's arm was slung around his neck, but he hardly seemed to be supporting her. He lowered her to a patch of ground that was grassier than the others. And then, to Meiling's surprise, he knelt in the rain—his lips thinning with concentration—and slid his hands up from the ground. Under his movements, ice appeared, flowing from his fingertips. Round, extremely thick, and large enough for the three of them.

He was fashioning a shelter of ice.

She stared.

Fen gave a shuddering laugh. "Never battle Shang during a storm," she croaked.

Meiling tilted her head, furrowing her brow. Images of him fighting flickered across her mind. How *had* he been able to fight three powerful wielders at a time? He'd been so restless and anxious from the storm, and now, despite his exhaustion, he was still using his magic.

That sort of power was unlike anything she'd seen before. Had the storm made him that powerful? Instead, she asked, "Is there any way to start a fire in this rain?"

"Maybe," Fen answered, wincing as she spoke. "Pine needles dry fast. Bark usually is dry on one side. Some wood under fallen logs might be dry. But it's a long shot."

Meiling pursed her lips, running her hand up and down the panda's back to comfort it. It still hadn't stopped cowering, and she didn't blame the poor thing. Shivering, she pulled her cloak tighter around them both. Pine needles. Bark. Wood under fallen logs.

"Meiling," came Shang's low voice.

She glanced back. He winced as he got to his feet, straightening to his full height in the darkness. "Yes?"

"I'll do it. Go inside the shelter."

He might be standing strong now, but he could topple at any minute. She shook her head. "I will be back shortly. I won't go far."

"Meiling—"

Setting her jaw, she marched away, wishing not for the first time that she'd been born a fire-wielder. It would make this situation much less complicated. Then again, if she'd been born a fire-wielder, they wouldn't be in this situation in the first place.

The panda let out a little whimper.

"Don't worry, we'll have a nice fire going soon. Then we can all warm up." She stroked its head and barely pulled her hand back in time to keep from being bitten. "But *you* need to be behave."

She started by peeling bark off a few different trees, but everything was soaked through. Gritting her teeth against the cold, she searched further, glancing back every few minutes to make sure she wasn't wandering too far. A bolt stabbed through her heart at the thought of getting lost. She quickly dismissed it. If she screamed, Shang would hear her.

Her boot kicked a stone. A very large stone. Meiling looked up.

And found herself standing before what seemed to be the remains of an enormous stone building. *What in the seven valleys?* Her breathing quickened with hope, and she moved faster, dodging around collapsed and half-buried stones, until she found a sheltered section with a roof and walls.

Better yet, the ground was littered with dry brush.

“Meiling!” came a distant call—Shang.

“Here!” she shouted back, and the panda grunted in annoyance. Wrapping herself up against the rain, she hurried back the way she'd come.

When she reached the horses, Shang was gripping his arm beneath the burn. His shoulders sagged, and he dropped his hand when she came into view. “There you are.”

“I didn't go far,” she said, blinking against the droplets falling into her eyes. “I found a shelter where we can stay. There's plenty of brush. It's just ahead, a short distance.”

The darkness made it hard to read his expression.

“Show me,” he said with a grunt, untying the horses' leads. “If it is good, I'll come back and get Fen.”

Meiling led the way, trying not to shiver. “Is she alright?”

“She'll be fine.”

What about you? she wanted to ask.

When they reached the ruins, Shang let out another grunt, clambering over fallen stones behind Meiling until they reached the part still standing. He ducked beneath the stone roof, through a curtain of dripping rainwater.

“See?” she said, kicking the small sticks and brush littering the ground. She led him past the half-collapsed sections to the mostly enclosed room she'd found. A room plenty big for the three of them and the panda.

Shang gave a single nod of approval that probably made Meiling's stomach warm more than it should have. “Will you start the fire while I fetch Fen?”

She gave him her affirmation and hurried to comply, mostly because she was frozen and dying for a scrap of warmth. Not to mention it about killed her that the cub shivered against her.

It took some time to retrieve the tinderbox from Fen's saddlebags and collect a pile of brush and small sticks for the fire. Some of it wasn't as dry as she hoped, but surely she could get it to light, right?

As she pulled the steel and flint from the box, Shang helped Fen into the room and leaned her against the frigid stone wall. Then he collapsed beside her with a groan, his head falling back.

Meiling's fingers shook as she struck the steel and flint for a spark. The brush was still too wet, and the sparks wouldn't catch. It was a challenge to see over the top of the panda's head, but she couldn't set it down for fear it would be too cold. She hoped her silent companions weren't paying her any heed. Like they usually did.

Swallowing her frustration, she struck harder, again and again. Her hands would not stop trembling from cold and aftershock—phoenixes *scorch* it all. Her grip slipped.

She let out a small cry, dropping the flint as blood welled and spilled over her hand. She'd cut open two fingers. Looking up, she found Fen curled in a wet, freezing lump against the wall, utterly oblivious. But Shang's black eyes had seen her carelessness.

The heat of embarrassment burned her cheeks. Her companions had wounds she needed to tend; Shang's tunic had been entirely burned away on one shoulder and his other arm looked black where the flame-dart had struck him. Not to mention Fen, who'd nearly had her life sucked out of her by the wind-wielder and might have other wounds besides. They'd worked so hard for her to escape unscathed, and she caused injury to herself just by trying to light a fire.

"Bring it here," Shang's low voice sounded.

Meiling's face flushed deeper, making her cheeks tingle in the cold. "I'll bind it. It isn't deep," she said, shrugging against the pain.

He eased back against the wall, keeping his eyes on her and the fire she was trying to light.

She clutched her fingers to her chest and asked, "Which horse has the bandages?"

"Mine," he responded.

Meiling nodded and got to her feet to brave the rain. Shang had tied the horses beneath a stone overhang, giving them shelter from the drizzle and piling their saddles to the side. She found the medical kit wrapped tightly in one saddle bag. Thank the fathers, it was dry. She grabbed a sack of food and two canteens of water as well, then made her way back into the shelter, wetter than before.

Her blood dripped on the medical kit, smeared her sleeve. A sigh escaped her lips as she pulled the gauze from the pack and settled on the ground beside the pile of kindling. "Knife?" she asked.

Shang patted his belt and frowned. "I lost one," he muttered to himself, and then pulled a small one from his boot. He held the blade and offered her the hilt. She took it and quickly cut a strip of bandage. After pouring water from her waterskin on the cut, she proceeded to fumble with the gauze, wrapping it around her still bleeding fingers. The cut was deeper than she realized, and it stung more with every passing minute. Blood dripped onto her sash holding the panda and dribbled down her knuckles.

"You'll bind it poorly with one hand," Shang said. "Come here."

She wanted to draw back, to insist she could do it, but . . . he was right. Wounded pride was preferred to foolishness. She scooted closer to Shang, holding out the gauze and offering her fingers.

Wordlessly, he took her palm and tilted her hand so he could squint at the cuts. He bound them carefully and wiped away the smearing blood, despite how his icy hands shook as he worked. Did his skin almost tingle against hers? Perhaps an after-effect of using so much magic?

Once he was finished, however, he didn't let go of her hand. He pulled it closer, frowning as he turned it over, inspecting it carefully. She said nothing, merely canting her head to one side as her eyes flitted from the knot between his brow to the bandage on her fingers.

What are you doing? she wanted to ask.

He gestured for her other hand, and she hesitantly obliged. He subjected this one to the same scrutiny as the first. Why did it feel like he read all her secrets in the lines of her palm, the creases of her knuckles? Why did she feel so oddly exposed?

"No scars," he said quietly, almost disbelievingly.

She bit her lip, a pang hitting her in the chest. She tugged gently on her hands, and his eyes shot up to hers, so large and black in the dimness. He released her, and she wrapped her arms around her panda as she shivered with cold and relief.

"Of course I don't have scars," she forced herself to say. "I didn't go to the Academy."

She couldn't quite bring herself to say, *"I have no magic."* Yet even so, the words rung in the air, full of deception. Did he hear the unspoken falsehood?

That gaze meeting hers was too impenetrable to imagine his thoughts. He'd overcome his disbelief at the sight of her hands, and it made her wonder if he'd ever seen hands that weren't riddled with scars, surrounded as he'd always been by magic-wielders.

"You will have scars now," he said.

Her heart stuttered. Did he know she had magic? Did he suspect?

It wasn't until his eyes shifted to the bandage on her fingers that she realized what he meant. Pursing her lips, she turned back to the fire, taking much more care with striking the flint. It wouldn't light, not until it occurred to her to use a piece of gauze to catch the spark. This time, after a few strikes, the fire caught. She blew on it carefully, coaxing it until it crackled and spat. She held her shivering hands as close to the flames as she could, extra cautious with the binding on her fingers.

But she could not linger, no matter how exhausted and cold she was. She had more work to do. She peeled off her wet cloak and laid it near the fire to dry. The shelter was already warmer, despite the frigid stone. Untying her soaked sash, she set the panda down on the ground, and it huddled in a little ball of fur by the fire. Lucky thing didn't have wet clothes to worry about like the rest of them.

Meiling held out the little sack of food to Shang. His eyes had closed, so she said, "Eat."

They flashed open, meeting hers. Firelight gleamed in those dark pupils. He accepted the sack but did not open it. She frowned. Now, by the glow of the dancing flames, Shang looked even worse than she'd realized. He'd been cut above his eyebrow, his shoulder burn moist and blistering, with his hair and clothes singed.

She couldn't help her grimace as she gathered the gauze, knife, and medical kit. "Let me tend your shoulder."

He shook his head slowly. Meiling shuffled to his side and leaned forward anyway, her hands outstretched.

"No," Shang barked, immediately drawing backward.

She lowered her brow in a glare. "You forget I come from a family of fire-wielders. I will not hurt you." Her soft tone turned earnest. "Trust me, Shang."

That steely gaze held hers . . . and slowly melted, enough for the pain and exhaustion plaguing him to shine through. Defeated, he exhaled and closed his eyes. With a determined set of her jaw, Meiling reached for the ties of his cloak.

He flinched, turning his face away from her, but didn't stop her. As she peeled off his cloak, she tried to ignore the way his chest rose and fell swifter with each breath, as if it took every ounce of his self-control not to jerk away from her.

She paused, suddenly embarrassed to attempt removing his outer robes. But she needed to help him, personal embarrassment notwithstanding.

He spared her, however, leaning forward and shrugging his good arm out of the sleeve. The other arm required more help, and his jaw tightened as she carefully eased the fabric away from the burn. It landed with a sodden smack on the ground, pooling at his waist. His garments were soaked through to his skin, and his tunic clung to the toned muscles of his torso. He braced himself, but a shiver escaped him, anyway.

She took the knife and slowly began cutting away the fabric around the burn. She should ask him to remove his shirt entirely, both to aid in treatment and warming him up, but the movements would be too hard on the injury. Especially where his shirt stuck to his wound. So she cut around the area until the burn had space to breathe. She worked carefully, refusing to be clumsy despite her own chill. She rummaged through the sack until she found the salve she needed. Slowly, despite Shang's winces, she gently rubbed it into the burn, avoiding the blisters.

"This should provide relief," she mumbled. Once she was done, she unwrapped a long stretch of gauze and began binding the wound. His eyes remained closed, squeezing tightly every so often in pain. Meiling bit her lip when he cringed. She tied off the bandage. "Now your other arm."

He said nothing, merely unfolding it from his waist and turning it so she could access the wound.

She set to work. The dart had only grazed him, so the burn wasn't nearly as bad as his shoulder. Within a few minutes, it was bound as well. "Any others?"

Shang opened one eye, closed it, and shook his head. A cursory glance revealed no other injuries besides the shallow cut on his forehead. Was it still bleeding? She leaned closer, trying to get a better look. Carefully, she brushed her thumb just above the cut.

His eyes snapped open, arresting her so suddenly that she froze, her thumb still hovering at his skin. She'd been so focused on whether he was hurt or not that she hadn't registered how close her face was to his, how her mouth drifted so near his own.

He caught her wrist, quickly averting his gaze and swallowing. "It's fine."

Meiling drew back. He released his grip immediately. She shifted toward Fen, attempting to disguise her flush by untying the shifter's sopping cloak and setting it near the fire to dry. Fen startled awake, growling wordlessly.

"You'll catch cold," Meiling whispered. "Come closer to the fire. Are you bleeding or burned?"

Fen obeyed, crawling so close to the fire that Meiling put out a hand to keep her from drawing too near. "Just bruised," she muttered. "I've never . . . They were . . ."

"It's all right," Meiling said. "You fought bravely, and we escaped. That's all that matters. Here, eat something. Sleep."

"Someone has to stand guard—" Fen protested, her eyes clearing in the firelight.

"I'll guard. Go to sleep."

Fen's face twisted in confusion, but she needed no more encouragement. She curled up near the fire, the color finally returning to her face, and slept. The panda cub scooted against her legs, laying its head on top of her knee before yawning and letting out a huff. It promptly fell back asleep.

Everyone was asleep and tended to. The fire started, the horses sheltered. It may not have all been done as well as if Shang had done it, but it would have to do. Now that everything was taken care of, Meiling's shoulders dropped with exhaustion. She was wearier than she'd ever been in her life. Her fingers burned where she had cut them, and her eyelids dragged with heaviness.

She lay down in a shivering bundle near the fire, and let her spirit fly free.

CHAPTER 10

ALL NIGHT, MEILING guarded the campsite, hunting for the glow of souls, and occupied herself with distressing turns of thought.

Brigands.

Those wielders who had attacked them were brigands—criminals who exercised their magic outside the emperor's sanction. But who were they? And why had they come for her?

Why had that evanescer come for her at the palace?

This wasn't merely coincidence. They had to be connected, which meant that someone was trying to take her. But how would they already know she had fled the palace, much less tracked her down? It seemed impossible. No one knew about this except her parents, Fen, and Shang. Unless the fact that Fen and Shang had been dropped from their appointments raised suspicion?

She dropped her face into her hands. This was too confusing. How was she to make sense of this by herself?

As Meiling floated through the dying storm, free of the chill of her body, she tried to piece everything together.

They hadn't tried to kill her.

That was obvious. They wanted to kill Fen and Shang, her protectors. They wanted to kidnap Meiling. How else could she explain the fact that she had not been killed? She'd been next to helpless, with no weapon and no skills in self-defense—all while carrying a fathers-cursed panda cub, no less. If someone wanted her alive, what use could they have of her? Perhaps her royal blood was intended to be used as leverage, as a means of power in negotiation to make her father capitulate to demands. Or perhaps someone had learned the secret of the cursed princess, that she wasn't as magicless as everyone thought. But *how*?

A sudden thought seized her.

Was her use of her magic even now—was it illegal? She was not a sanctioned magic-wielder. She was not employed in the service of the empire. That hadn't seemed to matter before. But now . . .

Dread settled into the pit of her soul. That explained Pa's last warning to her, not to tell anyone about her magic. If she did, if someone found out . . . She could be tried for treason. Burned as a criminal or slow sliced to death. Not even her Pa could circumvent the law, not unless he wanted to sacrifice his entire family to execution.

She'd be a brigand.

Or was she already that?

She shuddered at the thought. She may not be like the brigands who'd attacked them, but that did not make her magic use legal.

Whatever the case, she couldn't tell Shang or Fen. She couldn't tell anyone. She must hope that Shang and Fen would defend her from these mysterious enemies, get her to the fortress, and that her parents would quickly make the palace safe enough for her to brave the return journey.

Then she would resume her life as the cursed princess, such as it was.

Meiling did not wake Fen and Shang in the morning as the sky brightened. She rose early, stoked the fire, and did what she could to prepare for the day's travel. *If* Fen and Shang were well enough to travel.

The panda remained curled in the crook of Fen's knees, but it watched Meiling's movements, its rounded ears twitching.

There was nothing to be had for a warm meal, but maybe there was *something* else besides rice cakes and jerky. She ducked out of the shelter quietly. In daylight, it was easier to see the stretch of tumbled stones for quite some distance. Fallen, broken pillars lay half buried by dirt, with scraggly shrubs forcing their way up between cracked paving stones. Temple ruins, perhaps? She almost rolled her ankle, stumbling through the rocky remains to the horses' saddle bags piled near the animals. Her horse whinnied softly and nuzzled its face into her shoulder.

"There, there, my sweet one," she chuckled. "Don't turn invisible on me today, all right?" She stroked the horse's gray neck, admiring the beast's elegant stature that belied its graceful power. How majestic a horse was! She liked hers especially. Something about it belonging to her made it even more beautiful.

She didn't neglect the other horses, however, and took a few minutes to give each of them a little love and affection. It garnered mixed receptions from the animals. When she rummaged through the saddlebags, she was surprised to find what she was looking for: a small pot and tea leaves.

Quietly returning to her sleeping companions, she made the tea and silently bemoaned her lack of a strainer for the leaves. She was carefully pouring the tea back into one of the waterskins when Shang's voice startled her, making her spill a few drops.

"It's so late!" He jerked up from the ground and winced at the movement. His shirt had dried in the night, and it hung stiffly on his frame, the cut hole showing the bandage and just a tad of muscular chest and arm. "What are you doing? We must be—"

"You needed rest," Meiling said. "How's your arm?" She handed him the waterskin. "Drink."

He eyed it suspiciously. "What is it?"

Did he think she was trying to poison him? Why in the seven valleys would she do such a thing when she was all but helpless in this wild, *mó guǐ*-ridden countryside?

"Tea," she said, pressing it into his hands with a slightly annoyed cock of her eyebrow. She tossed him a hunk of traveler's bread. "How is your shoulder?"

He caught the bread and took one swig of the hot tea, then another. "Better," he grunted.

She smiled. "I'm glad to hear it. I will be back shortly. There's a stream nearby and the horses will be desperate for water by now."

"Don't go," Shang said immediately.

Meiling paused, pulling at one of her sleeves self-consciously. "Why?"

"You have no protection," he said, as if it were the most obvious thing ever. "No magic."

Did he suspect her?

Despite her rising alarm, she clenched her teeth and stared back at those calculating black irises as if his words had no effect on her. "It's midmorning. The sun is bright. Little mischief happens at such times. You and Fen are not recovered. I'll be quick."

His face darkened as the sun streamed in between the gaps of stone and cast bright rays across the ground. He quickly disguised any grimace as he sat forward. "Mischief? I suppose you mean like last night?"

Meiling would have grinned her own mischievous smile, but she kept her face calm and determined. "I'll be quick," she repeated and scurried out of the shelter, ignoring his further protests.

She shook her head as she knelt to unbuckle the three horses' hobbles. The leather was stiff from drying in a knot and the task proved especially difficult with her two fingers bound in a bandage. Her fingernails were red and stinging by the time she loosened all three beasts and collected their leads.

The three horses followed her with ears cupped forward as she led them toward the stream she'd seen last night while floating. If she was correct, it was not too far away, just a little in that direction there . . .

The sound of rushing water was her first indication that she'd chosen the right direction. The mud was the second. Her boots slugged in the wet ground whenever she did not take care to search for the grassy spots. Fen's horse kept stopping to lower its head and chew vacantly at the bright green stalks. "Ach, come, you stubborn thing." She tugged its lead and its ears went back. It swished its tail, glaring stupidly at her, and then followed with stomping hooves.

The stream was flooding.

It was much wider and swifter than last night. The engorged stream nearly swallowed up the bank, and she was forced to take great care with each step.

She tied the horses to a tree branch close to the water and let the parched horses drink their fill. While they lapped, she precariously slogged her way to a dry, grassy spot overlooking the stream. Her boots were filthy, with large squishy chunks of mud lining the edges and smearing up the sides.

She plopped down on the grass and smiled.

There was something about sitting in a place like this, with the sun beating down on her, the wind ruffling her hair and caressing her cheek, letting her eyes feast on the beauty of the green forest and the sparkling, gurgling stream, that was so much better when she was awake. She pulled her messy, tattered braid over her shoulder and unwound it leisurely, letting her fingers linger on the softness of its silky texture. For just a single minute, she let her hair fly free in the wind. It made her feel a little wilder and a little freer. Practicality quickly won over sentiment, and she braided it again.

Something moved on the other side of the stream.

She leaned forward, sitting up in a crouch, eyes squinting. A chattering sound made the horses whinny, stomp their legs, and flatten their ears. Except Fen's, which continued drinking.

She held completely still.

Something red scurried beneath the underbrush. And then a flash of brilliant blue.

She drew in a sharp breath, eyes flying wide. *Oh fathers.* Heart beating fast, she scanned the surrounding area, searching for an escape route.

Why hadn't she listened to Shang? She should have waited until he could accompany her or let him do it himself. She had no way to defend herself, or—

The horses. They were even more helpless than her, tethered at the edge of the water. She certainly was *not* about to leave them there and flee for help. Slowly, each movement deliberate, she slid from the grassy perch to the mud on the bank of the stream. As she moved, one of the hidden creatures chortled. She froze.

It darted out to the water, in full view of her.

Its body was the size of a dog, long and sinuous. Red, glittering scales ran the length of its thin, reptilian body. The creature spotted the horses with gleaming, golden eyes and reared back on its hind legs, flexing waxy, almost translucent wings. It spat warning puffs of smoke at the horses, which pulled at their leads and brayed anxiously.

A dragon.

Meiling's focus did not leave the dragon as she moved steadily closer. Her hands went clammy, but she dared not move to wipe them on her garments. The *mó guǐ* ignored her and seemed torn between intimidating the horses and getting its drink. Its forked tongue slid between sharp teeth and curled in the rushing currents of the bloated stream.

She slipped in the mud and flailed her arms to catch herself.

Golden eyes snapped to hers.

She froze, even as her foot kept sliding ever so slightly in the muck. She barely managed to trap her scream behind gritted teeth and a braced jaw.

The dragon screeched, flapping its wings, and spit little bursts of flame—still warning, but threatening.

"Shhhh, my beautiful one," Meiling said, her hands outstretched toward the creature on the opposite bank. "I mean you no harm. I just need to get my friends here, and then I'll leave you alone. How's that?" She smiled with closed lips so the dragon would not see her teeth and misinterpret her gesture. "I won't tell the others."

As she spoke, she continued her slow trek toward the horses. She cooed sweet words, and the dragon's wings drooped slightly. It cocked its lizard-like head at her, and its tongue flickered.

When she touched the first horse, the dragon screeched again.

"Hush!" she cried, still softly. "They'll hear you and they'll kill you. I don't want you to kill me or my friends here, and I don't want my other friends to kill you. So stay quiet, stay on your side of the water, and don't blast us with fire, alright?" She smiled her tight-lipped smile again, biting back a whimper of fear.

The dragon blinked its cat's eyes at her, thrice in quick succession, and cocked its head to the side. Then it scooted further down the stream, away from them, and with a wary eye on Meiling, began drinking.

She quickly untied the horses and began clambering up the bank with the three beasts in tow. The dragon, alerted by their movement, puffed out its chest again and spread its wings, but did no more. When they were a safe distance away, it lowered itself to the water again. Meiling breathed a long sigh and nearly collapsed in relief. But she gritted her teeth, dragged Fen's horse away from another snack, and squared her shoulders to face the others.

"See?" she said when she entered the ruins to find Shang working to disguise signs of their occupation. "Nothing terrible happened."

Hopefully, her smile didn't look too awkward or tense.

He looked up, his expression taking on the cold indifference she had grown accustomed to. He wore a fresh tunic, not the one she'd cut up last night. One glance at him and she could hardly believe he had been so badly burned yesterday. Either his pain tolerance was very high, or that salve had worked faster than expected. Possibly both.

"We're leaving," Shang said. "Fen's been repacking the saddlebags."

"Where's the panda?"

"Don't know, don't care."

She shot him a glare before hurrying to find Fen, who was sitting beside the pile of saddlebags, the panda sprawling between her legs. The shifter rubbed the cub's lower abdomen, a focused line appearing between her eyes, her tongue sticking out between her lips.

"Do you feel better?" Meiling asked.

"Can't you see I'm busy?" Fen growled—and then yelped as the panda let out a happy chirp, flapping its arms toward her.

Meiling hid a smile. Fen was fine, it seemed.

When she turned to leave, something hit the back of her head and fell over her, blocking her vision. She threw up her arms, scrambling to pull the fabric away from her head—only to discover it was her cloak.

"That's yours," said Fen from behind her with a little snicker.

Meiling tamped down on the sudden bubbling of irritation inside her chest. She didn't bother responding, instead merely clasping the cloak around her throat and marching away.

Of course Fen wouldn't be different after last night. Meiling had thought they'd be more of a team now, but apparently that was a flawed assumption. Fen would be Fen, and that was that.

Within a few minutes, after Shang finished disguising the area as their campsite and the horses were resaddled, they mounted. Fen had the panda tied to her front, its arms and legs free to flop at its side.

"You need to get rid of that thing," Shang growled at her. "It's nothing but a liability."

"His name is Bo," replied Fen haughtily. "And his wound isn't fully healed yet."

Shang said nothing more, coming to Meiling's side to hoist her into the saddle. She merely smiled sweetly at his hard face.

"I think I can do it," she said.

He blinked. Then he twisted on his heel and, in one deft movement, leapt into his horse's saddle. He didn't even look over his shoulder to see whether she got along or not.

She did. After a few deep breaths, after her heart rate skyrocketed, after she nearly fell just from getting her foot in the stirrup, she mounted her horse. She did it, albeit not gracefully.

"What are you smiling about?" Fen asked sourly.

Meiling grinned. "It's a beautiful day."

And each day, she was stronger than the day before.

CHAPTER 11

"THERE WAS SOMETHING strange about those brigands," Fen said to Shang while she let the panda gnaw on her hand. "They weren't employed in the emperor's service, obviously. But it wasn't just that. Their magic felt . . . *unnatural.*"

Meiling's head cocked at this. "What do you mean?"

Fen cast an irritated look over her shoulder, as if she hadn't expected Meiling to be listening. "If *you* had magic, Princess, you'd feel the difference. Magic flows. Theirs was *forced*. Like their magic wasn't their own."

"Or not entirely their own," Shang said coolly. He turned in his saddle to give Meiling a pointed look. As if he expected her to know something about it. Her face must have reflected her bafflement, because he narrowed his eyes and turned ahead.

He hadn't forgotten about the inn, then.

They traveled along the stream Meiling had visited earlier and she prayed desperately that they would not come upon any of the dragons from earlier. She wasn't sure exactly why she wanted her little dragon spared—*they were dangerous*. Yet something about that one's golden eyes made her think it did not *want* to be a threat to human civilization. It only wanted to be left alone.

The horses' hooves sunk into the rain-softened ground, a safe distance from the swell of the stream. Each step was a *pop*, like the mud was not ready to relinquish its hold. *Squelch, squelch, squelch,* they traversed in the sunlight.

The world was more beautiful after a storm, Meiling decided firmly.

"Not entirely their own?" Fen repeated. "How so?"

"Her Highness the Queen probably has a theory or two," Shang said, his head tilting slightly in Meiling's direction again.

Her focus snapped sharply. "My mother? What would she know?"

"She never told you about her . . . *friend*? From her Academy days?" Shang asked, peering at her with that dangerous glint.

The implication of that word *friend* made her stomach sink like a rock in a lake, stunning her into silence. Had there been someone before Pa?

"So she has told you something."

He *did* suspect her. Surely that was what that slow, calculating smile meant. He'd tucked away her knowledge of their pursuers and he was determined to discover her. He baited her, waiting for her to falter, and when she did, he would do . . . something.

What could he gain from unraveling any mysteries shrouding the shamed princess?

Perhaps he intended to leverage his knowledge of her secrets or crimes, whichever he discovered. Could he blackmail her? Force her to gather information, say or do something she did not want, or something worse? He was ambitious, determined, and cunning, but how vicious was he? What was he willing to do to accomplish his goals?

Despite everything, Fen and Shang clearly still hated her. She'd been a fool to think she'd made progress with them.

"She has told me nothing," Meiling said. "I know nothing of what you speak."

Shang didn't believe her. It was plain on his face, in the twist of his lips. His distrust carved itself into every line of his handsome face.

He thought her a liar.

Meiling dug her nails into the pommel of her saddle.

"The queen? What does she have to do with anything?" Fen asked Shang, completely ignoring Meiling. When he didn't answer, she peppered him with variations of the same question.

He let out an annoyed breath and flicked his gaze to her. "The queen has little to do with anything. Rumor has it that she was friends with one who defected from the Academy. One defect who is causing a stir in the barbarians amassing in the north."

"Where did you hear this?" Fen hurled the question at him. "We had the same masters, and they *definitely* did not cover this in our classes."

"Independent research," Shang said.

Inside, Meiling's hackles raised and despite her lack of battle training, she almost wanted to sling a punch at Shang for speaking of her mother like she was some enemy spy.

No one was better or more loyal than her mother.

For one with a shoulder that must be hurting even now, Shang sat with his back straight in his saddle. Despite the underlying accusations of his words, the ones he used were careful and well-chosen to appear harmless to anyone but Meiling. She tried not to hate him for the growing number of negative assumptions he made about her and her family. If her father knew how Shang spoke about his wife and daughter . . . A few words, and Meiling could utterly destroy Shang's life and future.

She ground her teeth together and gave her head a little shake. *No.* She wouldn't stoop so low. Even if Shang wasn't suffering from wounds on her behalf.

The stream was so glutted after the storm it could almost be called a river. Meiling tried to distract herself from the burning frustration in her chest with the sights and sounds of rushing water, the towering trees and the wet foliage that glittered like emeralds.

Something scuttled on the opposite bank.

Meiling closed her eyes as her heart sank. The dragons were still here. Maybe the others had missed the sound? It was a ridiculous hope. Shang and Fen were warriors, their senses attuned to any suggestion of danger.

As if on cue, Fen's head whipped to the side like a dog catching a scent. "Dragons. Look, three of them! You can get the blue, I'll get the green and yellow ones."

Meiling found a strange solace in the fact that her little red one was elsewhere.

"There's no need. They haven't seen us, and they won't bother us if we leave them alone," Shang said, dismissing Fen's eager gaze with a wave of his hand.

Those words brought a burst of hope to Meiling's anxious heart. She knew dragons were monsters to be killed, but these seemed almost harmless. Perhaps it was their beauty that made her want to spare them.

"Not slay them? But they are a danger to humanity! It's our *job* to kill *mó guǐ*," Fen protested, her body almost flickering like she itched to shift. "You'd better not be growing soft on me, Shangdi."

His gaze slid past her to the opposite bank, where a long yellow tail flicked beneath a bush. The blue one wasn't even hiding, but coiled around a tree trunk in the open. Its scales gleamed sapphire, glittering in the sunlight. So, so beautiful.

"We're in the middle of *nowhere*," Shang retorted. "They're not endangering humanity here."

"But what if they're free to breed uncontrolled? Their population will explode! They will terrorize and kill any traveler come this way." Fen's hand gripped her knife hilt with the tightly coiled patience of a huntress. "I can kill them quickly."

The panda batted a paw toward the knife, leaning its chubby head closer to sniff it.

"There's no need," Shang repeated with a glare. "It's more trouble than it's worth."

Or perhaps he suffered more from his injuries than he let on?

Fen's lips pulled back from her teeth in a snarl, but she stayed put.

They rode for several long minutes in silence. Meiling hated that every time she was angry at Shang, he did something like this that made her *not* dislike him as much as she wanted to. Despite the burning in her chest whenever she remembered what his words implied about her mother, she couldn't help but be thankful for his intervention against Fen's bloodlust.

Hopefully, they wouldn't stumble across any more dragons.

But then Fen's eyes suddenly locked on the back of Shang's head. She ripped the knot free of the sash tying the panda to her chest, leaned to the side and dumped Bo in Meiling's lap. Then she folded into a hawk, leaping into the air, and flew back the way they'd come. Her horse continued walking as if it did not notice the lack of a rider or the sudden slack of reins.

"No!" Meiling cried, wrapping her arms around the cub's flailing limbs before it fell off the horse. "Shang! We have to stop her!"

Shang said nothing, merely shot a dark look where Fen had disappeared and tightened his fists around his reins. Why didn't he do something? He was the only one who had any measure of control over her—

Meiling turned her horse around, clutching Bo tighter to her.

"What are you doing?" Shang demanded.

"She can't just kill them! They didn't hurt anything!" she cried, surprised by her own force of will and emotion. She was about to kick her horse into a gallop, but Shang reached over and deftly snatched her reins from her hands.

"It's too late," he said. "You can't stop her."

"I can try!"

But even as she spoke, the hawk came flying back. It hovered over the saddle and then folded back into that tall young woman. Fen said nothing, only plopped back like nothing had happened. Her back was straight, a tiny, self-satisfied hint of a smile playing on her lips.

"Thanks for holding him," she said as she peeled Bo from Meiling's arms and pulled him into her lap.

Shang dropped her reins, and they all continued riding.

Meiling stared with utter disgust at Fen. She let her horse fall a little further behind her companions. Or was *companion* too warm of a word for them?

As they rode, she couldn't help but shed a tear.

"We have to cross eventually," Shang was saying reasonably.

And Fen was responding impetuously, "Let's cross later. Maybe it'll lighten up downstream."

"Unlikely," Shang said. "Too much farther, and we'll be traveling outside our way. Besides, *you* won't have to get wet. Only the rest of us."

"Why can't you freeze a bridge for us?" Meiling asked.

Fen choked on a laugh.

"It would flood the area and prove counterproductive," Shang said, too simply.

"Besides," Fen said, chortling a little. "With your luck, you'd slip and fall in anyway."

Meiling glared at her back, swallowing the anger rising in her throat, burning her tongue. With effort, she drew in a deep breath and let it out between clenched teeth. She shouldn't let herself be ruffled by Fen's comments.

But they were just so *unnecessary*. And so rude.

Shang looked at Meiling, and something sparked in his eyes. She couldn't make out what, but it seemed negative. Was that disapproval directed at Fen or Meiling? "I'll go first with Fen's horse. You follow," he said.

"On my horse?" Meiling asked.

Fen smirked. "Unless you want to swim." Then she dumped a squirming Bo in Meiling's arms.

Meiling kept her horse at bay while Fen folded into a hawk and flew across. She landed as a human, and Meiling still couldn't quite make her brain understand what happened when she shifted. Shang already held Fen's lead in his hand and waded into the stream, guiding both horses after him. Fen's horse planted its hooves on the bank and Shang growled at it while pulling harder on the lead. His horse flattened its ears, but obeyed.

Meiling followed hesitantly, quickly discovering the water was much deeper than she expected. Shang wasn't even half-way before his robes and trousers were soaked to his thighs, and by the time he reached the middle, he was waist-deep.

The horses put their ears back, whinnying nervously.

"Follow!" Shang barked at Meiling.

She took a deep breath and urged her horse deeper. The mare tossed her head, ears back, and stamped her front hoof. "Come on, my pretty girl," Meiling soothed. "It's only a little stream. Keep going, that's it."

The water was shockingly cold as it enveloped her feet. She tried to hold her feet up, so they did not get wet, but after a few more painful steps deeper, it proved impossible. Especially with Bo trying to eat her arm. She let her feet fall and seize up from the cold. She drew deep, steadying breaths and kept softly coaxing her horse in further.

Of course, Shang didn't flinch from the icy water. Half his body must be numb now that he was almost to the other side. He glanced over his shoulder. "Move faster!"

Meiling glared at his back.

Something flashed in front of her.

She instinctively ducked, dropping the reins to shield her face from claws and clutching her arm tighter around the cub, but realized it was only Fen in hawk form. It screeched as though amused it startled her. Then it dove back in, snatching up a squawking Bo in its talons—presumably to carry him to shore.

Meiling's horse, however, was not amused.

Before she could grasp at the reins again, before she could scream, before she could even catch a breath, her horse reared and shrieked in terror. Meiling flailed her arms, scrabbling desperately for purchase and finding none.

She tumbled off the saddle into the rushing, freezing river.

Cold stunned her body. She plunged into the swift currents, smashing her back into something hard, knocking air out of her chest.

Breathe! She needed to breathe!

Her limbs turned to lead, stiffened almost beyond use. She frantically clawed at the water, her eyes open desperately wide and freezing in their sockets.

She was going to die. This was death. A panicked, wretched—

Something pulled tight around her neck, nearly choking her and making her last reserves of air gush into bubbles. Had her cloak caught on something? She was buried beneath the pressure of the rushing water over her head. She couldn't rise!

Panic overwhelmed her.

And then—air.

She gasped, choked, coughed up water. Something warm held her tight as the icy currents swirled around her. She coughed again—into Shang's chest. Then she became aware that he was shouting. At Fen.

She could only suck in lungful after lungful of blessed air and clutch fistfuls of Shang's tunic. One of his arms held her against him, while the other gripped his horse's saddle to keep them both from being swept away. They moved slowly toward the shore, where Fen was back in human form, reaching to pull Shang's horse out of the currents.

"Don't bother getting your boots wet," Shang snarled at her when they were finally nearing the bank. He released his horse and bent, scooping up Meiling out of the water to carry her to shore.

She trembled with cold, completely soaked head to toe, but all she could think about was how wonderful each breath was in her lungs. She clung to Shang, breathed heaving gulps of air. The water fell away with each step until they were on the dry—well, dryish—ground. He lowered his hold under her knees to allow her to stand. But as she tried to gain her balance, his wide hand planted on her head and pushed down.

Pushing her onto a rock to sit, she realized when she hit it hard. She chattered, wrapping her arms tightly around her middle.

"Your cloak," Shang ordered Fen while angrily bending to unfasten Meiling's. His hands were ice blocks fumbling at her throat. He peeled away the wet cloak and snatched Fen's cloak from her outstretched hand. Not gently at all, he wrapped the dry cloak around Meiling.

This done, he whirled on Fen.

"What were you thinking?" he exploded. "You compromise our mission. Do you realize the girl could have died? Do you realize our lives would have been forfeited? I don't care how stupid you think this assignment is—you will *not* allow your feelings to hinder your duty. Understand?"

"It's not *my* fault that her horse was spooked!" Fen shot back. "I had to get the panda!"

At the mention of her horse, Meiling glanced over to see all three horses safely on dry land. Fen was soaked to her waist. She had retrieved the horses while Shang saved Meiling.

"Did you expect to do something stupid and get a pleasant outcome?" Shang snarled mercilessly. "I don't *care* about the panda, and if you are determined to let it interfere with your duty, I *will* get rid of it. Don't tell me it's injured, and it needs your help. The daughter of your *emperor* is in your care. And while we're on the subject of duty, you need to stop being so cruel to her. Enough with it all, Fen!"

"I don't see *you* bowing to her and praising her grace and majesty!"

Shang stepped closer to Fen, water dripping from his clenched jaw, the darkness of his eyes sucking the sunlight out of the world. And Fen, to Meiling's shock, actually stumbled back a step.

"I don't care if you hate her or if you hate this mission," said Shang, dropping his voice to a low, menacing rumble. "I don't care if you're a dragon-blasted shifter with a temper you can't control—*learn* to control yourself, Hu Fen. You'll be the death of us all unless you stop putting your feelings ahead of your duty."

Fen stared at him, eyes wide and flashing with hurt. Then she whirled on her heel, huffing as she stormed toward her horse, scooping up the panda on her way. Shang's glare didn't shift away from her.

Meiling's teeth chattered, and she pulled Fen's dry cloak tight around her wet shoulders. Her back ached where she'd hit the rock, but she got to her feet.

"Shhh-should we b-be m-m-moving?" she stuttered.

Without waiting for their response, she walked on stiff legs to her horse. Did she have the strength to mount? She looked back to find Shang and Fen both staring at her.

"W-we are t-traveling more t-today? Right?" she asked, one eyebrow raised.

Shang strode toward her, not looking her in the eye, and offered her a boost into the saddle. Fen mounted, also refusing to meet her gaze.

The rest of the day, they traveled in silence and wet clothes.

CHAPTER 12

THANKS TO THE warm, bright sun, Meiling was mostly dry by the time they stopped to camp, except where she'd been sitting on the saddle. Shang left her to dismount herself, apparently confident in her recovery from her earlier swim. Fen took care of settling the horses for the night, Shang assembled the tent, and Meiling busied herself lighting the fire while the panda laid on its back beside her, munching on bamboo.

No one spoke for a long time. Not until Fen shoved Meiling's cloak into her face.

"Take your smelly cloak and give me mine," she growled.

Meiling stopped arranging the sticks she'd collected to unfasten the clasp around her neck and pull the cloak away from around her shoulders. She held it out to Fen, meeting her eyes. Fen looked away quickly. She snatched the cloak and turned on her heel.

So she *did* feel guilty.

Meiling braved a glance at Shang. He was focused, his brow relaxed, as he fastened the corners of the canvas tent to the stakes. But the tension in his shoulders told her he was a tightly coiled spring, ready to burst forth at any provocation.

He finished his work and looked up, catching her studying him. She did not let her gaze flee away, but instead held his firmly.

"Let me look at your shoulder," she said. When he looked like he was about to refuse, she added, "A little more salve will help with the pain, and you'll need fresh bandages after the river today."

His eyes were so dark in the twilight.

He didn't say no, which she took as a yes. She scrambled to her feet to fetch the supplies, and returned to find Shang had set himself near the unfinished fire, awaiting her ministrations. Did she mistake the line of pain in his face? Perhaps the thought of relief was more than he could bear after hiding the pain all day.

"Let me start the fire," she said, setting the pack of medical supplies next to Shang. "It'll give me better light to work by."

He said nothing.

Fen distributed waterskins, strips of jerky and rice cakes, then sat down across Shang, quietly watching Meiling strike the steel on the flint. With both of their eyes on her, she dared not be so careless as to injure herself again. Even as she struck the metal and rock, her fingers throbbed in fear of another biting incision.

Bo rolled around behind her, tangling his paws in the folds of her cloaks. Little squeaks punctuated his movements, and by now, he'd almost chewed through his bandage. He seemed to be healing very quickly. Did that mean they'd have to release him back to the wild soon?

Eventually, the fire crackled and gained strength. The horses chewed noisily nearby, mingling with the familiar sounds of the night—singing bugs, the swoosh of a gentle breeze rustling leaves overhead, and Meiling could easily imagine the stars' whispers above her.

She approached Shang where he sat, the fire hot at her back, and knelt next to him. For a split second, his eyes met hers, and she hesitated. Chewed the inside of her cheek. Then he looked away and shrugged out of his outer robes, undoing the front laces of his tunic. Carefully, as though the movement brought pain, he pulled the neckline to one side, over his bandaged shoulder. There was the tiniest flash of a wince on his face, but he masked it quickly.

"I'm going to unwrap the bandage," she murmured softly, shifting so she could better see by the firelight. She had removed the bandages on her fingers earlier—they were so wet and had served their purpose—so she worked with no impediment.

When she pulled back the last layer of bandage, her fingers brushed his skin and he shivered. Probably from the bandage finally peeling away from the wound or the startling cold of her fingers. It was hard to see clearly in the firelight, but she told him what she saw.

"It's a little pale, puckered in some areas. A couple of the blisters burst, but it is looking much better than yesterday." She attempted a reassuring smile. He wasn't looking. She continued her work, pulling out the salve. "I will apply the salve now."

He did nothing except stare into the fire, but with each application, his body tensed beneath her rubbing fingers. A muscle in his neck, then jaw, twitched as she moved closer to the blisters.

"There," she announced with another missed smile. "I'll rebind it. It should feel much better in the morning." The fire itself popped much louder than she spoke, and Bo had snuggled next to Fen's boot. If she did not hover near his ear, she would think he could not hear her soft whispers.

She cut a long stretch of bandage and Shang obliged to pull the neck of his tunic over a little more so she could loop the soft gauze under his arm and over his shoulder.

"Done." She tied the knot, her tongue stuck into her cheek. She pulled away, and he readjusted his tunic. "What about the other one? It should be much better."

Face still tight and expressionless, he rolled up his sleeve where the other bandage was bound around his forearm. When she pulled it away, it was so much improved that she announced he shouldn't need another bandage for it. She did take his forearm in both of her hands, though, turning it upward, and gently worked more salve into the area.

Once she was done, she packed the supplies back into their pack. The top of her bent head prickled, as though in response to his gaze following her movements. She looked up, found him staring at her. She almost frowned at the strange way the fire gleamed in his dark pupils. But she snapped shut the kit and stood.

She froze at his voice.

"I know you're hiding something," he whispered, his voice edged in darkness and low enough that only she could hear.

She stood, stunned. Her breath escaped her lips in a whoosh, her eyes widening.

He knew about her magic. Or suspected it.

And what would he do if he found out? Would he expose her before the courts to get his appointment back? Expose her father as a liar? Would her secret magic bring a centuries-old dynasty to its knees?

She shot a glance at Fen, who seemed completely absorbed in sharpening her knife and ignoring the panda chewing on the top of her boots. Meiling's mouth opened, but she clamped it shut. There was nothing she could say to Shang, not when he looked at her like his hunted prey. Wordlessly, she turned around and carried the pack to the horse, silently fuming as she went.

This was how he repaid her kindness?

What happened to him telling Fen to stop treating her cruelly?

She was tired of this. Sick of the way they constantly reminded her that she was *less,* less because she hadn't gone to the Academy, hadn't touched a weapon in her life, because she was forced to keep her magic a secret.

Stalking back into the ring of firelight, she crossed her arms over her chest and asked boldly, "Shang, would you teach me self-defense? In case we're attacked again."

Fen's eyes went the size of saucers. Her eyebrows shot up, and she turned her surprised gaze from Meiling to Shang. "Teach *you?* You'd do more damage to yourself if you knew anything."

Shang's cool eyes slid from Meiling's determined brow to Fen's mockery. When he looked at Fen, something flashed in his eyes. Anger at her words? Or a desire for revenge? Would he train her to spite Fen? Her hopes rose.

But he shook his head and returned his gaze to the fire. "Nothing you could learn in the span of a few short evenings would be helpful. Fen's right; a little training would pose more danger than anything else."

Perhaps he decided he preferred to spite Meiling by refusing to help her. That, judging by the ever-so-slight lift of the corner of his mouth, was very possible. Or maybe he genuinely did not think she could learn anything of use in so short a time.

"Leave the fighting to us," Fen said, her voice too eager. In the flickering flames, she suddenly took on a wolfish sort of grin. Meiling could have sworn those fangs reappeared.

"May I have a small weapon, at least?" she pressed. "The illusionist—"

Shang was shaking his head again, not letting his eyes stray from the dancing fire. Then he seemed to reconsider, and he shrugged. He reached into his sleeve and extracted a small penknife. "Here."

Fen howled with laughter. The panda barked in response, scooting away from her.

Meiling accepted it with heated cheeks, sliding it up her own sleeve. "Thank you," she managed to mumble, despite how fat the words weighed on her tongue.

It had grown so much darker in a matter of minutes. The last light of dusk had fled away, leaving the heaviness of midnight, despite the early hour. Meiling retreated into her tent, Fen's laughter still ringing in her hot ears. The moment she moved back the flap, she cursed herself for not getting her bedroll. She was surprised to discover that Shang had already arranged it for her. Cocking her head, she let the tent flap fall closed behind her.

Exhaustion grappled at her, tangling in her hair, reaching for her mind, and she was strangely cold. Not bothering to undress, she snuggled into her cloak and blanket on the bedroll and fell fast asleep.

She hovered over the campsite, watching Fen talk to Shang. Fen kept reminding him of various funny or shocking stories from Academy days—definitely an attempt to weasel her way back into his good graces.

"Remember when that good-for-nothing Jizi challenged you to a duel because the girl he liked had set her sights on you? And then you *demolished* him." Fen laughed.

"Was that why he challenged me? I thought he just wanted to practice with me," Shang said. "Who was the girl?"

"Li Feiyan, the healer. You did not know she liked you?"

The kind girl who had spoken to Meiling at the Graduation festival?

He shrugged. "I knew of her. Everyone was excited about her. First healer in ages. What was she, a year behind us?"

"Aye, though she should have been two years behind us. They accelerated and abbreviated her training so she could serve the people while still at the Academy. She was always busy."

The panda curled up by the fire, always near Fen, and fell asleep.

Story after story passed. For as headstrong and impulsive as Fen was, she knew Shang. Much better than Meiling did. With each story Fen told, she stroked his ego. They were stories about Shang winning a battle, outsmarting a classmate, one even of a prank Fen had tried to get Shang to join. He'd said he did not have time and could not risk getting in trouble. But then the prank went off without a slip, apparently thanks to some evanescer named Kai, and the masters never knew about it. The way Fen spoke about it, it was clearly one of her most proud accomplishments.

Then the direction of the conversation shifted.

"I never expected this to be our first assignment," Fen said, sourness edging her words.

Shang didn't respond, but there was no denying what the clenching of his jaw meant. He was still angry about losing his appointment, despite how he tried not to show it.

"I curse the day she was born without magic. Just because the emperor wants to keep her tainted reputation far away from the prince does not mean our lives have to be ruined," Fen growled.

A jolt went through Meiling's spirit. That was what they thought this was? A ploy to separate her scorn from her honored brother? It was *nothing* like that.

Or . . .

No. Meiling would not give voice to the terrible thoughts swirling in her mind. Her parents never lied to her. They might withhold information, but they would never lie.

She found herself sinking closer to the ground, and her presence shrunk into a small, dense mass. She listened as the conversation descended even further.

"If only she wasn't so *annoying*." Fen held her knife to the fire, turning it this way and that to see the flames reflected in its gleaming blade. "Pompous, superior, and so judgmental! She tries to sound smart and sweet by asking so many questions. And then she's utterly helpless. Not only in battle, but she couldn't even mount a horse or start a fire. Have you noticed how long it takes her to light the fire? She moves so slowly, as if the wood must be *just so*."

Shang was staring at the fire without speaking. But when she mentioned the horse and the fire, his lips pursed ruefully.

It was as though Fen's dagger plunged straight into Meiling's heart.

"Here, Shang," Fen stood up, mimicking Meiling's soft voice. It came out ridiculous, stilted, and harsh from her mouth. "Let me care for your wound." She tossed her hair over her shoulder and batted her eyelashes.

Shang said nothing, ignoring her.

Then Fen said, "It would be so easy to pack up and leave her here. She'd become dragon food before midmorning. Or we could—"

"Watch your tongue. Our lives are forfeit if harm befalls the girl," Shang interrupted. "Do not speak of ways to dispatch her. I don't want to hear any more of your complaints about her."

"You can't stop a girl from dreaming," Fen grinned wickedly. "Here, I'll take first watch."

Meiling drew back when Shang approached the tent to sprawl out in front like previously. Fen kept her knife out, twirling it dangerously in her fingers, staring at the surrounding area. Every few minutes, her gaze dropped to Bo, sleeping by her boots.

"Your gift," Ma had called her magic.

It was her curse. A curse deeper than the shame she bore.

Here she had been, thinking they had made progress in their relationship. Shang did not trust her, but she had thought herself of some use. *Helpful.* They spoke like she only served to slow them down.

Pompous? Superior? Judgmental?

Those were severe charges indeed. Meiling might have had trouble breathing through her pained, constricted chest if she were in a physical body. But she was spirit and could not feel those physical symptoms of distress. Instead, all she could feel was an aching, throbbing heart.

She floated away from the fire, away from Shang, away from Fen. She fled as far as she could go, as high as she could fly, until her soul tether pulled taut, stopping her flight. Pulling at it, she wheeled back, and lurched forward. Tried to claw her way further, to disappear into the stars and never wake up again.

It was fruitless.

She couldn't break the tether, couldn't lose herself in the midnight sky.

It hurt. It hurt very much. Possibly more than anything else she had experienced. It should not hurt her—their opinions of her did not *really* matter. They could think what they wanted. But their opinions *did* matter. Their words did hurt her. And as she floated, suspended above the world, so far away from those glistening diamonds above, a temptation grew so great it nearly overwhelmed her.

This was how people grew hard, cold, unfeeling. They were hurt, and as a result, they pulled away. Brick by brick, they built wall after wall of disappointment, fear, and resentment. She could almost feel the brick and mortar in her shadow hands. It would be so easy.

But she could not escape the memory of her mother. Ma, the elegant and stern queen of the emperor. She was not hard and cold. She was brave.

Then there was her younger sister. Pretty, fierce, little Hou. She loved as fiercely as she fought at the Academy. Could Meiling let herself become hardened when she still had a little sister to love? What would Hou learn if Meiling began building walls around her heart?

She didn't want to be hurt.

She also didn't want to be hardened.

What if she returned to her family after these months, only to find that she was a completely different person? And not in a better way?

She thought of Fen and Shang. Their personalities were very different, but they both harbored a deep cynicism about life. So much doubt, distrust, and coldness. Perhaps they did not think so, perhaps they ought to be so for their careers.

Meiling did not want to be like that.

The fight in her soul melted into a sad sort of determination. A resolve.

She let the imagined bricks and mortar fall out of her hands.

She refused to believe that strength was only found in physical might and supernatural powers. Value didn't come only from utility. She refused to close her heart to the beauty that was still very much present in the world, in this empire.

Meiling let her vision trail along the landscape below her, blanketed in thick darkness. There were the mountains they skirted, so high, jutting, craggy, and black. There was the valley, stretching as far as she could see. Forest, fields, and farmlands.

She closed her eyes and imagined sitting on her cliff back home, overlooking the ocean. Never had she suspected how she would ache for that view. Being away from her family . . . How much longer could she go on without them? Perhaps this would have been easier with kinder protectors, but it hardly mattered. She missed her siblings, her parents, and each echo of Fen's word and glimmers of Shang's twisted lips in her mind drove a knife further into her homesick heart.

Suddenly, a fiery orange glow blinked a long way away, catching her eye and causing her heart to lurch. Meiling tugged on her tether and realized it ran straight to that glow.

Her soul plummeted.

Mó guǐ.

CHAPTER 13

MEILING HURTLED THROUGH the air, as fast as she could, back to the campsite.

Please let it not be too late. Please let it not be too late.

When she got closer, orange glowed so brilliantly it almost concealed the birdlike, feathered body that hovered dangerously over the campsite. Its wings of flame dissipated into smoke, its beak dripping fire and snapping in anticipation of the kill.

A phoenix.

Meiling's heart almost stopped. She had to resist the terror that tried to pull her spirit back into her body. The phoenix couldn't see her, so she fled past it, through the treetops, and burst into the campsite.

Shang lay sprawled where she'd left him, asleep by her tent. Fen's head leaned heavily on her fist, elbow propped on her knee, with eyes shut and soft snores escaping her throat. Bo sprawled spread-eagle at her feet, his fluffy white belly upturned.

They were utterly helpless against the circling, predatory monster.

She couldn't warn them! She had to rush to her body and scream for them to wake up before the phoenix could—

It dove. Straight for Fen.

Meiling acted before she thought.

She sent her spirit hurling into Fen's mind.

And found herself floating in a vast, wild field. In the distance, the rooftops of a village were visible. Gray sky cast overhead, long stalks of brown grass waved beneath. There was no sign of the phoenix, of the campsite, of a sleeping Shang.

PHOENIX!! Meiling screamed in Fen's mind. *WAKE UP!*

Suddenly, Fen's eyes opened, and it was like Meiling saw double—the grassy field and the campfire. One blink, and she was seeing outside Fen's eyes. A second blink, and she floated under cloudy sky.

Rapid fire thoughts burst through Fen's mind.

Except they weren't articulated thoughts. They were instincts.

Mó guǐ! Roll! Duck! Monster, monster, monster! Kill the monster!

Fen's body reacted to the heat of a narrowly missed burst of flame and claws from the phoenix. Meiling felt Fen's tension, felt how her training overtook her limbs, felt the sudden burst of thrill and adrenaline.

Shang. I need to wake Shang! thought Fen with a burst, her voice echoing into Meiling's awareness.

"Shang! Phoenix!" Fen screamed.

Fen turned away from Shang, despite Meiling scrambling to see if he woke. Fen did not doubt that Shang was awake and immediately readied for an attack. But Meiling wasn't so sure.

Fen's thoughts had one focus, with no room for anything else.

Kill the monster.

There was power in Fen's limbs, a feeling so entirely unfamiliar to Meiling. This was what it felt like to be strong. But then an alarmed thought crossed Fen's mind.

I can't shift.

It was a realization that crashed into Fen's core and echoed into Meiling's. Fen could not shift because it required close combat. And if she got close to a phoenix, she would burn. The *mó guǐ* was almost more element than physical.

The waves of confusion and frantic alarm, mixed with the rush of addicting adrenaline and the thrill of challenge, plowed into Meiling's conscious. Fen was crippled, almost like she'd broken a leg. It frustrated her but also enthralled her.

The next panicked thought: *Bo! Keep Bo safe!*

Completely disregarding everything else, Fen swept up the cub in her arms and tossed him into the tent with Meiling—as if that would keep him safe. Then he was gone from her mind.

All this happened in milliseconds.

Meiling had no use here, not in this strange place—not anymore. With a blink, she launched herself into the gray sky.

And found herself flying free in the air above the campsite. She whirled, gaze latching onto the phoenix preparing to dive again.

Below, Shang had scrambled to his feet and braced himself for the attack. Fen searched the ground for something . . . stones? A long strip of leather dangled from her fingers. A sling.

The phoenix dove for Shang's face. A streak of fire in the night sky, brilliant and deadly.

He hurled an ice bolt at the oncoming blast of fire. Then he leapt out of the way and the phoenix screeched an earsplitting cry as it narrowly avoided crashing into the ground. The force of that cry shattered into the spirit dimension where Meiling floated. To her horror, her soul tether trembled, as if it were about to break.

A new fear tore into her heart. The thought hadn't even occurred to her before. Could her tether be broken? She couldn't break it, but could others—like the phoenix—break it? What happened if it broke?

Leather cracked below her, and Fen sent rock after rock hurtling toward the blazing phoenix. It wheeled around too fast for her and almost chomped its beak down on her neck. But in a flash, she shifted into a tiger and the phoenix missed. Fen swiped a claw-tipped paw at the phoenix with a roar. She tore through flames and yelped, shifting immediately back into human form, and clutched her hand.

Shang flung bolt after bolt at the beast. His face twisted in focus and heat as he fought. His bolts were the biggest she had ever seen him throw, both thicker and longer. He hurled them like javelins into the sky. If he had hope of any ice piercing through flaming feathers to tender flesh, he had to make them bigger.

But such a weapon was unwieldy.

The phoenix whirled and wheeled, snapping and flaming. Fen and Shang were both disadvantaged in this fight. Neither could use their weapons and magic as they were accustomed.

Shang switched from ice bolts to a *jiaun*. He slammed two arrows into the shaft. "Distract it!" he called to Fen.

"I'm *trying*!" Fen shouted back, diving to avoid being annihilated by a searing burst of flame. She rolled into a crouch, swung her sling, and launched her projectile. It hit the phoenix's feet, making the *mó guǐ* let out another soul-shattering screech.

Meiling clung to her tether as the dangerous tremors reverberated through her spirit hands.

Shang took aim.

Something fiery dove from above.

A second phoenix.

And then Meiling was diving faster, desperate to reach him before the second phoenix did. She tore into his mind, landing in a wide, vast hall. It was barren, dark. The ornate curtains flowing from the towering ceiling all the way to the polished floor were drawn across the windows. Pillars with winding, curling decorative dragons lined the huge, empty space.

ROLL TO THE SIDE! Meiling screamed in Shang's mind.

Confusion rippled through the room, and Meiling's vision switched to Shang's as he took aim at the first phoenix.

SECOND PHEONIX IS DIVING FOR YOU! MOVE!

Fen's scream, echoing through the cavernous room, was what finally made Shang dive and narrowly avoid being decimated by the second phoenix's fatal blow. Heat blasted through his body, but just missed him.

The thoughts roiling through Shang's body felt—for *felt* was a better description than *sounded*—much different from Fen's.

He constantly took stock of the battle. *Fen, there. The first phoenix, there. The second, about to dive again—at Fen. I can hit it.*

Meiling saw through Shang's eyes the sights on the *jiaun* he held. The weight was familiar in his hands, as he calculated exactly where to aim, when to take a shot, noting the *mó guǐ*'s speed so his arrows did not miss.

He released the string.

As soon as he did, frustration flooded his body. *Ach, not close enough!* One dart struck the low underbelly of the second phoenix, but the other barely missed. *A second earlier and it would be dead.*

Pain flared in his shoulder. Sharp, burning pain. He shoved it away without a consideration as his eyes roved the battleground. *Fen!* He blasted a wave of ice just above Fen as both phoenixes bellowed fire toward her. The ice evaporated instantly, but it gave Fen the split second to roll out of the way. Power coursed in his limbs, as he carefully calculated every use of his magic, almost *measuring* the size, the temperature of his ice.

The girl! Where is Meiling? The thought shot through his mind with something akin to panic.

"Find Meiling!" Shang shouted to Fen. "Guard her!"

No! Meiling cried in his mind. *They can't see me—they don't know I'm here too! Leave me!*

Shang's arrows careened wide as an avalanche of confusion rolled over him. Fen was already going to obey, leading the firebirds right to Meiling's prone body and exposing their vulnerability. Meiling tore through the ceiling of Shang's mindscape and darted into Fen's. She hurled down through a gray-cast sky.

Ignore Shang! she shouted. *Fight! Kill! It is better if the phoenixes don't know about Meiling!*

A flash of inarticulate confusion. Then Fen whirled on her foot and slung a stone straight into a phoenix's open mouth.

Now that *is a shot.* Fen's satisfaction flooded every inch of her body with electricity.

The phoenix sputtered on its own flame and lost its balance. Before Fen could load and launch another stone, two arrows struck the phoenix's flaming neck. The phoenix froze midflight and fell.

Fen's body exploded in thrill and adrenaline. Pride too, but this rush, this high that Fen felt was . . . It was pure exhilaration.

This was why she loved killing *mó guǐ.*

Fen was already swinging her sling toward the second phoenix. But Meiling flew out of Fen's head as the deafening snap of a soul tether tore through the ether. The writhing spirit rose out of the mass of feathers and sputtering flame. It was . . . enormous. The long, shapeless mass kept rising. It snapped an owl-like gaze at her.

You protect them, it accused. Its voice—if it could be called a voice—was not furious. It was far darker, far deadlier. *I will break your tether and bring you with me.*

You cannot break it, Meiling said.

No, but my master can. There was a flash in that massive black shadow. A flash of blue fire. And then the shade was dragged upward, far away from Meiling.

When she pulled her gaze away from it, the second firebird was nowhere to be seen. She shot upward in the air, just to make sure nothing glowed nearby. There, getting smaller on the horizon, being swallowed up by the night, was a hiccupping glow. The one Shang shot but hadn't killed. It fled.

Fen and Shang, chests heaving, stared at one another. Shang sat down heavily, a hand drifting toward his injured shoulder. Fen plopped across from him, her singed hair sticking up at weird angles, her eyes alight with wildness.

"Are you hurt?" he asked her.

She shrugged and hid her burned palm close to her leg. "Nothing I can't take care of."

Meiling wanted to enter Fen's mind again, just to see if she felt any guilt for falling asleep on guard. But she restrained herself. She would not gratuitously exercise her magic.

Her magic.

The battle delayed the shock of her realization, but now it hit her full force.

She could enter people's minds. She could enter their *minds*. Feel their thoughts. She remembered Fen's bleak mindscape of a gray and brown field, Shang's gloomy, stately hall with drawn curtains.

"Check on the girl. I'll grab the medical supplies," Shang said, already turning toward the horses. "Then you'll have to scout to ensure the coast is clear."

Fen bristled under his order but obeyed. She strode toward Meiling's tent, not caring to quiet her footsteps. She flung open the flap, and her lips parted in a snarl, then let the flap fall closed.

"The girl sleeps soundly along with the stupid panda," she announced, shaking her head while tilting her eyebrow in scorn. "All that racket, and she sleeps through it. Reason number one hundred fifty-two she would make a terrible warrior."

Shang's head shot up from the saddle bags. Even the darkness couldn't hide the sudden pallor of his face. "She is still asleep? She is alive, right?"

"Yes, she's breathing."

He blinked, looking off into the dark forest. He grew quiet, thoughtful. That gleaming light returned to his eye. His fingers slowed their work until they stopped entirely. He stood so still, so contemplative.

What was he thinking?

She could find out.

Her fingertips buzzed with the realization of her unexplored magic. It would be so easy. She could prepare herself for whatever he would say or ask tomorrow. She would not be as startled as she'd been when he threatened her after she bound his wound.

No.

She would not do it. She would not give into these urges. Their minds were not hers to explore. Would she want them rifling through her mind? No, of course not. She had already invaded their minds out of necessity. She would only do so when she had no other option.

She fluttered above the campsite while Shang bent over the charred remains of the fire bird. "Two of them," he muttered.

"Aye, and we killed one for sure. The second may still die."

"When have two phoenixes ever been seen in the same vicinity?" Shang asked, thoughtful again. He shook his head. "Something is strange about this."

Fen was busy nursing her hand with salve and fresh bandages, but she looked up. When she cocked her head, her features flickered, and she looked like a questioning, ear-raised wolf. "You're right. That *was* very strange. What could it mean?"

Shang holstered his *jiaun* and replaced it in his belt with his knives. "My guess is that we'll find out sooner rather than later." His gaze flicked to the tent, his brow tightening. That cunning light returned to his eyes, replaced by what could possibly be a flash of understanding.

Something tightened in Meiling's stomach. Something deep and foreboding.

Had he . . . figured it out?

Unconsciously, she drew away from by the fire. She didn't want to leave them again, in case another *mó guǐ* happened upon them. But she also didn't want to hear them continue to talk, too afraid of what they might say. She stayed near enough to spot any glowing mass, but she tangled herself into a denser part of the forest where she was more alone.

Here, she could fortify herself for whatever Shang would do in the morning.

CHAPTER 14

MEILING TOOK A few minutes after she woke up to braid her hair, straighten her tunic, and tie up her bedroll. Bo sat in the corner of the tent, watching her with slowly blinking eyes, his bandage slipping down his belly. Outside, the early morning birds chirruped and whistled, one to another. The fire crackled, followed by a hiss as someone poured water on it.

She bent and pulled back the canvas flap so she could slip into the dawn. And immediately froze.

Fen and Shang both stared at her.

Shang smiled—something she had never seen in full. This was not a true smile, however. This was the smile of a cat cornering a mouse and gearing up to torment it before devouring it. His smile might have made him more handsome had its danger not completely counterbalanced the effect.

"Good morning, Highness," he said. "Come, eat. We ride soon."

A wolfish sort of tension lined Fen's face. They sat on the ground waiting for her beside the doused fire. Around the campsite were patches of blackened ground, where every living thing had been annihilated by phoenix fire. Meiling's eyes darted around the camp back to the two tall, seated forms eyeing her like prey.

Bo hopped out of the tent, bounding straight to Fen and wrapping himself around her boot. She kicked him away. He only came back, hugging on tighter. Any other day, Meiling might have smiled.

They could not hurt her. Not while their mission was to deliver her hale and whole to the fortress for safe keeping. Despite that, a shiver ran down her spine. She paused, still bent in the doorway of the tent. She looked from Shang to Fen and back again.

Shang chuckled. "Come. It's only food."

He knew. He dragon-blasted knew. He had figured it out and now believed he could intimidate her into admission.

"What's in it, poison?" Meiling asked, refusing to come closer. She braced herself, tightening every muscle to run—not that she could outrun them. A pang of helplessness flashed through her, but she swallowed it down her knotted throat.

Shang gave a short laugh. "You don't have to eat. We can ride now. You choose."

She straightened, her bedroll and blanket tucked under her arm. She decided to not answer and walked straight past them toward her horse, which was already saddled for the day. Their eyes prickled on the back of her neck as she stood on her tiptoes to pack her bedroll and blanket.

She was delaying. They knew it too.

She turned, crossing her arms over her chest, and arranged her features into a look that she hoped told them she was not scared of them.

Shang stood. Dawn light caught in his glittering black eyes; the loose fit of his clothes unable to hide the strength of his purposeful movements. A warrior of the Academy, their best and brightest.

He'd already demonstrated his prowess and power in battle. He was almost . . . *menacing* as he stared her down, shoulders back and one hand resting on the hilt of his knife.

It was positively irritating.

He couldn't hurt her. His career would be destroyed forever. He would never risk that. Raising herself up to her full height, she lowered her eyebrows and refused to be intimidated. "You're trying to scare me," she accused, too quietly.

"Huh?" Fen barked.

"What did you say?" He craned his neck.

She swallowed and gritted her teeth. "You're trying to scare me. I don't know why, but that's what you're trying to do."

He raised an eyebrow.

"There's no need for whatever secret cunning you two are plotting. We can talk about whatever is wrong, like adults," she said, lifting her chin a little more. "I kindly ask you to stop your ruse."

Shang met her eyes. Surprise flickered in his gaze, but it was followed by a new light. He was testing her. Analyzing her strength of will.

"I'll eat while we ride," she said.

"Take down the tent, Fen," Shang ordered, keeping his gaze on Meiling.

Fen shot a quick glare at him and then huffed her way to the tent, ignoring the somersaulting panda at her heels.

After one long moment, during which Meiling nearly broke his stare half a dozen times, Shang took a step. Then another. Closing the distance between them, blocking the rising sun with his back. Unintentionally, she curled inward toward her horse, and only realized it when his eyes flicked down, registering her movements. She forced herself to let go of the saddle and face him.

"I *said* you can stop trying to intimidate me."

He grinned, teeth flashing in the early dawn. "The princess needs assistance mounting."

Something flared inside Meiling. A fire. Like the one that had coursed through Fen last night. She was angry—*furious* that he should play such games with her. He might like to see her squirm, might try to intimidate her into telling him a secret, but it was cruel. And Meiling was not completely helpless.

She touched the penknife in her sleeve, a tiny weapon that she could not wield effectively, especially against him. But he saw the motion, and she hoped he knew she was serious when she spoke. "Tan Shangdi, if you threaten me, frighten me, or try to coerce me, I will report every instance to my father, the emperor. He will have your diploma retracted, and you will have no appointment. Your career will be ruined. Do not terrorize me, understand?" She went almost lightheaded at the rush of blood through her veins as she spoke those quiet words.

She'd found her weapon, sharper than Shang's ice shards or Fen's claws. Cursed or not, strong or not, trained or not, Academy graduate or not—Meiling was a princess. The daughter of the emperor.

She was not helpless. Not now, not ever.

Shang blinked, then his eyes narrowed.

"The *princess* can mount by herself, thank you," Meiling said, and nodded toward Fen. "But your comrade might require assistance with the tent."

Shang tilted his head, and his conniving smiles disappeared. The dangerous look in his eye, however, did not. With one swift step, he closed the gap between them, stepping so close to her that they were nearly chest to chest.

Meiling stumbled backward into the horse, which stomped a hind hoof in response. Her brow furrowed, her mouth opening to reiterate what she'd just said—apparently he hadn't gotten the message—when his hand darted out and snatched her chin.

The breath in her lungs wheezed out in a gasp as his cold fingers tightened their grip. She tried to twist her head away from him, tried not to give in to the sudden bubbling of panic.

"Look at me," he growled.

At least *that* she could ignore. She kept her gaze focused over his shoulder, even when he tilted her chin up toward his face.

"Look at me."

"No."

"*Look* at me, Meiling."

The last was spoken with such authority, she flinched. She didn't want to. Fathers, she *hated* herself for how her eyes lifted to his like a penitent child's. She was certain her terror was clear in them. But when he spoke, every thought eddied from her mind.

"You have magic," he said. "Mind magic."

She stared at him, so startled she couldn't say anything. She tried to wrench herself free of his grasp, tried to push back on his chest. But he snatched her wrist, doubled it behind her, and pulled her against him so she couldn't fight.

"Let me go," she gasped, her free hand clenching in his tunic, her nails digging into the fabric.

"You don't deny it."

"What? Deny what?" Meiling sputtered quickly.

"Don't play stupid," he snarled. "Your games have fooled us long enough. Last night, you spoke in both of our minds. While you slept. You knew about the brigands at the inn."

She was dumbstruck, at a complete loss for how to respond. Should she lie? Could she phrase it so she did not tell a straight denial? What could she even say?

If she couldn't convince him that she didn't have magic, he could ruin her. Her family. Her father.

She hesitated too long. She twisted her face away from Shang's unrelenting gaze. To her surprise, he let go of her chin.

Fen stood off to the side, arms folded across her chest, Bo wrapped around her leg, staring at Meiling like she was a *mó guǐ* herself. Shang's face was cut as though from stone, sharp and cold. He was quiet. No doubt his mind worked out all the possibilities, trying to decipher what this could mean and imply for their journey—both what was past and what still beckoned ahead.

And how he could leverage this to his advantage.

"If you have magic, why didn't you go to the Academy?" Fen demanded, stalking a step closer.

Meiling glanced from her, up to Shang, who still stood much too near for comfort. He studied her closely, waiting for her answer.

"Why did you lie to the empire?" Fen continued. "Why did you make us all believe you were cursed? Why are we on this dragon-blasted journey in the first place? Is it because of your magic? What is going *on*?"

A sob caught in Meiling's throat. She tried to swallow it, but it bubbled up against her lips. She pressed the back of her hand to her mouth, her chest too tight to draw a full breath.

The secret was out.

Were all those years pretending to be something that she wasn't, bearing the scorn of her people for naught? Had she paid the price, only to find that what she'd bought was dust? Was all the shadow-dodging nothing but a wind that brought no rain?

The edges of her vision started to go black, closing in on the sunlight.

Shang's arm slid around her waist just as her knees buckled. She fell hard against his chest, trying to blink away the darkness, but it closed in, sure and steady.

"Mount up, Fen," barked Shang as he bent, hooked an arm under Meiling's knees, and swept her up into his arms. "We need to leave."

"But she needs to answer our questions!"

"She can't answer them very well if she's unconscious, now can she?"

Meiling clutched fistfuls of his robes, trying not to cry despairing tears against his chest. She couldn't begin to imagine what would happen, what they would do. Would they betray her?

"I saved your life," she whispered against his collarbone, the words like a plea.

"What?"

The world was too hot, her heart roaring in her ears as she fought to keep from fully passing out. "I saved your life," she said again, louder than before. It came out like a croak. "Both of your lives."

He stopped walking. She tilted her face up toward him, blinking hard. Slowly, her vision cleared. Enough to see his stone-cold expression.

"And you might cost us our lives," he replied.

Some grateful warrior he was.

"Are you going to betray me?"

His throat bobbed, his gaze fixed stolidly ahead. "I suppose that is to be seen, Highness." He lowered his grip on her knees, allowing her to find her footing. Ironic as it was, he was the only firm thing in a world that spun before her, and she found herself clinging to the man who just admitted he might betray her secret. The only thing keeping her conscious was his arm around her, and the wads of his robes in her fists.

"Can you stand?" he asked. "You're white as a sheet."

If he let go of her, she would black out and crumple to the ground. But she hated feeling helpless, so she nodded.

He didn't let her go, though, perhaps unconvinced by her answer. Instead, both of his hands grasped her waist firmly, and she sucked in a sharp gasp of surprise as he lifted her up. Into the saddle of his horse, she realized belatedly. He swung up behind her, settling further back in the saddle to accommodate her sideways position. She was warm again, and she had no idea if it was due to her lightheadedness, the startling heat of him against her, or her own flush of embarrassment as his arms reached around her to grip the reins.

Then, to her surprise, his hand wrapped around her, gripping her shoulder, and pulled her to lean back against him. Her forehead rested against the column of his neck. He smelled like leather and pine, a startlingly soothing aroma. She stiffened.

"Try to stay conscious," he said. "We have things to discuss."

“In that case,” Meiling mumbled, his rapid pulse beating beneath her temple. It was only a touch slower than her own. “I’ll just pass out.”

Did he just snort? It was so subtle she couldn’t be sure.

“Ready?” he barked to Fen.

“I’m ready for *answers*.”

The horse lurched into motion beneath them, and Meiling closed her eyes against the rocking movements. Never had she gone from the thrill of discovering she wasn’t as weak as she’d always thought, that her magic was an untapped well of power, to crashing down into the realization that it was empty.

That no matter what kind of magic she had or didn’t have, she would always be a slave to her own helplessness.

CHAPTER 15

IT'S TIME TO talk," said Shang after a half hour of blessed reprieve and silence.

Meiling shook her head. His impatient exhale stirred the top of her hair.

"No more faking fainting to get out of questions," said Fen. Bo was strapped to her front again, but today he wiggled much more than before. Every few minutes Fen barked at him to stop chewing through her sash or to hold still. Once, the cub even growled back at her.

"You have magic," Shang said, ignoring Fen and the panda. "Something pertaining to mind-reading or mind-manipulation. Explain."

Meiling said nothing. It would be stupid to answer their questions and confirm their accusations. She had not given a verbal admission yet. Perhaps if she said nothing more, her innocence could be preserved before the courts. If she said too much to Shang and Fen, then they could be used as witnesses to her unsanctioned wielding of magic.

"He asked you a question!" Fen barked. "Answer him!"

"She won't answer," Shang said, with an understanding nod. "Because she's a *brigand*."

At that, Meiling snapped her eyes up to his, the fire returning to burn in her gut. "I am not! I am no brigand."

"You are not employed in the emperor's service, though, are you? You are a rogue magic-wielder. That makes you a brigand. Should you be discovered, you'd be condemned to death. Which is *quite* a serious situation indeed for you." He continued his slow nodding, one hand resting on his leg while the other gripped the reins of his horse. He seemed to chew on his next words before saying, carefully. "Since we are not threatening one another . . . Let's say I have a *deal* for you."

Meiling bristled, sitting up straight in the saddle. "No deals." She had to fling out both hands, one grabbing the horse's mane, the other grabbing Shang's arm, to keep from falling.

He pulled her back against his chest. "This one works in your favor," he said, and she didn't like his tone. "I propose an exchange. You tell us everything you know about your magic, the *real* reason behind this journey, and how you're connected to the barbarians. In return, neither Fen nor I will breathe a word of your magic to anyone else."

"*What*?" Fen demanded. "You're bargaining away our power over her?"

So he wasn't going to betray her? And he was going to make sure Fen didn't either?

Why didn't this feel like a good thing?

"Would you rather be dead, Fen?"

"Dead? I'm failing to see how this relates—"

"We've been attacked once already by brigands, and I'm inclined to believe the phoenixes last night were connected. Somehow. There is something we don't know about this mission that has put us at a disadvantage that could cost us our lives. And *she* knows what it is." At this, he took hold of her chin, tilting her head back so he could meet her gaze. "Don't you?"

She stared up at him, lips parting, and swallowed with effort. His own mouth was so close to hers and staring into his eyes was like staring into a glacier under a starless, midnight sky.

He let go of her chin. Her head sagged forward, and she stared at the golden glint of sunlight on emerald foliage, growing dizzy watching the trees move past them.

"So, Fen, how much do you value your life?"

Fen only growled in response, turning her back to them. Bo gnawed on her braid.

Shang continued. "We already know you wield magic, *Highness*. We can decipher with reasonable certainty many of the aforementioned things. And we are under oath to the *emperor,*" he said the word deliberately, "to report brigands to him. So, as you see, I offer you your life."

He looked more like he offered her death and an eternity of torture in *diyu*.

Meiling swallowed. "Why should I trust you to keep your oath to me, when doing so would demand you break the oath you made to my father?"

"Would you rather I keep the oath?" Shang asked easily. "You have no choice but to trust me. And Fen."

"And Bo," said Fen, who looked about ready to explode with impatience.

Meiling turned Shang's words over in her head. He was right. He'd cleanly maneuvered her into a corner and left her no choice. No choice but to entrust them with the secret of her soul.

The fire in her blood died. She lowered her head, slumping in defeat against him. "What do you want to know?" she asked finally.

She felt rather than saw Shang's smile. She shuddered.

"Describe your abilities. In detail," he said.

Ahead, the sun crested the horizon and spilled into the forest. The ground grew rockier, making Meiling terrified their horse would slip. She pulled her cloak tighter around her shoulders, but she wasn't cold. That is, the breeze *was* a little chilly. It tugged dead leaves away from the trees, spinning them in the air, and then depositing them onto the ground. Autumn would be here soon. But that wasn't why she needed the security of her cloak bundled around her.

Shang did not hurry her as she found the words. Fen, on the other hand, grew antsy with expectancy. She twirled the reins in her hands and dug her nails into the leather. Her lips compressed for a minute, followed by puckering and opening them like she had something to say. Mercifully, she kept quiet except to snap at Bo when he wouldn't stop wiggling or made too much noise.

"I do not know what my abilities are," Meiling admitted after several long minutes.

"That is not a sufficient answer. But I will help you get started," Shang replied evenly. "You can enter minds or speak telepathically."

Meiling glared up at him, grinding her teeth in agitation. "I did enter your minds last night."

The confession made the air freeze. Shang and Fen's cheeks paled slightly, despite the fact that she only confirmed what they already knew. They seemed to grapple with the implications of that statement. Did they think she had entered their mind several times, even frequently? The last thing she needed them assuming was that she used her magic flippantly. Quickly, she said, "That was the first time I'd ever done such a thing. I only did it to save you both."

"Explain how you saved us."

The blood drained from Fen's face. She had not told Shang that she'd fallen asleep on guard. Now Shang would require an explanation. Meiling should not feel guilty for tattling on Fen, but she did anyway.

Meiling closed her mouth. Fen watched her carefully.

"You promised to tell everything," Shang pressed. "How, specifically, did you save us last night while you were asleep?"

Meiling glanced at Fen. "I saw the phoenixes before you both did. They moved so fast; I had no choice if I was to warn you before they killed you."

Shang lifted his chin, his jaw twitching.

She'd just told a warrior that he would be dead without her. It served him right if he was offended. Hopefully, he wouldn't press her more. Let him think this was the extent of her magic.

"How could you see the phoenix first if you were asleep?" Shang asked.

She was a fool for hoping. Nothing could get past him. She tried to steady her breathing and keep herself upright in the saddle. His threat echoed in her mind as her tongue cleaved to the roof of her mouth. "My magic . . . I can . . ." The right words escaped her. How could she describe it?

"You can what?" he prodded. Was that apprehension gleaming in his dark eyes? His brow lowered. "Everything, Highness. That was the deal."

She glanced sidelong at Fen to find she'd wrapped the reins around both hands repeatedly and was squeezing them tightly. Her eyes dilated to the point that they almost took on the glassy sheen of a ferocious animal.

She closed her own eyes and focused on making her voice stable. "When I fall asleep, my spirit separates from my body. I can . . . I can see *mó guǐ* and magic-wielders from a distance—their spirits glow, you see."

"Everything," Shang said when she stopped speaking, his voice rumbling in his chest against her.

Qilins curse this helplessness that seeped into every single bone in her body! Why could she not lie? Why did the words, *"That is all,"* refuse to pass through her lips? The truth came tumbling out, despite how her mouth burned with the confessions. "I can move through walls, I can fly. I do not have a body; I'm just spirit, and I can fly wherever I want, watch anything, listen to anything—"

Fen whirled. "You're saying that you've been eavesdropping on us when we had no way of knowing, and that you've been in our minds when we didn't ask? What kind of power is that, anyway? I've never heard of such a thing!"

Meiling swallowed her next words.

Shang said, “You can go as far as you want?”

“Until my tether pulls taut. Then I cannot go further,” she mumbled.

“Your tether?” Shang prodded.

She loathed him for his refusal to back down. She hoped he could see that loathing simmering in her eyes as she tilted her face up to meet his gaze. “It binds my spirit to my body. So I can return later.” Should she tell them about how the firebird’s tether snapped when it died? Absolutely not. Yet somehow, the next words slipped free of her lips, anyway. “I think . . . I think we all have tethers. Whether they are different lengths, or it requires a unique magic to leave the body, I don’t know.”

Shang went quiet, considering. After another minute, he said, “You can enter minds. Can you control them?” His voice softened just barely enough to make Meiling want to trust him and share everything. He almost seemed like he was more curious than conniving now.

Or maybe his voice softened because he was afraid of what her answer would be.

She refused to trust him. She still had to answer him.

Meiling scrunched her brow in concentration. She closed her eyes, the vision returning of his mindscape: the long, grand hallway with the dragon pillars and closed curtains. “I don’t think so. I think I can mainly listen to thoughts . . .” Her voice trailed off, broken by a new consideration.

“What? What else?” He straightened behind her, and his gaze prickled on the top of her head.

“I might be able to search through memories,” she said. “I haven’t tried, but I think I could.”

Fear flickered in Shang’s eyes and he turned them away from Meiling to stare at the back of Fen’s head. “You can only access these powers while you sleep?”

Meiling nodded.

"Who knows of your magic?"

She shifted uneasily against him. "My parents. Now you."

More silence.

Then, "The brigands . . . They knew, didn't they?"

Why did the air keep going colder and colder? With each question, her hands went more numb. "I don't know what they knew. They were coming for me." She reached up and tucked a stray hair behind her ear, keeping her eyes downcast.

Fen exploded. "The emperor did not think it was important that we knew she was being hunted? That is *crucial* information!"

"They didn't know. That is, they thought if I was gone from the palace, they wouldn't know where to find me." Meiling's brow puckered. "I think if they had thought I was being hunted, they would have sent more wielders."

"But they knew someone was after you?"

Hesitantly, she nodded. Fen gusted out a whoosh of an exhale.

"How did they know?" asked Shang.

Memories crashed into her mind, of flashing purple and sweat, a leathery hand reaching for her, the cries of her guards, the pained surprise of the intruder when he was shot. Pa vaulting over her bed and shoving her into a corner.

"Because someone tried to abduct me the night before we left," she said.

"*What?*" Shang demanded. "You were almost *abducted*? Tell me what happened, Meiling."

Several minutes later, once she had relayed the entirety of the evanescer episode, and Shang's face was twisted in a mix of fury and consternation and Fen had taken to ranting aloud about how they *should have been told*, Meiling mumbled, "Is there any food?"

"Oh, yes," Shang said, and if she didn't know better, she might have thought that was chagrin in his voice. He looped an arm around her waist, holding the reins, and leaned back to rifle through the saddle bags. Once she was eating, and beginning to feel significantly less lightheaded, Shang returned to their conversation.

"They didn't think anyone would discover you'd left the palace," he said. "Aside from a *mó guǐ* or two, we shouldn't have encountered any problems. Nothing that we weren't trained to handle."

"So . . . let me get this straight." Fen twisted in her saddle to stare back at them. "This mission has nothing to do with what we were told, but is instead a race to get a magicless princess—who actually *does* have magic, despite the lies we've been told—to safety before whoever wants her catches up. Oh, and before we get eaten by *mó guǐ*."

Shang nodded. "Seem right to you, Highness?"

Meiling nodded numbly.

"Is that everything? Or are you hiding anything else from us?"

"That is everything."

"Good. Now, tell me about your connection with the barbarians."

Her head swiveled fast as lightning, and she turned earnest eyes up to Shang, who was staring down at her. "I truly do not know anything about the barbarians. Except that they're amassing on the northern border and might try to conquer Zheninghai. That's all I know."

That wasn't entirely true. She knew the traditional blessings Ma always mumbled over her food before eating—one of the few things she retained from her own Butagin heritage. There were other things she knew, stories Ma had told her when she was a child, the stories passed down from her Lao Lao when she was young. Of a land with blistering winters, of a people who made buffalo tents on wheels so they could always be traveling to keep their herds fed and watered.

None of that was relevant to what Shang asked her.

"How did the emperor and queen discover your powers?" he pried.

When would he run out of questions? When would he stop holding her life and secret over her head? When would he simply leave her *alone*?

"Before I was born. My mother had a vision," Meiling ground out begrudgingly.

Silence reigned for the span of several heartbeats, and she was just beginning to hope this discussion was over. But, of course, Shang wasn't done. "From this point forward, we must work together. You possess magic like us—"

"She is not like us!"

Shang fixed Fen with a face of pure indifference. "She wields magic. Like us."

"Clumsily and sneakily!"

"But still wields it." His eyelids lowered slightly, betraying his annoyance. He turned to Meiling. His words were sharp, almost threatening. "While you are under our protection, you will obey our rules. Do not enter our minds without either our explicit invitation or for an emergency. Do not listen to our private conversations."

This must be part of *the deal.*

"Yes?" Shang prompted. "You understand?"

She gave him one of his own icy glares. "Yes, I understand."

"We work together now," he said, looking from Meiling to Fen, daring either of them to argue.

Neither did. They rode on in silence.

Meiling felt like she'd just sold her soul to *diyu.*

CHAPTER 16

THEY CONTINUED TRAVELING for hours. The landscape grew even rockier and steeper, forcing them to slow their progress. At some point, Shang deemed Meiling recovered enough from her near-fainting spell to sit atop her own horse "without toppling over," as he put it.

She said nothing all afternoon, occupied by her own thoughts, drinking in the vast, brilliant green scenery, as if it could erase the numb fear eating away at the back of her mind.

Fen and Shang rode ahead together, whispering back and forth so she couldn't hear. Bo's contributions to the conversation were clearly audible, however, and ranged from sporadic enthusiasm to growling irritability. Sometimes she could make out a word or two from Fen, but Shang kept his voice controlled, and it was too deep for her to discern the words, anyway.

To their left, rice terraces cut into the hillside, like bright green stairs, just waiting for her to run up them barefoot. If they traveled down into the valley, they would find a village tucked into the sunshine and fertile grounds, wouldn't they? Not that it mattered, since they stayed off the main roads and avoided villages like death.

Shang stopped his horse.

Meiling peeked ahead, trying to get a glimpse of his face or what lay ahead.

"Something's not right," he said sharply.

"I'll scout ahead," Fen said, her eyes bright with brimming excitement. For the first time, Meiling knew what thrilled through Fen's blood. She dumped Bo into a saddlebag, which he protested avidly before he seemed to realize it was the bag with cut up stalks of bamboo. Then she folded into a hawk and flew high above the treetops. Meiling could only catch snatches of her through the breaks in the shimmering, green foliage above them.

"What do you think—?" Meiling was starting to ask.

"Hush!" Shang hissed, spreading his hand back toward her while keeping his sharp eyes fixed ahead. He swung his long legs over the side of the horse and dismounted. His boot crunched on rock when he landed.

He flicked both wrists, filling them with tiny, gruesome ice shards. He stepped quietly ahead, slowly. His head twisted quickly from side to side. He halted silently, staring ahead.

Meiling tried to stare ahead too, but the only things ahead were towering trees with gray bark and vines swinging between them. The vines themselves, thick and green, hung with more vines. Roots from the trees twisted out from the rocky ground, almost seeming to wrap around the large rocks jutting out of the increasingly steep incline. No sign of anything out of the ordinary.

Shang's horse nosed the grass, taking a few uninhibited steps toward the edge of the trail they traveled. Should she dismount, too? She decided against it; if Shang had wanted her to dismount, he would have told her. Besides, being on horseback gave her an advantage to flee.

Did they think they heard or saw *mó guǐ*? Or more enemies? Her heart rate increased to a nervous *thud, thud, thud.* If she were asleep, she could scout the area easier than both of them.

Fen landed as a crouched human, one hand on the ground, next to Shang. "All's clear from above." Then she shifted into a huge, snarling wolf. She stuck a wet, black nose to the ground and sniffed her way ahead.

Shang watched Fen intently. He spared a cursory glance back at Meiling, presumably to ensure she was still where he'd left her. Fen moved quickly, following scents off the trail, then returning and rushing after another. Her shaggy, dark gray coat shone coarse in the sunlight. When she had progressed further, her haunches tightened. She released a growl through barred fangs.

"What is it?" Shang whispered, tense for attack. The ice glittered in his hands from refracted light, casting little rainbows on the ground, his horse, and a nearby tree trunk.

The wolf turned her enormous head around to look at Shang, eyes beady and intelligent.

Something snapped.

Whirling movement plunged toward Fen. She leapt aside, howling ferociously at the . . . the . . .

Vines?

Meiling almost screamed when Fen's hind legs were caught by the tangling, twisting, lurching vines. She howled again, trying to bite the vines as they dragged her off the trail, across the rocky ground, and strung her up between the trees.

She shifted into human form, but the vines lashed out in a net, catching her before she fell free to the ground. An inhuman roar wrenched from her throat as vines latched onto her wrists and ankles, stretching out her limbs tightly.

Shang's eyes darted about frantically, covering every inch of ground.

"What are you doing? Help me!" Fen screamed at him.

"If I'm caught too, we're doomed."

Fen screamed again, pulling at her limbs with all her might.

"Is it trying to kill you?" Shang cried in alarm. "Or restrain you?"

"I don't know!" she wailed.

"Stop fighting it!" Shang ordered, taking another step closer, hands outstretched.

Fen cried out. "If I stop—"

"It'll kill you if you don't! Stop fighting it!" he yelled.

She cast a frightened look back at him. Her panic was so strong it made Meiling's heart clench. She sagged in the vines' grip, and they relaxed as well, dropping her a foot in the air and leaving her suspended.

A magical trap.

Shang took a tentative step closer. He halted immediately, peering up and down suspiciously.

Before he could make another move, the vines struck. They shot out, lacing around Shang's ankles so fast he only sliced through one before he, too, was being dragged. He let out a vicious cry when another caught his swiping, ice-armed hand and yanked him upward into Fen.

It was like the net and restraints were alive, almost hungry. And two victims would not satisfy.

While Shang was grabbed, more came for Meiling. She screamed, trying to turn her horse around and urge it into a gallop. But the vines snatched her wrists and her waist, yanking her off her horse so hard she hit the ground with a force that knocked the air from her lungs.

The vines dragged her, ripping her along jagged rocks, but she could not think about the cuts scraping her back, nor the pressure around her waist that threatened to squeeze her in half. She couldn't breathe—couldn't breathe, couldn't breathe, *couldn't breathe*! She was going to die.

This was it.

She tried to breathe, but despite how she gasped, she couldn't get air. *In, in, in!* No air came. She panicked, drowning on land. She tried to cry out for help, but she couldn't speak. Not without air.

"Breathe," a female voice assured. "Keep breathing. You'll be all right. Don't panic. Breathe."

Fen?

Through her bug-eyed vision that saw without seeing, she perceived a face hovering over hers. But she had to focus. Slowly, air started coming. Tiny sips at first, but after a few more minutes, big gulping gasps. Bit by bit, the panic eased, replaced by coherent thought. She could breathe. Think. She became more aware of . . .

"Getting the wind knocked out of you is the worst feeling," Fen was saying, her voice strangely sympathetic. "You never get used to it."

Meiling let out a squeaky scream. She hovered high in the air, suspended only by the death grip of vines on her body. Below, so far below, sharp rocks protruded from the ground, ready to impale her if she fell. Her panic returned in full force. She wrenched against the vines. They tightened, stretching her arms away from her body until it hurt.

Meiling screamed a real scream—one of terror and pain.

"It's all right. Calm down. Stop struggling."

That was Shang's low voice. And it sounded . . . behind her?

She stopped struggling, trying to breathe. The vines relaxed, making her fall slightly and bump into someone. She whimpered with the effort to hold still as the panic coursed through her.

"Deep breaths. You're still winded," Shang said. "Hold still. Breathe."

Meiling shuddered, knowing she would vomit if she looked down. "What do we do?"

"We wait until we're calm," he said.

"Are you scared?" she asked.

There was a small pause. Then, "Yes."

Somehow, his admission soothed her. Like her terrified hysterics were justified. She took one deep breath, then another. Then she took in their orientation. She hung primarily from her waist, arms held over her head, and both dangling feet fastened. Her weight was distributed enough that no single vine was excruciating, though everything was painfully tight.

Fen's face was right near hers. She hung almost entirely upside-down from both feet, her hands brought out wide on either side of her. Shang was mostly behind her, except for one leg, which was fastened at what looked to be a strange angle, almost tied to one of Fen's hands. When she relaxed fully, she bumped against Shang's back behind her head and shoulders.

"All calm?" Shang asked. "Fen?"

"Yes," Meiling quivered.

"Yeah. I'm calm. But I'm furious," Fen said tartly. "Especially that my stupid panda is just eating his bamboo as if nothing is happening."

"Forget the panda. We need to make a plan. Let's start with the basics. This is a magic trap, set by someone to presumably catch *mó guǐ*. It's triggered by magic. We all wield magic. So we were all taken," Shang began. His breaths were fast and shallow, like he also fought away the frantic rush.

"What kind of idiot sets a trap that will catch the emperor's wielders?" Fen growled. "Who *can* set a trap like this? Whoever they are, they're a dragon blasted, phoenix scorched—"

"A guardian would," Shang said, as if it were the most perfectly obvious answer. "To trap *mó guǐ*."

"We're in the territory of Ganhai," Meiling started to say. How ironic that she was actually applying some of the things she learned while holed up in the library those many hours.

Fen's too-close face snapped to hers and it contorted in pain at the movement. "We know, brainless."

Meiling returned her gaze and continued speaking as evenly as she could around quick, near-frantic puffs of air. "And their guardian is Zuan Wan, who has magic pertaining to manipulating vegetation." She could not see Shang's face, but Fen seemed to be surprised.

"Indeed," came Shang's thoughtful reply. "Zuan Wan must have set this. Which means he almost assuredly had no intention of catching wielders. This means that there must be some manner of getting free. It seems to have been designed for squirming, thoughtless *mó guǐ*. Which we are most certainly *not*."

"My nose itches," Fen said, wrinkling it.

Now that Fen said it . . . Meiling's nose started itching too. And her arm, just above where the vines were cutting off her blood flow and turning her hands red.

"Do either of you see anything strange? A pressure point for the spell or anything similar?" Shang said. "I'm looking on my side."

Meiling pulled her gaze away from Fen's dangling braid and tried to study the trees and vines. Not every vine was engaged in holding them captive; some hung uselessly nearby. They might not all be spelled. She tried to trace her eyes along them, trying to find where they took root. It gave her a headache trying to follow the twists and tangles. Or perhaps she already had a headache.

"If I can fall asleep," Meiling said, "I could probably find something. Magic usually glows."

"No one can fall asleep like this!" Fen snarled, moving slightly. She gave a short cry when the vines tightened.

"You can lean on me if it would help," Shang offered.

"I don't know if I *can* fall asleep," she said, trying to force her tense limbs to relax. As she relaxed, she lowered until she rested against Shang's back behind her head and shoulders. It was taut and hard, not exactly the most comfortable pillow. "May I . . . enter your minds? It might get us out faster than if I had to fall asleep several times."

"You are *not* entering my mind," Fen snapped.

There was silence.

"Shang?" Meiling prompted, too softly for him to hear.

He heard anyway. "Yes. Alert me if you do."

She tried to shift, but the vines tightened and she let out a small cry. She steadied her breathing, relaxed her muscles. The vines relaxed, and she closed her eyes. When she did, the bright sunshine turned the inside of her eyelids red. The vines' hold on her waist suddenly turned crushing. She was even more aware and tense with her head leaning on Shang's back. His own strain coursed through his body and into hers, each of his muscles tight with tension. Not quite a relaxing touch.

Falling asleep like this was impossible.

She tried to slow her breathing, to take one big soothing lungful steadily after another. Her heart rate slowed down almost imperceptibly. Shutting her eyes tighter, she tried to imagine she was back home, in her soft bed. Her mother had just said goodnight and was leaving after blowing out the candle. Meiling could almost hear her soft footfalls . . .

No, she couldn't imagine it. Not with these vines crushing her.

She tried something else. She imagined curling up in a ball on the tent floor. The wrists of her sleeves and the ankles of her trousers were far too tight, and she wore Shang's belt notched to the tiniest, most constricting hole. The thought made her almost smile, but she caught herself. The vines around her stomach loosened.

Patiently, Meiling took every sensation and rewrote its story to convince herself it was safe enough—that she was tired enough—to fall asleep. It felt like a hundred years, and it might have been a full hour, but Meiling was so concentrated she did not realize when she actually drifted to sleep until her soul slipped free of her body.

Relief coursed like water through her. Now they had a chance of getting out of this.

CHAPTER 17

WITH AN EXHILARATED cry of relief, Meiling extricated her soul from those cursed bonds. She startled to find Fen staring at her sleeping face with a wild ferocity. She never could have fallen asleep if she'd known Fen stared at her like *that*.

Shang was in a much less comfortable position than she was. His back arched almost painfully as he was held up by his limbs, his stomach and hips overhanging the rocks below. His body was completely still, but his eyes darted through the foliage, ever focused and razor sharp.

Meiling searched as quickly as possible. A cursory glance over the entire area showed no stark glows. Perhaps it would be easier to see them at night?

She picked one vine and, placing one shadowy tendril of a hand on it, followed it around and around the tree branches. The further she followed it, the thicker the vine got, and the more vines converged. Finally, on the ground, by the base of one of the big trees they were suspended between, she found where the vines took root.

Still no glow.

She stared, stumped. How could a trap be magical if it didn't glow to her sight? Or did only souls glow?

Then an idea struck her. She couldn't dig, so she slid into the earth like she did with walls. The difference was immediate. It resisted her, only allowing persistent, sluggish movement as though she slogged through syrup. Nevertheless, she pushed onward against that resistance. She only had to go a foot or two—

There!

Just below the surface, in a tangle of roots, a massive green glow seeped through the dirt. It was an eerie, froggish-green color, so bright in its tiny space that it made Meiling wince. The moment she stopped forcing herself deeper, the ground promptly spat her back out, sending her reeling.

She tumbled through the air, head over heels, then wheeled and backed toward Shang and Fen. She hesitated just above his arched back, where his long hair had nearly come free of its neat queue. A sense of guilt and exposure crawled up her spine. Perhaps it would be better if she woke herself up to tell them.

Her heart beat faster at the thought of entering his mind when he *knew* she was there. But no, this was the quickest way for them to be free. Falling asleep once was miracle enough; she wasn't foolish enough to believe it could happen again.

With a wince, she cautiously slid into Shang's mind. When she should have found herself surrounded by bone and brain, she floated down through the gold-encrusted ceiling of a grand hall.

It had changed.

The floor was dusty, not as brightly polished as before. One of the columns started crumbling, as if under terrible pressure. Cracks ran up the spines of more columns, through dragon tails and wings and jaws. The hooks rattled on the curtain rod, making the crimson fabric flutter.

Thoughts flew in rapid succession through his mind.

Is the girl asleep? Is she in my mind yet? Will I feel a difference? If Fen dares to make a sound . . . If the girl doesn't find anything . . . We've lost so much time already. I need to think of another plan. One of Zuan Wan's minions might come check the trap soon. That could be hours; could be days. If we are here overnight, we'd be a feast for mó guǐ. Fen could shift again and try to escape. Could this spell get distracted? If Fen shifted again and again, could it grow preoccupied with her to allow me to slash free? How would we brace our fall? The girl couldn't survive such a fall. Fen could shift. I'd . . . manage something.

It was such an avalanche that it knocked Meiling backward. Panic laced every thought, but he fought to keep calm. His body ached from how he was suspended, and she realized . . . he was afraid of heights. She glanced at the cracking columns. The spidery breaks kept forming, all the way up to the painted red and gold gilt ceiling.

I'm here, Meiling whispered into his mind. *I found something.*

He simultaneously tensed and sagged in relief. He spoke aloud to Fen, "She's in my mind. She found something."

There was a gasp of relief and then a small cry of pain from Fen. His mind-voice was tight when he spoke.

What did you find?

I found what you spoke of—the curse center? What did you call it?

Pressure point, he responded.

It's underground.

His hope dashed slightly, and bits of plaster fell from the ceiling. Meiling rushed on quickly. *Just below the surface. If you could throw something sharp, like one of your ice bolts, it should penetrate it.*

Where is it? he demanded.

This was the part that Meiling was unsure about. *It's at the base of one of the trees. The vines converge into one mass of roots. May I see through your eyes? To try to show you?*

He gave an inarticulate, grunting concession. She blinked into his vision and found herself staring at a tall gray trunk right in front of his face. All around, vines hung, ready to snatch and bind.

Not that tree, she said. *Can you tilt your head to the right?*

You can't control it? he asked. *Control me?*

She shook her shadow head, but then said, *No. I don't think so.*

Slowly, painfully, with tension binding every limb tightly, he craned his neck, expanding her view.

There. The one in the middle.

With the big knot in the front?

No, no—the other middle one, she responded sheepishly.

Oh. I see the vines now. Where is the pressure point?

It's . . . Meiling paused, trying to find the right words. *Between the two large roots that come out from the tree. They make a sort of horseshoe shape. In there is the pressure point.*

So far away. His stray thought was not intended for her. *How can I . . . ?*

She went silent, chewing with shadow teeth on shadow lips. *Can you move fast enough to throw it before the vines react?*

But a plan was already forming swiftly in his mind. She blinked back to his mindscape as it shimmered at the apse of the hall. A ball of light and spirit, bright ice blue. Then she realized it was part of his spirit. It glittered like diamonds, whirling in a circle, growing thicker and larger with each pulse of his heartbeat.

Her lips parted in awe.

Meiling? Are you still there?

Hearing her name echoing through the hallway, spoken with his voice, made her almost jolt upward in surprise. *Yes,* she said. Then, after a second's hesitation, added, *Your plan is blue. Sparkly blue.*

Confusion and surprise rolled through him. Was that also a trace of amusement?

You can see it? he said.

She nodded. *Yes.*

Do you think it's a good plan?

Why did it matter what she thought? Wasn't she the stupid princess who was supposed to fold her hands and shut up? *I do think it's a good plan.*

Satisfaction moved like a wave through him, and some of his tension dissipated. The cracks in the columns of his hall retreated.

Do you want me to stay longer? Or wake up? she asked.

Stay. A moment longer. Then he was speaking aloud to Fen. "You need to shift as fast as you can into different animals. Try to keep the spell busy. I need to shoot the pressure point."

Meiling blinked to his vision and found Fen's eyes bright with the thrill of battle.

"It will be my great pleasure," she said with a devilish grin.

A small inkling emotion of Shang's washed through Meiling. Amusement. And an even tinier inkling of . . . affection.

As if remembering Meiling was in his mind, the emotions were swiped away almost faster than she could catch them. But not fast enough, and now she tried to make sense of them.

Did Shang have a sort of fondness for his wild, impulsive comrade? They hadn't been romantic feelings, but there had been a distinct warmth. She never would have guessed such a thing from how he spoke to her, so often rebuking, so often arguing.

Meiling had the sense that if she wanted to, she could dig deeper into his emotions, pry into the most secretive parts of him until she knew him better than he knew himself.

"Let me know when," Fen said.

Shang's mind completely focused on how to hit that soft spot on the ground. He twisted ever so slightly, trying to get at a better angle, but his movements were met with the tightening of his bonds. Frustration swept through his soul. Meiling listened quietly as his calculating thoughts spilled onto the hall floor and ricocheted off the walls.

He thought so differently than she did. It was not just that he thought different thoughts, or thought about different things. He saw life and the world differently from her. *How* he thought was so different from her. It fascinated her.

He remembered her. *You still there?*

Yes, she answered. She almost defensively reminded him that he'd told her to, but stopped herself. *How should I keep from falling?*

I . . . don't know, he admitted. "Fen! If we successfully destroy the trap, would you be able to keep Meiling from falling?"

Two times in the last few minutes, he'd used her name. Instead of simply referring to her as *the girl* or *Highness.*

"Impossible to know," Fen responded. "We don't know what will happen if we break the spell."

She's right, Shang thought to himself. To Meiling, he said, *We'll keep you from falling. But if something happens . . .* Meiling saw through his eyes how he tilted down to look at the ground, felt how his stomach fluttered with dread. *It's not that far.* A blatant lie. *You can survive a fall such as that.* Not quite a lie, but he didn't think she could survive it. *But you need to roll when you land to keep from injury. Understand?*

What about the rocks? she squeaked.

He let out an audible sigh. *I won't let you get hurt.* Those words were paired with a swift, deep determination—a determination wrought of iron.

She believed him. Not because he knew how to save her, but because Shang was a man of his word.

I trust you, she whispered.

At the sound of her words, a strange and unnamable emotion flashed through Shang. Perhaps it held the slightest hint of warmth.

You can go now, he said.

Do you want me to wake up? Or wait a bit longer?

Wake up.

She floated upward, into that golden ceiling, and slid out of his mind. She regretted it, if she was honest. There was so much he knew that she did not, so much mind to explore. But she respected his privacy—had invaded more of it than he likely realized—and would not overstay her welcome. She regretted that it was pain and panic awaiting her in her own bound body.

With a lingering sigh of reluctance, Meiling braced herself and slipped back into her mind. She blinked awake.

And what a rude awakening that was.

CHAPTER 18

THE MOMENT SHE opened her eyes, panic closed around her chest like an iron cage. She gasped, breathing heavily. The vines constricted, making her gasp again and struggle desperately to *not* struggle. Shang's back hit hers and somehow being within close physical proximity after being in his mind flustered her even more.

She remained suspended high in the air, that wretched vine wrapped far too tightly around her waist. Fen's face hung red near hers.

"Nice nap?" Fen asked.

Meiling did not answer, partially because if she opened her mouth, she'd scream, and partially because Shang shouted.

"Now!"

Suddenly, she was suspended with her face far too close to a roaring tiger clawing at the vines. Now she did scream, and tried to scramble away by instinct, but the vines pulled taut and painfully tight.

Then Fen was a bird, a coyote, an elephant. When she shifted into an elephant, several vines snapped and Meiling found her nose pressed into the folds behind the elephant's ear. The strangest smell assaulted her lungs. She let out a cry, trying and failing to keep still while terrifying animals flashed and clawed and trumpeted so close to her.

Something hit her shoulder.

She looked just in time to watch Shang's ice bolt plunge straight into the soft soil beneath the tree, where the vines converged. He cried out as he did it, as if the motion were excruciating. The vines holding Meiling shuddered.

"Meiling!"

She twisted to see Shang catch hold with one arm and leg of a branch as he broke free of the vines. He wrapped the other leg around the branch and reached out toward Meiling. She twisted awkwardly as Fen shifted into a hawk and disentangled herself.

Snap!

Shang swung out further just as Meiling tried to launch herself toward him. The vines broke.

She started slipping.

She would hit the rocky ground and spill her guts beneath the trees.

An arm grabbed around her waist, gripping the vine that was still tied tightly around her, and pulled her out of the air just before she fell. Her forehead hit the bark hard. Stars spun in her vision, dizziness whirling her thoughts. Somehow, she clung to the underside of the branch with one arm and leg, and Shang's neck with the other arm.

He was gasping. Her lungs heaved along with his. She was almost upside-down, holding onto the branch and Shang. He kept that iron grip on her waist. His face was very close to hers, but he didn't look at her. His eyes darted around wildly, then squeezed shut with a grimace. "Fen!" he cried.

The hawk had already lighted on the nearest branch and shifted. Fen was in motion instantly, moving to crouch on their branch.

"Meiling!" Fen called. "Let me pull you up!"

Meiling shook her head frantically. "I'll fall if I let go!" she wailed. A tear squeezed out of her eye.

"You won't . . . fall," Shang said, his eyes finally meeting hers. His were so close, round and terrified and so black. "You said . . . you trusted . . . me," he gasped. "Let Fen . . ." He trailed off, grimacing again.

"Meiling!" Fen shouted. "I've got you! Give me your hand!"

With a cry, Meiling let go of Shang's neck and flailed her arm toward Fen. Fen caught her above the elbow, straddling the branch, as she pulled.

Meiling's leg was wrenched free of its hold on the tree and she squeaked, certain she was about to be dropped. Her legs dangled over the drop, one arm in Fen's yanking hands and the other holding on to the bark for her life.

Fen let out a great roar and pulled with all her weight. Meiling flopped onto the branch with a cry of relief. But before she could relax, Fen was tugging her upright. "Away!" she said. "Get on this branch. Shang needs room to climb up."

With near useless limbs, Meiling crawled to the higher branch. Her palms scraped on the sharp bark. This trembling was going to make her lose her grip and topple to her death.

Fen was attempting to haul Shang up with loud grunts. He gasped when, by a combination of their strength, he pulled himself onto the branch. He straddled the branch and leaned against the trunk, closing his eyes, but then opening them a split second later. Perhaps afraid he would fall. He glanced at Meiling.

"Thank you," she chattered.

He nodded and said nothing, closing his eyes again while bracing himself with his hands.

Meiling turned her attention to Fen. "Thank you."

Fen breathed hard but tried to shrug nonchalantly. "It was nothing."

Shang gasped a half-laugh. "Nothing," he repeated.

"If only both of you could fly, too," Fen grumbled. "Then it really would be nothing."

Meiling laughed. Much harder than the words merited, but she was near delirious at this point. And then both Fen and Shang were staring at her, and she couldn't stop giggling. Perhaps she *was* delirious. She shut her mouth and tried to breathe deeply.

"Let's get down," Fen said.

The thought of climbing down a tall tree after nearly plunging to her death made Meiling wince. She summoned her courage and did not hesitate when Fen offered her a hand. Each movement was painfully slow and shaking. Shang took the lead, climbing down and finding the best path. Fen was nimblest, but she was shockingly patient as she aided Meiling. Not, of course, without a few barbed words.

"Pick up the pace! You're slower than a line for sweetheart cakes at New Lights!"

They were almost to the bottom. Shang swung from the lowest branch and rolled when he landed, springing back up to squint at Meiling and Fen's progress. "It's a bit of a drop at the bottom," he shouted upward.

They reached the last branch. Meiling's legs quaked on the branch. She was so ready to be back on the ground again. She settled herself into a sitting position on the branch next to Fen, who eyed the ground.

"Here," Shang offered, coming to stand below the branch. "I'll catch her."

"You'll break your back," Fen snorted.

"She's not heavy," he said. "It's only a few feet."

This seemed like a questionable plan of action. Nevertheless, she scooted to the edge of the branch. "Any particular way you want me to fall?"

He positioned himself directly beneath her, holding out his arms. "No. Just don't leap over my head."

"I'll do my best," she said, smiling despite herself. Why was everything so hilarious when she was terrified?

He gave her a narrow look, as if he had no idea why she was smiling. He probably thought she'd lost her mind. It hardly mattered. With a deep breath and a squeak, Meiling pushed herself off. She didn't know if she was screaming—it sounded perhaps like someone was. The fall was short, but every second was an eternity of weightlessness.

And then she stopped falling.

She blinked open her eyes and found herself staring at Shang's face, caught in his arms. She had not died. He'd caught her, like he said.

He was already setting her down. She stumbled on her feet, but he gripped her upper arm to keep her from falling.

"I feel like a baby learning to walk for the first time." She laughed again, taking a tentative, trembling step. They were back on the ground—everything was wonderful in the world! They had escaped, and she had helped. She grinned, silly with relief.

Fen swooped down and then shifted into herself. She eyed Meiling oddly. "Did you drug her?" she asked Shang with a raised eyebrow.

Shang's black eyes darted to Meiling while she was still grinning stupidly despite her best attempts to compose herself. His eyebrow quirked. "No, but it's not a bad idea."

Meiling's eyes flew wide.

Then it was Shang who was smiling. At her. Without a dangerous undercurrent. It was a mischievous smile—almost a smirk.

If her mind had felt addled before, now it was even worse. She spun away, almost pitching forward, looking for her horse. Spying her pretty gray dappled mare, she stumbled over to it along the rocky ground.

Bo had either jumped or fallen out of the saddlebag and rolled around on the ground with his bandage fallen around his hips like a loincloth. Meiling laughed, swaying as she crouched beside him and rubbed his head. "You're so adorable," she cooed. "So fluffy."

He batted at her hand, grabbed it with his paws, and pulled it to his mouth to chew.

"No, no!" Meiling laughed again, drawing her hand away and nearly falling as she tried to stand.

She wanted to collapse into bed and sleep for hours—except her mind was too loud. She was not *tired*, per se, but her body shook from the strain. All she wanted to do was collapse somewhere and listen to people tell funny jokes and laugh until her sides ached.

She was mad. Utterly mad.

She had never been so terrified in her entire life.

"We'll keep riding," Shang said, his voice mostly normal and even, as if they had not almost been ripped to pieces by spelled vines. "But the day is lengthening, and we'll need to stop soon." Then he eyed Meiling. "Keeping that vine as a memento?"

She looked down and found the vine still knotted around her waist. She laughed again, pulling out her penknife. "I finally get to use it!" she said, grinning to keep from laughing.

Shang looked almost concerned as he mounted his horse. His brow wrinkled, and hesitation sparked in his eyes. Fen was tromping back out of the forest, bringing her wandering, baleful-eyed horse after her. She scooped up the panda under one arm, and its limbs flopped with each of her steps. "You are *strange* when you're scared."

She had to stop laughing! But how could she when everything was hysterical? She breathed through her teeth, trying to compose herself. *Breathe, breathe, breathe.* She needed to mount—yes, that was something to focus her mind on. She had no strength, but Shang had already mounted. Which meant that, strength or no strength, she needed to do the same.

Suppressing weakening giggles, Meiling heaved her weight up and successfully ended up back on the ground.

"Need help?" Shang asked, his voice tinging with annoyance.

"I'll manage," she said as she attempted another leap into the saddle.

Almost.

She *almost* successfully got her leg over the other side of the horse. If only this horse wasn't tall! And it seemed like she twisted the saddle with how much weight she placed on the one stirrup.

Shang moved to dismount.

With a determined, bounding leap, Meiling flung herself upward. Her ankle made it over the saddle. After that, it was only a matter of scuffling and scooting until she was finally settled in the saddle.

Satisfied, Shang turned his horse around and let Fen take the lead down the rocky terrain.

Meiling imagined what she must have looked like, jumping and crawling into the saddle. She nearly burst into another fit of laughter, but instead controlled it to an incessant chuckle that she tried to hide by ducking her head.

Shang caught it. He twisted back to look at her and proceeded to roll his eyes.

She grinned stupidly.

They must think her an *absolute* idiot.

She was so relieved to not be dangling high above sharp rocks, tangled up in vines. So, so relieved.

CHAPTER 19

SHANG CALLED AN early stop for the day. He gave no explanation, and neither Meiling nor Fen asked. Apparently, they were all still a little rattled after the vines. Her giggles had faded hours ago and now her mind pulsed with a dull throb, trapped inside her aching body on this jerking horse. She hoped Shang would come and help her down. She was so exhausted, still weak from earlier, and she didn't want to muster the energy to dismount. But Shang did not so much as glance at her as he dismounted, tied his horse, and set to work. She sucked in a breath of air and forced her stiff body into motion.

It might not have been the most graceful dismount—it definitely wasn't—but she didn't end up flat on her back. She celebrated by arranging the fire after fishing through Fen's saddlebags for the tinderbox and gathering whatever small brush and sticks she could find nearby. Since it was still bright out, she didn't light it yet, opting instead to ensure everything was prepared so they wouldn't have to hunt for wood in the dark.

"Go water the horses," Shang ordered Fen, pulling the saddle off the last animal.

"Once I'm done helping the panda," replied Fen archly.

Shang let out a deep sigh, setting his jaw. "You know you cannot keep it."

Fen looked up from where she inspected the cub's healing wound and gave him a wolfish growl. As though daring him to try to take it from her.

"It's already endangered us, and it's healed. You need to let it go."

"It's not *fully* healed."

"Don't make me get rid of it *for* you."

"If you hurt him—"

"I didn't say I would hurt it."

"You'd be killing him to throw him out in the wilderness now! He's just a baby!"

"It's old enough to survive on its own, and you know it."

Bo squealed and flapped his arms, nearly making Fen lose her grip on him. Meiling smiled, drawing her cloak closer around her as she gave a little shiver. Her smile quickly faded. Shang was right. They couldn't keep bringing a pet along with them.

What if they encountered those brigands again? Or another *mó guǐ*?

Even if the panda would struggle on its own, it would probably be better off than continuing with them.

"Horses, Fen," Shang ordered.

Fen shot him a dark look, but set the panda down—away from its pile of excrement—and stalked to the horses, grabbing their leads. "Come on, you big idiots."

"Are we still near the stream?" Meiling asked. "Is that where you're taking them?"

"We've been following it all day, *Highness*," retorted Fen.

A muscle jerked in Shang's jaw, but he remained silent as he unpacked a few things from his saddlebags, including a fresh quiver of arrows for his *jiaun*. What did he need that for?

Meiling bit her lip, not wanting to voice her request. In the end, she didn't know when she'd get another opportunity. She swallowed her fear as best she could and said, "Would there be part of the stream that's not so . . . rapid?"

"What is it that you want?" Shang asked, cutting off Fen's reply.

"Um . . . a bath?"

She had never been so stinky and disgusting in her life. Shang and Fen might be used to the grimy, unwashed life, but Meiling didn't know how many more days she could tolerate wearing the same three sets of clothes.

That is, she'd tolerate whatever she needed to tolerate. But if she could take a bath, perhaps wash the clothes she wasn't wearing . . .

"There's soap in your saddlebags," said Shang crisply. "Stay with Fen. Fen, don't let her out of your sight."

"I do *love* watching royals bathe."

For once, Meiling was glad for Fen's sarcasm. She hurried to her saddlebags, rifled through them until she found an unscented block of lye. There was no towel, of course. She'd just have to use her cloak.

This was going to be quite an adventure.

She gathered up her dirty clothes and the soap. And then, to her surprise, a folded blanket landed on top of the clothes in her arms.

"Take that," Shang said with a grunt. "The water will be very cold."

Meiling blinked twice at him, then gave a small smile and nod in return. He turned his back to her, busying himself once again with his *jiaun* before she could thank him. Adjusting the string or something?

She shrugged and hurried after Fen and the horses. And Bo, who scampered on all fours at Fen's feet to keep up with her.

It wasn't far to the stream. The water level had gone down since her previous . . . ahem, *swim*. It was still fuller than it should be, judging by the number of trees with submerged trunks, but the flow was wide and sluggish. Nothing like yesterday. Meiling glanced back toward the camp, holding her bundle tighter to her chest. She let out a sigh of relief when it wasn't visible through the trees.

Fen brought the horses down to the bank, and Bo followed, almost pitching himself into the water with his enthusiasm.

"Well, get busy, Highness," she said, folding her arms over her chest.

Was she intending to just stare at her like that? Not even feign interest in something else? Meiling sighed, trying not to care as her cheeks flushed hot. She'd just have to pretend Fen was one of the maids who regularly helped her bathe at the palace.

And she'd have to move quickly if she wanted any hope of washing her clothes before Fen got bored.

Giving one last glance back the way they'd come, confirming there were no male gazes in the vicinity, she stripped as quickly as she could and stepped into the stream before she could stop herself.

And nearly screamed as the icy water closed around her body.

Fen snorted. "*You* were the one who wanted to bathe."

Meiling's teeth chattered as she ducked deeper into the liquid ice. Her hand shook as she reached for the soap. She could hardly convince her limbs to work as she scrubbed her skin. How did Shang handle being an ice-wielder? Was he cold all the time? Only when he used his powers? Or was he resistant to the cold?

Ugh, this was utter misery.

She worked as quickly as she could, despite her frozen limbs. Fen threatened her wandering horse with mane braids if he didn't cooperate. All while the panda—apparently feeling much better—rolled around on the ground and attempted to climb one of the trees on the bank of the stream. He quickly gave up, resorting to sniff her pile of clothes. He took special interest in the blanket Shang had given her, rubbing his face on it and chewing on the corner.

Just her hair now. Meiling gritted her teeth, bracing for the shock, and then submerged her head.

Could eyelashes freeze? Hers froze. The cold was so intense it seemed to burn straight through her lids into her brain, paralyzing her. She barely managed to scrub the soap into the roots of her hair before she was simply *too cold.*

She rinsed her hair, tuning out Fen's haranguing of the animals until she let out a high-pitched shriek.

"Put that back, you four-legged terror or I swear I'll shave you bald! Bo! Get *back* here!"

Meiling opened her frozen eyelids, and then opened them some more as bile burned in the back of her throat.

Bo had sunk his teeth into the blanket and bolted for the forest, running for all he was worth. Fen tore after him, yelling obscenities and cursing his mother. *No,* Meiling wanted to cry, but she couldn't find her voice. She whimpered instead, shivering so hard she could barely control her movements.

She had to get out of this stream. Blanket or no, she'd freeze to death if she stayed here. She forced her legs into motion, crossing her arm over her chest as she reached out with a numb hand for her cloak. It wasn't thick and warm like the blanket, but it would just have to do.

Drawing it tightly around her body, she dropped onto the grassy bank in a sunny spot. *Just a few minutes,* she told herself, teeth chattering as she trembled from head to toe. Once she was warm enough to move, she'd get up, dry herself off, dress, and then figure out how to wash her clothes.

"Meiling!"

That was definitely a man's voice. *Shang's voice.*

She was still too cold to move, but not too cold for the sudden, all-consuming burst of panic. "Sh-shang?"

His footsteps pounded toward her, slid to a stop, and then he was kneeling over her, a hand gripping her shoulder. "Meiling, what happened? What's wrong? Are you hurt? Fathers, you're cold as ice! Where is Fen? Who screamed?" He flung his own cloak over her, and despite it belonging to an ice-wielder, it was *so warm.*

"S-she's chasing p-panda," Meiling managed.

Shang let out a growl, but made no comment about Fen or the panda, which was an odd relief to Meiling. "Are you hurt?"

She shook her head.

"Just cold?"

A trembling nod.

"From the river?"

Another nod.

"Where's the blanket I gave you?"

"P-p-panda."

Shang sat back on his haunches, shoulders sagging as he ran a hand down his face. He looked like he'd just had a heart attack, whether from Fen's shriek or finding Meiling curled up in a ball by the river or both, she wasn't sure. She drew both cloaks tighter around her, far too aware that she wore nothing beneath them.

Shang seemed to realize the same thing at once, because he withdrew his hand and pointedly averted his gaze. Just in time for Fen to come marching back, a floppy, upside-down panda in one arm and the blanket in the other.

She met Shang's dark glare with one of her own. "I was getting the blanket for Her Highness, so don't lecture me."

He didn't lecture her. One look from him was lecture enough—though possibly not for Fen. He held out his hand for the blanket, and she tossed it to him. With a quick sweep, he added the blanket to the two cloaks, and despite her shivers, Meiling chuckled. "I th-think I can—"

"I'll carry you back, and then you can dress in your tent."

That bolt of panic lashed through her again. What if the cloaks slipped while he carried her? What if—

He reached toward her, to tuck the blanket around her. She caught his wrist, stopping him.

"I'm f-fine," she said. "I'd still like to wash my clothes, if that's alright."

It was only then that she noticed the loaded *jiaun* hardly a foot away from her, as though he'd flung it down when he'd dropped to her side. She ducked her head a little lower in the folds of the blanket as Shang's jaw worked.

He stood, snapped something on his *jiaun,* and holstered it. Then he grabbed the pile of clothes she'd taken off—leaving the other pile she'd set aside for washing—and tucked it under his arm. What was he . . .?

Then he crouched next to her, and she barely had time to yelp before he tucked the blanket tightly around her and scooped her up into his arms.

"Shang!" she cried, clutching the layers of fabric closer as her wet hair dripped down her neck and back.

"I don't have the choice to leave you," he said, his low voice as cool as ever. "You cannot stay here by yourself."

With that, and nothing more, he marched back up the slope to the campsite, dodging around low shrubbery and ducking under branches. Between the layers of fabric and his body heat, the coldness started slipping away, replaced by warmth. Except her wet hair.

She didn't dare cling to Shang's neck for fear of dislodging the blanket, so she dug her fingernails into the thick material and squeezed her eyes shut as a gentle breeze blew against her bare feet.

"We're at your tent. You can open your eyes now."

"Oh!" was all she could manage as he bent, setting her on her feet and opening the flap of her tent. She hugged the blankets tighter around her and couldn't bring herself to glance back at him as she scurried through the opening. They closed behind her, and she plopped on the ground, holding her cold fingers over her warm cheeks. The blankets sagged from her shoulder.

Movement made her glance up frantically.

Shang's hand had thrust through the flaps, holding her clothes. She grabbed them quickly, and his hand retracted.

"Oh fathers," she groaned, and a little shiver raced down her spine with another bead of water dripping from her hair. As quickly as she could, she dressed, pressed as much of the water out of her hair as she could, and combed her fingers through the knotted strands. It took much more time than she liked, but part of her was glad to have a reason to not leave the tent just yet.

Once she was through, she paused. Took a few deep breaths with her eyes closed.

She didn't want to go back out there.

Maybe she could stay here. It would mean skipping dinner, and yes, she was famished, but would it be *that* terrible?

She let out a soft groan, pressing the heel of her palm into her eye socket. It would be cowardly to keep hiding in here. With one more fortifying breath, she gathered her cloak and Shang's and the blanket—all varying degrees of damp—and ducked out of the tent.

The sun was just setting, sunlight fading to dusk.

The panda lay on his back in the middle of the campsite, gnawing on a shoot of bamboo, heedless of Shang stepping over him with a pile of sopping wet clothes over one arm. Was that a clothesline? Where had he found the string?

Were those *her* clothes?

Had someone . . . washed them? Shang had made Fen do it, hadn't he?

She swallowed, then hurried to his side as he draped the pile of wet clothes over the line. "I can do that!"

He glanced down at her. Without a word, he returned his attention to the dripping clothes, grabbed the topmost garment—one of her tunics—and wrung the water out of it before hanging it on the line.

The next thing on the pile was one of her underthings. She snatched it quickly before he could grab it, wringing it out with twitching fingers, and then suffered a long internal debate about where to hang the garment. Would it be worse to scurry back to her tent to . . . lay it out on the ground? She opted to hang it on the line, hoping beyond hope that he either wouldn't notice or wouldn't care when she half-tucked it beneath the tunic he'd already hung.

It was a little ambitious to think Shang wouldn't notice. He noticed everything.

Trying not to betray her embarrassment, she added the cloaks and blanket to the pile before grabbing the smaller items to wring out. They worked in silence as the sun descended, casting the world deeper into shadow. Meiling still hadn't lit the fire, but it wasn't like she was about to leave Shang to wring out her clothes by himself. He was apparently determined to finish the job.

There were so many things she wanted to ask him. Questions about the Academy, about his studies, his magic, his family. She doubted he would be interested in answering such questions, so she kept quiet except for a quick, "Where's Fen?" The horses were back, hobbled at the edge of the campsite, so she couldn't still be down at the stream.

"Hunting."

Did that mean they wouldn't be eating jerky tonight? Meiling bit her lip to keep from grinning in sudden anticipation.

"How long will she be gone?"

"She'll be back soon."

Hardly twenty minutes passed before Fen returned with a brace of rabbits, during which they finished hanging the rest of the clothes and Meiling set to work finishing the fire she'd started earlier.

"See these rabbits?" Fen said, stopping and glaring down at the panda still lying in the middle on the campsite. "This is going to be you if you don't behave."

Meiling's eyes widened, and if she hadn't clapped her mouth shut, she might have burst a shocked, *"Fen!"* She stole a glance at Shang. His hard mouth twisted just slightly in amusement.

Bo flung his stubby legs wide and squeaked at Fen, abandoning his bamboo.

"What are you doing with the *jiauns*?" Fen asked, glancing at Shang, who was seated with one of them in his lap, the other propped up next to him.

He didn't look up. "Recalibrating and checking the strings."

Fen gave a little shrug, setting the rabbits down on the ground.

Meiling didn't want to watch her gut them, so she bent her head, focusing her gaze determinedly on the wood she arranged and definitely *not* on the glint of the knife in Fen's hand.

"You forgot the first step!"

Meiling startled, looking up to find Fen hovering over her work.

"Remember the—oh." She peered closer and ignored Meiling's bewildered face. "Oh," she repeated, gruffly. "I couldn't see it well. Never mind. I'll get some bigger logs to last us through the night before I start these rabbits." Then, "Have you seen your face? You have a knot on your forehead the size of Zheninghai."

Meiling let out a relieved puff of air and continued her work as Fen stalked away from the campsite, heading into the forest before the sun fully set. She tentatively reached up to her forehead. There was, indeed, a large bump. It ached when she touched it. So *that* was why her head had been hurting all afternoon. It must have been from when Shang grabbed her out of the air and pulled her into the tree branch.

Had that only been this afternoon?

"Come here." Shang's low voice sounded from across the campsite.

"Why?" Meiling blurted, frowning at his commanding tone.

"So I can ice your forehead."

"I'm almost finished with the fire," she said, a tinge rebelliously. She never would have disregarded her parents' instructions so flippantly. But Shang was not her parent, and she was discovering that rebellion was surprisingly thrilling.

He did not press her as she struck the flint and steel together, trying for a spark. Nevertheless, his gaze burned like frost on her face.

Now that Fen had pointed it out . . . Her head really did hurt. She tried not to let the throbbing overcome her vision or slow her work.

At long last, the fire caught. She blew on it, coaxing it higher, brighter, hotter. Delaying more than necessary. It was silly, really, but she was getting tired of being ordered around.

She half expected Shang to repeat his command, knowing she would break and obey. But he did not. Instead, he gathered his long limbs, stood, and walked over to her side. Where was Fen? Why was she taking so long?

Why did Meiling even want Fen here?

Shang knelt next to her, one knee planted in the ground. She sighed, scooting so she faced him. Hesitantly, she peered up at him. But he wasn't looking at her. He studied her forehead. "It's swelled a lot in the last few hours. Here."

Before Meiling could protest or pull away, he caught the back of her head with one hand and pressed his other hand, palm down, against her brow. Her eyes flew wide at the sudden cold, her mouth gaping. He did not hold ice to her head, she realized belatedly. Instead, his hand was ice-cold, but in a very strange, completely unexplainable way, his hand was still warm. It was like the relief of ice on an ache without the burn. She closed her eyes. This was perfectly soothing and entirely unsettling. The throbbing behind her eyes eased. His hand at the back of her head, pressed over her braid, was warm too. Not cold at all.

It was very fortunate indeed that he did not hold ice, for it would be melting against Meiling's flaming skin, dripping into her eyes and down her cheeks.

"Th . . . thank you," she stuttered, opening her eyes to find his gaze fixed on her face. A tiny gasp caught in her throat.

He let go of the back of her head, but kept his palm pressed to her forehead, cupped over the bump. "A few more minutes should be enough . . ." he murmured. "To make the swelling reduce."

Minutes? She wasn't sure she could last seconds. It was soothing, but he was too close. This was too long, too uncomfortable. She couldn't . . . Fen might walk up at any minute, demand to know what they were doing, and she would be too embarrassed to answer, making it seven times worse.

Shang seemed to have none of these thoughts. He pulled back his hand for a second, eyeing the bruise, and then touched the edge of the knot with his thumb. She winced. He replaced his hand, and a shiver raced down her spine.

She looked at the ground. Swallowed. She did not want to know if he studied her face, or if he was completely preoccupied by his work. She twisted the sash around her tunic in her fingers, a habit she inherited from Ma. For a moment, her self-awareness was caught away at the thought of her mother, missing her family, and longing for home.

Fen's crunching footsteps made Meiling's eyes fly wide, and she jerked back from Shang, cheeks flushed. He tilted his head at her, his gaze raking over every hesitation in her face. As though he read each thought careening around her mind. Then he stood and held out something in his hand toward where she sat on the ground.

Ice. He held out a chunk of ice to her.

She took it and mumbled a nervous, "Thank you." Her fingers almost stuck to the ice, but she held it to her forehead and immediately felt the difference. It was so much colder, harsher. She alternated which hand held the ice to keep her fingers from freezing.

Even though Shang returned to his spot and stared at the fire, she could have sworn his attention lingered on her.

"You wouldn't believe how much dead wood there is around here," Fen announced, entering the firelight and stomping to the fire to dump her impressive load nearby. "So ice-man helped you out, I see. A pity, since you could have *almost* passed for a horned qilin."

Rabbit meat and rice were practically delicacies after how sick Meiling was of jerky and rice cakes. She ate gratefully, and if Fen wouldn't snap at her, she might have thanked her. Alas, she didn't trust the shifter to not turn a thanks into an insult. Without a word to the others, she finished her meal and retreated to her tent.

It struck her as a little strange after all they'd been through today, but she couldn't forget the conversation she'd overheard only last night. Whatever camaraderie she thought had grown throughout the day was only a tiny step forward from her companions mocking her behind her back, from Shang threatening her this morning.

Pompous, superior, judgmental. That was what they thought of her. She would do well to remember that and not try to push the bounds of their friendship. Not try to pretend she was one of them or hope they could accept her as a magic-wielder like themselves.

Maybe in time, they would see more of who she actually was, not who they assumed her to be. Maybe they would esteem her—not quite as much as they esteemed each other, but she wasn't asking that. She only wanted them to not hate her.

Why did she even care?

Was it because their thoughts and feelings of her reflected the general population's, and if she could convince them she was more than they had thought, then perhaps the masses would believe one day? Was that why she couldn't get over this need to be understood for once in her life?

She pulled back the canvas flap, silently thanking Shang for always setting it up for her. He had set up her bedroll, too. She undressed quickly and lay down, the smell of grass and dirt filling her nostrils.

The night passed too quickly. Her few short hours of freedom and quiet slipped away like her wraithlike form in the depths of midnight. Her mind was too full, too full of faraway visions of flame-blasting phoenixes—why had there been two?—Shang's dangerous smiles and threats, their promise to not report her illegal magic use, the snaking, tangling, spelled *mó guǐ* trap.

Crowding those images were memories of her family and her increasing homesickness. Would Pa and Ma have sent her away if they had known what they would encounter along the way?

The thought brought back memories of the cloaked figures at the inn. The fire-wielder, the wind-wielder, the illusionist. Who had sent them? What did they want from her?

So many questions, so few answers.

Meiling did not dare stay too near the camp, neither did she dare let it out of her sight. She stayed on the fringes of the campsite, flitting around the forest, thinking and thinking. And looking for *mó guǐ.*

Fen took first watch; Shang took second.

It was during Shang's watch that the panda uncurled itself from the crook of Fen's knees, hopping on all fours to where he was seated by the fire, watching the camp. Meiling hesitated in her own rounds, waiting as the panda scurried to Shang and stood on its hind legs before him.

Shang's hard-edged expression softened—just slightly—as he reached out and patted the cub's head. The cub tottered back to the ground, sniffing his boots. Shang leaned back to rifle through the saddlebags. Withdrawing a shoot of bamboo, he held it out to the cub.

It sniffed the offering, then accepted it between its teeth, nose twitching.

With that, and nothing else, the panda turned—

And ran off into the wilderness.

Meiling's jaw dropped while Shang's set in a determined line as he watched it leave. Part of her panicked, the need to retrieve and protect the cub so sharp she could hardly ignore it. But there was no denying that. No matter how much she liked having the furry little guy around, the panda didn't belong with them. It belonged in the wild, and apparently it had decided it was time to go home.

That didn't stop her from following it a little ways, and it didn't stop the way her soul drooped.

Impenetrable midnight faded to the purple night before dawn. The early streaks of sun painted the sky pink. Fen wasn't going to be happy when she woke up.

CHAPTER 20

MEILING HUDDLED NEAR the edge of the camp as Shang rose from where he had been keeping watch. He stretched long arms behind him, a mere silhouette against the rising sun from her vantage point. He refastened his hair in its queue, straightened his tunic. Then he knelt, tapped a sleeping Fen, and turned to search the world around him.

"Time to wake up, Meiling," he said, staring in the opposite direction of where she even now floated closer. "Wherever you are."

She blinked in surprise, then returned to her body, her fingers vaporizing as she tried to feel along her soul-tether binding her. She placed one tendril of shadow that might have been a toe back in her body and slowly slid all the way back.

Her eyes blinked open.

It was still dark in her tent. She sucked in a deep, lingering breath, stretched, and went about her preparations for the day.

"Where is Bo?" came Fen's sudden demand from outside the tent.

Meiling closed her eyes, exhaled. This wasn't going to be pretty.

"It left."

Silence.

Then: "What do you *mean*, Shangdi, that he *left*?"

"I mean exactly what I said. He left. A few hours ago."

More silence. Meiling cringed. She parted the flaps to her tent, just enough to peek through. Fen's back was to her, her hands clenched at her side, her legs braced wide as she faced an unperturbed Shang.

"You didn't stop him?" she demanded.

"He's a wild animal. He's not your pet. You saved him, nursed him back to health. Now he's back where he belongs."

Fen didn't move. Didn't say anything. And that, to Meiling, was more alarming than anything she could have yelled in Shang's face. Who would have thought that the angry shifter was the one to get the most attached to the cub?

Shang went back to packing up their campsite. Fen stayed where she was.

The last thing Meiling wanted to do was walk out into *this*, but it wasn't as though she could hide in her tent all day. She gathered what scraps of courage she could and slipped out of the tent.

"Did you see Bo leave?" Fen snarled, whirling on her.

Meiling startled. She stumbled back when Fen took another menacing step closer.

"Did you see when he left?"

She nodded.

"Are you now as heartless as Shang too?" Fen demanded. She loomed closer and closer. Did she even realize how threatening her posture was? But there—past the barely contained rage—her eyes shone too brightly. Her mouth twitched, her chin quivering.

"Oh Fen," Meiling said softly. "I'm so sorry."

Fen stared at her, shock widening her eyes as they filled with tears. "Sorry?" she croaked. "*Sorry?* You're *sorry* that I lost the one thing I cared about on this whole fathers-forsaken mission? This mission that has ruined my *life*?"

"Back off," Shang growled, grabbing Fen's shoulder and yanking her back from Meiling. "She's your princess, and this isn't her fault."

"Not her fault?" Fen snarled back, whirling on Shang. "*Everything* is her fault! If she hadn't had her stupid magic, then we wouldn't be in this position in the first place! I'd be heading north with my battalion! *You'd* be working in the palace, just as you always wanted. You're supposed to be my ally here, Shang! But you just keep taking her side because . . . because . . ." Fen glanced back at Meiling, angry tears streaking her face. "Because she's *pretty*!"

Meiling shrank back.

"Enough!"

"You know it's all true!"

Shang took two steps closer until he towered over Fen. "Pull yourself together. This is pettiness. You are a *warrior*, not a sniveling schoolgirl. I need to be able to count on you. You cannot lose your head over an animal."

Fen glared up at him, tears dribbling down her cheeks. A barely contained volcano, about to erupt. But Shang didn't back down. He faced that explosion, ready to take it. To fight it.

Meiling stared at them both, backing up slowly. And barely kept herself from tripping over a tree root.

The sound startled Fen enough that she broke Shang's gaze, wiped her cheek with her sleeve, and stormed away. Meiling let out the breath she'd been holding, her shoulders sagging. Oh fathers, this was just too much drama first thing in the morning. She went to rub her forehead, only to wince as pain radiated through her skull. *Right*. She'd forgotten about the bruise. The swelling had gone down mostly, but any pressure was too much.

Shang spared her a glance but said nothing, taking down her tent quickly while Fen took out a fraction of her anger on the saddlebags, loading them onto the horses with just a tad too much force.

Today already loomed so long and dull ahead of her.

It wasn't until they were mounted and already traveling that a thought suddenly occurred to her.

Shang's burns. She hadn't rebandaged them last night; she'd forgotten everything when he had caught her head and held his cold hand to her forehead. Had Fen bandaged them? Had he himself done it? If so, when? She might have missed it during the night, since she did not stay very close to the camp. She hadn't watched Shang's every move—had preferred to not look at him at all—while he was on guard. He might have done it himself.

Or perhaps he wore the same bandage and hadn't applied the salve. He might have borne the pain like a fool, despite aid being near at hand. Whatever had happened, she determined to look at it later and make sure it was still healing properly. They needed to keep it from growing infected. Burns were serious injuries, though one would never guess with how Shang carried himself.

She chewed on her lip, peering at him between loose strands of her hair. He was so smart, so careful, so intentional, so strong in so many ways. He would call out for reinforcement when he needed it. But about some things . . . he would never admit a weakness. And that was a fault of his.

Meiling eyed his impassible, stalwart back ahead, his queue falling between his shoulder blades.

What sort of family did Tan Shangdi come from? She should know, considering he was the darling of the Academy. But she had stopped paying attention to the individual graduates. They ran together through the years. Because while Shang was the wonder of this year, there had been another last year, and the year before, and so forth. It was an endless supply of talent that Meiling could never be part of.

Could she have been the top of her class? She would be graduating in three years if she had joined the Academy. Instead of being the cursed princess, the one always shunned from moving in the circles her birthright demanded, she could have been a star pupil herself.

But what did it matter? She was being a fool, wasting her mental energies imagining life at the Academy. A useless endeavor. And truly, becoming a warrior and fighting *mó guǐ* didn't exactly suit her temperament. That wasn't what she wanted.

She wanted to not be misunderstood.

For hours they rode. If Fen and Shang talked, Meiling couldn't hear it. She doubted they did, however, with the rage simmering beneath Fen's surface. They rode near several villages, but never close. She shuddered, remembering the last time they had ventured into a town. Perhaps the weather would remain clear and there would be no need for an inn.

Hopefully. This would be the worst time to deal with another bout of Shang's storm-angst.

Fen held up a hand. They all stopped. Meiling's stomach plummeted.

She shifted into her favorite long-winged hawk and launched herself into the air, leaving Shang to catch the reins of her horse. He glanced back at Meiling and motioned her closer with his free hand.

"What—" Meiling began in a whisper.

"Hush," Shang said sharply as he tracked Fen's flight over the treetops. She dove.

Mó guǐ? Another magic trap? The enemies from the inn? Something else?

She came careening back at a breakneck speed. She didn't shift into her saddle like normal, but dropped onto the ground next to her horse. Her muscular frame tensed with preparation for battle, and her eyes blazed. Those eyes also held . . . fear? A tinge of panic?

The rage was gone.

She ran to Shang's side, grappling for his arm to pull him off his horse. "Come! Come! It's the healer—they've kidnapped her! We've got to save her!"

Meiling's stomach and chest tightened. The healer, as in the Academy student? The one she'd met back at Graduation? The kind, smiling Feiyan?

Shang pulled his arms out of reach and glared at Fen. “What are you talking about? Who has kidnapped whom?”

Fen had that *look*. Battle lust and terror mingled in the set of her jaw, the gleaming in her dark eyes, the tension in her shoulders. “Li Feiyan, the healer, has been kidnapped by the brigands from the inn. They have her bound nearby. We can save her!”

“The brigands? Fen, are you out of your mind?” Shang reached down from his horse and snatched one of Fen’s tugging, insistent arms to restrain her. She shot a furious look at him, trying to wrench free. “We cannot rescue the healer. That would put our own mission in jeopardy. We need to get out of here as fast as we can. Mount your horse!”

Fen gaped at him. “You’re going to leave Feiyan to those monsters? I’m telling you; we can save her!”

“If it is indeed the healer, you can be sure an entire company of wielders will be dispatched to rescue her. *They* will save her. We have a separate assignment. We obey our orders.” Shang’s hard face could have been carved from stone.

Fen stared, jaw sagging, hands twitching. *Stunned.* She stepped backward, almost stumbling. “You wouldn’t . . . I can’t . . . believe . . .”

Meiling’s heart ached with every fast beat.

Shang’s brow narrowed. “Mount your horse, Fen. Once we finish this job, you can save your friend. If she hasn’t already been saved.”

Fen stared at him a moment longer, her features settling into disgust. With a whirl of her cloak, she stalked back to her horse. “I’ll take up the rear,” she spat. When she wheeled her horse around behind Meiling’s, she did not so much as glance at her.

Meiling’s head whirled. *Their enemies were so close*. And Feiyan was in their clutches? What did they *want*? Had they hurt her? Her breath came fast. She didn’t even know who was right between Shang and Fen. In principle, she agreed with Shang and knew he called the right move for their party; there was no doubt a rescue party had already been dispatched for the healer. But those wielders were not here now. Shang and Fen were here now.

If Meiling had been kidnapped, she wouldn't want capable people to walk past simply because it wasn't their assignment to rescue her. But it wasn't so simple as that. Engaging with their enemies without reinforcements put Meiling and their entire group at incredible risk. Shang was thinking practically.

Seeing Fen so stricken, and so soon after she lost the panda, was nearly more than Meiling could bear. She could almost feel the throb of Fen's heart behind her. Or perhaps that was Meiling's own heart, aching with the terrible imagined fate of poor Feiyan.

She turned to look back at Fen, afraid of what snarling, tormented face would meet her. Instead, her heart lurched, her breath snagged in her throat, and she choked, "Shang!"

He twisted in his saddle. His eyes rounded to the size of wide, black moons. Then his brow furrowed, and he gnashed his teeth.

Fen's horse tromped listlessly after them, the empty saddle rocking on its back with each apathetic step.

Fen was gone.

CHAPTER 21

"WHAT DO WE do?" Meiling cried.

"Grab the reins," Shang snapped.

She reached backward, almost toppling off her saddle in her attempt to snag the reins. Finding the lead, she was about to tie it to the horn of her saddle, but Shang held out his hand for it. She gave it to him.

"We're going after Fen," Shang said, drawing the horse alongside his and pointing where she'd dived into the treetops as a hawk earlier. "That's where they must be."

"We?" Meiling squeaked.

"I can't leave you alone, now can I? Phoenixes scorch that Fen! *Fool*. But you need to stay far enough away from the battle, and you'll stay mounted so that you can flee if necessary."

"What about you?" she asked, her own terror coursing through her veins at the prospect of another battle. She rubbed her sleeve up and down, letting the friction warm her arm despite the heat overhead. What about Shang's injured shoulder? "Will you try to rescue the healer, then?"

He did not look at her as they rode closer to the spot he'd pointed to. "I'm rescuing *Fen*. Idiot girl!" He sprang from the saddle, drawing a sheathed broadsword from his saddlebags and buckling it to his back before holstering a loaded *jiaun.* He glanced back at Meiling, his eyes catching a strange light. In two strides, he was standing next to her horse, placing one hand on the neck of her horse, the other gripping the reins she held.

His face was so intense she couldn't look away.

"Don't come near the fight," he said, his voice threaded with darkness. And . . . *earnestness.* "Stay here and if the battle takes a turn for the worse, Meiling, you *run.* Don't wait for us. Go that direction. I'll catch up and find you."

He held her gaze for a long moment. Meiling's throat went dry. He hadn't promised that *they* would catch up. He promised *he* would. Which meant if he couldn't save Fen, he would leave her behind.

He'd let his comrade die to fulfill his duty to keep Meiling safe.

He turned and ran into the forest, hardly making a sound despite his swift progress. She watched as he disappeared, heart in her throat and a sense of helplessness settling heavily on her shoulders.

If only she could fall asleep, then she could be of some use to them. But there was no way she could fall asleep like this, not mounted on a horse with the threat of battle tasting like sour wine on her tongue.

It was only a matter of seconds until the first bursts of shouts, roars, and colliding magic met her ears. She gasped and her horse nickered nervously. The fight was much closer than she'd originally thought. If she moved forward a little, she might be able to catch a glimpse . . .

A scream, much nearer than the earlier ones, burst into the air, loud and terrified. She gripped her reins, glancing around with wide eyes. Should she already run? Surely they couldn't—

Two figures broke through the trees. A man and a girl.

Meiling pulled back in her saddle, biting a scream between her teeth. *The illusionist.* He dragged a bound, screaming, and kicking girl after him.

Feiyan.

She wrenched in his hold, yanking back on the iron grip with which he restrained her. She was dirty, bruised, with a bloody gash across her collarbone. The illusionist limped as he dragged her, his thigh wrapped up in stained bandages where Shang had pierced him with a horrific ice bolt outside the inn.

How had he not died from such a wound? He was ghastly pale, seeming to act in strength not his own.

The healer shrieked a string of curses at him. "May you be devoured in *diyu* for all eternity! Let me go, qilin spawn! Monster fodder! Phoenix-scorched, dragon-blasted—"

The illusionist cuffed Feiyan in the jaw so hard she cried out and stumbled to the ground. But then she was fighting again, yanking and pulling and biting and kicking with all her might.

The illusionist's eyes latched onto Meiling.

His focus broke, his mouth falling open. The girl brought her elbow sharply into his stomach and kicked his shin with all the power she could muster in her lithe body. He yowled, wheeling back, and then smashing his fist into the girl's face just as she, too, saw Meiling.

Those eyes, so dark and beautiful and fierce, burned in Meiling's memory.

Feiyan crumpled.

Fire burst above the treetops. A ferocious roar tore through the air.

The healer went limp in the illusionist's arms as he hefted her over his shoulder. Her bound wrists dangled in the air. But instead of running away with his captive, he ran toward Meiling.

She screamed. She kicked her horse into motion—only to pull her horse to a screeching halt as the ground split apart in front of them. The earth opened, a vast, black, and hungry canyon. Rocks splintered, tree roots ripping to shreds.

Meiling choked on her own terror, pulling backward on the reins before they could gallop to their deaths. Rocks skidded beneath her horse's hooves, cracking and bursting as they fell into the dark abyss and smashed on the edge of the sheer rocky drop.

But no.

Her rational mind caught up to her instinct. This gaping hole in the earth—it was only an illusion. It certainly looked real, but it couldn't be. She should keep going; she wouldn't fall to her death. Nothing would happen if she rode straight into that hole.

Her hesitation, her momentary flash of panic, was all the illusionist needed.

A hard blow hit the back of her head. Meiling slumped in the saddle. Her vision went black.

Her soul burst free of her body with such a force that she went flying into the air, wheeling and careening. She whirled, looking down in time to see her body fall from the saddle into the illusionist's free arm.

She screamed inaudibly.

The illusionist, now with two unconscious and limp girls in his arms, let them both fall to the ground as he caught the reins of Meiling's speckled horse. He glanced back toward the emanating glows between the trees. Then, with a grunting heft, he slung the healer over the saddle of the horse. Panting heavily, he reached down and lifted Meiling.

She sent her spirit hurtling through the trees, toward the battle as fast as she could.

It was a blur of orange, red, ice-blue, and a steel gray glow. It was such a flurry of fireballs, ice bolts, gusts of wind, and tiger teeth that she couldn't tell what was even happening.

She burst into Shang's mind.

The illusionist is kidnapping me! she screamed into the familiar grand hall of his mind.

His entire body balked at the sound of her voice. *Meiling! Where are you?* His thoughts immediately shifted from battle instinct to trying to spot an opening to escape the battle without leaving Fen for dead.

Back where you left me—the illusionist knocked me unconscious. He's putting me and the healer on my horse to get away.

Fight back! Shang shouted back, strained so much that plaster fell from the ceiling overhead. *Get in his mind!*

I'll try to slow him, Meiling said, and then zoomed out of his mind. Why hadn't she thought of using her magic that way? Probably because she hadn't been trained for battle. She zipped back to where the illusionist guided her burdened horse away from the fray. Gritting spirit teeth, she flung herself into his mind.

She found herself standing in a world so vibrant, so full of color, that she was temporarily overwhelmed. She stood at the center of an explosion of radiance, blinding light fracturing into diamond glitter. Slowly, the light clarified, until the emerald shifted into brilliant green trees, the diamond fractals into vivid rainbow flowers. A flagstone path paved the ground beneath her feet, and the sky sparked clear sapphire blue overhead.

If this was her mind, she'd never want to be anywhere else.

The beauty was dazzling.

But when she blinked, her vision switched to see out the illusionist's eyes. Her mind almost broke at the realization that he was seeing double out of his own eyes, too. Which meant Meiling saw triple—his vibrant mindscape, the forest where he dragged the horse after him, and another image entirely.

An illusion he was trying to create.

She jolted as a sudden realization struck her.

He wasn't articulating his thoughts. His mind was near silent. His thoughts were . . . not quite emotions. Emotions were tangled in them, but they weren't his own. They were the emotions he was trying to project and capture.

He built, taking elements of his own vivid imagination—which was some strange conglomerate of emotions, pictures, and music—and mixed it with reality, fashioning a glimmering image that spewed refracted rainbows.

What could she do in this mind? Should she try to tamper with his illusion? Should she talk to him and tell him what to do? Hope he'd listen and think it was his own voice? That had worked on Fen, but not Shang. Something told her it wouldn't work here either.

He was so focused. So incredibly focused that he wasn't thinking about where he was going. Could she try to guide him back to the others? She could tell him to turn. Would he listen? Could she do something else? Plant an impression or something? Could she manipulate his emotions?

She had no idea, and time was quickly running out. She spoke, whispering. *Left here.* Could he even hear her, with how soft her voice was? Could he even process her words while so focused?

But then she blinked back to his vision, only to discover that he *had* turned. He operated on instinct while absorbed in the illusion he spun.

Turn here.

He turned.

Meiling almost laughed with ecstasy. But she clapped her lips shut and then, on impulse, tried to glimpse the illusion he created as he guided the horse and his captives directly back to where they'd come from.

She blinked into his third picture—

And lost control of her own mind as an image flooded her awareness.

In the background—not part of the illusion—a tall, strong ice-wielder fought with shocking skill for his youth. At his side, a ferocious tiger barred her teeth and launched herself into the thick of the fight. They battled a red-eyed fire-wielder and a deadly wind-wielder.

Then, the illusion bursts into reality. Meiling sees herself kneeling on the ground, bound with her hands behind her back. The illusionist holds her close, his arm looped under her elbows, holding them up at a painful angle. Meiling sees herself wince in pain, sees her hair loose from her struggle. She bleeds from gashes on her arms and face. The illusionist holds her with a knife under her throat. He orders the ice-wielder and tiger to cease their fighting, else the princess will die. He threatens by slicing that knife across Meiling's jaw, drawing a thin line of blood. She cries out, her eyes wide and full of terror. "Please," she whispers to the ice-wielder and tiger. "Please!"

The illusion shifts slightly, and Meiling sees what will be. The ice-wielder will pause, stricken. The tiger will shift back into her more vulnerable human form. Both will look into Meiling's eyes, see her fear and pain, both will feel their defeat and their failure. They will drop their weapons. Knives and ice will clatter to the ground. Claws will be retracted. And then the fire-wielder will blast them with fire from behind. They will crumble, fall. They will die.

No! Meiling screamed. *They will not die!*

The illusion trembles, buckling under the weight of her words and the break of focus. She kept shouting, too afraid that he'd already projected the illusion to Shang and Fen. *They live! They see through the illusion, they know it's false. They don't stop fighting, they don't care about the vision-princess. They defeat the brigands!*

The illusion broke. Agony crashed into her spirit, the agony of that soul-shattering of a stained-glass vision. Meiling screamed. The sound reverberated through the garden as if it were an empty chamber, hollow and cave-like. As she opened her eyes, the vibrant garden shivered on the edges. As if this brilliance, this unnatural beauty, was also an illusion.

She had to escape this mind. She shot up into that shuddering sapphire sky, out of that horrible, lovely, deadly mind.

When she flew free, the wind-wielder grabbed and yanked the come-to healer off the horse. The healer tried to scream, tried to fight, but the brigand was too strong and sucked the girl after her as she ran, ran, ran.

The brigand almost snatched Meiling too, but Shang leapt into Meiling's saddle, behind where her body was slung across it, and he nearly sliced open the brigand with an ice bolt. Shang kicked the horse into a gallop just as the fire-wielder came after them. Fen mounted her horse and urged it into a breakneck pace to catch up to Shang. The illusionist had fallen, clutching his mind on the ground.

Meiling's spirit dragged along after her body, away from the brigands and their prisoner. *Feiyan!* she tried to call after the poor healer, but she had no voice in this cursed ether, this world between worlds.

She gave up and raced to where Shang and Fen rode hard. Sweat gleamed down his face as he drew in ragged, gasping breaths. He leaned down into the horse as it galloped through the treacherous rocky ground and between the reaching branches of the forest. One hand clutched the reins, his other planted firmly on the back of Meiling's limp body slung over the horse's shoulders.

Fen's shoulders slumped with the same exhaustion as Shang's, but her face wasn't flinty like his. It bore a mingling of frustration, fear, and fury. She could almost hear Fen's thoughts—

"We were so close!" Fen shouted to Shang. "We could have saved her!"

"And we were so close to losing the girl!" Shang snarled back. "Don't speak to me about the healer!"

Meiling flew alongside them as they fled, until she got close enough to dive back into her body.

She rammed into a wall instead.

Pain radiated through her soul. She blinked in surprise, bewilderment. Then, the panic hit.

She couldn't get back into her body.

Don't panic. Don't panic, she told herself, trying to calm herself. *Be rational.* She reached out for her soul tether in desperate hope.

Something like a gasp of relief escaped her. There it was, loose but holding. She was still tethered to her body. Being knocked unconscious, then, must be different from falling asleep. She couldn't return to her body at will. At least, temporarily.

She forced her heart to slow, took something resembling a deep breath, and did the only thing she could think of: she slid into Shang's hallway mindscape.

Shang? she called, glancing up at the ceiling. It patched itself together as the adrenaline and fear pulsing in his veins slowed.

What? he answered sharply.

I cannot reenter my body, she said, refusing to retreat from the bite behind his tone. *I'm still connected, but I cannot enter.*

We'll figure that out later, once we're safe, he said, almost too quickly. *Leave my mind.*

I'm leaving, she said, slipping out and barely restraining a growl of annoyance. Let him be unconcerned! It wasn't as though this had never happened before and she might forever be locked out of her body.

Was this what Pa meant when he said if people knew of her magic, she'd be *"put to sleep?"*

Eventually, Shang and Fen slowed their horses.

"Can you scout, Fen? Make sure we're not being followed?" Shang asked, and just as quickly shook his head. "No, Meiling," he called into the air. "You scout."

The request surprised her. Fen raised a glowering eyebrow at Shang. He ignored her and led on, his hand still planted on Meiling's back, his fingers digging into the folds of her robes.

She flew higher, scouring the distance for any telltale glows. When she found nothing, she flew below the treetops, squinting and hunting for the smallest sign, the smallest glow.

Nothing.

Relief flooded her.

She returned to find Fen and Shang riding at a slower pace, Fen in the lead this time. Where was Shang's horse? Had they left it behind in their bid to flee quickly?

Fen's face was a thundercloud of barely contained fury.

Shang's expression, on the other hand, betrayed no emotion. Meiling hovered nearby, unsure how to report that the area was clear. Did he want her to enter his mind?

She hesitated.

That was when Shang bent, carefully lifting her limp body from where it was slung over the horse. He pulled her upward, arranging her so her head lolled over the crook of his elbow, her hair falling loosely over his arm and in her own face. His other arm, previously under her knees, shifted her into more of a sitting position in front of him on the saddle.

Her arms hung from her shoulders, like a floppy ragdoll's. Shang pursed his lips, took a deep breath. His thumb brushed the hair out of her face. Meiling's heart thudded through her tether. What in the seven valleys was he . . .?

"You're taking a million years," Fen barked.

Shang's gaze moved from Meiling's face to glare at Fen. "Her deadweight is heavier. Hard to get into a proper position."

"Just get it over with!"

His lips pulled back from his teeth in a snarl. Shifting Meiling's body again in his arms, he leaned down, bringing up the elbow her head rested against.

His lips pressed against hers. Gently, hesitantly.

Meiling's soul lurched, jolted, screamed. She flew backward, stumbling on nothing but air and landing in a heap of shadow on the ground. Her tether pulled taut, drawing her back to her body with ferocity.

She shrieked, pulling against it, desperately afraid to wake up to Shang kissing her.

His brow puckered as he kissed her. Perhaps he felt her resistance, wondered why she had not blinked awake, why her lips were still so unresponsive.

"Is she awake yet?"

Shang growled in his throat, and his soft, tentative kiss changed. He kissed her deeper, harder; his jaw set in a determined line. Lightning flashed through her soul. It dragged her back, no matter how hard she resisted, as though she were a fish reeled in by a line.

Her eyes flew open to find her range of vision completely occupied by Shang's too-close face. The rush of awareness flooded her with sensations she couldn't understand, couldn't process, couldn't fight against. His mouth moved against hers, warm and soft. Gentle, but firm and insistent. He held her limp body close in his arms. She didn't know if the heat exploding across her was from his proximity or the furious blush roaring across every inch of her skin.

Then she was fighting, pushing away from his chest, flailing her arms and legs—desperate to get away.

Shang's face pulled away. He fought her, restraining her from knocking herself clean off the horse. "She's awake, Fen." With that, he wrapped both arms around Meiling's middle, pinning her flailing limbs to her side, and held her tightly against his chest. "Calm down. You'll knock yourself off the horse. See? You're awake now."

Meiling tilted her head, blinking up at him with wide eyes. "You . . . you . . ." She was still too stunned. Unconsciously, when he relaxed his hold, her fingers moved to her lips.

His eyes glittered down at her like black diamonds. His lips had been so warm on hers, but it seemed hard to imagine looking up at him now. It was like a wall of ice slid into place over his features. "First kiss, hmm? A pity it was under such circumstances."

He said it like he'd kissed dozens of girls.

"The other horse?" she croaked.

"Lost," said Shang.

"She is *not* riding with me," Fen growled, her voice uncharacteristically quiet.

"We'll get another one?" Meiling asked. "Or . . . can't Fen just turn into a horse?"

Fen scoffed darkly, as if the suggestion was utterly ridiculous. The battle hadn't vented her rage, then.

"Apparently you're riding with me," Shang said, with an irritated gaze cast toward the shifter. "It's a waste of her energy to shift and walk the whole way. She needs to be ready to fight."

Meiling swallowed, too flustered to reply. She kept her head lowered, as if that could hide her while she sat sideways, pressed against Shang's chest. *Get control of yourself! Don't cry in front of them.*

He had only kissed her to wake her up. She should view it the way he did, almost transactional. One kiss in exchange for consciousness.

She should thank him, be grateful, be glad she wasn't shut out of her body forever.

But she wanted to shiver as vulnerability swept over her. He should have *asked* first. They could have waited to see if it was even necessary. Now she would always have this memory, these feelings that would creep upon her when she was least expecting it.

Memories of warmth and softness. Of being *kissed* by a *warrior*. And by Tan Shangdi, no less.

"This is not an arrangement conducive to riding all day," Shang said, carefully disentangling himself as he dismounted. "Halt, Fen."

Fen let her horse take several more lumbering steps before she pulled it to a stop.

Meiling kept her focus on her horse's mane.

"Adjust yourself, Highness."

Keeping this dignified was going to be a challenge. She chewed the inside of her cheek as she twisted, trying to keep her balance before she pulled her leg over the horn of the saddle. When she wobbled, Shang caught her arm, steadying her. His gaze burned into the side of her face, but she *would not look*.

Clinging to his arm, she straddled the saddle, scooting forward as much as she could. Would her face ever cool? This blush was hot enough to carry with her through the rest of her life.

Then, apparently because she was a masochist, she glanced at Shang.

Their gazes locked. It was hardly more than a second. That second was enough to burn the handsome lines of his face, his *lips*, into her memory.

He just kissed me.

Shang's foot was in the stirrup when he paused to glance at Fen, at the hard set of her shoulders. His mouth pursed into a tight line. Then he mounted up behind Meiling, reaching around her to grab the reins.

He was too close. Perhaps on a cold day, having his warmth around her would have been more tolerable. It was still summer, however, and his nearness made her sweat. Flushed and flustered, she kept her head low to stare at the horse's gray mane and block out her back pressed against his chest. She imagined away his exhales in her hair and tried to not stare at his muscular forearms on either side of her.

"No sign of pursuers?" he asked.

She only shook her head. She did not trust her voice.

Could they *please* camp soon? Could they please get to the fortress—now?

Perhaps she would allow herself a tear or two. Too subtle for her companions to notice, but enough to relieve a fraction of the pressure building in her chest.

She let one tear escape and trail quickly down her face. After that, she just had to wait until nightfall to let her haggard emotions sort themselves out in the darkness and privacy of her tent and her shadow wanderings.

She only had to survive until then.

CHAPTER 22

THEY HAD TO stop after pushing the horses so hard. When Shang ordered Fen to find the nearest water source, she didn't fight or protest. She did delay, however, and that was enough to make Meiling's insides knot.

Shortly, stopping by a spring so the horses could drink their fill, they dismounted. Meiling put several paces between her and Shang as he and Fen brushed down the horses.

No one said a word.

Until, at long last, Shang said, "Scout the area and make sure we're safe."

That was when Fen threw down her brush. In three paces, she'd stormed to him, sticking her face close to his as she snarled, "*Stop* ordering me around."

Shang didn't flinch, merely tilting his head down toward hers. "Then don't make me ask for things you should already be doing."

Meiling gulped, glancing between them and their frosty glares.

"We should have rescued Feiyan," Fen growled.

"You shouldn't have come on this mission," Shang growled back. "I don't care how skilled of a shifter you are. Your hotheadedness makes you incompetent. You're a liability, not an asset." He took one step forward, until they were nearly nose to nose, and Meiling hardly breathed as she watched. "We'd be better off if you hadn't come."

Fen's fist flew. Shang ducked to the side and blocked the blow. She threw another punch, and he blocked it again.

Meiling gasped, covering her mouth with her hand as she scrambled backward. She needed to do something! Throw herself in the middle of their blows, perhaps? That hardly seemed like a good plan.

"You don't care about anyone but yourself!" Fen snarled, pummeling blow after blow, trying to force a retreat from Shang. "All you care about is prestige and prominence. Your *duty*. And you'd sacrifice everyone along the way!"

She kicked at the side of Shang's knee, but he grabbed her leg and threw it to the side so hard that she flipped, landing on all fours in the dirt.

"You just nearly sacrificed the *Emperor's daughter* to your enemy for your so-called care of others!" Shang hurled those words down at Fen as she rolled into a crouch. "Is it because you value your friendship with the healer so much? Or because you wish to punish Meiling for ruining your life—perhaps in the same way you wish to punish your father for ruining your family? Did you really care about that panda, or are you just angry that someone who should have protected you when you were vulnerable betrayed you?"

She launched herself at him. "How *dare* you!"

Then they were rolling on the ground, knees and elbows and fists crashing. Meiling screamed into her sleeve, backing away. She had to stop them. They'd pummel each other into a pulp. Shang was still wounded, for the father's sakes!

Fen was on top, trying to pin Shang and slam her knee into his face at the same time. He fought her, dodging and evading, but didn't throw blows back. Oh fathers, oh fathers, oh *fathers*!

"Stop! Stop!" Meiling cried, finally mustering the courage to run forward and grab hold of Fen's robes. "Please stop!"

Fen flung an arm back in a blow so powerful it knocked her clean to the ground. Meiling hit grass, her body rattling from the impact, her head spinning. She scrambled to get her arms under her, pushing up.

Shang flipped Fen onto her stomach, pinning her legs with his and yanking her arms behind her at a terrifying angle. She gasped, wrenching and twisting to get free. He held her fast.

"Qilin spawn!" Fen shrieked, spine arching as she threw her hips to dislodge him.

He said nothing. Strands of his long hair fell in his face, his powerful arms lined with tension—and was that a slight grimace of pain? Fen didn't stop shouting at him, spewing insult after insult, curse after curse. He didn't move, didn't relent.

She isn't shifting. The realization left Meiling half-dazed. If Fen shifted, this fight could have gone very differently. Shang couldn't wrestle a tiger to the ground, right? He could kill one, but he wouldn't kill Fen. *Right?*

But Fen didn't shift.

Suddenly, the anger in her voice choked into something different. Something that sounded a lot like tears. Meiling got to her feet, not bothering to brush the dirt and grass off her robes. Shang didn't acknowledge her, keeping a tight grip on Fen as she sagged against the ground. Sobs shook her shoulders, her whole body.

Oh Fen.

Shang let go. She collapsed, curling up into a ball as she cried. He didn't move away from her, but sat down beside her and laid a hand on her shoulder. Still, he said nothing. He didn't have to say anything.

Meiling sniffled, fighting vigorously to keep her own tears contained. How could anyone *not* cry if *Fen* was crying?

Slowly, Fen's tears eased. She sat up, breathing shakily. She whispered something to Shang, something that looked like, *"I'm sorry."* Shang squeezed her shoulder in response and got to his feet, picking up the brush she'd thrown.

If Fen would have accepted it, Meiling would have offered her own comfort. A hug, a hand on her shoulder, a sympathetic look. She refrained. Fen would only take any attempt at comfort as patronization.

A sense of lostness swirled around her soul.

Shang and Fen might argue and fight viciously, but a deep bond burned between them. A bond that came from spending their lives at each other's side at the Academy. They were comrades, brother and sister. Shang had gone after Fen when she attempted that rescue of Feiyan when he should have left her for dead.

Fen's hurled accusations that he cared for no one but himself weren't true. Not one bit—and she knew it. They cared enough about one another to struggle and strive together.

Meiling didn't have that. She wanted it. She wanted *friendship.*

But was it even possible to be friends with someone like Shang or Fen when they'd known each other their whole lives, and she'd only just entered the picture?

"Highness," said Shang, rousing her from her thoughts. "It's time to mount up."

Now that she no longer rode so far behind the others, Meiling couldn't miss the bits of conversation that drifted between Shang and Fen. Plans for how much longer to ride, how far they were still from the fortress, should they stop for food or hunt more for meat, and little bits here and there about Academy things.

At first, Fen was quiet. Her red-rimmed eyes and flushed skin kept Meiling from peeking at her too often. She longed for some distraction from Shang's arms around her, but their party remained silent for almost an hour until *finally*, Fen asked, "Did you restring my *jiaun* when you had them out?"

"I restrung and recalibrated both of them," Shang replied.

And that was the end of the tension that had hung so heavily between them since Fen discovered Bo gone.

Perhaps they were taught comradeship at the Academy; how to work together on missions, how to hunt and fight together, knowing both would make mistakes aplenty.

When they lapsed back into silence, there was nothing to guise Shang's heart pulsing against her back. This proximity was driving her utterly mad. She needed a distraction, and if the others wouldn't provide it, she'd just have to provide it herself.

She needed to make conversation.

Clearing her throat to speak, she said too quietly, "You don't throw ice balls."

"Pardon?" Shang asked, behind her. His chest vibrated with his voice.

She hated repeating herself. She said louder, "Your ice. You don't throw ice balls. Why is that?"

"Not as effective," he said immediately. "Not as deadly as shards or bolts and takes more moisture. I'd sooner throw a rock in a sling."

"So your magic does depend on moisture in the air." Meiling had long suspected this, since observing the effect the looming storm had on him. "Are winters hard for you?"

"Another reason shifters are superior," Fen said from ahead, lifting her chin haughtily, though the bravado seemed more forced than usual. "If you were a shifter, you'd never have to worry about those sorts of confines."

"If I was a shifter, I'd wield my abilities very differently than you," Shang replied coolly. "All magic has its confines."

Fen gave another "Bah!" Then, "What do you mean, wield them differently?" She sat up straighter in her saddle, eyes flashing.

Meiling wanted to glance up and see what his face betrayed, what sort of look he fixed upon Fen. But she could not bring herself to turn and arch her neck around. By the time she had made the necessary adjustment, he would be likely looking down at her with a raised eyebrow.

"I would shift into different animals. Smaller ones," Shang said.

"Smaller? You could be crushed easier!"

"Smaller animals are smaller targets. They can often move faster and hold an element of surprise that a monstrous tiger cannot. A viper's bite will destroy an enemy in a few minutes," Shang said, with a shrug that Meiling felt against her back.

"Do you know how easy it is to kill a snake? Especially compared to a tiger?" Fen had whirled to face him, even as her horse continued forward. "Besides, the injury translation between a smaller animal and a human is horrible. If you shot me as a snake and then I shifted back into a human, it'll be like having a spear through my chest instead of an arrow!"

Injury translation? This wasn't something Meiling had heard of with shifters. Not that she'd studied shifters all that closely.

Shang shrugged again. "Smaller animals come with some different risks. I think those risks, when exercised properly, could be deadly weapons."

"That's easy for you to say, ice-man." She faced forward in her saddle again and kicked the horse faster.

Meiling, holding onto the horn of the saddle with one fist and grasping horse mane in the other, half turned her head back toward Shang. She stopped herself, however, and faced forward.

Shang remained silent behind her.

What had he said about Fen's father? That he'd ruined her family, that he hadn't protected her when she was vulnerable?

She wanted to ask Shang about it. Not to pry, but to understand, if she could. Fen had an undeniable cruel streak, but that wasn't all there was to her, and perhaps if Meiling understood her better, she wouldn't be so hurt by those cutting barbs. Who had Fen been before the Academy? What sort of family did she come from? Was she descended from a long, powerful line? Or had she been like Ma, whose magic came from seemingly nowhere?

What about Shang?

Meiling licked her lips, then braved a tentative, "Shang?"

"Hmm?"

"Do . . . you have siblings?"

Silence. Then: "No."

"Are your parents still alive?" was the next question that hopped onto her lips. She quickly tossed it away and asked something a little more tactful instead. "Where do your parents live?"

"My father lives in Guihou. A day's journey from Suguan."

A wave of sadness washed over her. When had he lost his mother? When he was a child? Or recently? She wanted to murmur a soft, *"I'm sorry,"* but she held her tongue. Parting her lips, she turned over her next question carefully in her mind.

"Do you intend to interrogate me for the rest of the ride?"

Was that deep tone laced with annoyance?

It was hard to tell. Either way, the question itself seemed indicative enough of his willingness to continue the conversation. She shut her jaw with a click, unable to help the tiny prick of pain at the apparent rejection.

Whether he came from a long line of ice-wielders or from the millet farms of north Zheninghai, it didn't matter. Both were pressured positions. When the entire economy of the empire depended on the distinction between wielders and non-wielders, it was hard for anyone to not bear some measure of expectation.

Pressure was applied to wield magic when such a thing was impossible, curses were slapped on disappointing, magicless children, and there was always the burden to prove a special talent, a gifting, anything to secure an illustrious career and honor for the family.

Competition in the Academy was fierce. Everyone had something to prove. Everyone struggled to keep their head above the rising tidal wave of expectations, just to get a little sip of success.

Those expectations did not disappear even after the hope of developing magic had long vanished. Meiling doubted she would ever face the people of Zheninghai, or meet the gaze of a courtier, and not feel like a failure.

"We are the balance," Ma often said. Not everyone could be a powerful wielder, not everyone *should* be a powerful wielder. If everyone in the world was like Shang, her father, or even Fen, the world would be an explosive place to live.

Especially if there were a lot of Fens.

Meiling wasn't like any of them. She fit nowhere. As much as it rankled her to hear anyone describe her Ma as a low magic-wielder, it was true. Ma had sporadic visions; she couldn't control her magic. She had been a typical country girl who woke up one day with magic and was sent off by her hopeful family to the Academy, only to be faced with the insignificance of her magic upon arrival.

It had cost her much. She'd fought tooth and nail to succeed, and in the process had done far more for her family by catching the interest of the Crown Prince than she ever could have done with her magic. She'd done well in the end, graduated with honorable marks, and was offered the hand of a prince.

But that didn't change the fact that she was a low magic-wielder. Which Meiling was *not.*

She could control her magic. She had unique powers, so unique she was not even sure what category they were supposed to fall under. Mind manipulation?

Or something else entirely?

Her lack of Academy education, and the secrecy of her magic, would forever be the dividing line between her and her peers. Between her and Shang and Fen.

She belonged nowhere.

Her mother tried to make her feel like she belonged with her and others like her, but she didn't. Not truly.

Meiling told herself she didn't mind being different. She had spent much of her life escaping to abandoned sunspots in quiet libraries. She never wanted to be like Fen or Shang or her siblings Yun and Hou.

All she wanted was a place to belong. *People* to belong with. She wanted to not feel like a burden or a mistake or a failure. She wanted her tall, strong, powerful father to be proud of her.

Instead, she was being carted across Zheninghai to be discretely stuffed away into some fortress full of powerful wielders who would ignore her until it was time for her to be carted back.

Would Shang and Fen escort her a second time? Surely not. They would be trying to salvage their careers after such an ill-timed assignment as this.

Meiling was tired of it all.

She would just have to content herself with her hours of freedom at night, and in the day, she would just have to keep working to prove she was of some value.

Meiling wanted to ask Shang about Fen's family.

He dismounted behind her with a little sigh—probably thrilled to not be crammed into a saddle with her for the duration of the night—and turned to help her.

She was dragging her leg around over the horn of the saddle, moving slowly due to the aches of her body. Sitting two in a saddle apparently left one sorer and stiffer than expected. Per the usual, Shang did not glance at her as he reached up, grasped her waist, and hoisted her down. For once, Meiling was disappointed. She gripped his forearms and tried to catch his eye, to communicate she wished to speak to him.

He was either determined to ignore her, or it had not occurred to him to acknowledge her. He strode past her with the horse, leaving Meiling standing behind him with parted lips.

"Most of our food was in your horse," Fen said to him.

He cast an icy glare over his shoulder. "So it was."

Fen snatched up a few rocks, tested the weight in her palm, and slipped her sling free. "I'm going to hunt us something."

"With your sling? That's an improvement on last time. I do tend to prefer my meat not mauled," Shang retorted dryly.

She glared at him and stalked off into the twilight. Before she was entirely swallowed in the darkness, she called out, "Make sure you've got a fire roaring, Princess."

Meiling raised an eyebrow after her and then headed toward Fen's horse to hunt for the tinderbox. Shang already had the bedroll, tent canvas, and spikes under his arms. He set to work silently.

She bit her lip as she set down the tinderbox. She needed to collect wood, but should she take advantage of Fen's absence to ask? Or should she first ensure the fire was ready? She hesitated for a moment, then she too left the campsite to hunt down wood.

She was not in the mood for Fen's ire if the fire was not ready when she came back.

It was hard to see in the darkness, but Meiling was quite used to navigating at night. It was easier in shadow form when she didn't have to worry about stumbling on rocks or holes in the ground or banging her head into low-hanging branches. But there was something magical about a forest in the dark that could be experienced better in a physical body. Twigs snapped beneath her weight. Bugs sang their unique songs—some pretty, some loud, some almost squeaky. The moon hung delicate and low in the sky in a perfect, slender crescent. She stopped to peer up at it through the black branches twining overhead. It was so big, so low, that she could almost believe that if she were in her spirit form, she could fly high enough to touch that pointy tip. Slide shadowy tendrils along those milky curved edges. What would a moon feel like?

The wind tugged at her hair, and she let out a sigh. It whispered to her to hurry, so she could go to sleep and be free. But when she slept, she could not feel the wind in her hair, its coolness against her closed eyelids and its soft, tantalizing brushes on her lips.

If only she could experience the whispering stars along with the whispering wind.

She turned and trudged back to the campsite, arms full. Shang had finished setting up the tent and now tended to the horses. Meiling again paused, glancing at him. She licked her lips, trying to summon the courage to break the silence.

No, she'd finish the fire first.

She worked quickly. She had just finished, was just summoning the courage to ask Shang—had talked herself through a bout of wondering if she *actually* wanted to know enough to ask—when tromping footsteps made her heart sink.

Slumped her shoulders and sitting down by the fire, she drew her legs up to her chest and wrapped her arms around them.

"Your cloak," Shang said suddenly, dropping it next to her and striding to the other side of the fire. He sat down cross-legged.

Oh. Of course. She had taken it off earlier while riding because she had been so *hot.* She picked it off the ground and plucked away accumulating leaves, mumbling, "Thank you."

"How's that for record time?" Fen said triumphantly, marching into the firelight and holding up two lifeless rabbits.

Shang gave one nod of assent and stretched out an arm for one of the rabbits. Fen sat next to him and soon, both were gutting and skinning the rabbits.

Last time, it hadn't bothered her much. This time, however? Meiling's stomach convulsed. She tried not to think about how those pretty little things had only been alive mere minutes ago, had not even known what happened. If she dwelled on it, her heart would ache too much for her to eat. And she needed to eat. Her limbs trembled with hunger even as she tried to hide from the smell and view of the rabbits.

"The princess has never seen an animal butchered?" Fen smirked. "Did you think they just showed up on your table cooked to delectable perfection? That there was no blood and guts before that?"

Meiling was grimacing, wasn't she? She swallowed thickly and said nothing, trying to pull her features into indifference.

She glanced at Shang and found him watching her steadily. His knife hand slowed until it had stopped moving entirely, and he stared at her unabashedly. Almost . . . challenging. But challenging to *what*?

Meiling blinked away quickly. She sucked in a breath through her teeth, tightened her arms around her knees, and stared into the flickering fire.

What did they want from her? What did *Shang* want from her?

She couldn't shake the feeling that he still watched her. Was he thinking about her magic? Trying to plot how he could use his knowledge to his best advantage? Planning how he could use this interruption to his benefit?

She would never know.

There came no chance to ask him about his earlier comments. They ate; Meiling enjoying the savory tenderness of meat after so much jerky, despite how it landed hard in her stomach. Waterskins were passed around.

Meiling swallowed her knotting fear and asked, "Shang? How is your shoulder? May I look at it?"

Fen's taunting mimics echoed in her mind as she spoke. She braced her spine against them.

His gaze flicked up to hers. "It's fine," he grunted, a hard steel entering his eyes.

"May I look at it? Make sure it is healing as it should?" she pressed. "It's been two days."

"I rebound it yesterday. It is fine," his voice had a slight edge, one that made her want to shut her mouth. "Besides, the medical supplies are all gone."

She bit her lip. At her silence, Shang glanced up at her again. She looked away and couldn't bring herself to keep pressing. After a few minutes, she retreated to her tent.

Fen's chattering at her back, she lifted the tent flap. It was coarse and thick in her grasp. She hesitated one moment longer, fingering that flap. Should she have fought him more? *Why* did he insist on being so cold? With a little shake, she pushed the flap aside and entered the darkness of her tent, shutting out the firelight behind her.

If he wouldn't let her tend his wounds, that was his problem, not hers.

It was time for her to sleep. *Finally.*

And perhaps she'd have a chance to ask Shang about Fen.

CHAPTER 23

SHANG WAS ON watch first.

Meiling hovered just beyond the firelight. It played on his solemn face as he stared into the flickering flames, cutting the sharp angles of his face even harsher. He looked so stern. If he would soften his features into a genuine smile, he would be the most handsome man she'd ever seen. But his lips were pursed into a tight, thin line and despite how tired he looked, his eyes were sharp. He seemed lost in thought, but she suspected his senses were on high alert for any unusual or unexpected sounds, sights, or smells.

Should she do it?

Her reasonable mind said no, he would not want her in his mind uninvited. He would get angry. But her irrepressible curiosity argued that perhaps he would not mind. Perhaps he would find the conversation a welcome break from the monotony of his long watch.

As if he hadn't had an opportunity to speak with her all day.

But Fen had been there the whole time, and he seemed to be more reserved when she was present. Perhaps if given the chance to speak privately with Meiling, he'd take it.

She flitted further away, still watching him. No, she shouldn't do it. It was not important enough. Curiosity over Fen wasn't worth the possibility of angering Shang.

But that wasn't the real reason, was it?

She drooped closer to the ground, her shoulders sagging. No, this wasn't about Fen. This was about herself, and wanting to know if there was a part of Shang that wanted to talk to her when no one else would interrupt, when there was no risk of Fen's mockery.

It had been so long since she had a warm conversation. She was used to loneliness—that was her lot in life—but this journey was another, deeper brand of loneliness. At home, she'd had Ma and Pa, and to some extent, her siblings. Ma had been there when Meiling had been just a child, weeping because she had no friends like her brother Yun. Ma had held her then, and while it hadn't lessened the pain, she hadn't been truly alone.

These long days were getting to her.

By now, she'd given up hope Fen would ever care about her. But Shang? He'd staunchly defended her, no matter his personal opinion of her or this journey. He'd given her chances when Fen had only scoffed.

And there were moments—small, almost indiscernible moments—when that ice had thawed toward her. Maybe he didn't hate her.

She needed to know.

But this hounding *fear*! What if he was angry with her? She would never know unless she tried. What if he was happy?

Was she insane? Why would he be happy to discover her in his mind?

Meiling's thoughts spun round and round. She hated herself for this indecisiveness. She should be firm, stolid! There should be no room for fear in her heart. If he was angry, then she would have learned her lesson. If he was not, then was there a chance she could find a friend in him?

Curse you, Meiling! She gnashed her teeth together. Maybe it wasn't her lack of magic and combat training that made her useless; maybe she was useless because of her constant indecision.

She was done being afraid. She would stand up to her fears, would face the consequences of her actions. No more hesitating or indecision.

She would do it.

Before she could change her mind, despite how her fear grew and tugged her back toward her body—a feeling that seemed so gentle now compared to the force of Shang's kiss—she rushed in a blur of shadow across the campsite.

Into Shang's mind.

When she floated down into the grand hall of his mind, the first thing she noted was that it was dimmer than usual. The curtains were drawn tighter. A cursory glance revealed that, thankfully, all the pillars and the red-painted plaster ceiling remained intact. No cracks wrapped like long-legged spiders around the pillars and dug into the sinuous dragons carved there. *—ride hard, could make it in four days. Perhaps five. The money almost gone, unless the emperor gave some to the girl, which seems unlikely. Foolish Fen and her impulses! We'll need to find a village to buy supplies. Or Fen will need to maul us more food. I should make her ride with the girl. They'd fit better in a saddle. No—she'd torment the girl. There would be so many supposedly accidental spills we'd deliver a concussed princess to the fortress. Renshu would have been far more suited to this assignment. But we must have a woman wielder for the girl's sake. This would have been much easier if we were protecting a prince instead of a princess. More helpful in battle, and Renshu could have come instead of Fen.*

Shang's thoughts spilled over Meiling, so fast that she could hardly process them. So his mind was, indeed, very active despite his lazy posture. Not only that, but while his mind flew through plans of the journey ahead, the back of his mind—it was like a whisper of trained instinct toward the back of the hall—was busy processing the surroundings.

Her vision caught along doors she hadn't noticed at both ends of the hallway. The apse held doors to either side, despite how in the very center were three panels the size of doors. Facing the other way, she found many more doors. Or were they cabinets?

As much as she wanted to stay silent, poke around, and listen to his thoughts, she shouldn't. She had already listened too much. He would be furious if he knew.

An idea hit her. What if she went into his memories, found his memory of earlier today . . . and discovered what he'd been thinking while he kissed her?

Her fleshless form heated. And no matter how much she was tempted, she thrust the idea away. That wasn't fair to him. Besides, what did she hope to gain from that knowledge?

Shang? she called softly.

His stream of thoughts stopped abruptly, and the room went darker. *Meiling? What are you doing in my mind? Is there danger?*

No, no danger! she assured quickly.

Surprise shot through his mind, followed by a burst of anger that radiated all the way through her tether to her sleeping body. Oh fathers, he was mad.

Of course he was mad! Why had she even considered that he wouldn't be?

I . . . Forgive me—I . . . Was she a spluttering idiot? She sounded like one. *I wanted to ask you something about—*

How long have you been in my mind? he growled.

I just entered—

Get out. His voice was calm, controlled, but she stood inside him. There was no hiding from the tight restraint flooding his mind, or the simmering force beneath that restraint. *Get. Out. Now.*

I'm leaving, Meiling choked.

She fled. As fast as she could fly, she exploded out of Shang's head, reeling into the ether between worlds. She choked again, sputtering. She hovered high above the ground, the campsite. Below her, Shang stood, glaring around at the campsite.

He was speaking. Oh fathers, she did *not* want to know what he said. If she stayed this high, she wouldn't hear. She could hide from his words. But despite herself, she drifted low enough for his quiet, but dark and dangerous voice to fill her senses.

"Don't invade my privacy. Apparently I wasn't clear enough before, so I'll say it again. Don't invade my privacy."

I won't. Never again, Meiling whispered without voice.

He settled back down, still glaring at the empty sky, but sealed his lips tightly together in a frown.

Meiling fled. Away from the campsite, away from him and his frown, away from her body, away from the everlasting tension between her and her protectors. She wanted to scream, but she was too broken to scream. Too torn open, too shattered.

And it wasn't because he had been angry.

It was because, beneath the anger, he'd been . . . *disappointed.* As though he'd thought better of her but had been proved wrong. Whatever progress she'd made toward gaining his respect was completely gone.

It shouldn't *matter*.

He shouldn't matter. Not really. Not truly. He was only her protector, only her escort. She probably would see him very little the rest of her life; with him being the illustrious Tan Shangdi, powerful ice-wielder and Academy favorite, and her being the cursed princess.

She shouldn't care what he thought of her. She shouldn't care that he was disappointed in her, that his opinion of her had fallen.

But she did care. She cared so much.

His disappointment and disapproval gored her more effectively than any *mó guǐ*.

She couldn't escape, would never be free. It didn't matter how high she flew, how far she fled, she was still tethered to her body, to her shame, to her disgrace, to her failure. She was still tied down to this horrid journey, this horrid *life.* Hated, hunted—what had she ever done? She'd only tried to be good, to do good. It didn't matter. None of her efforts mattered.

Ma. Pa. Yun. Hou.

She spoke each of their names without voice, formed the syllables with no tongue or lips. What she would give to go home, to see them again. To be wrapped in Hou's fierce hugs, to be safe in Pa's shadow, to smile at Yun's contagious excitement for life, to drown in the loving warmth of Ma's soft brown eyes. No matter how much Meiling failed, Ma looked at her like she was the one thing in the world she was most proud of.

Meiling's spirit convulsed, shuddering and trembling. She had no tears, could find no relief from the knife in her soul. So she wept as only a spirit could weep, her heart bleeding inside her chest.

Movement behind her startled her.

She turned, spotting Shang standing in the distance. She convulsed again, harder, faster. But she floated closer, afraid to see and afraid to not see. Maybe he'd caught sight of a *mó guǐ,* or sign that their pursuit had caught up to them.

She flitted closer, still shuddering and twitching, still hurting.

Shang frowned, but not in anger, rather in confusion. He picked his way quietly across the campsite. Toward Meiling's tent, skirting around Fen's sleeping body.

She almost tore her gaze away, a fresh wave of shaking washed through her soul. Maybe he thought she hadn't left his mind. She waited as he crouched on the ground, brow puckered, head down, ear leaned toward the canvas.

It was only then that she heard what he heard—soft weeping. Shallow, tremulous gasps for air.

She was crying. Her body was crying in response to the pain in her soul.

Meiling froze, dread knotting into a rock in her stomach. She tried to calm herself, to quiet her spirit's convulsions. Slowly, breath by breath, the sound of weeping quieted until it was only a sporadic, shuddering gasp here and there. This, too, calmed.

Shang's head lifted, his dark eyes piercing into the night sky, like two glittering black stars. Meiling held perfectly still. Her body might have stopped breathing.

He stood. Glanced around warily, as if he suspected she watched him. Then he straightened his tunic and strode with less care than before back to his spot by the fire. He sat on the ground, one long leg stretched out, the other bent. He rested his elbow on his bent knee and let his gaze gloss over as he stared at the fire, leaning his chin on a clenched fist.

Meiling couldn't watch anymore. She grasped her soul tether in one hand and followed it back to her body.

She hovered for a moment above her tightly curled form. Her dark hair splayed on the ground, over her face, hands clutched under her chin. Her face was wet, tearstains on her clothes and bedroll. Occasional shudders escaped her parted lips.

With something like a cry of pain, she did something she hadn't done in many years.

Meiling slid back into her body to sleep. *Fully* sleep. She didn't want to think thoughts or feel the pain for another moment. She couldn't.

Blessed oblivion welcomed her.

CHAPTER 24

FEN WAS TALKATIVE the next morning, spewing story after story from the Academy to Shang. He remained quiet. Never once looked toward Meiling, never once let his glimmering black eyes settle on her. He nodded and grunted in response to Fen, but mostly ignored them both and set about preparing for the day's travel.

Meiling blinked back the fog in her brain. She huddled in the folds of her cloak, not bothering to redo her braid, and instead left it in shambles. So *this* was why everyone seemed so tired in the morning. If she didn't know better, she'd think she had slept a full day, or perhaps been trampled by a horse. Her eyes were puffy to the touch, and she hoped Fen assumed it was from sleep.

Shang wouldn't be fooled, of course.

He stood, signaling that it was time to ride. From her vantage point, hunched on the ground, he seemed so much taller. She quickly averted her gaze, lest he catch her staring. It was a silly fear; he was utterly set on refusing to acknowledge her existence.

"Your bruise is spreading," Fen said, squinting her eyes at Meiling's forehead.

"I don't think bruises spread," she responded quietly.

Fen huffed, but said nothing more.

Meiling scrambled to her feet. Each movement sent a fresh wave of aching pain through her body, and she barely bit back a moan. Every step closer to Shang and their horse was difficult, though the pain seemed to be less and less physical.

He would not look at her, not as he helped her into the saddle. He did not place her foot in the stirrups; those were for him. Hardly after she had settled, he swung up behind her. He grasped the reins, encasing her between his arms. He said nothing, but a small sigh escaped his lips and rustled the hair on top of her head. She pulled her cloak tight around her, but it could not block out the feeling of his chest at her back, his knees fitting into the crook of hers.

She hadn't grabbed the horn or the mane of the horse before Shang kicked it into motion. A startled grunt escaped her throat. She lurched forward in surprise, but he caught her around the waist and held her steady, pulling her firmly against him.

All without a word or an acknowledgement. She fisted the horse's mane in her hands. *Fine*. She had only to play Shang's game back and ignore him just like he ignored her.

"West," Shang's voice reverberated through his chest. He pointed.

Fen gave him a look. "I know where west is."

They rode away from the sunrise, into the dark forest. Fresh sunlight cut through the boughs and foliage, streaming in beams and patches. It lit the path before them.

Four days. That was what Shang had thought last night. Four more days and then she could be free.

Unexpectedly, Meiling found herself mourning the loss of the panda cub. She'd been so caught up in Fen's wrath yesterday that she hadn't stopped to process her own sadness. There had been something much brighter and warmer about their travels with that squirming little bundle of black and white fur. That brightness and warmth was gone now.

Four days.

"You two stay here," Shang said, crouching and spying through the foliage into the town where they were to buy food. "Don't do anything stupid while I'm gone." He fixed a warning look on Fen.

He had successfully ignored Meiling all morning and into the afternoon. Even when he helped her dismount from the horse, he so thoroughly ignored her that she almost checked to make sure she was in her physical body. Now, as he took the lead of the horse that formerly belonged to her, he did not give her the slightest glance or word in acknowledgement.

Meiling ignored him, too.

He strode away toward the town, tall and confident. She looked down and focused on untying the ties of her cloak. It was nearly sweltering.

Fen glared after Shang. "Stupid? What does he think I am? Some idiot apprentice?" She stalked around the little clearing where they were to wait. "Now I'm stuck with *you* while he sees and talks to real people again. He always takes the adventure for himself," she muttered, withdrawing her knife and spinning it around her fingers alarmingly fast.

Meiling had to look away from the knife so she could think about something else besides getting murdered by a careless flick of Fen's wrist. It made sense why he went instead of Fen; an unaccompanied woman traveling through these parts could only be a wielder, and they needed anonymity. Fen would be too easily noticed.

Meiling could not blame her, however, for feeling cast aside.

She set herself down in the dirt, swiping away the hair that kept falling in her face. Despite the recent wash, her clothes were already stinking again. The thought of four more days in reeking garments was unpleasant. But at this point, if her smell bothered Shang while riding so close to her, then he could arrange a stop by a river. He could buy a lump of soap to replace the one lost in his horse's saddlebags.

She would not ask for special treatment or complain. She would not be a high-maintenance *princess.*

The thought of another river bath made ice trickle down her spine. How could water be so cold in the summer?

"I'm going to scout," Fen said suddenly, catching her knife by the hilt and shoving it into her belt. "Don't move or I'll flay you alive."

You might not have to, Meiling thought silently to herself. She only nodded and grabbed a nearby stick to trace lines in the dirt. She happened to glance up in time as Fen rolled her eyes and folded into a bird. The bird flew away, into the forest.

Meiling contented herself with drawing characters in the dirt.

Home is by the ocean, she wrote, only half thinking. Would Liafugen have a library? Would she be able to use it during her time there?

Fen's horse was wandering.

She stood, stepping around her characters and after the nosing horse. "Bik, there's grass over here, too. Come back."

The horse's ears perked forward, and he raised his long neck, staring at her with empty eyes.

"I know you're hungry," Meiling whispered with a small smile. "Come back over here." She stroked the beast's beautiful mane, its coarse hairs rubbing between her fingers. Then she grabbed the horse's lead and started pulling him back.

Approaching footsteps made Meiling whirl. Was Fen back already?

But it wasn't Fen. It was Shang.

She immediately turned back around, fixing her attention on the horse again and pretending to be busy stroking it.

"Where's Fen?"

His question startled her enough for her to turn and glance at him. There was something . . . Why was he looking at her? And without malice or indifference, for that matter?

"Scouting," she answered quietly, averting her gaze.

"Did she say how long she was going to take?"

"No."

There was silence for a moment. He tilted his head to one side, then took a step closer. "Meiling . . ."

Her eyes shot up to meet his. She held perfectly still, wary, and leaned closer into the horse. Her heart picked up an odd, syncopated rhythm.

"While Fen's gone . . ." He paused, his jaw twitching slightly. He looked away, studied the ground. "I—I wanted to . . . apologize. For last night and today. I know you meant no harm. Will you forgive me?" At this, he looked up, eyes meeting hers with an unexpectant softness.

His words barreled into Meiling like a brigand's fireball. She stared at him, her mouth agape, as she took a step back. His gaze tracked her movements carefully.

"Forgive you?" she asked breathlessly.

"You don't have to," he said. How had she never noticed how large and round his eyes were? "I know I have been . . . unkind. Impatient."

This was nothing like the Shang she had grown to know. But she'd known him only a few days; there was certainly much more to learn about him. Was this contriteness, this humility a side he tried to avoid showing to people?

Wasn't this exactly what she'd wanted from him last night?

"Of course I forgive you," Meiling sputtered. She should say something else, but all she could do was stare at him stupidly, like he was a ghost. Or a *mó guǐ*.

"Thank you," he said, and gave a small smile. One full of warmth. She had been right; a smile made him handsome beyond description. Not only was it beautiful, but it was oddly vulnerable. The way he cocked his head, the curve of his lip, all spoke of slight uncertainty.

But something felt wrong. She couldn't believe this was real, couldn't believe that Tan Shangdi would ever apologize to her. And why *now*?

He seemed to note her hesitation, her wariness, as she stayed near the horse and away from him. He frowned slightly. "Are you afraid of me?" He took one step closer.

She stepped back involuntarily, swallowing heavily. "Yes."

He smiled again, this time gentler. "You need not fear me. Come here. We will go find Fen."

Something . . . something was not right . . .

But what could not be right? She was so disarmed and flustered by Shang showing an unexpected side to him. Was she so unwilling to accept any goodness from him? Was she to distrust him for showing virtue?

One of his eyebrows quirked and his smile faded, showing the Shang she'd come to know. Stern, taciturn, reserved. "What's wrong, Meiling?"

Could he just *stop* saying her name? He said it so gently. It was so beautiful on his lips. Unwillingly, the memory of his kiss assaulted her mind. Of his arms holding her close, the way his mouth had moved against hers.

She could not bring herself to come closer to him. The way he beckoned, the way he took deliberate steps toward her . . . Had his eyes always been so round?

Something was wrong.

There was no denying that insistence in her gut as her soul writhed within her. "Shang . . ." Her voice quivered. "I . . . I don't . . ."

A roar split through the air.

Claws, black stripes, and orange fur pounced on Shang from behind.

He screamed.

Meiling screamed too, lurching forward with arms outstretched. "Shang!"

He cried out as a huge tiger claw raked across his chest, slicing through clothes and flesh. His face contorted with pain. Meiling rushed forward without realizing it, shrieking and calling for Fen.

But the tiger was Fen. She knew the tiger was Fen.

Fen would never attack Shang.

Despite her rational mind telling her this couldn't be Shang, Meiling tried to grab the tiger's front leg and yank it away with gasps to spare his life. The tiger roared in her face, making her fall to the ground, screaming, and throw her hands over her face.

Then the tiger pounced again, knocking Shang to the ground. Before she could scream again, powerful jaws snapped down on his neck. And *ripped.*

Shang went still.

The tiger stepped back, growling with visible fangs as the body . . . *melted.*

Into a silver fox with nine tails.

Meiling choked on a sob, pressing her face into her hands.

Fen shifted into her human form, looking grimly down at the monster. Then her battle-lust filled eyes fixed on Meiling. "It's hard enough to kill a fox spirit without you trying to save it!"

"I'm sorry," she whispered, lowering her head. "Thank you . . . for saving me."

When she expected a digging insult, Fen said nothing, only giving the fox spirit's limp body a nudging kick.

"How did you know it wasn't him?" Meiling asked, afraid to hear the answer.

There was no mockery in the lines of Fen's unusually serious face. "The key to fighting the lure of a fox spirit is to know your own weaknesses. You're not trained as a warrior, but if you were, you'd have seen the inconsistencies. Where was Shang's horse? The food he was supposed to bring back? When has he ever smiled like that? *Never.*"

So she had watched the entire exchange. Meiling's face heated.

"You didn't know with complete certainty that it wasn't him," she said, afraid of the answer.

Fen shrugged, giving a dark grunt. "You can't know for sure with fox spirits."

"So . . . you kill and hope your guess was right?" She almost stuttered on the words.

"Basically," Fen said, not seeming to either notice Meiling's shock or have any of her own. She looked down at the body, gored from her teeth and claws. Then she looked up, a strange glint in her eyes. "What was he apologizing to you for?"

Meiling drew in a shuddering breath. "Nothing."

Fen eyed her suspiciously, but didn't press the issue. "I need to burn the body. Far enough away that no one will smell it. Don't move while I'm gone. And no falling for more fox spirits. I can't have you dying on me. Shang would murder me." She gave Meiling a fierce look of warning and snatched up a handful of still-twitching tails, mounted her horse, and rode away.

Leaving Meiling completely alone. Yet again.

She tried to remove the images fighting for ascendency in her mind. She never wanted to remember Shang's throat being torn out. Or the way he'd spoken gently to her and smiled.

Shang is still alive, she told herself, still reeling. *And he is still mad at you.*

Another set of footsteps made her whirl where she stood.

Shang. With his horse and a full sack. His footsteps slowed when his black eyes—less round than the apparition's—caught sight of Meiling. "Where's Fen?" he barked.

Was this the true Shang? It certainly seemed so. His brow was knit, face flashing in irritation at finding her alone. But could she be sure? Meiling touched the penknife in her sleeve without thinking. He noticed, and his eyes narrowed.

"Burning a fox spirit," she said without ceremony.

He froze. The horse stomped its hooves, ears flattening.

"A fox spirit?" he repeated, his gaze roving over Meiling for injuries and then the surrounding area. "Are you hurt? Is Fen alright?"

"We're both uninjured."

"Good. Come quickly. We need to catch up with her. I don't like either of you being alone out here."

She drew back instinctively. He certainly *felt* real. There wasn't a sense of wrongness in the air like before, and it was unlikely that two fox spirits would be in the same vicinity. Nevertheless, Fen had explicitly said not to fall for any more fox spirits, and she didn't want to be foolish or hasty. She was alone and unguarded. A perfect target.

Shang's eyes narrowed again at her, brow puckering in confusion. Then his face cleared with sudden realization. "Oh. I see."

Meiling blinked at him, her sluggish mind taking a moment to understand *what* he'd just realized.

Oh.

She quickly averted her gaze to her toes, too embarrassed as heat burned up her neck. Of *course* he deduced the fox spirit had manifested as him. Wonderful. Just *wonderful.*

"Here, look," Shang said, withdrawing a knife. Her eyes widened as he pressed the tip of the blade into the pad of his fingertip. Blood welled, red and glistening like a ruby. He held up the bleeding finger to her. "Visions don't bleed."

"How do I know it's not part of the vision?"

He should be irritated, but he did not seem to mind. Perhaps he preferred her skepticism.

"Toss me your cloak," he said, tucking his knife back into his belt.

Meiling obliged. He caught it with his free hand and pressed his cut finger into the fabric. Then he tossed it back. She caught it and looked.

There. There was the blood stain.

"How do I know you're not lying to me?" Meiling asked, folding the garment over her arm. "About the bleeding."

Shang had started loading the food he had procured into the saddlebags of the gray horse. Rice, rice cakes, and more dragon-blasted jerky. His fingers stilled their work. "Did the fox spirit bleed when Fen killed it?

The image flashed in her mind of Shang lying on the ground as a tiger sank its fangs into his throat. She winced, almost sick. But he was right—there had been no blood.

"I thought so," said Shang, buckling the saddlebag closed and turning toward her. "Come. Let's go find Fen. Or are you still afraid of me?"

Meiling searched his black eyes for any reason to disbelieve him. "Yes," she said finally. "I am still afraid of you. But I will go with you."

When he looked at her, it was like he carved open her mind and read every thought flashing through it. It was more unnerving than when he ignored her. He stepped to the front of the horse and laced his fingers together to help her mount.

Meiling forced herself forward, trying not to betray her lingering doubt with slow steps. After all—if he was a fox spirit, would it matter if she walked slowly or quickly to her death?

She reached Shang, and he did not lunge for her throat or bare fanged teeth. He waited and then hoisted her up onto the horse. He grabbed hold of the saddle, stuck his foot in the stirrup—but paused. His gaze caught on the characters drawn in the dirt. He stared at them for a moment, then turned back to the horse. Meiling gave him a sidelong glance and found him studying her again.

"You should be dead," he said at last. He mounted up behind her, all but wrapping his arms around her when he grasped the reins.

"I suppose that is what you and Fen are for," Meiling mumbled.

"Lucky for you," he rumbled behind her.

She tilted her head. "I don't imagine my parents would have sent me on a dangerous journey without protectors."

"I don't imagine they would have," he agreed.

A long silence passed as he guided their horse along the trail Fen had left behind through the forest edging the village.

Heart throbbing painfully in her throat, Meiling sucked in a deep breath to summon her courage. It would be easier to say nothing. But . . . but she should. Licking her lips, she said softly, "I am sorry."

"Hmm?"

She breathed another deep lungful and said louder, "I'm sorry. About . . . last night."

He stiffened behind her. Just slightly, but it was there in his chest, racing down along his arms. "Let us not speak of it."

She lowered her head, staring down at the horse's mane, the clomping of its hooves. Her stomach plummeted and tears threatened, but she refused to let her emotions control her. Last night, she had violated his privacy against his explicit desires. She apologized. There was nothing more she could do. If he would not accept her apology, that was his problem and none of her business.

Stink of scorched flesh assaulted her nostrils. Meiling recoiled, accidentally leaning backward into him. She quickly recovered, sat up straighter, and held the scratchy folds of her cloak over her nose.

A strange noise sounded ahead. It was like the tinkling of bells, of many chimes. How odd.

Shang tensed behind her. The hand holding the reins slid to her waist, his palm splaying across her stomach and pulling her tightly against him. A protective gesture. Meiling tried to ignore the sudden hammering of her heart and glanced to find his other hand full of ice shards. This close, they almost looked like refracting crystals.

Another strange, bell-like sound. Then a roar.

Shang leapt off the horse in a flash. *"Fen!"*

CHAPTER 25

SHANG TORE THROUGH the branches. Meiling, not knowing what else to do, followed as quickly as she could on horseback, urging her horse forward with kicks and nudges.

"Fen! Fen!" he shouted, his voice full of terror and sudden desperation. A sound she had *never* heard from him before.

He burst into a clearing, Meiling fast on his heels. She pulled her horse up abruptly. The stink was so alarming, so noxious, she almost choked.

In the middle of the clearing, a fire burned the remnants of a silvery body, now charred black. To one side, a tiger crouched, snarling, backed against a tree. Opposite the tiger stomped three of the strangest creatures Meiling had ever seen.

They had deer-like bodies with stomping, cloven hooves. Their bodies were lithe but strong, dense with muscle like Fen's tiger body, only far bigger and fiercer. Two had antlers with many tips, long and tall and proud. The third had a single horn at the crest of its brow. Fangs dripped blood and fire from their strangely snouted mouths. One of the beast's scales glinted gold with a fiery red mane and beard. Drops of flame fell onto the beast's beard, sizzling where they landed. The other beasts possessed bodies of jewel-like brilliance. One was sapphire blue, with a crimson mane. The next was amethyst purple, radiant and dazzling in the sunlight. Its mane was black, and its single horn shone like the purest star.

Though she had never seen them in real life, she immediately recognized them from statues, tapestries, and rugs all over the palace.

Qilins.

Alone, they were some of the deadliest monsters. And they were never alone.

The three qilins—there were more nearby—approached Fen with glassy, beady eyes and hungry, chomping jaws. They cornered her, coming nearer and nearer. She growled and barked, shrinking into herself more as she exposed her fangs.

Shang acted before Meiling could finish processing the scene.

He flicked his wrist and instead of ice shards, he held ice bolts in each hand. He flung them as hard as he could with impeccable aim at the gold qilin nearest Fen. The ice sunk deep between the shoulder blades of the *mó guǐ*.

It keened a roaring sort of wail—pained and terrifying and horrible all at once. Meiling covered her ears at the sound. Bells coughed and sputtered, a sound too strange for her ears, for her mind to comprehend.

The qilin fell. The bells clattered to silence.

Meiling shielded herself instinctively with an arm against what would be a rushing, whirling, furious spirit. But her spirit was tucked deep inside her physical body while she was awake, and the *mó guǐ's* spirit could not hurt her now. Not her spirit, that is. Her body was completely vulnerable.

The other qilins attacked.

Lowering its single horn, the purple one pawed the ground, and charged for Shang. The sapphire one lunged for the hunkering tiger.

Meiling cast around desperately for the other horse. There! Bik whinnied, pulling at his ties to the tree. She kicked her horse to his side, too afraid to look behind her. The last thing she wanted was another searing memory of her companions being gored.

She jumped down from the saddle, a painful jolt shooting up her legs. She stayed in a crouch for one moment, breathing, and dared a glance back to the others.

The sapphire qilin sank its wide maw of fangs into Fen. A roar split the seams between reality. The pain of that roar hit her very soul. Her throat closed, her heart stopped.

Fen fell.

The qilin backed to skewer her in the gut with its horns. It pawed the ground, snorting its bell-like sound.

Meiling had to do something—had to intervene.

She leapt to her feet.

An ice bolt shot into the sapphire qilin. It shrieked like the clanging of dissonant chimes. Shang cried out, though Meiling could not tell if from pain or strain.

She stumbled back, scrambling toward Fen's bound horse. Her fingers tore at the lead, and it tumbled free of its knot. "Steady, steady girl," she gasped. The horse whinnied and jerked backward, jolting her to her knees in the dirt. She got a foot up, planting it firmly and pulled against the horse's fighting.

"Bik, you will be all right. Come, it's okay." Her voice sawed roughly in her own ears, fragile, half choking. Not at all reassuring to the frantic horse. "Come, my sweet one, stop *fighting* me!"

Then, on a stroke of fortune, or perhaps misfortune, Meiling looked behind her.

Another qilin, this one shining like red copper, pawed the ground and lowered its antlers at her.

Her heart stopped. There were more in the forest behind it—one, two, four, *five* more?

"Shang!" she screamed.

The *mó guǐ* would attack any second. It would gore her, and then the two horses.

Bik almost broke free of her hold. Now the other horse shrieked its own bray of panic. She couldn't restrain one, much less both.

She faced the qilin. And there was herself—reflected in its glassy eyes. Its mouth dripped fire, searing its beard, and scorching the earth where it landed. It had only to open its mouth wide and blow, and she would be incinerated.

"Easy, there. I won't hurt you," she said in the most soothing voice she could manage.

"What are you doing?" a voice cried behind her.

Suddenly, she was tackled. She hit the ground hard, rolling to a stop. She gasped, blinking against the dust in her eyes up at Shang, whose weight pressed heavily on top of her, his forearms braced against the ground, framing her face.

For a brief second, his eyes met hers.

He leapt up, dragging her painfully after him, his hands so cold they burned. She stumbled for the horse leads while Shang shouted at her.

The qilin had apparently little interest in the horses, for it turned toward Meiling again. It opened wide its mouth—

Meiling threw herself to the ground.

Blistering hot and cold met over her head.

A gaping maw spewed fire, and Shang faced it straight on, legs braced wide, and hands outstretched and shooting ice, face contorted. Meiling screamed, then flung her arms over her head. The sound was like nothing she'd encountered before—an unnatural, hissing scream.

Then the sound stopped.

"Get up!" Shang shouted at her.

She did not even look before she jumped to her feet. She sprang and caught the lead of Fen's horse before it could gallop away into the forest. If they could mount the horses, they could escape.

With a burst of sudden strength she didn't know she had, she mounted Fen's horse. In front of her, Shang had caught the lead of the gray horse, but instead of mounting, he aggressively stormed the qilin, forcing it to retreat.

Another qilin in the forest reared and opened its mouth to blast Shang. Meiling urged her horse to where Fen had fallen. She was about to leap down when, miraculously, Shang was beside her with the other horse.

"Stay!" he shouted at Meiling as she started swinging her leg.

Two qilins charged toward them. She screamed and fell against her horse's neck, clutching it, as her horse reared back and shrieked. Only a miracle kept her mounted.

She didn't know how it happened. Somehow, both qilins collapsed in their charge to the ground, letting out a cacophony of shattering bells. Somehow, Shang was in the other saddle with Fen's bleeding body slung in front of him.

Somehow, they were running, escaping, fleeing for their lives.

Meiling glanced behind as the qilins followed them. The one in front, an emerald green one with a flame-red mane and beard, opened its mouth to burn them. "Shang! Behind!" she screamed.

He twisted and barely managed to put up his hands and meet the fire with a blast of ice. He cried out, his face twisting.

"Faster, faster!" she urged her horse. Perhaps she cried in her terror. She wasn't quite sure. She only knew that if they didn't move fast, they'd be dead.

Shang caught up, riding alongside her.

She wanted to glance behind her, to see if they were being pursued, but she needed her focus to not get slammed by branches. There was no getting used to fleeing for their lives!

She spared a glance for Shang. He leaned close to his horse, eyes blazing with battle and terror and danger. His shirt was torn in a few places, and she thought she saw blood. Wind caught the strands of his hair that had come loose of its queue.

They rode longer than they probably should at that speed. She struggled more with each second, barely keeping from flying off the saddle. It was hard to dodge through the forest, over the uneven ground, beneath scraggly branches, and not go plunging to her death.

Once, she risked a glance behind, but there was nothing.

Shang did not stop, however.

Not until they broke out of the forest, skirting along open fields between the foothills and a shining lake. Shang pushed them further, faster, even as Meiling considered letting go of the reins and tumbling to her death. She was so exhausted, so weak after the adrenaline rush. She couldn't hang on much longer.

Shang slowed, signaling to her.

They stopped near the shore of the lake, hidden in a protective cluster of pine trees. The late-day sun blistered straight into their faces, through the parting arms of the evergreens.

He jumped off the saddle and landed on unsteady feet, pitching forward and barely catching himself before he fell. His hands trembled violently when he reached back, pulling Fen's body off the horse and carrying her to the ground.

"Meiling! Hurry!" he shouted.

She'd already dismounted, grabbed a waterskin, and rushed after him.

The horses, foaming and breathing heavily, took themselves to the lake to drink. She didn't spare the effort to hobble them. She couldn't think of anything else as she knelt by Fen's body, opposite Shang.

Her eyes were closed, her face pale. Blood soaked through her garments; blood that still gushed out of a nightmarish wound in her shoulder and neck. Shang leaned over her, pressing a hand beneath her jaw for a pulse.

"She lives." His breath whooshed out of him in relief.

"Cut away the fabric," Meiling ordered quickly. "Where are the medical supplies?"

Shang lifted his face toward hers, his jaw slack and his brows drawn in anguish. "They were in my saddlebags."

Meiling gritted her teeth. She glanced down at her own tunic and immediately began cutting the excess off the ends with her penknife.

"Here, use mine," Shang said, flinging off his outer robes and ripping his overshirt off without bothering to undo the front laces.

Meiling's eyes widened at the blood seeping into his undershirt in multiple places on his torso. "You're bleeding, Shang!"

He shook his head. "Fen first. We must save Fen!" His breath shuddered out of him much too quickly.

Don't panic, don't panic.

"Cut her shirt," Meiling repeated, grabbing Shang's tunic, and ripping it into long, thick strips. "She's bleeding fast. What can we do? We have nothing to stitch her with."

"We'll have to cauterize it. Here, you do this." He shoved the hilt of one of his knives into her hand. "I'll start the fire."

Fen's face grew paler by the second.

Meiling jumped up and ran to take his place and began working, her fingers shaking as she stuffed the makeshift bandages against the wound. "Stay with me, Fen," she whispered, putting pressure against the bleeding. Her voice kept catching, kept quivering, but she didn't stop speaking. "You're going to be all right. We'll have you better in no time."

Her hands grew steadier as she pressed the fabric against Fen's neck and shoulder, and with the other cut away her shirt from the wound with Shang's knife. Blood soon soaked her fingers, rolling in dark, crimson streams to the ground.

"Shang!" she cried. "Is the fire ready?"

"Almost!"

"Hurry!" she gasped, grimacing down at Fen's ghastly face. "I can't stop the bleeding."

"I'm heating the blade!"

With the first press of the hot blade against the wound, the smell of seared flesh nearly made Meiling vomit. But she held herself together. A scream burst from Fen's throat.

"Keep going," Meiling said. "I'll hold her down."

He looked up, the hot knife in one hand, and his face was stricken.

"Don't stop! Hurry!" She pressed her knee into Fen's good shoulder and pinned her arms.

Fen screamed again.

Shang choked, hands trembling as he worked. "There. It's done."

The burned flesh looked horrible, but it no longer bled. They had no salve. Nothing besides the bandages. So she took the rest of the strips from Shang's shirt and bound up the wound as best as she could. She could only pray there would be no infection.

Fen had grown still. Meiling bent over her, checking for her pulse. It was slow, weak, but it was still there. Shang knelt beside her. "Do you think she'll live?" His voice was so low, so quiet, so tense, she almost did not hear him.

Finished with her work, she sat back on her heels. Almost collapsed from her own shuddering limbs. She kept herself upright; she still had to tend Shang. "Time will tell," she said. Then, "You're hurt!"

He looked so pale himself, so weak. Now that Fen was out of immediate danger, he wavered on his knees, looking like he might collapse any second.

"Shang!" Meiling cried, rushing to his side. She caught him, looping his arm over her shoulders and easing him to the ground next to Fen. Would he pass out of consciousness? "Stay with me, Shang. Hold on. Stay with me."

He forced his eyes open. They cleared, and he took a big, gasping breath. His jaw hardened. "I . . . am . . . fine."

"Don't pass out, understand?" Meiling said sternly. "I need your help to remove your undershirt. Otherwise, I'll have to cut it off. Stay awake, Shang."

"Fine, fine, fine!" he growled with a tight grimace. "I only want to rest for a minute . . ."

"Don't sleep. Not yet. You hear me?"

"I hear you," he croaked. He lifted himself on one elbow and together they wrestled his undershirt off, which Meiling set aside for bandages. She helped him to lie back down so she could inspect his wounds, his muscular torso rising and falling rapidly beneath her fingers. Sweat slicked his skin, catching on the light of the dying sun.

"These don't look so bad. Still bleeding, but I think we can fix that," she said, bending closer to the wounds. There were several punctures in his torso and arm, but none near as severe as Fen's. She couldn't help a small gasp of relief. His burned shoulder was poorly bound from his own attempt at bandaging it.

She set to work immediately, cutting his undershirt into strips, washing the wounds, and binding them. Light faded fast, and she didn't want to be working in the dark. "You're going to be fine, I think. Roll to your side."

He winced with every movement. "Of course I'll be fine." Then his eyes opened again, and they fixed on her so intensely that her fingers slowed. "How . . .?"

"Don't worry yourself. Here, drink." She pressed the waterskin to his lips, reaching under his head, shifting him so he could lean on her knee.

He drank, gasping between swallows. When she pulled the waterskin away, he fell back to the ground. He closed his eyes, breathing hard. "How will we make it?"

Meiling's hands froze.

She had been so caught up in tending their wounds, binding this bandage around Shang's ribs, that she had not realized how dire their situation was. She shook herself and tied the knot tightly, resulting in another grimace from Shang. "We'll make it," she said firmly. "We're close. We'll make it."

His gaze was clearer, darker. "Who will protect you?"

She raised an eyebrow, grabbing another strip of shirt. "I suppose I will. Roll again."

He closed his eyes, shaking his head. "You're helpless. You'll die without us."

"You forget I have magic too," she chided, even though they both knew any of the *mó guǐ* they had encountered would have gobbled her up. And then there were the brigands pursuing them.

"Useless magic," Shang muttered.

Meiling's eyes widened, her hands growing very still.

He opened one eye. "In battle."

She gave him a glare. "Stop trying to convince me that we're going to die. You'll scare me."

He quirked an eyebrow. The faintest of smiles pulled at his lips.

She decided that was a good sign. "If I'm so helpless and useless, you'll just have to get better quickly. We both know Fen can't fight anymore. Now hold still. Lift your arm so I can get this bandage tied properly." She puffed against the hair falling in her face, brow furrowing in focus.

He lifted his arm obediently. She set to work tying the bandage, staunching the flow of blood.

"It's getting so dark," she mumbled. "At least I'm almost—"

Something warm brushed her face. She glanced up, startled, and found Shang staring at her, firelight shining in his eyes, as he slid his fingers down her temple and cheek. Carefully, he tucked her unruly hair behind her ear. Then his fingers trailed to her jaw, his thumb brushing her chin.

Her breath caught.

"I didn't say *you* were useless," he said softly.

Her lips parted, chest squeezing far too tight. A deep flush turned her cheeks hot. With effort, she tore her eyes from him and grabbed the last bandage. His hand slid from her face, but his gaze didn't shift away. She tried to ignore it as she leaned over him to access the last wound. She pulled her hair over one shoulder, so it didn't trail across his chest.

"We'll make it," Meiling said with finality. She tied off the last bandage and said, perhaps a tad too briskly, "I'll get your cloak and some food from the saddlebags. You stay here. You can sleep in a minute. After you eat."

"Meiling—" He caught her hand just as she was about to get to her feet. She froze, watching in shock as he drew her knuckles to his mouth and pressed a kiss to them. "Thank you."

She stared at him, stunned.

His lips were so soft and warm against her skin. Her stomach clenched, her heart twisting into a knot that nearly made her gasp aloud. Then he dropped her hand, letting his fall heavily to the ground and closing his eyes.

She sucked in a sharp breath, then shoved her feet into action, moving stilted like a puppet on a string. She would focus on tending the horses now, getting their food, on her own exhaustion. Not on the way her hand curled in toward her heart, as if she could bottle up the feeling of his kiss and store it inside her forever.

She hurried after the wandering horses on the edge of the lake. Everything hurt—aching muscles and scrapes and a few very shallow cuts bled along her arms. Perhaps whipping branches when they had galloped through the forest? It did not matter. None of Meiling's aches could be considered until the others were settled. She would have time to worry about herself later.

Forcing one foot before the other, she finally reached the edge of the lake where the contented horses lapped and grazed on the soft, green grass.

"You two look happy." She smiled at them, digging into her own saddlebags first for the food Shang had packed earlier. Her horse gave an acknowledging whinny and craned its neck to nuzzle her. She returned a small, shaky laugh and pet the horse on its velvety nose.

She gathered her bedroll, all the cloaks and blankets she could find, food, and another waterskin. Determined to carry everything in one load, she could hardly see where she walked. Her knees almost buckled.

"Just a little longer," she told herself under her breath.

When she made it back to the clump of evergreens where Shang and Fen lay, Shang's eyes were closed, and his breaths were shallow.

"I told you not to sleep yet," Meiling huffed, leaning down to set her bundle of things on the dirt.

"I'm not asleep," he growled, with his eyes still closed.

"Oh, good," she said, trying to hide her own fatigue. "Here, I brought you something comfortable to sleep on." She pulled her bedroll from the pile, as well as a few rice cakes and jerky, and knelt beside him.

He half opened one eye. "I'm not sleeping on your bedroll."

"Don't be all tough. You're injured and this will help you sleep better. Which will help you heal faster." She rolled it out beside him and reached to help lift his shoulders.

"I'm not an invalid," he retorted, pulling away from her hands and moving himself without assistance to the bedroll. Stopping suddenly, he glanced at Fen.

"No, stay," Meiling said quickly. "We shouldn't move her yet. I'll make her comfortable." While he glared at her, she unfolded the blanket and draped it over him.

"Meiling, stop—" He pushed himself up on one elbow.

She crossed her arms and cocked an eyebrow at him, ignoring the sudden fluttering of her heart. "Stop what?"

He stared at her for a long, silent moment. His head tilted and his breathing increased. As if every moment sitting up was painful. He laid himself back down, shaking his head and saying nothing. Like he wasn't sure he knew what he wanted to say, or how to say it.

He didn't protest as she gave him food and more water. When she offered to help him sit up to eat, he silently shook his head and propped himself up on his elbow again.

"Now you can sleep," Meiling whispered as he leaned back with closed eyes.

His brow pinched, mouth opening before closing again. His throat bobbed.

Turning back to Fen, she tucked Shang's cloak around Fen. She added Fen's cloak too, to ensure she would be warm all night.

Finally. Everything was dealt with. She had arranged both for sleep, fed the fire, gathered extra wood, and hobbled the horses. Exhausted to the bone, she fastened the clasp of her cloak around her neck, wrapped herself up in its folds, and laid down on the grass for sleep near Fen.

A sigh escaped despite herself, a sigh from the depths of her soul. She closed her eyes—and then opened them again. Her gaze settled on Fen, her head lolling to the side. Pursing her lips, Meiling sat up again, unfastened her cloak, and folded it into a little pillow. Oh so gently, she lifted Fen's head and slid her cloak underneath and laid her head back down.

Satisfied, Meiling curled up in a ball. At least it was not cold.

Not *very* cold.

She shivered a little, but decided she was only being dramatic. Squeezing her eyes shut, she let her exhaustion claim her.

They would make it. They *had* to.

CHAPTER 26

MEILING REFUSED TO let her spirit drift far away. Though the moon and stars reflected in the shimmering lake, though the countryside gleamed in the pale glow of night, she would not give into the temptation to fly far away and abandon her troubles.

Instead, she scouted.

She didn't let herself be lazy either, and only hunt for the glow of magical threats. She searched hard for even the most basic of dangers—snakes, wildcats, wolves, hogs, anything. Shang and Fen had protected her from so much on this journey. She would not let them down now.

Her soul hung low in the sky, drooping toward the ground.

Shang was right. How could they possibly make it? Had even a day gone by where they had not run aground of brigands or *mó guǐ*? Even if Shang were at his best, Fen was incapacitated. She would be another liability. How was Shang to protect them both, especially while injured?

Meiling was not about to pretend she would be any help in battle. If they encountered brigands, they were done. If they encountered *mó guǐ*, they were done. Especially if they encountered another herd of qilins or a phoenix. If they happened upon another fox spirit . . . If one appeared again to Meiling as Shang, would she fall for it this time? What if he was not nearby? Even if she recognized a fox spirit, she had no means of killing it.

What if Fen took a turn for the worse? What if Shang woke up feverish? What if he was worse than he was letting on, worse than she thought?

Why couldn't Meiling have powers that were easily wieldable in battle? Shang was right; hers were of hardly any use unless she was asleep. Even then, she could not kill. Not that she very well *wanted* to kill.

A cry split through the night.

She tore back to the camp. Her eyes darted to the fire, dying to embers nearby, and the three slumbering forms. One writhed, moaning loudly. Meiling dove back into her body. She sat up with a heady rush of sensations. Her head pounded. She blinked away her dizziness.

Then she was instantly at Fen's side.

Fen cried out again, the firelight catching on beads of sweat pooling on her forehead and soaking her hair. She tossed her head from side to side, moaning. Her eyes stayed closed, as if she were still asleep.

"Shh, it's all right. Shh, Fen." She repeated her name softly, gently stroking wet hair out of her face. She was burning to the touch. "I know it hurts. But everything is going to be all right."

A pair of bleary eyes blinked opposite Fen's writhing body.

"You can go to sleep, Shang," Meiling whispered. "I'll stay with her."

He slowly eased himself into a sitting position, staring down at Fen. His black eyes turned almost liquid in the darkness of the night. A few of the bandages wrapping around his torso were lightly stained with blood. His hair fell loose, long, and black.

"Go to sleep, Shang," she repeated.

He ignored her, reaching out to touch Fen's burning forehead. He withdrew slightly at the heat, but then placed his full hand over her forehead. A shudder cascaded through Fen's body, escaped her lips. She calmed almost immediately at the cool of his hand.

"Shang—"

He looked up at her through the strands of hair that fell in his face. "Stop worrying, Meiling. I'll stay with her a little more. You sleep."

She wanted to protest, but she could not find the words or strength to do so. Instead, she nodded. She laid down, her eyelids so heavy—

Her spirit floated free of her body. She wanted to continue scouting the area, but she could not bring herself to leave Fen's side.

She looked so horrible. Her usually bright red glow had dulled. It pulsed faintly with threads of life. Shang, who still sat beside her with his hand pressed to her forehead, glowed his striking ice blue, but even his glow was subdued.

A pang shot through her heart. Was there anything more she could do? Anything that she was not already doing?

Shang's eyes moved from beyond Fen to Meiling's huddled frame in the darkness. His tired eyes narrowed. Then, with a grimace, he stood. He leaned down and grabbed his blanket. With slow, but surprisingly stable steps, he left Fen's side and came to stand over Meiling.

She watched, her soul frozen, as he stooped and draped the blanket over her body. He stood there for half a second longer, looking down at her, and then he strode back to the bedroll. Wincing, he lowered himself next to Fen and placed his hand on her forehead again.

"I know you're watching," he said aloud, though still quietly enough to not disturb Fen. "Don't neglect yourself or you will fall sick and then you'll be of no use to anyone."

Meiling started, pulling back a little. She wanted to reply something about the same applying to him, but she couldn't. Not without entering his mind, and she was not going to make that same mistake again. A dozen different replies sprang to her lips, but she could say nothing. Not without a voice.

Eventually, Shang withdrew his ice-cold hand from Fen's still body and lay down on the bedroll. He lay on his back, one arm under his head, looking up into the starry sky. Was he not cold, all bare-chested like that?

He can't hear the stars whisper. Did he even know they had voice and song? No, how would he?

He fell asleep.

Night bled into midnight, into the wee hours of morning, and then dawn was born. Soft, beckoning, whispering, promising. The morning light stained the sky above and reflected in the lake, and Meiling desperately hoped they would make it.

"Wake up."

Shang's eyes flickered open at the sound of her voice. Meiling withdrew her hand from his shoulder and stood. She smiled and said, "Good morning, Shang."

His eyes widened, looking past her to the sky. "It's so late! Why didn't you wake me earlier?" He tried to scramble to his feet, winced as he grabbed for his side, and then stood more slowly. "Now we'll lose our progress and—"

"It's still early. We all needed sleep. Fen, especially," Meiling said, indicating Fen with a nod of her head. "Everything is almost ready for us to leave. We only need to eat, roll up the bedroll, find you a shirt, and help Fen onto a horse."

Shang looked down, having apparently forgotten his shirtless state. He glanced around the camp, seemed to note the doused fire, the tethered horses, and packed saddlebags. That attention shifted to Meiling, as though surprised by what she'd done on her own. Last, his eyes fell on Fen, lying still beneath two cloaks.

"Can she be moved?" he asked.

Meiling's lips tightened. "What other option do we have? Any minute, the brigands or any number of *mó guǐ* could stumble upon us."

He was already nodding, his dark eyes roving the landscape with that calculating look of his. "Our best hope is arriving as quickly as possible, within reason with Fen's injuries." His gaze fell on Meiling. "You ride Bik. I'll take Fen with me."

She nodded. She bent and started rolling up the bedroll.

"I'll get that," Shang said, crouching next to her.

"I'll do this while you eat. Then we load Fen?"

She looked up to find his eyes on hers, his jaw hard even as something uncertain flashed in his pupils. Her hands slowed her work, her head tilting in question.

"I'll find a shirt," he said, turning and stalking toward the horses.

Meiling found her breath again and focused on the task in front of her. Within a minute, she had tied up the bundle and hurried to fasten it to the back of Bik's saddle.

Shang shrugged himself into a spare shirt, pulled on his robes, retied his hair, and found some breakfast to nibble. "When I bought food, I'd intended for Fen to hunt. I didn't buy enough—didn't have enough money—for all the food we'd need."

"You can hunt, though, right?" Meiling asked, standing on her tiptoes to tie the bedroll.

"Fen's better than me." His mouth twisted like the admission tasted sour on his tongue. "I can't very well leave you two at the camp unprotected while I hunt."

"I'm sure we'd be fine for twenty minutes."

He gave her an annoyed look. "It'll take me more than twenty minutes. Without Fen's shifting abilities, I can't find prey so quickly."

She finished tying the bedroll and lowered herself from her toes to the pads of her feet. "I'm sure we'll think of something."

For all Shang's faults, he would not let them starve or die without a fight. She knew that much about him.

Getting Fen on the horse was no easy matter. After bringing the dappled mare closer, she and Shang knelt on either side of Fen's unconscious body. Meiling carefully pulled back the cloaks at her throat to check her wound.

"It looks like it's healing properly," she mumbled, grimacing despite herself, and then redid the bandages. "I wish we had some salve. Some broth. Tea and tonic for her fever. And a dozen other things."

"Help me lift her," Shang said, sliding his arms under her knees and shoulders. Meiling did the same, and together they stumbled, trying to carry her deadweight between them as carefully as possible. His arms trembled slightly against hers, and she was afraid he pushed himself too hard, but she held her tongue.

He, staggering a little under the weight, heaved Fen up into the saddle. Meiling caught her and steadied her as much as she could until he mounted behind her, wrapping a strong arm around her waist as she lolled forward. With his free hand, he tilted her head back against his shoulder. He grabbed the reins.

Meiling hurried to Fen's brown horse after retrieving their cloaks from the ground. Bik looked back at her with large, stupid eyes as she gripped the saddle and braced herself to mount. She refused to look back toward Shang, knowing he would be judging her harshly. Instead, she wrestled her foot into the high stirrup—if only the horse was a little shorter!—and with a grunt, heaved all her weight upward. She managed to end up in the saddle. With a little grin of triumph, Meiling looked back at Shang.

He gave her a nod, then turned his horse toward their long day of riding ahead. She pulled her cloak around her shoulders, fastening it, and followed him.

CHAPTER 27

"HOLD HER UP so she doesn't fall," Shang said, dismounting out of the saddle. He moved slower than usual, though his face was hard. Occasionally, in the past two days, Meiling had caught tiny flashes of pain across his face. But while he was still called to lead their little party, he would not give in to the smallest grimace.

"I won't fall," Fen slurred, slumping in the saddle.

Meiling stood on her tiptoes, trying to avoid Fen's weak swatting and prevent her from falling to the ground. Once Shang had dismounted, he reached up and hefted Fen down into his arms.

"Spread out the bedroll for her," he said through clenched teeth as he shifted Fen's inert weight and strode with swift, blocky strides.

Every time Meiling tried to fight him about his overexertion, he only gave her an icy look and continued whatever he was doing. So she held her tongue now and swiftly unfastened the bedroll.

Shang had found a little cave in the foothills of the mountains for them to rest in tonight. She crouched under the low opening into the darkness beyond, blinking into the dimness, and unrolled the bedroll.

"Deeper into the cave." Shang's voice was laced with strain.

Rolling her eyes to herself, she grabbed the bedroll and pulled it until she could hardly see. Shang seemed satisfied, so she cleared away the rocks and laid the bedroll down on the hard ground.

He heaved Fen down onto it.

"You couldn't be a little gentler?" Fen groaned, squeezing her eyes in a wince.

Shang stood over her, a frown on his face. "Perhaps if you were lighter."

"Bah!" she spat halfheartedly. Her words were hardly discernable. "I'm sick of riding with you. I want my own horse."

"You are not ready for your own horse," Meiling said as she knelt next to the wounded warrior. "Soon, but not yet."

"You dare challenge me?" she slurred. "I'll fight you!"

"Yes." Meiling couldn't help her smile. "And for once, I think I could actually win."

A soft snort sounded from Shang just as he turned to retrieve their saddlebags.

"Phoenixes scorch you both," Fen muttered grumpily. Then she cringed and moved her hand toward her shoulder.

"Be still. Don't touch it. You'll be fine."

"It aches," she whimpered. "*Hurts*."

"I know. You're healing. Don't worry," Meiling said, tucking Fen's cloak around her both to warm her and to restrain her. "I know it hurts, but it will heal. Shh."

This had happened at various times over the past few days. Fen would grow aware of her surroundings, panic, whimper, and then fall back asleep. It always happened when they unloaded her, but sometimes it happened during the day while they rode. And when it did, it was the strangest thing to hear Shang try to soothe her with quiet, gentle words.

"I can't calm her," he had told her earlier that day after attempting to soothe Fen. "You're better at it than me."

Meiling had attempted to hide her blush as she led her horse close until she was leg to leg with him and leaned over to clasp Fen's hands and whisper to her. Shang watched her every movement, but she had mustered her strength of will and focused solely on Fen.

Now Fen was finally falling asleep. The puckered lines of her brow smoothed slowly until her breathing grew shallow and even. Her face was pretty in sleep, when it was not twisted in her wildcat snarl.

Footsteps crunched on the small rocks littering the cave floor behind her. Meiling looked up toward the fading light as Shang's tall frame silhouetted in the cave's opening.

"I collected enough brush and tinder to start a fire. You can light it while I get the rest of the things from the horses and settle them for the night," he said, dumping his armload on the ground next to her. He pulled something out of his pocket and handed it to her.

The tinderbox.

She nodded, even though she wasn't sure he could see it in the dark, and set to work.

Her fingers trembled a little as she arranged the fire and fumbled with the tinderbox for means to set the blaze. She let out a long stream of breath into the dank, cool air. She had to pause in the middle of striking the flint. Her arms . . . well, *all* of her was so weak.

But if Shang knew how exhausted she was, how weak she was, he would further overextend himself. He was already struggling.

They were all struggling.

Was it possible that they could still make it?

If they rode hard enough and if *mó guǐ* or brigands or rough terrain did not slow them, they could arrive by dusk tomorrow. They were so close, and yet so far. She wasn't sure if she was strong enough for another day.

Well, she would just *have* to be strong enough for another day. There was no other option. Not if there was to be hope for Fen's recovery. Not if there was hope that Shang would survive how hard he pushed his wounded body.

The fire crackled and spewed smoke into her face. She was coughing and waving away the smoke when Shang returned. He set down their sack of dried rice, a little pot, waterskins, the blanket, his cloak, and a few other things.

She expected him to sit, but after he deposited his load, he stood and turned to leave. He pulled a strip of leather—his sling—from his belt. It hung from his hand as he started walking away.

"Shang," Meiling called softly after him.

He stopped, shoulders braced, and tilted his head enough so she could see his glare. He said nothing. From this angle, the firelight did not betray how filthy and full of travel grime his garments were.

"We have enough rice. You don't need to hunt," she said.

"Not enough for tomorrow." His low voice reverberated through the cavern walls.

"We'll arrive tomorrow."

He let out a long, deep breath. That breath was enough to tell Meiling what went through his mind. It made her strength crumble and her shoulders sag even more. She fought to be unwavering in her determination, no matter how desperately hopelessness clawed at the inside of her ribs.

She pursed her lips and bit the insides of her cheek. "If we don't arrive, you can go hunting, then." She held her breath, hoping he would not continue arguing, hoping he would stop and rest.

He tilted his head forward, toward the mouth of the cave where the last reaches of dying sunlight shone. His fist clenched around the sling he held in his hand. Then, wordlessly, he turned and stalked back to the fire. He sat and leaned back against the wall of the cave, letting his eyes fall to where Fen lay nearby.

Meiling was already preparing the rice. She waited for the water to boil and opened the small, limp sack to peer inside.

"Is there enough?" he asked quietly.

She nodded and forced a reassuring smile. Once the rice was cooking, she fixed the sternest look she could muster on Shang, arms crossed and face firm. Another thing he'd been difficult about the last few days—allowing her to tend his wounds.

But tonight, he relented almost immediately.

"Fine," he said, shrugging out of his robes and unlacing his shirt with shaking fingers. They twisted together, caught, and fumbled with the ties. A low, guttural growl of frustration sounded in his throat.

Meiling pretended she didn't notice his struggles and set herself to stirring the rice with a stick from their fuel pile. She wanted to offer help, but he hated her help. Especially with things as basic as removing a shirt.

He gasped when the garment was loose enough, and she scooted closer to help him get it over his head. The exertion left his chest heaving against his bandages. She began the process of unbinding, cleaning, and rebinding, blinking every few seconds to clear her tired vision.

Sweat slicked his cold skin. Despite noble efforts, he flinched at her touch and pain flashed across his face when she ran a wet cloth over the slow-healing wounds. His muscles guarded against her, stiff and untrusting.

"Shang," she wanted to whisper, to plead gently. *"Relax. Trust me."*

But Shang didn't like being spoken to like a child. She needed another way to get his mind off the pain. She needed to distract him.

"You've had large ambitions," Meiling started.

"I *have* large ambitions," Shang corrected through gritted teeth. He twitched when a lock of her hair brushed his skin while she worked.

"You must have something specific that you are working toward. What appointment—?"

He didn't answer. Meiling looked up from his bandages to find that his eyes had shot to hers, his face surprisingly near.

"What appointment did I lose, you mean?" he said.

She swallowed, and couldn't decide if there was an accusation in his voice or not. If the sharpness was because of closely harbored bitterness, or because of the pain of her work. She met his scrutiny, her hands slowing to a stop. Whatever he saw in her face, she believed she saw more in his. She held back sharp words, pursed her lips tightly.

There *was* a bite to his words. Not as much as maybe there had been before, but it remained. Yet, she was almost certain the reason he brought this up now had nothing to do with his lost appointment, but rather because she, Princess Meiling, the cursed princess of Zheninghai, was seeing him at his lowest. His weakest. And he grappled for any defense, any advantage he could press.

What did he have against her, the girl whom he'd come to rely on so heavily these last few days? It wasn't her uselessness now.

It was the fact that they were here in the first place.

"The same," she said, refusing to take his bait.

Long minutes dragged by in the growing darkness of the cave. The fire burned brighter on her work when she was careful not to let her back block the flickering light. She untied the knot of another bandage and carefully removed it, biting back any hint of queasiness at the sight of the wound. She tried not to let out a breath of frustration as his judging eyes fixed on her work. Or her. She was not sure which was better. All she knew was that she was trying to do this as quickly and gently as possible so she could move back to the opposite side of the fire. Away from his determination to keep his defenses up against her.

"Military strategist."

Shang's echoing voice startled her enough to make her hands jump. She hoped he did not notice. His voice reverberated in the cavern, and it was not his cruel, dark voice. It was quiet, with a tinge of defeat.

"Why?" she asked, keeping her tone controlled.

He shrugged, but the tightening in his jaw betrayed the movement—a foolish one. "It would always be interesting, and I would devote my life to the protection and prosperity of the empire." Then his voice took on a different note. One almost . . . impassioned. "It would be important work. I'd build strength out of nothing. Take something weak and make it impenetrable."

She tied a knot on one of his bandages. A spasm jolted through his body.

"Careful," he growled.

"I'm *being* careful," she said softly, with a pointed glare at him. "There aren't many strategist positions open very often, are there?"

"There was only one when I graduated."

He'd gotten the appointment. She didn't have to ask; she could tell by the tone of his voice and the light in his eye. And now, it would probably be filled when he returned to Suguan.

Instead, she asked, "Do many people strive for such positions? I know the Emperor's Guard and territory guardians are very popular positions."

He scoffed. "No new graduate is being assigned the position of a guardian. Perhaps some foolishly think they'll be the first. I do not understand why anyone wants to be in the Emperor's Guard. It's only a position of honor, but how often does the Emperor's Guard do much beyond escorting His Imperial Majesty down the streets of Suguan for a festival? The strategist positions are few, and they are indeed competitive. Which discourages many people from applying. But the people who *do* apply are either completely disillusioned about their abilities or they are formidable opponents."

He was proud he'd received the appointment. She could see it in how he straightened his shoulders and back as he spoke the words, how he tried to hide the pain even more, how he tried to force his hands to stop trembling.

Part of her considered how easy it would be to slip in a small remark about how impressive it was that Shang had been appointed.

How easy it would be to stroke his ego. She might be impressed—she *was* impressed. But she refused to flatter him, to make him like her more. She wouldn't manipulate him.

His chest heaved with each breath. She tried to work quickly, but she also needed to be gentle. She currently tended his worst wound: a puncture between his ribs. Not deep, thankfully. But painful enough for him to cringe when she set to rebandaging it.

"Try to calm your breathing," Meiling said, bent over his torso. "I can't tie this properly."

His glare was withering. But his chest slowed its rapid swelling and contracting enough for her to fasten the bandage.

She asked another question. "When did you know you wanted to apply for the position?"

He was still glaring. She ignored him.

"When I was seven," he said. Then, more urgently, "The rice."

"Oh!" Meiling jumped to her feet, whirled, flustered that she had forgotten, and hurried to the pot to stir the food. She pulled the pot off the fire and set it on the ground to cool. She cast a sheepish look Shang's way. "I'm sorry that cooking is not one of my skills at the moment."

He did not respond.

Meiling scooted back to his side. "One more," she said, moving toward his burned shoulder.

He pulled back like a scared hound dog.

She let out a long exhale. "Shang. Please."

He shook his head, holding his hand over his shoulder. And then—he bit his lip. Subtly, but it was enough to betray him. She glanced from his face to his hand on his shoulder. Realization flooded.

She immediately pried his icing hand away from his shoulder. He growled and tried to protest, but she was too determined and pulled open the bandage. Her eyes widened, her mouth forming a little O. "Shang! It's infected! Why haven't you let me look at it? You've been riding for days with your shoulder this bad? What were you thinking?"

"Because you would flap around like a headless chicken if you saw it," he muttered. "There wasn't anything you could do. Not without the medical supplies in my saddlebags."

"Shang!"

"See? You're doing exactly what I said. Leave it alone. I'll get it treated when we arrive." He tried to swat her hands away, but she was insistent.

She firmly shook her head. "This is dangerous. You shouldn't be carrying Fen. We need to—"

He bolted upright, reached out in a flash, and caught her upper arm, dragging her closer to his scowl as she gasped. "We need to *what*? We need to get to the fortress. Now you know the full reality of the situation. It doesn't change that we need to get there. We may arrive in pieces, but by all the fathers and lights above, Meiling, we're going to make it!" He released his grip on her and fell back against the wall of the cave, as though all strength had fled him.

She crawled away, her arm aching where he had grabbed her. She wanted to bury her head in her hands and cry. But she swallowed the lump in her throat and looked down at her robes. With a burst of anger, she ripped a long strip from one of the inner layers, finding the cleanest part she could. The sound careened in the echoey space, loud and sudden.

Shang's eyes widened where he was sitting. She snatched up the strip of robe and planted herself next to him. It was not often that something fierce burned through her blood, but it burned now.

"We're making it whole, Tan Shangdi. Not in pieces," she growled, lifting his arm. "Now let me clean and rebind this." *You fool,* she wanted to add.

His brows raised in surprise, and perhaps that was a tinge of guilt shining in his eyes as he watched her work. She tied off the last knot and marched back to the pot to distribute their meager supper.

All was quiet, awkward silence, giving her time to wonder how exactly to distribute the rice without bowls or utensils of any kind.

It also gave her time to listen to her own words rattle around in her head.

In the end, she plopped the pot between her and Shang, reaching in and pulling out a piping hot bite of sticky mush. She ate without a word, her lungs burning as her limbs trembled. He scooped out bites after her, eating slowly and letting the food cool. Meiling just popped it in her mouth and let it burn.

His voice startled her. "What do you want to do with your life, Highness?"

He was asking about *her* life? After ignoring her for this entire journey as much as he could? After all his implicit accusations? And . . . everything else? Her fragile control broke into pieces.

"What do a cursed princess's life dreams mean to you?" she snapped harshly, angrily. "What does anything I want matter to you? Or to anyone?"

Her outburst caught up to her. She shut her mouth with a click. Her head swiveled to the side, away from Shang's perceptive gaze. Now *she* was the fool, expressing more of her true feelings than was wise.

"I was merely curious," he returned coolly.

She was weary of dueling with him. Too exhausted from the past few days, from the strain of their struggling journey and caring for the injuries of their party. She didn't want to keep fighting, didn't want to straddle this line between animosity and something like comradeship. It was so deeply draining.

She lifted her chin, giving a little sniff as though that would help her regain her control. When she spoke again, her voice was rank with bitterness. "The most I can hope for in this life is to find a powerful magic-wielder willing to marry me and pray I can redeem my shame through the bearing of powerful, magic-wielding children."

Silence hung suspended like moisture in the air, thick as a blanket, coating the lungs with each sucking breath.

She scooped another handful of hot rice and ate it vigorously to satiate her gnawing hunger. But it was not enough. It could not cure her limbs of their quaking.

"Is that what you want?" Shang's question was quiet.

Meiling forced a dismissive shrug. "I suppose."

"You're not usually one for lies, my princess."

Something like a knife stabbed her chest. The sticky rice lodged in her throat. She almost choked as she swallowed. An unbearable urge nearly overwhelmed her to draw her knees to her chest, plant her face against them, and release a torrent of weeping. She grabbed a waterskin and gulped down water, trying to hide her emotion.

He saw it all. She knew he did. She dared not look at him, dared not meet those cold eyes as he analyzed her weaknesses.

"I'm tired," she whispered, almost choking again.

Quiet. Then, in a voice that was so soft it almost sounded like a plea, he spoke.

"*Meiling.*"

That was it. She couldn't control it anymore. The tears came, bursting like rivers down her face. She pressed the heel of her hand into her eye, trying and failing to staunch the insistent sobs.

"I'm sorry," she gasped, unable to look at him. "I'm just tired. I can't . . . I can't argue with you tonight."

She pulled her cloak tightly around her shoulders and got to her knees.

His hand darted out, catching her forearm. "Meiling," he said, much sterner this time. "Come here. Please."

Her shoulders drooped as she covered her face with her hands. As if that could hide her tears from him. "No, I don't *want* to talk anymore! Just leave me al—"

Even while he was injured, her strength was no match for his. He drew her to his side, ignoring her whimpering protests.

"You don't have to talk," he said. And then his hand was on the back of her head, pulling her close.

For a wild instant, her eyes dropped to his lips, her tears freezing their descent down her cheeks. But he didn't pull her in for a kiss. No, he drew her gently against his bare chest, letting her head rest against his heart. His arm wrapped around her, his hand reaching up to tuck the hair falling in her face behind her ear.

That was when her tears burst anew. She curled into him tighter and sobbed.

"It's alright," he whispered, leaning down so his mouth hovered just above her forehead. "Sweet Meiling, it's alright."

Sweet Meiling?

Why did he call her that? Why was he comforting her at all when it was his fault she was crying in the first place? There was nothing to be done but let the tears flow faster, releasing her pent-up anger and fear.

His voice took on a raw edge as his fingers trailed up and down her back, catching in her hair. "I'm sorry. I'm so sorry."

"I'm trying," she gasped. "But it's never enough. I can't make you and Fen stop hating me. And now we might die in this wilderness."

He let out a soft groan, though she wasn't sure if it was from his wounds or her words. He twisted toward her, his other arm coming around her. The muscles of his abdomen flinched in pain, but he pressed her tightly against him and leaned his head on hers. His heart thudded against her wet cheek, speeding up with every fast inhale.

"I don't hate you," he said, his voice almost pained. "And I will *not* let you die."

A gasp of relief gusted out of her lungs, a sob dying in her throat. He didn't hate her. *He didn't hate her.* She shuddered, feeling small in his arms . . . and so *safe*. She buried her hot face against him and drew in one deep breath after another.

"We will make it," he whispered.

Then he slumped, falling back against the wall of the cave, one of his arms slipping away as he groaned again. The other arm, however, remained wrapped around her, keeping her pressed to his side.

She sniffled. Blinked damp eyelashes and drew in a shivering breath, peering up at him. Slowly, she pried her hand off his chest, scooting to get her feet under her. But his arm tightened in response, his head dropping to lie against hers. Her cheeks flamed.

His eyes were closed when he whispered, "Please stay. Your nearness is . . . soothing."

Her lips parted, a flush spreading down her neck. She couldn't find her voice. She just swallowed thickly, then laid her head back down on his chest and tried to calm her racing heart.

A satisfied sigh stirred her hair.

CHAPTER 28

IT TOOK HER longer than normal to fall asleep, what with being held in the arms of a warrior, her cheek brushing against bandages and his words echoing around in her head.

Sweet Meiling. I don't hate you.

Her whole body rose and fell with each of Shang's breaths. They grew even, shallow, and when she peered up at him from beneath crusty lashes, his eyes were closed, his mouth opened slightly.

Finally, her own exhaustion won, and she drifted into slumber. Her spirit rose out of her body, and for a long moment, she couldn't help but stare at herself asleep on Shang with his arm around her. His long legs sprawled out, his back leaning against the slanted wall of the cave, with one hand resting on his bare abdomen. She curled into his side, so small compared to him, even with how trim he was. Her head lay above his heart, her long hair covering most of her face and falling to pool on the floor.

He wanted her there. Close to him. Which seemed completely incongruous with the cold indifference he'd given her this entire journey.

She shook herself.

They were exhausted, pushing themselves to the ragged edges of endurance, and if they were both more impulsive than normal, that didn't mean he truly cared for her. It wouldn't make up for the fact that he would bring her to Liafugen and leave her there, possibly to never see her again.

She needed to focus.

While physical exhaustion didn't drag her spirit, emotional weariness however . . . that was a toll she carried with her, no matter how far from her body she flew. She flitted away from the three slumbering bodies to the mouth of the cave. Their horses were tethered just outside, sleeping peacefully on their feet.

Moonlight poured like liquid silver over the vast countryside. Meiling's heart ached at the darkness, the shadowy landscape of her kingdom, the stars blinking and whispering above. It was probably her imagination, but the whispers seemed louder tonight. Almost as if she reached high enough, if everything else was silent in the world unfurling below her, she could discern the words they spoke.

Except . . .

It was a different language. Meiling somehow instinctually knew it. Still hovering by the mouth of the cave, still floating just beyond the reaches of the campfire's flickering flames, she reached up a tendril of shadow that might have been a hand. Reached high, toward the stars.

She had not told Shang what she wanted. When she was no more than a spirit tethered to a weak, frail body, she was so close to what she wanted. It was like trying to grasp hold of something with short fingernails—it bit into the pads of her fingertips, tasted so close on her tongue—but she could not catch hold. It was agonizing and frustrating and hopeless.

But Meiling's life had no time for dreams save those she lived at night. She had no use for the treasures she clutched to her spirit-heart. No use, except save one crucial purpose that no one else knew. She looked down to find that her hands glowed with imaginary, glittering diamonds. She held them close. Moonlight reflected off their cut facets, but the true brilliance of these gemstones came from the light shining in the center of each.

Her dreams. She held them for one sole, terrifying purpose.

To not lose herself.

To not let herself be swallowed up in failure that was not hers, in disgrace shoved upon her from birth, to not be devoured by despair at the life ahead of her. Even now, she fought the temptation to pluck each one up and snuff out its light between her fingers. To give in to the madness.

She wasn't thinking straight. She was too weighted down by the disaster of this journey, for it truly had been a disaster in every sense of the word since the moment they took that one fateful step out of the palace gates and into the wild country beyond.

There was nothing to do but set aside these feelings, the overwhelm surrounding her, and attend to her duty.

Meiling left the cave and began her guard. She hunted for anything glowing in the forest. Brigands, *mó guǐ*, anything.

Their luck had been too fortunate for the past two days. Weakened, slowed—yet they encountered no contest to their travel. Even at night, when she scoped out the area, she had seen nothing. Not even the distant burning of a phoenix on the horizon.

Somehow, she just knew tonight would be different.

Her soul lurched when she spotted a glowing through the trees. Dread knotted tight in her stomach. She sped toward the glowing until she was close enough to discern three separate glows. A fiery orange glow, a dull, bluish-gray glow, and a mesmerizing glow of flickering rainbows.

Heaviness sank like a rock through her soul. *The brigands.* They were so close. Within a few li of where they now slept, bone-weary and vulnerable. Did the brigands know how close they were?

Worse than finding them, however, was the slicing realization that followed.

The healer wasn't with them.

Had they . . . *killed* her?

That seemed a foolish move. Whatever drove these brigands, she couldn't be *that* foolhardy, right? No matter how stubborn the healer might have been.

She must assume the healer was somewhere else. Rescued, perhaps?

She flitted closer, slowly, still afraid that by some work of dark magic they could see her. Hadn't Fen said their magic felt strange? Even as Meiling studied the glows emanating from the three bodies, she couldn't help but agree. It was almost as if the glows *sounded* wrong. As though the light was . . . *dissonant*.

Two brigands slept in the clearing, next to a dead fire. They slept on the ground, bundled up in their cloaks. If their souls had not glowed, Meiling never could have found them in this darkness unless she had carefully combed every inch of land along her soul tether. The third brigand—the wind-wielder—sat awake to guard the camp.

She floated into the camp, staying high above to avoid any unnatural perception on their part. From this vantage point, they hardly seemed any different from Fen and Shang sleeping in the cave. But they did not look wounded. In fact, the terrifying wound Shang had dealt the illusionist seemed mysteriously healed.

Shouldn't they be stalking, lying in wait, and then pouncing upon them while Meiling and her protectors slept soundly? Perhaps they didn't know their quarry was so close.

She needed to know for certain.

If they knew where they were, she would need to rush back, wake Shang, and they would have to leave.

She kicked herself for not killing the fire before she had gone to sleep. The smoke could give them away easily. Yet more proof she had not been raised a warrior.

But Shang had not done it either.

If the brigands didn't know, then perhaps Meiling could watch them all night and wake Shang early in the morning—after a night of much needed, uninterrupted sleep—to flee.

Taking a deep breath, she plunged into the mind of the slumbering illusionist.

And was immediately overwhelmed.

Flickers of the mindscape she had last seen in this mind burst in her view. She caught glimpses of that vivid garden, blackened by night, with diamonds sparkling in the sky overhead and a moon that glowed nearly as brightly as the sun, yet without making it seem any less like midnight.

Mingled with those glimpses were flashes of other things. When she focused, when she let her straining mind go, there were splotches of a deeply dark cave. One very different from the cave she now slept inside. It was so hard to tell with the tiny snatches, but this cave seemed truly terrifying. It felt like . . . death.

This mind always peeled back layers of reality, and one minute she saw the illusion of the beautiful, moonlit garden, and then the next instant part of it was stripped back to reveal the cave. Then there were parts pasted in front of the garden. Moving parts—not scenes.

Running people. They were shadows, sometimes dark and sometimes bright with flashes of faces and clothes and limbs. Some laughed, some cried, and others opened wide black mouths and screamed. One shadow pricked her awareness as familiar, vaguely familiar. How she picked it out of the crowding shadows, she had no idea.

But she snagged on to that bit of familiarity in this wildness and ran after it. She chased after it, into the garden, deeper into the dark cave, through throngs of screaming and laughing shades that tried to pluck at her awareness.

Come back to me! she cried, suddenly afraid to lose herself in this mind. The shadow turned, looked at her, and then kept running.

Follow me, the shadow responded.

A girl's voice. A *familiar* girl's voice.

One minute, Meiling was bursting through a picket gate, down a flagstone path, through a winding terrace of climbing, reaching, thorny roses. The next, almost nothing was visible in that swallowing, devouring darkness dripping with something wet.

Blood.

If she'd had a physical body in this mind, something wet might have splattered up her legs as she ran barefoot through thick liquid. Jagged rocks would have pierced the soft skin of her royal feet, and her blood would have mingled.

Then she was in both places. Something else flashed in front of her, something so bright it almost blinded her into madness. Was that . . .? She didn't know. But it flashed again, closer, this time brighter than before. It broke through the illusion of a willow. Or did it press itself on top of the willow? She tried to catch a good glimpse before it was gone.

Was it . . . the palace?

Her home?

Bizarre images and scenes popped up randomly, seeming somewhat interconnected with each other, but too quickly for her to comprehend. The shadows followed the scenes, moving and repeating and shifting.

Was he dreaming?

The shadow girl ran nearly beyond her reach. Meiling chased faster, feeling like she should be gasping for air, even though she had no physicality here.

Here. The shadow girl stopped and looked back. Her face was visible for only an instant. But that face burned in Meiling's memory. A young, beautiful face, with eyes like a midnight sky full of glittering stars. A determined brow, a jaw set to fight.

The healer.

Feiyan, Meiling whispered.

This is where he keeps his memories, she responded, pointing with one flickering, fading hand.

Meiling followed her gesture.

It was a canyon. Full of mist and shadows, flashes of light and darkness. It cut wider and deeper than she could tell from where she stood. The jutting canyon walls glowed red, orange, and dusty brown in the half-light between night and dawn. Something like a sun shone behind heavy clouds, illuminating the seeping mist. It stretched for li upon li, as far as she could see.

Are you one of his memories? Meiling asked.

The shadow girl did not answer. *Don't talk too much. He'll hear you and wake up. He'll know what is happening. Go into the canyon and find what you're looking for.*

Then the girl vanished.

Having no other choice, she flew over the edge of the canyon and plunged into the depths of the mist.

CHAPTER 29

MADNESS SWALLOWED HER in one huge gulp.

The mist surrounded her, suffocating and clenching around her spirit form. She should not feel it, since she had no physical form. But this was not a physical place. This was a wild, dangerous mind.

She flew toward the bottom, searching for a sign of—

Something writhed. Not one thing—*many things*. Sleek bodies coiled in constant motion. The fog lifted just as she got close enough to see . . .

Snakes covered the ground. Slithering, lisping, fanged snakes.

Meiling screamed, banking upward just as several snakes struck into the air at her shouldn't-be-real-body. A cry caught in her throat and, as if responding to her own nightmares, the mist faded, and movement stretched for hundreds of li in either direction. Snakes of all shapes and sizes and colors. Some were as thick as her waist, while others were hardly longer than her hand.

But then they shifted, and they were spiders. Huge, crawling, carnivorous spiders. The mist surrounding her was no longer mist, but silky, sticky, grasping spider web. It latched hold of her struggling limbs, pinning them in place until she couldn't move. She fought, pulled, but the more she resisted, the more the spider web caught hold of what shouldn't be real, until she was being bound up in a cocoon of webbing.

Spiders started crawling upward toward her.

Meiling screamed.

It's not real. It's not real, she told herself.

She was only spirit. She had no physical body they could harm. But these were not physical spiders. Did that mean they could kill her? Could the snakes—did she see snakes slithering between the skittering, amassing spiders?—be as venomous to her soul as her body?

It did not matter. The webs were *not real.* Perhaps she could be hurt, but she could not be confined. She could not be captured.

With a scream of determination, she forced her mind, forced this *world* to bend to what she knew to be true.

She tore free of the bindings, shooting upward in the mist. But as she flew higher, the ground shifted below yet again. Peeling back layer after layer, flickers of weak and strong illusions, all fighting for ascendancy.

Meiling squeezed her eyes shut. Darkness filled her vision. Blessed, uncomplicated, unshifting darkness. Her spirit heaved as though she ran for her life, terror shaping every thought. Nothing was solid here, nothing was truly real. How far would she need to go to discover what was real?

She kept her eyes shut until she could calm her frantic heart and her raging fears.

Her own mind was safer than any other. She needed to stop trying to understand what was happening in this mind. She just needed to find his memories. Specific memories.

She opened her eyes.

The canyon had shifted once more. Snow fell from the sky, flickering into fire . . . then rain . . . then arrows. The walls moved. They had been moving this entire time. Growing, shrinking, pressing in and out.

Was it . . . destroying memories?

With the boundaries of the canyon always shifting, did it crush into oblivion the memories that lingered on the edge?

It did not matter. She wasn't going to figure it out. There was no understanding the illusions threatening to overwhelm her. She wouldn't let the way that the canyon flickered back into a cave, then a garden, scare her.

There had to be something true here. Something that would guide her. This was someone's mind, after all. Not a monster's. A human's.

If a human's thoughts were incohesive and shrouded in lies and laced with deception, surely there was something else . . .

Meiling closed her eyes again. Darkness.

There.

Hovering above the illusion of the deadly canyon with her vision cut off, something pulsed against her awareness. *Emotions.*

How had she missed them before? They throbbed with such deep life and love, heartbreak and pain and sorrow. Emotions radiated and called to her from the canyon below. Emotions so strong, her heart might break with their burden.

She chose an emotion.

Or, perhaps more aptly, an emotion chose her. Meiling wanted to sit and think and try to imagine what emotion might lead her to the information she needed, but there was no way she could guess. He could have been happy or sad or frustrated or anything when they camped for the night. Was there a way to access recent memories?

It did not matter.

The strongest emotion grabbed hold of her and pulled her at a dizzying speed down into the canyon, into the mist that wasn't mist.

Sorrow.

Meiling felt it before she saw it. Suddenly, she was a little girl—

Meiling sat in a dark cave. Thin little arms wrapped around her dirty, grimy body. Confusion beat through her heart. It was so dark, but Ma had said to wait here. So she did. She waited for her ma to come back. It had been a very long time.

But she waited patiently.

Ma and Pa had gone into the back of the cave. She did not know why. She looked back the way they had come, hoping to see a sliver of light in the darkness. But there was no light.

She waited and waited.

Something wet ran into her feet. Water? It seemed warm for water. She touched it with her finger. It was sticky.

Ma had said to wait.

So she waited, even as the sticky, warm liquid pooled around her where she sat. She waited, and she thought about butterflies. Butterflies were beautiful.

They never came back for her.

Meiling gasped, suddenly freed of the memory. Her heart cried even as her mind wrestled with comprehending this memory. It felt so real, so like her own.

This was a frequently accessed and also frequently suppressed memory. How Meiling knew that, she had no idea. It was a memory with memories, linked to even more memories. Grief, coping, wrestling. Strings like spider silk linked this memory to countless others, threatening to drag her through their ranks.

She was never going to find what she looked for in this mind. Not in a timely manner.

She might lose her sanity and her heart might break into a thousand pieces if she stayed to rifle these memories. If she continued to *relive* these memories as he had experienced them.

She fled upward, desperate to be free. Into the clouds, the moonlight, into the tree branches, through the top of that cave—

Meiling spilled out of his mind, reeling with shock and horror.

It was dark. It was night. Overhead, stars shone. They were speckling dots of light surrounding the moon. Evergreens stood tall around her. The three brigands lay below her, two asleep and one awake.

She crumpled into a pile of shuddering spirit on the ground. Already, the things she had seen in his mind began slipping away, so much of it too strange for her to describe with words. While he slept, he looked so . . . *normal.* Except for his pulsing rainbow glow, he looked like the fire-wielder next to him, or even Shang. He was just a man.

How did a man possess such a mind? How did he feel so deeply? How could he function while his mind stirred with madness?

Meiling would have to enter a different mind. The wind-wielder was still awake, still standing guard.

Which would be better? A sleeping, dreaming mind? Or an awake, alert mind?

It was riskier, but she decided an awake mind would be simpler. Slogging through one mindful of crumbling dreams was enough.

She didn't *want* to. She wanted to hide, to find some time and space to be alone and process what she had experienced in the illusionist's mind.

But she didn't have time. She slipped into the wind-wielder's mind.

She stood in the middle of a busy, bustling village. Women in colorful robes laughed as they walked by with baskets of food and jars of water. Children darted in between them, tripping and squealing. Men went about various tasks of varying importance. Down the street were two magic-wielders. They wore the typical village patrol uniforms and badges on their belts. Wardens.

It was so loud.

Meiling strained, but the wind-wielder's thoughts were lost in the cacophony of the village.

Shut up!

The order came booming from overhead, but the people didn't seem to hear. Instead, a huge gust of wind billowed through the village, making the people brace themselves. As soon as it passed, they returned to their business, quieter than before.

Their faces weren't clear. When she tried to focus her gaze on any one person, they grew fuzzier. If she looked at the entire village, however, the people turned clear and solid.

Find the memories. It was so easy to get distracted. But she needed to focus. Needed to know if the brigands knew where they were. She floated down the street, uncertain and confused. The further she went, the louder the people grew, and the longer the village stretched out before her. Her brain turned muddled, once again overwhelmed.

One mind was not made to comprehend another.

On impulse, she floated up the steps to the front door of a thatched house. Not knowing what else to do, she peered into the open doorway.

Light met her gaze. Not the expected darkness of a dimly illuminated hut.

And there was the wind-wielder, kneeling before a tall man in a dark cloak. His robes were much finer than the wind-wielder's, black and well-tailored to suit his tall frame. He struck Meiling as similar in age to her father, but the furs he wore around his shoulders and the tight braids lining his scalp were very different. He mumbled words in a foreign language—a language she was shocked to recognize, if not understand. It was the tongue of Butagin. He directed these words at a burly soldier beside him wearing heavy pelts to ward off cold.

Then he shifted his attention to the wind-wielder and the two other brigands kneeling on either side of her. The illusionist and the fire-wielder. He switched languages to Meiling's familiar tongue.

"Be swift, my friends. Every minute you are gone is a minute that delays our freedom. Complete my collection of wielders with the healer, the guardian, and the princess. The empire of Zheninghai has ruled

long enough on the blood and tears of the weak. It's time to show them what true magic and true power are."

Meiling clung to the doorframe. She tried to get a good glimpse of the tall man, but the closer she looked at him, the blurrier he became. This woman remembered impressions, then, not details.

This had the feeling of a recent memory.

She fled away from it. Despite her fear, her mind struggled to understand this dream, to understand how she might find what she needed. She floated again amid the street, people wafting like specters past her.

There had to be a faster way than flitting door to door. How did she recall information and memories to her own mind? The din of the village grew louder again. Meiling almost screamed in frustration for them to be quiet so she could think.

But that would betray her presence in this mind.

She closed her eyes, trying to calm her frenzied spirit. She pictured moonlight, the stars above her, and the tension eased slightly. Could she use her own thoughts to direct this mind to show her what she wanted?

Phoenixes scorch complicated minds! Dragons eat unorganized thoughts!

It would be far easier to access Shang's memories.

An undercurrent of anxiety blew by on a gust of wind, toppling baskets of food and blowing children's hats away. Meiling froze as the stench of smoke wafted past her. *She could smell here.* It was a startling realization that only served to discombobulate her further.

Then—an audible thought: *They must be nearby. We have to find them. If she gets to that fortress first . . .*

The wind grew stronger, washing away the anxiety with determination. The determination smelled like strong, cold iron.

We'll get them.

That was it. That was what Meiling had been hunting for.

The brigands did not know where they were. They knew they were close and where they were going, but they didn't know their exact location.

She whirled upward, out of that mind, then stared down at the three figures below her. Even a few minutes inside a mind betrayed much about a person. Her gaze lingered on the one brigand whose mind she had not braved.

The fire-wielder. The one with the burning red eyes. Perhaps another time she would have that . . . *pleasure*.

She fled back to the cave.

CHAPTER 30

SHOULD SHE WAKE Shang and Fen?

They could get a head start on the brigands. Maybe it would give them the one sliver of advantage they needed against their foes. Meiling ducked into the cave's entrance, flying toward the light of the dying fire and the three slumbering figures around it.

She jolted involuntarily, the image of her and Shang sleeping bringing back a rush of memories. His gentle words, warm touch. Calling her *sweet Meiling.* Things that she didn't have time to process right now.

She returned to her body.

It took everything to suppress her groan and peel her salt-crusted eyelids open. What had been a blessedly painless existence only a second ago was now an awareness full of aching and blurry vision.

Carefully, to not rouse Shang, she lifted her head from his chest and disentangled herself from his arm. She shivered, pulling her cloak tighter around her shoulders and getting to her feet. She hadn't expected to feel so bereft.

But that wasn't important right now.

She grabbed her waterskin and poured a stream of water on the fire to snuff it. With its last embers dead, the cave plunged into pitch darkness. She shuddered, searching with wide eyes, but even the prick of moonlight from the cave's opening wasn't enough. Half-awake and half dead, she crawled on hands and knees to Shang's side, hoping she wouldn't accidentally bump into him in the process.

His face was turned so she could barely see it. His brow had smoothed, the tension finally gone from his body. He slept soundly, sweetly, soaking up the rest he so desperately needed.

Meiling's tongue caught in her mouth. Her hand hovered over his arm, ready to gently rouse him. But his face . . .

She couldn't do it.

Her hand fell back to her side.

He would hate her for this. He would get up, sling Fen over his infected shoulder, and drag them to die of injuries and exhaustion mere hours from their destination.

More than anything right now, they all needed sleep.

Brigands or no brigands, they could not outrun anyone in their current state. They would have a better chance after a few hours of rest. Shang would kill her in the morning.

But he would only have the strength to do so because she let him sleep.

She, on the other hand, had nothing left. She crumpled to the floor where she was, by Shang's knees, and immediately fell asleep again.

"Wake up," she whispered.

Shang's lids fluttered. His mouth opened. She clamped both her hands down over it. His eyes widened, then narrowed. One hand came up and grabbed her wrist, about to wrench her grip away.

"Brigands," she said, her voice barely audible. "They're near."

Shang's eyes widened again. He pulled her hands away from his mouth, and was immediately captain of their group again, drawing himself to his feet with hardly a grimace. "How close?"

"A few li, would be my guess," Meiling said. "But I'm not good at estimating. They're in the forest. They don't know where we are, but they do know we're going to Liafugen."

"Are they searching for us?"

"They're asleep."

"Do we have time to pack up?"

"I . . . already did. We only need to get Fen up."

Shang blinked. He cast a look around the campsite, over at Fen's sleeping body. His gaze shifted back to Meiling, lips parting. He swallowed and turned away from her, clearing his throat softly. "You should have woken me sooner. I would have helped."

It was still dark, but she could have sworn his ears flushed red. Was he remembering last night?

"It was just packing things in bags," Meiling said briskly, hoping his mind was still too sleep-fogged to notice the weariness in her tone. "We need your strength for things like lifting Fen."

He knelt beside Fen, frowning. "How do you know that they know our destination?"

"I went into their minds last night." She couldn't help her shudder and how her head shook from side to side. "Terrible minds. Yours is so much cleaner."

He blinked in surprise, raising an eyebrow, pausing with his hand on Fen's shoulder. He opened his mouth, then closed it. "I suppose I am flattered."

Meiling blushed, feeling suddenly foolish.

But Shang did not seem to notice, preoccupied with trying to lift Fen.

Within a few minutes, they were mounted up and riding again, the sky still dark with night. Meiling directed them silently, giving a wide berth around the area where the brigands slept. Fen moaned softly, and Shang clamped a frantic hand over her mouth. She wriggled in his arms in response, brow furrowing tightly.

Would this be enough of an advantage to ensure their safe arrival at the fortress today? The wind-wielder seemed to believe that stealing her out of the fortress would be nigh impossible, which was very encouraging at least.

Once they were there, they'd be safe.

Once they were an hour or two past the brigands' campsite, Shang spoke, tilting around Fen's lolling, groaning head. "Did you learn anything else in the brigands' minds?"

They rode side by side now. His hair was a mess, several days' growth of stubble on his jaw, but instead of making him appear haggard, it made him seem harder. More dangerous. He eyed Meiling with a sidelong glance.

"I did," she said softly, her brow wrinkling as she tried to form cohesive thought from what she had seen. "It was so strange. The illusionist's mind . . . It was illusion upon illusion and if it hadn't been for Feiyan, I wouldn't have found his memories at all."

Shang looked at her with something between awe, terror, and complete bewilderment. "The healer?"

Meiling shook her head, pressing her fist to the space between her eyes, squeezing her eyes shut. Those images played out before her memory, of Feiyan's running, flickering shadow. How could she describe it? "I think she was a memory . . ."

"What?"

"I think her memory betrayed him," Meiling said with a wince. Her mind constricted tightly, painfully. She shook her head again. "The illusionist's mind . . . I didn't end up finding much of importance there. It was too confusing."

He nodded hesitantly.

"I found something in the wind-wielder's mind, however. It was a memory of their leader. He spoke the native tongue of Butagin. He was tall and . . . very fuzzy. All of them—everything was fuzzy. But he mentioned the healer . . . and me."

"You?" Shang's face darkened, his arm tightening around Fen's waist.

"I assume he meant me. Considering that the brigands are now hunting me and not my sister, that I am aware." The thought of little Hou being hunted made Meiling's heart clench. "He said to find the princess to add . . ." Her voice trailed off. It was almost too strange to say. But Shang's eyes bored a hole through the side of her face, and she had to finish, even if she didn't want to. ". . . to add to his collection of wielders."

She peeked at Shang.

He faced forward, light blazing from his black eyes. His jaw worked.

"You know what is going on, don't you?" she said. "From your . . . independent research?"

He acknowledged her question with one brief sidelong glance.

"You know who the man was. You know why he wants me."

"The man is likely Fang Zedong," Shang said coldly. "Magic-wielders have been disappearing from across the empire. Vanishing from their posts and appointments without a trace."

"What?" Meiling breathed. "How do you know this? How does no one else know this?"

"Some people know, but not many. It's been a secret for years now as the emperor's spies try to uncover the truth." He shifted Fen in his arms and pain flashed across his face. "Fang is the one behind the amassing armies of barbarians in the north. There's long been a suspicion that he is behind these disappearances, even though no one could prove it. Some thought the disappearing wielders were defectors." He tossed her a dry look. "These abductions might suggest otherwise. Nothing is certain, but there are rumors he has learned by some dark magic how to harness other wielders' powers against their will." His voice lowered, and he glanced up at the foliage arching above them. "It is also rumored that he can . . . *enhance* their powers."

"Like the brigands," she breathed. "That's what Fen was talking about."

"Fen didn't know what she was talking about. But yes, that is what she noticed."

Meiling paused, her mind working through the implications behind his words. Suddenly, she looked up. "You knew . . . from the beginning. Or, at least, from the inn. Who was pursuing us. That was why you were so suspicious of me." Her horse's hoof caught on a rock and slid slightly beneath her. The air fled her lungs, her heart lurching as she caught the reins harder. "How do you know all this?"

He gave her another sidelong glance. "I make it a point to understand the dangers my country faces."

That wasn't an answer.

"Your mother . . ." he started, then stopped.

Meiling whirled. "What about my mother? What does she have to do with anything?"

His black eyes met hers. "Rumor has it that she was *friends* with this Fang Zedong while he was at the Academy."

The way he said *friends* made something dark as night slide down her spine. For the first time, a deep seated fear squelched her curiosity. She didn't want to know what he meant. In fact, she would rather know just about anything else in the world.

Had there been someone before Pa? If so, why had he defected from the Academy?

It seemed impossible that someone as good and kind as Ma could have any connection to an Academy deserter, much less one who currently worked to capture magic-wielders. There was a story here—one she didn't know.

However the dynamic had played out, it hadn't just been Ma and Pa. There had been someone else.

This Fang Zedong.

"She tells Security her visions, you know," Shang continued. "I don't know if she tells all, but she tells many. Good and bad."

"Why?" The words slipped out of her mouth unbidden. "That is . . . if they are glimpses of the future, then what would be the purpose of sharing? If it's going to happen, anyway?"

"Not all visions tell the future. Sometimes they are warnings. Things that *could* happen."

"How do you know the difference?" she asked.

He shrugged his good shoulder. "A high magic seer can tell."

But Ma was a low magic seer. Why did Meiling feel the anger rising in her breast at the thought of her mother being a low magic-wielder? Why did it bother her?

Because Ma was not defined by her magical abilities. To classify her as a low magic-wielder was to lock her in a cage she did not belong in.

"How does Fang Zedong know of my magic?" she asked. "No one knows except me and my parents. And now you and Fen."

"Two of the missing wielders are high seers. He might have used them to discover the wielders he wanted to capture. You could have been one of them." Shang kicked his horse faster up a steep incline.

She followed, leaning forward in the saddle to keep from falling backwards off the horse. "But *why*?"

"He's building an army."

Her breath came faster. "But . . . but Zheninghai is the largest empire in the world. Butagin cannot compare in strength. How could . . .?"

Shang's hand fisted tighter around the reins. "That seems to be where *you* fit in."

Her? What advantage could she give Butagin over Zheninghai? Capturing the healer was obvious—no one else could heal with a touch like she could. She'd be a valuable asset in a war. But Meiling?

Fen interrupted her thoughts with a moan. "Idiots." She slurred the word, making it sound more like *iduts*. "May your souls burn in *diyu*. May you get lost in labyrinths for all eternity!"

"Harsh curses for your saviors," Shang muttered.

"May phoenixes rend your soul!" she shouted, suddenly lurching forward in the saddle.

Shang caught her, wrapping his arms around her torso to restrain her as her head thrashed, trying to bash into his. "Hush, Fen. Hush, hush."

She fought harder, and even in her weakened state, she was surprisingly strong. Not stronger than Shang, but enough to make him struggle to keep her in the saddle.

"Meiling," he called, glancing back at her. "Calm her!"

She hurried forward, sidling along Shang's horse. "Shh," she soothed, reached out for one of Fen's hands. Fen yanked against her touch and moaned at the pain.

Then her eyes burst wide, unseeing, and she screamed.

That scream echoed into the forest, bouncing off the eastward rockface and footholds of the mountains. Silence descended on the trees around them. Winding, swallowing all noise. Like the silence of death, of the terror before death.

Fen slumped back against Shang's arms. He turned horrified eyes to Meiling even as dread and terror roiled in her gut.

"Maybe . . . the brigands didn't hear," she whispered.

Shang looked at her. Hopelessness writhing in his gaze.

She felt faint suddenly.

"Hurry!" Shang leaned forward, holding a now-limp Fen close, and kicked his horse into a gallop.

Meiling raced after him.

Dread filled her from head to toe. Any moment, she imagined the brigands to come bursting out in front of them, flinging incinerating fireballs and sucking the air out of their lungs. And that illusionist . . . Meiling shuddered again at the memory of his mind.

What was someone with that sort of mind capable of?

Something blue glittered in front of them.

Shang dragged his horse to a staggering halt, and Meiling went shooting past him, unable to control her horse like him.

"Meiling!" he cried.

She was finally able to stop. Right in front of a large, glittering dragon.

Its eyes glittered like multifaceted jewels, and it cocked its head to stare down at her, its reptilian body moving with deadly grace. It flapped waxy wings, spreading them wide and high. It opened its mouth. There was light—fire—building at the back of its throat.

"Meiling!" Shang snatched Bik's bridle and pulled them out of the way as the blast flew wide.

The dragon shrieked and flew into the air, circling and aiming.

Shang quickly gathered himself, whipping a *jiaun* from his saddle and slamming two arrows into it. He glanced down at Fen frantically, then at Meiling, then at the dragon overhead.

"It's scared of us!" Meiling shouted, tugging at him. "We need to run!"

"It'll pursue!"

The dragon wheeled and twisted in the air, charging straight for her. It opened its gaping, fanged mouth.

Shang tried to grab her, but she leaned down and spurred her horse into a gallop, barely dodging the burst of flame. Bik whinnied, tossing his head as a wave of heat washed over them. But Meiling didn't slow, and soon Shang was galloping beside her. He leaned close to his horse's neck, keeping Fen close as he gripped his loaded *jiaun* in his other hand.

They rode hard. Shang frequently looked back to see if the dragon pursued them. Meiling focused on riding. It wouldn't come after them.

They could not sustain travel at this pace.

Too soon, they were forced to slow. Her heart hammered in her throat. Shang looked wild, overcome by his warrior instinct. He glanced down at Fen in his arms.

She would be the death of them.

Shang gasped heavily and lifted his hand to briefly touch his injured shoulder. Suddenly, he seemed more exhausted than ever. How was he standing the pain?

How could they make it?

They had to make it. They *would* make it.

Any minute, the brigands could descend upon them. Any minute, a *mó guǐ* they could not fight could emerge from the depths of the forest. Every shadow, sound, and slight disturbance sent Meiling's blood surging through her veins.

For hours, they rode in silence, nerves jumpy. The moment a branch cracked, Shang whirled with a fist full of ice. Once, he glanced at Meiling. There was too much in those eyes. He was stretched almost to the breaking point, but he would get them to the fortress if it killed him. This was his duty, after all.

His life was forfeit if he failed.

They could not fail. They would make it.

Each minute was an hour. Each hour was a decade. Time dripped by like thick blood in between their fingers. Agonizingly slow.

"We're almost there," Shang whispered suddenly.

Meiling looked up just as they emerged from the forest.

Ahead, on the crest of a hill far away, but still within view, stood a tall, proud, mighty fortress. Its walls were strong, its towers high. Their beloved flag flew from each tower, brilliant crimson waving in the wind.

Meiling gasped. A bubbling, desperate laugh escaped her lips. "We've made it!"

His eyes narrowed. "Not quite yet."

In front of them stretched a lush, green valley. A deep chasm cut through the center of the valley, with a long bridge stretching over it to a road that lead up the hill to the fortress.

"Just a few more hours," Shang mumbled. Relief lined his face, but it was hesitant, unlike hers.

"I can't believe . . . I can't believe we've almost made it. Shang, it's so close!" Meiling was laughing outright now. "All that and we're *finally* almost here. It's so, so close! I've never been so impatient to arrive in my entire life! We can get the care you need for your shoulder, and we can save Fen."

Shang tilted his head around Fen's to look at her. His face was still very guarded, but—

He *smiled.* At Meiling.

It was better than how she had imagined, better than even the fox spirit's portrayal of his smile. It was a little crooked, and it stretched his upper lip thin until it almost disappeared. This smile was so much more real, so much warmer, so much more perfectly imperfect.

It ensnared her, like a beautiful soprano voice might halt her tracks, make her lean closer to appreciate it more. Her cheeks flushed with a pleasant warmth, her stomach stirring as her own hesitant smile grew in response to his.

"Let's hurry," he said, and looked away.

She ducked her head to hide her blush, pulling her cloak tighter around her. Which was stupid, because she was warmer than she had been all day.

"You never told me what you wanted to do with your life." Shang's voice broke through the silence that had fallen. "Since we're so close . . . I might not have another chance to ask."

Her eyes snapped to his, but he was not looking at her. He stared straight ahead at the bridge they needed to cross to reach the fortress.

He was right. Once they arrived, what opportunities would they have to see each other? Not many. After all, Shang and Fen were only her protectors. They were not her *friends.* With how treacherous these last few days had become, she'd been so consumed with thoughts of just *arriving.* They had to get to the fortress. It was a matter of life and death. She could not think past arriving.

Now that she stared up at that bulwark on a hill . . . What sort of life awaited her inside?

Would she be able to visit Fen and Shang as they recovered from their wounds? What if one of them took a turn for the worst? What if Shang's body gave out after the strain he'd borne these last few days?

No, no, she couldn't think like that. They would heal. There was no other option.

What happened once they *did* heal?

Would they stay at the fortress? Surely not. They would make the journey back to Suguan and would salvage their careers. Shang would try to recover his dream appointment. Fen's battalion would have left without her by now, so she'd have to . . .

Pa would make sure they were rewarded. But how much reward could he give to them after completing a journey this secretive?

When the time came, other wielders she did not know would escort her home. She would do this all over again, but with new people who did not know about her magic and who still thought of her as the cursed princess.

There was the added concern that now other people knew about her magic. What if it got out, somehow, despite Shang's promise? What if her magic was found out, and she had to face trial for being an illegal magic-wielder?

Suddenly, the fortress did not seem quite so welcoming as before.

"Meiling?" Shang prompted after her silence stretched long.

She turned to him and suddenly remembered his question. "Oh. Forgive me. I was thinking . . ."

"I noticed."

She glanced at him. He didn't give her that cold stare she was so used to. His gaze . . . it was not hostile. It was *almost* gentle. Not quite, but almost.

"Your life. You want something else," he said.

She glanced down, found herself fingering the edges of her cloak and the stitching in the saddle.

"I told you mine." He raised an eyebrow. "It's only fair if you tell me yours."

"Yours was easy," she retorted. "Because yours is something you can do, something you *will* do. I know you will reach your ambitions. It's not the same for me."

His face took on a strange expression. She didn't know what it meant.

"That's unfortunate," he said at last. "Because you're still in my debt. So you must tell me. Silly or bold or ridiculous, you're obligated."

Was he . . . *teasing* her? Or just prodding her for information?

Why must her hot cheeks keep betraying her? "I'll tell you only if you promise me something," she said, her voice unintentionally growing quieter.

He craned his neck to hear and nodded.

"No holding this over my head like my magic, understand?" She tried—and probably failed—to make herself look fierce.

He smiled again. It was a small smile, but it was still a smile. And Meiling was still lost when it fixed on her.

"You're stalling," he said.

"If I say it, you're going to think it's anticlimactic—"

"Still stalling."

"But—"

"Meiling!" He was grinning now. "Stop overthinking everything."

She wanted to draw back, to be insulted. But she couldn't. Not when he smiled. And then the worlds were tumbling free, despite herself. "I want to see things. I want to experience places across the empire, across the world! I want to see different places and different people. Hear different languages. I don't want to do it at night while I sleep. I want to do it in my physical body, so I can smell and taste and feel. I want to read everything I can, and then I want to *see* it. I want to know things because I've lived them. There's so much beauty in the world and I can see pictures of it in the palace, but I want to see it with my eyes. In the sunlight. Touch it with my hands and feel the wind in my hair and the ground beneath my feet."

Now that she'd started, she couldn't stop. "I cannot go far in my dreams, you see. I'm restrained by my tether, and it won't let me go. I want to be *free* to find beauty."

She stopped. Caught a gasping breath.

She wanted to look at Shang, but she was too afraid. He must think her silly. Ridiculous. There was no hope for such a life for her, not when she was the cursed princess cooped up at the palace. Not when she was doomed to live in a world where she would be forever defined by what she was not.

Not when she was destined to redeem herself through the bearing of magical children.

"I hope you can," Shang said.

The softness in his voice surprised her. She still couldn't bring herself to look at him. He might be watching her carefully, or perhaps he focused on the horizon—on their destination. She was too much of a coward to find out.

For one who could enter minds at will while she slept, she could not guess what thoughts rushed through Shang's head, what he might be feeling.

The bridge loomed ahead of them, still so far away. It was still so far away. When would they arrive? When could they be done with this journey?

When would she say goodbye to Shang?

She should not care. It did not matter. But she *did* care. It *did* matter.

It mattered so much.

A tear slid down her cheek. She allowed no more to fall.

There was no point in discussing what would happen after they reached the fortress. Meiling knew as well as Shang what was to be generally expected. She would be sequestered for her safety. Protected by strangers. Loved and cared for by no one.

Shang would leave.

She would likely never see him again except at festivals or banquets, but even that was very unlikely. How often did she see magic-wielders besides the Palace Guard and the Emperor's Guard? Especially young wielders, new graduates? Not very often.

Perhaps in many years, when Shang inevitably rose through the ranks, she would see him more often. He would wear distinguishing robes with a red sash. He would marry, of course. Some beautiful, magically talented girl with skill and honor to her name. Perhaps another ice-wielder to preserve the bloodline.

And Meiling would wait. *Wait, wait, wait.* Until some foolhardy graduate would approach the emperor for the hand of his daughter.

How long until that happened?

He had already received requests for Hou's hand, young as she was. But as far as Meiling knew, no requests had come for her.

Perhaps she would see Shang again at a festival. The Festival of New Lights or maybe next year's Graduation. There would be another celebration at the palace, one cramped with bodies in fine, embroidered robes. Perfume and the scent of melted wax would fill the room. She'd be there because she was obligated to, but she would stand at the back of the room, watching for a familiar face among the sea of nobility. The usual shroud of discomfort and lostness would settle on her shoulders. Every time she moved, she'd be wary of casting her shadow too long.

Then she would look up—and he'd be there.

He'd be tall and handsome and strong and everything he was supposed to be. And the thing was: she knew he'd notice her. He noticed everything. She wouldn't be invisible to him. He'd see her and meet her gaze. It might be months later, or it might be years. But their eyes would meet again, and she'd fall into those black depths. Memories of these weeks, of working and struggling together, of their *kiss*, and everything else, would pass between them. He would nod once, acknowledging her, but he wouldn't approach her. He would turn back to his conversation, his own duties, as he always had. After all, she would no longer be his duty.

And her?

Well, she would watch the world unfold from the shadows. Just as she always had.

They rode in silence. Penetrating, heavy, deepening silence. Down into the valley, their horses clambered. Meiling clutched the reins, squeezing her knees into the horse's side, and tried not to be flung headlong. Fen's head sagged in front of Shang. He looked weary as he tried to hold her up.

Just a little farther.

They reached the valley. Their horses' hooves sank slightly into the soft grass. It was so beautiful; it made her already aching heart ache just that much more.

"Shang, do you—" she started to ask, turning toward him.

He froze. He pulled his horse to a stop, his face gone ashen.

Meiling knew before she slowly turned her head. She knew it in the pit of her stomach, driving like a knife into her gut. Her chest constricted and simultaneously loosened with imminent dread.

Ahead, standing between them and the bridge suspended over the chasm, standing between them and safety, between them and freedom, stood two brigands.

Red eyes glowed beneath a low-pulled hood. "You have finally arrived. And now you have no choice. No more running," he rumbled, his voice like the clashing of burning, sparking coal. "We fight."

CHAPTER 31

SHANG CAST A look toward Meiling. More than the sight of the fierce brigands blocking their path, that look shot terror into her heart.

He thought—he knew—he was going to die.

"No, Shang," she breathed.

His jaw hardened, his eyes turning to flint, and he leapt down from his horse, facing their enemies. Meiling scrambled off her horse to catch Fen's body before she fell. Her weight was too much, and Meiling only succeeded in shielding her body from the most of the impact. The horses bucked in terror as she crouched over Fen.

She pulled Fen's moaning head into her lap. Tears splashed onto her face. "I've got you. I've got you. I've got you," she soothed, even though Fen was not the one terrified out of her mind.

She almost did not want to look up, to see what was happening. But then a shock rushed through her body and a spasm followed it.

The illusionist.

Where was the illusionist?

She gritted her teeth against the whizzing buzz of Shang's ice. He might be sorely outmatched, but Meiling wasn't about to give up. Not yet.

She couldn't lift Fen into the saddle of the horse. She also knew that she could not sit here, waiting for the brigands to kill Shang and then come to finish Fen and capture her.

Her own life, Meiling realized with a dull thud, was not in danger. Fen's was. Fen, who lay in a stupor in her arms. Every moment they stayed here was another moment Shang was in danger.

She scrambled to her feet, ignoring the clash of magic, the whoosh of sucking wind. How long did they have until the wind-wielder managed to snatch away Shang's air and leave him choking at her feet? How long could he delay the inevitable?

No. She wouldn't let her fear for him paralyze her.

She latched her arms under Fen's armpits, ignoring her sudden cry of pain. She glanced around frantically. Behind and on either side of her rolled the open valley. No place to hide except perhaps on the far side of a single tree. Not a viable option.

That left the bridge. Could she drag Fen around the fighting, over the bridge, and up the hill to the fortress?

She had no other option.

With a guttural roar that hardly sounded like her own, she heaved Fen up and ran backward, toward the fighting. She dragged with all her might, ignoring the shaking of her limbs. Adrenaline raced and pulsed, and all she could think about was running.

Shang cried out.

She wouldn't look. She ground her teeth together, biting her lip, letting the blood flow. Tears flowed too, but she wouldn't look.

She dragged and dragged. The sound of the battle grew louder in her ears, clashing without rhythm. Wind almost knocked her over, but she would *not* let them take Fen too.

They would have to kill her before she let them have Fen.

Shang would die for her. She wasn't about to let Fen die, too.

Another cry from Shang pierced the air. Another knife to Meiling's heart. Tears blurred her vision, but she kept dragging even as her back threatened to buckle from the strain.

She glanced to find she was almost upon the fighting. Shang spotted her, saw what she was trying to do. In response, he stumbled back, drawing the fight away from the bridge. To give her a chance. He nearly paid for it with a fireball to the face, but he threw himself to the ground, rolling and springing back up as he sent ice flying.

Meiling stumbled, landed hard on the ground. Then she was up again, gasping as she dragged Fen. Why did Fen have to be so tall? So densely muscled?

In the corner of her eye, Shang staggered.

She was almost to the bridge. She looked back toward it.

A figure stood on the bridge, watching the battle raging between ice, wind, and fire. She'd never caught a clear glimpse of his face . . . until now. It was strangely beautiful, as though painted by a master painter. Where Shang was severe lines and harsh cuts, this man's features were finer, more delicate. Fuller, softer. His eyes latched on hers, full of whirling chaos.

She recognized him instantly.

The illusionist.

Meiling's feet betrayed her, and she stumbled to the ground. She lay there, frozen, for an instant as their eyes met. The vivid, unnatural, stunning beauty of his mind shone through his irises, giving her once more a glimpse of a child's sorrow. A dark night in a cave, alone and abandoned. Meiling searched a little deeper, and there was Feiyan's shadow, betraying him. There he was, dragging her away from a battle, carrying her despite how much she fought him.

And then Meiling understood. The one truth of his soul flashed through his eyes, and it almost seemed ridiculous now how obvious it had been in his mind.

He . . .

It couldn't be true. Couldn't be *possible.* And yet . . . he loved Feiyan. The girl he'd kidnapped, the healer he had broken. Regret spilled like bloody tears down his cheeks.

Meiling's mouth formed the words she could not utter. *"Help us."*

He understood.

Then she was leaping to her feet again, dragging Fen after her. The illusionist stepped aside, looking past her to the battle raging. Creating illusions to kill Shang.

Except . . .

Meiling glanced back. Shang's ice bolts and shards flew true, striking and wounding. Gusts of wind caught his feet, wiping him flat on his back, but never grabbing at his lungs. Fireballs arced wide, narrowly missing him.

The illusionist *helped* Shang. Even though he bled from multiple wounds and staggered, he was still alive. He should have been dead long ago.

It was too bizarre for her comprehension.

Meiling pulled Fen onto the bridge. It was surprisingly narrow, but bless the fathers, it was not a rope bridge. She pulled with all her strength, dragging Fen along the wooden planks.

"Don't let her escape!"

The shout came from the battle.

The illusionist turned toward Meiling, and a battle raged in his eyes. Her breath caught as his eyes slowly blackened, hardened, the light fleeing.

He lunged toward her.

His illusions snapped. His focus was broken. Shang's cry cut off abruptly.

Meiling should run as fast as her legs could take her. Should give up Fen for dead and run for her life to the fortress. She shouldn't care. Fen shouldn't matter.

Shang shouldn't matter.

But they did matter. There had never been a moment when they hadn't mattered to her. Even when Fen had been cruel to her, even when Shang had been cold—she had always cared.

She cared even more now.

She would not leave Fen. Even if hope was gone for Shang . . . she could save Fen—*just maybe.*

Meiling's eyes betrayed her.

She looked past the illusionist running for her. She looked past the bridge, past the brigands. She looked and found Shang clutching his throat on all fours. His eyes were wide with panic. His life was being stolen right in front of her.

Meiling looked down at Fen's limp form that she held. And her frantic mind cleared. She screamed with all her might, "*Let him go!*"

The wind-wielder's hold broke with a startle, and Shang sagged, gasping and choking. The illusionist reached for her, long fingers extending to wrap around her arm.

"Stay back!" she shouted at him, whipping out her penknife. She pressed the knife to her own chest.

The illusionist froze. The brigands stopped.

"I *will* kill myself," Meiling seethed. "I swear to you upon everything that is good in this world. I will kill myself if you don't let these two go." The words were pouring out of her mouth, and she meant every word more than she'd ever meant any words in her life.

"You won't kill yourself," the red-eyed brigand snarled. He raised a fireball over Shang's head.

Despite how her heart hammered viciously in her breast, despite how tears streamed down her cheeks, Meiling pushed the blade. She cried out as the blade pierced skin and blood flowed.

The wind-wielder knocked his arm aside. "Stop! She's doing it!"

Meiling's voice quivered. Her hands trembled so hard she could hardly keep the sharp point of the knife pressed into her chest. Her heart throbbed with such life and fear and pain. "Let them go," she threatened, gasping when she made good on her threat, pushing the blade a hair deeper until more blood flowed.

"Meiling—stop!" It was Shang's choking, broken voice.

"Let them go. Swear to me that you will let them go. You won't kill them," Meiling snarled. "You want me. Not them. Let them go."

The illusionist's beautiful face was contorted in shock and bewilderment. It was almost as if he could not think straight. She did not want to know what roiled in that wild mind of his.

"She's bluffing," the fire-wielder growled.

"I don't care," the wind-wielder snapped back. She shouted to Meiling: "You for them. That's the only deal we're making."

"Deal," Meiling said without hesitating. "But the moment you lay another hand on my friends, I will kill myself."

"Run, you fool!" Shang shouted, coughing, sputtering as he pushed up on his elbows.

She leaned down to brush a lock of Fen's hair out of her face. Fen blinked wide eyed at her, uncomprehending. "Phoenixes scorch your brains for dragging me," she growled. Then her eyes closed, and she slumped on the bridge.

There was nothing else Meiling could do for her. She stood and glared at the illusionist blocking her path. "Move aside."

The illusionist stepped out of the way but watched her closely. She kept her knife near her bleeding chest, poised and ready. She walked down the short length of bridge she had managed and stepped down to the grassy side of the valley.

Shang breathed heavily on all fours. His shirt was torn where something sharp had pierced his forearm—not fire—and the blood darkened his garments. Other parts of his clothes had been burned away, revealing scorched flesh beneath.

Bloodthirst burned in the fire-wielder's gaze. The hard-nosed wind-wielder at his side seemed to be the only thing restraining him from burning Shang into oblivion. How could she ensure they'd let him go?

Shang struggled to lift his head and look at Meiling. His eyes were so black, so pained, so despairing. "Meiling," he choked. "Don't—don't—"

She wanted to rush to his side, to whisper soothing words that she would be fine, but the fire-wielder reached out and snatched her arm. He dragged her to him and yanked the knife out of her hand. With one move, he flung it into the gaping chasm below.

"Take her." He shoved her to the wind-wielder. "I'll get rid of others."

"No!" Meiling screamed, fight surging through her limbs as she struggled against the wind-wielder's iron grip. "You said—"

"Ruogang, stop!" the wind-wielder snarled.

"What? *Why?*"

"Don't let them off so easily. Make them face their emperor—*alive*. Make them suffer for failing to protect his daughter. They want to blindly serve their emperor, so *let* them. Let them see how it feels to have the empire you served turn on you."

Meiling's blood ran cold. Oh fathers, she was right. That was what Pa had told Fen—that their lives were forfeit if they failed. They were going to die, anyway. But now, instead of dying honorably to save her, they'd be punished. Stripped of everything.

"No, no, no," she said, as if that could make this nightmare go away. Pa wouldn't kill her friends, would he?

The wind-wielder's voice darkened behind her. "Besides, *someone* has to tell the emperor that Fang Zedong declares war."

And then she was being dragged away from Shang, from Fen, from the fortress.

She glanced up the hill. Were those warriors streaming out of the fortress? They'd never reach her in time.

"Meiling!" Shang sputtered, reaching a limp arm after her. "Don't be stupid!"

Ruogang shoved her hard to her knees, and a little cry escaped her lips as he yanked her wrists painfully behind her. Her eyes locked on Shang's stricken expression as Ruogang bound her wrists so tightly the rope sliced into her skin. Blood still oozed from her chest, staining the front of her tunic. She went lightheaded, dizziness almost turning her vision black. This wasn't happening. They'd been so close—they *were* so close!

Somehow, her mouth was moving, forming words meant for Shang. "Everything will be fine! I know what I am doing!"

"No!" he shouted, dragging himself upward on one elbow. "You have absolutely *no idea* what you're doing!"

Ruogang yanked her to her feet, roughly dragging her with burning hands. The illusionist grabbed Meiling's spotted horse and brought it near for them to load up their prisoner.

"Don't—don't hurt her!" Shang cried. Desperation ringed his eyes like a deadly winter. Meiling could hardly bring herself to look at him, but she couldn't *not* look at him. She held his gaze, willing him to not look so horrified, so desperate, so *frantic*.

"Don't hurt her?" Ruogang sneered. "Like this?"

Before she could brace herself, his fist swung. Fire burst on her cheek and she fell to the ground under the shock and force of his blow. She braced herself, hair falling in her face, gasping in air as she stared at the grass beneath her. Her new burn throbbed as her head reeled.

Shang let out a strangled, unintelligible cry.

"Enough games. They're coming. It's time to go." The wind-wielder yanked Meiling back to her feet.

Within seconds, she was forced into the saddle, bound so tightly she couldn't hope for escape. She was vaguely aware of Fen screaming.

She was in a fog.

She twisted back and caught one last glimpse of Shang's strong, broken body lying defeated on the ground. His black eyes burned in her memory. Then they were galloping away to whatever fate lay waiting for Meiling.

At least . . .

At least someone had seen the fighting. At least some wielders were coming. At least they would find Fen and Shang and would tend their wounds, even if they could not reach the brigands. Even if they could not save her.

At least . . . At least *what?*

The fortress on the hill faded from view. Back into the forest, back into the *mó guǐ*-ridden countryside she'd just escaped.

At least none of them had died. Yet.

EPILOGUE

THEY TRAVELED UP a steep, winding road. It played out in front of Meiling's eyes like a reflection of the last time she had seen Shang and Fen. They rode up to a hilltop fortress, black and fortified and imposing.

A foreign flag waved in its towers.

The air was notably cooler. She wanted to pull the tatters of her cloak around her shoulders, but with her hands bound behind her, she could do nothing except let the wind whip it around wildly.

Ruogang took the lead, his narrow shoulders pushed back to make him seem more threatening than he was. His red eyes blazed with triumph as the large gates and portcullis opened and several figures emerged. Ling, the wind-wielder, held the lead of Meiling's horse and cast hostile glares her way every so often.

For one with such a loud, hectic mind, she was definitely the most reasonable of the three.

Shuren, the illusionist, followed. His face was downcast when Meiling peeked back at him. He was the quietest and had hardly spoken this entire time. He did what was asked of him, working silently and keeping to the fringes. They had hardly encountered any *mó guǐ* because he drew them away with his illusions.

As they approached, a strange smell caught her nostrils. She wrinkled her eyebrows. It was a smell unlike anything she had ever smelled before, yet a smell she almost recognized from a dream.

A *dissonant* smell.

Drums pulsed as they drew near. *Thump, thump, thump.* They hammered relentlessly as they approached. The closer they got, the better she could make out the tall figure in black robes waiting for them. His legs were braced wide, and a black cloak flowed in the wind behind him.

He was smiling. Grinning, even.

Fang Zedong.

Thump, thump, thump, the drums beat. Pulsing in time to her raging heartbeat and ragged breaths.

Then—silence.

He stepped forward and began clapping. "Ah, my guest of honor has arrived! Princess Meiling, cherished daughter of Queen Lu Liena, and the final piece to my puzzle. My sweet girl, you do not know how much I've longed for this day." He reached her side, smiling up at her like she was an old friend. It quickly morphed into a frown. "What? Devils you are indeed—why do you bind my princess?"

It wasn't his physical appearance that struck her. His face was rather plain, with rounded cheeks, a rounded jaw, and thin, scraggly eyebrows. His skin was pale, like he spent too much time safe in his fortress, cooped up in an office. But his height was impressive, and his build reminded her of Shang—slender and muscular. He was, after all, a former Academy student. It appeared he had kept up his training through the past twenty years. His hair was cut short, which surprised her, and instead of the typical queue, his scalp was lined with thin, tight braids. The beard lining his jaw was neatly trimmed. At this proximity, she could tell how finely tailored his garments were.

A gold clasp in the shape of a flower kept his cloak from blowing away across the hillside. A lotus. Around his throat was a rough brown cord, with a single wooden bead hanging from it.

His eyes were striking blue.

A bad omen.

Meiling was not usually superstitious, rather exhausted she was at being the object of it, but those strange blue eyes . . . Was there movement behind them? They shone far too brightly.

What lurked in his mind?

But even more striking than his eyes was the sheer magnitude of his presence. Power billowed out from him like ocean waves, rippling through the air between them.

He cut the cords digging into her wrists. The moment they were free, he snatched one numb hand and pressed his lips to their bloody filth. Her mouth opened, startled.

He slowly lifted his mouth and his eyes upward from her hands and smiled at her.

“Surprised you recognize her under all that dirt,” Ruogang muttered.

Zedong’s grin widened. Meiling’s skin crawled as his blue gaze raked over every curve and crevice of her face. “Oh, I certainly recognize her. She takes after her mother. Well done, you three. It is time we escort our beautiful guest to her new home.”

Meiling cried out. She hit the ground hard, barely catching herself on her stinging palms.

The ground was moist.

She scrambled to her feet, wiping her hands on her dirty robes as the cell door banged shut. Blackness swallowed her, blocking out all sight. She groped and found slick, freezing iron bars.

“Why, did they worry I was lonely?” a feminine voice chirped nearby.

Meiling gasped, jerking away from the iron bars. She backed up until she thumped hard into a cold stone wall. Something smooshed under her feet.

It stank.

Meiling almost vomited.

"How sweet of them to bring me a friend," the voice continued. "Let me guess—not a handsome prince to rescue me? Probably not a sage either. No, they wouldn't want me having access to sagely wisdom. Not that I would have any use for such a thing. I tend to prefer stupidity. It works just as well half the time and is *vastly* more fun."

Meiling blinked. She knew that voice.

"Not a prince. Not a sage. Hmm, that leaves only one option. You must be Princess Meiling. I do hope you brought a knife of some sort with you."

"Feiyan?" Meiling whispered, braving the blackness, and stepping toward the voice.

A laugh barked from the other cell. "In one guess! I'm impressed. Unless you cheated, of course. I have no tolerance for cheaters. Usually."

This did not bode well for Meiling's situation. Feiyan could not have been here very long, and she was already clearly going insane.

"You . . . you were in Shuren's mind. The illusionist's mind," Meiling blurted.

There was a tiny pause. "I should like to think so," Feiyan said. "He must have concussed me once or twice with those punches of his. Not exactly gentlemanlike. But I bit off his earlobe, so I suppose we're even. Sort of."

"What?" Then she shook herself, shoving away the confusion. "You were a shadow. I was trying to find his memories, and you guided me to them."

"Oh really? How resourceful of me!"

Meiling licked her lips and tasted blood.

"Look, princess, I've been hatching a plan." Feiyan's voice got closer. "Here, stretch out your hand. I'll heal you."

After a moment of groping, Meiling's hand grasped Feiyan's. It was warm, so alive. She was so reassured by that touch that she almost didn't realize the relief from the burning on her face and the stinging of her wrists. The aches spreading like a plague through her limbs washed away into nothing. Even the shallow cut in her chest and the bruise she'd had on her forehead, when she pressed on it, were completely healed.

Meiling gasped. "Th . . . thank you."

"Pfft. Anytime. It is my utter delight."

Silence fell.

"Back to business. Where would we be without business? Look, I've been plotting. I'm going to get out of here. You want to escape with me?"

Meiling's mouth twisted into the first smile in weeks, the first smile since she and Shang had ridden on the rise overlooking the valley and their fortress destination. The first smile since Shang had been smiling at her.

"I would love to escape with you."

Read on for an excerpt from Captive of Twilight and Treachery!

CAPTIVE OF TWILIGHT AND TREACHERY

THE GLIMPSE OF night sky visible through the small window of the bunkroom told Shang it was a couple of hours past midnight. Only the guards would be awake now. He eased of his bunk and slipped out of the room, silent as death, his clothes bundled to his chest. No one stirred behind him. *Good.*

The fortress hallway before him was bleak and dark. Nothing but a sconced torch in the main hallway beyond this one shone any light into this crevice of Liafugen. He dressed as fast as he could—in all black.

In the weeks since Meiling's capture, he and Fen had been kept at this fortress to rest and recover before returning to Suguan, but Shang hadn't been doing much resting.

It was quick and careful work to dodge patrol's prying eyes and sneak a few wings down to the infirmary. The only delay was when a feral-wielder with augmented hearing made his rotations close to where Shang was crouched in the shadows. He waited, not breathing, until the guard was long past before he moved again.

He slid the infirmary door open, ducking behind a changing screen before the medic on duty could see him. The infirmary was quiet, with Fen as the only overnight patient. She was finally sleeping soundly from dusk to dawn, instead of waking every few hours moaning with pain. The space between those moans had nearly shredded Shang's sanity when he'd been here. It was already too much that Meiling was captured, but to lie awake for hours hoping he wouldn't lose Fen too . . .

The medic probably spent most of the night dozing against his desk. Shang might check, but if he was wrong, he didn't want to risk getting discovered.

Any moment now.

Sure enough, a pair of running footsteps came straight for the infirmary. A groan sounded from the medic.

"If that is Yaozu and his delicate stomach again . . ."

Loud retching in the hallway dragged another groan from the medic. Paper shuffled and robes swished, and then his heavier footsteps thumped across the infirmary.

"All I want is one night in the span of a week where I'm not cleaning up vomit," he grumbled. Then he slid the door open. "Am I going to have to put you on a stricter diet, boy? This is the third time this week!"

Sorry, brother.

Shang leapt into motion, leaving the shelter of the screen. He skirted around empty bed mats, the medic's desk, the cabinets of herbs and medicines. Candlelight bobbed and winked against the darkness. His fast movements sent a sharp burst of pain down his spine. Cursing inwardly, he slowed just slightly, until the pain was only an ache.

The medic would have a fit that Shang wasn't following his instructions to rest and recover. If Shang listened, however, and waited until he was recovered, he'd find himself en route to Suguan for trial. Besides, there just *wasn't time*. It had killed him every waking minute to delay this long.

He reached the one bed concealed by a screen to block out the candlelight. Fen lay sprawled on her back, her mouth open. Her shoulder was freshly bandaged, the color returned to her cheeks. A small chest was at her feet, containing her clothes.

He dared not touch her for fear of waking her. The time he had was already slipping through his fingers. Still, he couldn't help mouthing a silent, *"Goodbye, friend. Heal quickly."*

Then he flipped open the lid of the chest, dug beneath Fen's robes, and pulled out the things he'd been slowly pilfering and hiding away over the last couple of weeks.

Extra knives. Rope. Flint and steel. Some food things. A mask and gloves. His father's signet ring. The broadsword he'd hidden in the tall potted plant by the bed.

The infirmary door slid back open, and the medic's voice carried through the small space. "Sit yourself down, boy. I'll brew you *another* ginger tea."

Shang buckled on his weapons silently, keeping his breathing steady to calm his heart rate. He slid the tight coil of rope and sack of food onto his belt. He hated that he didn't have a *jiaun*, but those were carefully cataloged in the armory. Even one's absence would have been noticed.

The earthy aroma of ginger was abruptly cut off when Shang tied on the mask, hiding his face except for his eyes. He drew the hood of his cloak low and pulled on the gloves.

He was just about to stand when he looked down—and found Fen's eyes wide open. Faster than a heartbeat, he clapped his gloved hand over her mouth. She lowered her brows, glaring at him. He held a finger to his masked lips, then let go of her.

She said nothing, just kept her eyes locked on his. Then she reached out and clasped his hand. Something inside him twinged with regret. He squeezed back. He hated leaving her like this. Hated it more than words. Fen was his comrade. Warriors didn't leave their comrades behind.

He forced himself to let go.

The moment Yaozu had his cup of ginger tea and the medic had left the infirmary to clean up the hallway mess, Shang slipped to the window. He eased it open, swung himself out onto the sill, and pulled it closed behind him.

If he didn't do this right, he'd be shot.

But if there was one thing his father had taught him from the moment he was born, it was that failure wasn't an option. Getting shot off Liafugen's walls was not an option. Even though he'd spent most of the last fortnight in the infirmary, he hadn't wasted a single moment. All those hours staring outside that infirmary window, he'd been planning. Watching the patrol rotation. Asking innocuous questions. Working out exactly how to pull this off.

He braced himself, then dropped onto the roof of the armory. Pain shot into his ribs as he rolled into a crouch. He allowed himself three seconds to press a hand to his side and wince. Then he was in motion again.

He slinked across the armory roof, to the edge nearest the parapets. When a patrol came near, Shang dropped to his stomach, laying flat on the roof, waiting for her to pass. The moment she was gone, he pulled the rope from his belt, worked a slip knot, and eased himself back into a crouch.

The loop he threw landed around a merlon. He counted to three, waiting for the window in patrols, and then tightened his grip on the rope and swung himself off the roof, landing with his feet flat against the side of the parapets.

Quickly, he pulled himself up to the parapet, fitting between the crenels.

And right in front of him, with his back to him, was an armed guard.

A comrade.

Sorry, Shang thought before slamming the side of his hand into the man's neck. He crumpled, and Shang caught him, easing him to the ground and hiding him in the shadows before unlooping his rope from the merlon and slinking to the opposite side of the parapet.

He ducked below a crenel, his hands working the rope into a different, more complex knot than the first. One that would support his weight but come undone with a sharp pull.

Voices drifted on the chill night wind. They came from below. Not a risk for him. Even so, sweat slicked down his brow, dampening his mask. Despite his carefully measured breaths, his heart raged in his chest.

He finished the knot, got to his feet, and slipped it around the merlon he hid behind.

Then, with a last check over his shoulder to be sure he hadn't been spotted, he swung himself out over the battlement. Hand over hand, his feet flat against the stone outer wall of Liafugen, he walked himself down the steep incline.

When he reached the bottom, his lungs were heaving. He yanked hard on the rope, and the knot came undone, falling around his feet. The aches plaguing his body grew more insistent, but he ignored them as he rewound the rope and hooked it on his belt.

One step down. Now he just needed to knock out the guards at the bridge over the chasm, and then the hardest part of the first half of his plan would be done.

After that, he had to get a horse. His father's signet ring would accomplish that.

The road before him was long, treacherous, even *traitorous*. Defying orders like this was enough to get him executed. The emperor would have his head—twice over. But Shang didn't care.

Not when Meiling was in the hands of a monster.

It had been hard enough to imagine leaving her alone in the hands of allies.

The few times he'd let himself imagine what Fang Zedong and his minions could be doing to her, he'd nearly lost his mind. Which he couldn't afford. He had to stay calm and rational. Recklessness wouldn't save anyone.

But when Shang snuck up behind the guards, all remorse that these men were his comrades was swept aside by the burning ice in his gut. As their unconscious bodies fell to the ground, he broke into a run and sprinted across the bridge. He only had seconds now before the fortress watch realized their gatekeepers were down.

So he ran, plunging into the darkness, ignoring the pain of his partially healed wounds.

Come hell, high water, *mó guǐ*, an entire empire—he was getting Meiling back. He swore it on the graves of his fathers, the grave of his mother. *Dragons*, he'd swear it on anything. If he had to tear apart both Butagin and Zheninghai to find her, he'd do it.

He was getting her back, or he'd die trying.

MORE FROM ANASTASIS BLYTHE

THE ZHENINGHAI CHRONICLES

Maiden of Candlelight and Lotuses

Guardian of Talons and Snares

Warrior of Blade and Dusk

Princess of Shadows and Starlight

Captive of Twilight and Treachery

Daughter of Darkness and Dreams

ABOUT THE AUTHOR

Anastasis Blythe makes her home in central Texas with her husband and their two adorable but rather whiny cats. When she's not writing, she is reading an unhealthy amount of fantasy novels, daydreaming about future books, and trying to keep up with the laundry.

If you would like free novels, regular behind-the-scenes updates on her writing, and an early peek at new book covers, join her community at Patreon.com/AnastasisBlythe.

CONNECT WITH ANASTASIS ONLINE AT:

Website - AnastasisBlythe.com

Instagram - @AnastasisBlythe

Facebook - Anastasis Blythe

Goodreads - Anastasis Blythe

www.ingramcontent.com/pod-product-compliance
Lightning Source LLC
Chambersburg PA
CBHW020241030826
48979CB00030B/2426/J

* 9 7 8 1 9 6 0 6 0 6 0 3 7 *